I0730779

J.P. JENTILE

Ogrino

The Ancient
Legacy

WORKBOOK PRESS
RECOMMENDED

WORKBOOK PRESS LLC
187 E Warm Springs Rd,
Suite B285, Las Vegas, NV 89119, USA

Website: https://workbookpress.com/
Hotline: 1-888-818-4856
Email: admin@workbookpress.com

Ordering Information:
Quantity sales. Special discounts are available on quantity purchases by corporations, associations, and others.
For details, contact the publisher at the address above.

Library of Congress Control Number:
ISBN-13:   978-1-956876-06-2 (Paperback Version)
              978-1-956876-07-9 (Digital Version)

REV. DATE: 05/11/2021

Ogrino,
The Ancient Legacy

Ogrino,
The Ancient Legacy

J.P. JENTILE

TRANSLATED BY ELIZABETH SIMON

CONTENTS

BOOK SUMMARY

Hunted by the Military Order of Legiferius, which seeks to eliminate all magical creatures, a young Ogre named Ogrino has lost his parents and his memory. He is adopted by the circus people and comes to live as a human boy. Discovered again by the Order, he escapes with help from the Pixie Razenbruck. Ogrino fights off a thousand dangers in order to spread the news of the Order's threat to the peoples of the Legendary World, including Delphoros, the king of seas; Precelestine, monarch of underground; and Themistomene, sovereign of the forests.

Ogrino wakes the dragon Metanor and even meets Felicia Regina, Queen of the Elves, who reveals to him his destiny. But will all this be enough to protect the Gigantum, the tree-father of all life, and preserve the Great Balance from the evil schemes of the Order's leader, the Magnus Legifer?

THE AUTHOR

J. P. Jentile was born in Paris in 1960 and spent his childhood in both France and Italy. As an economist and then an international banker, he has traveled all around the world, being in contact with different people and cultures and finding there an inexhaustible source of inspiration.

His career as a writer grew out of years of inventing bedtime stories for his two sons. An avid reader of Heroic Fantasy, J.P. is happy to share his passion, values, and vivid imagination with the general public through this first novel, which has already been a great success in France.

This book is dedicated to Annie, Sebastien, and Yoann, the apples of my eye; to Angela and Camillo, who gave me life and the confidence to go my own way; to Nonna for her undying affection; to the memory of Nicodemo; to my uncle Enzo, who passed on to me the desire to tell stories; and to all my known and unknown friends, who will enjoy this journey to the boundaries of the real and the imaginary.

THE FATEFUL HUNT

It all began on a beautiful, sunny spring day in the bosom of a dark and dense forest, the guardian of the fantastic Legendary World. Creeks burbled delicately over sun-dappled stones. The leaves of great majestic trees danced in a soft breeze. The joyous melody of many multicolored birds rang out above treetops and grasses, gladdening the hearts of all the forest's creatures. Everyone, from the biggest to the smallest, lived together peacefully in the harmony of the great chain of Life. In those times, all sorts of magical people lived in the thick, protective forests and also in any place where nature's strength and beauty reigned. They even lived in human cities, often without being recognized, because as time went on, humans became ever blinder—incapable of seeing or even sensing the innumerable creatures of the Legendary World. These beings not only lived among humans but also quite often helped them, or even threatened their safety, without the humans ever knowing.

Of this vast menagerie of strange creatures, one especially haunted the thoughts and fears of Man, all the more because it was not invisible. From time to time, its path and humans crossed, quite unluckily for the latter, since afterwards often nothing was found but a few scattered pieces of bone. Yes, the Ogres were like that—not aggressive or reckless, but gourmands, curious about new culinary sensations. This curiosity transformed them into quite a threat to the tender and succulent, plump little humans who dared to venture into the forests and disturb the peaceful lives of these enormous, kindly creatures. Ogres hate to be disturbed. It puts them in a rage; they see red, their eyes become bloodshot, and a terrifying hoarse cry escapes from their gaping throat. They begin to run, shaking the earth with their steps, and then nothing and no one can escape them, and it ends in horrendous carnage. Still, most of the time, they are calm, appreciating the beauty of their forest home and the soft whispers of wind and water. They play in waterfalls, catching fish as hors d'oeuvres, rabbits as a first course, and wild boar as their main dish, for, it must be said, Ogres eat a truly incredible amount—they gorge themselves to their hearts' content. Which is to say that humans are petrified of Ogres because many hunters have lost their lives to them. And from time to time, a toothless old Ogre, no longer able to chase down game, would end up on the edge of an isolated farm and devour chickens, ducks, cows, and pigs, leaving nothing more to a peasant family than their eyes to cry with. In order to fight this scourge, the villagers at first organized simple raids with pitchforks and sticks, but either they came back empty-handed after days of exhausting searching, or else their number had been reduced by half. 'We cannot tolerate this any longer!' the villagers proclaimed, and so in time, reinforcements were organized under the authority of the Militians of the Order. Staunch in the face of fear and danger, hardened to extreme situations, these formidable soldiers were without pity and led raids as one would embark on a war, only rarely taking prisoners. They took a perverse pleasure in killing. They were renowned for their cold efficiency and inspired as much admiration as fear, for their uniforms and their gazes were equally dark.

So it was that on a radiant morning, they arrived at a little village on the edge of the forest where the wagons of a circus were parked. Once more, the villagers had called upon the Militians to pursue a small family of Ogres that was threatening their flocks.

'All right, send these buffoons away. The area must be cleared within the hour so that we can use the space for our troops and weaponry,' Commander Erasmus said in a booming yet melodious voice.

He emanated a natural authority due to his unparalleled dedication and to a long military training, since, as a student of the Order, he had grown up from a young age in the heart of the Militia. Essentially the Order would systematically gather all orphans, abandoned children, and even boys from the poorest families who could no longer afford to feed them. All the children were then raised as soldiers according to the strict doctrine of the Order, destined to become part of the elite of Legiferius's armed unit: the Caste of the Commanders. It was they who then formed the Militia of the Order, often made up of peasants or laborers who would rather trade a sometimes-wretched life for the prestige of a uniform. And so the ranks of Legiferius grew from year to year, and it became a giant army.

Apart from the impressive number of combatants, Legiferius's army benefited from very sophisticated weaponry that allowed it to fight against a great many evil-doing creatures of the Legendary World. Each soldier was equipped with an efficient personal arsenal in order to be as independent as possible and be able to conduct his own little war. Thanks to these weapons, he was able to cause the enemy the most damage possible and come back safe and sound, or at least survive long enough for help to arrive. The uniform consisted of a soft leather helmet with flaps over the ears, a jacket and pants made of thick fabric with metal reinforcements on the shoulders, elbows, and knees, and high leather boots. But what was more intriguing was that all the soldiers wore curious orange-tinted glasses with leather straps. Rumor had it that these glasses allowed the soldiers to see the invisible creatures of the Legendary World—the Sprites, for example, who could infest a village and torture people with foul tricks like setting tripwires, breaking dishes, or making doors stick shut. As everyone knows, these creatures can become visible or invisible by turns, but thanks to these special glasses, the soldiers were always able to see them and chase them endlessly. And so, day or night, not one of those creatures could escape their piercing gaze. In addition to that, the soldiers had all sorts of strange weapons, starting with the crossbows that served to launch a wide variety of projectiles. These ranged from simple arrows to soporific green bombs, passing on the way by rockets, which exploded in a blinding flash, sticky liquids, boomerangs, exploding marbles, and nets. This armory had been scientifically developed by the Docts according to the characteristics of catalogued magical creatures. But in addition to these personal weapons, the Militia of the Order was equipped with combat horses, Terranefs, crossbow-catapult hybrids, portable dungeons, wheeled skiffs, and net-shooting cannons. All in all, a panoply of extraordinarily efficient weapons allowing each soldier to capture or destroy a great many enemies.

This mass of arms and equipment was assembled in the center of the village square, under the villagers' dumbfounded stares. Some were quite impressed by all the resources gathered, while others wondered if the ado wasn't disproportionate to the hunt, which was only meant to concern a two—or three-member family of Ogres. But Legiferius never took the slightest risk; success was their motto and anyway, one never knew what terrible perils one would have to face in these dark lands, where the beings of the Legendary World resided.

Once the equipment was set up, Commander Erasmus gathered all his sub-officers together in his tent to decide on a hunting strategy based on information the villagers had given. After a good half-hour, they left quite hurriedly, rejoined the Militians, and with all their equipment left immediately in groups of six to plunge into the dark forest along different paths. Fifty groups had formed like this and were walking along noisily, hitting one large hollow stick against another.

During this time, the family of three Ogres, far from suspecting the plan that was being hatched, was living in their little cave according to the peaceful rhythm of their forest life. Since the sun was at its zenith, this meant that it was time to eat. The mother Ogre was named Loganda, and she was fat and strong, with big round hazel eyes, a wide mouth full of pointed teeth, and long, russet hair. Her skin was tanned and she wore a deerskin dress. She had begun to collect berries and fruits before going to see if any rabbits, partridges, or other appetizers had been caught in the traps she had laid here and there in the forest. The little Ogre, named Ogrino, was dressed in a buckskin shirt and short beaverskin trousers and was playing next to his mother. He was trying to catch butterflies and bees, for Ogres are famous for being unafraid of stings. As for Hogar, the father Ogre, he had already been out a long time looking for big game and would no doubt return soon. Loganda wasn't surprised, then, when she heard the sounds of breaking branches as if someone were quickly approaching. However, she was shocked to see a pack of wild boars running toward her, frightened, and a herd of deer leaping all around. The Ogress hardly had time to pull her son from the wild herd's path so he wouldn't be trampled. When the animals had passed by, she listened carefully and heard something like a strange music coming from the south and the west. It was as if trees were continually crashing together while the noise got closer and closer. Then Hogar appeared.

He threw down the three boars and two deer he had been carrying on his powerful shoulders and said, 'It's hunters, a lot of them, and not like the others! This is the first time they've come so far into the forest. We've got to hide the little one away, and you too, so that I can face them without problems. Let's get back to the cave! On second thought, no—let's go north, toward the marshes. They won't dare follow us there!'

Hogar grabbed the child in his two enormous hands and lifted him onto his shoulders, grabbed his wife by the hand and began to run. They made swift progress. Bushes and undergrowth didn't slow them; even low-hanging branches splintered in their path. Ogrino was frightened. He lowered his head and clung as hard as he could to his father, watching his mother jump alongside them. After a long while of this frenzied running, the father stopped to listen and sniff. He turned up his nose to better catch the scent on the wind.

'We've gotten away from them. They're at least a hundred stones' throws behind. Let's rest a bit. We've got to find food! I'm very hungry . . . those imbeciles made us miss our dinner and that really has a way of making me mad.'

The only advantage gained by the pursuers was that with all that noise, the frightened animals were running off in the same direction as the Ogres, so much so that our fugitives found themselves surrounded by game. Hogar took a huge branch from a fallen tree and broke it to make a bludgeon. He began to run at the beasts that were fleeing the men. In the blink of an eye, he had killed two bucks, three wolves, four badgers, and six hares.

'This will tide us over until we are free from these troubles and able to have a real meal, worthy of us, with wild boar like they were falling from the sky.'

Hogar had barely finished his phrase when he hungrily devoured the three wolves and one of the bucks, leaving the rest for his wife and son, who began to feast—particularly Ogrino, who enjoyed the hares. After a meal, Ogres typically took a nap, but in this case, they kept walking since the sounds and especially the odor of the hunters had gotten much stronger. These were no villagers, Hogar was sure now. They were moving too fast, were unafraid to plunge into the forest, and seemed to be more organized than usual. The sounds they were making formed a semicircle, a sort of barrier that could close in on the Ogres and capture them.

For the first time in his life, Hogar felt that his family was really in danger. Until now, he had always taken great pleasure in facing these puppets, who came onto his land to pester him. They threw wooden pickaxes at him but their silver blades never hurt him any more than a snakebite, which is to say hardly at all. They hurled stones that only tickled him. So with a roar that was more laughter than scream, he would chase them away, jumping for joy that these little human creatures were so slow and fragile that a mere turn of the hand could break them in two. Perhaps, he shouldn't have left the forest that one day and devoured the large horned animals that lived near humans' houses. It was just that those beasts were delicious, quite fat with meat that melted in your mouth and most of all, not only could they not run quickly, but also they couldn't even jump over the low fences that generally surrounded them. It was really too tempting for Ogres to resist. And then the humans were also so tender and fragrant that when they came out of their little square caves, it would have been a shame not to have nibbled on a few for dessert. After all these years and especially during the harsh winters when game became rare, he had gone hunting on human territory several times and he must have eaten about a dozen of them in all. Maybe that was the cause of their spite today: they wanted revenge.

Man was a different animal from the others, for when Ogres attacked a pack of boars or even wolves, the battle could be very bloody, but the surviving animals would never try to avenge their comrades. It was as if this constant fight for survival was just part of the natural order of things and everyone knew it. Humans, though, not only held grudges after a battle, but might even exact their vengeance years later, after the Ogres had already forgotten all about it. They were a strange sort of prey, at once cleverer than others and easier to catch but mainly crueler. Hogar had seen several hunts led by humans. Often they killed just for fun, not to eat, which to an Ogre is unforgivable. They would kill dozens and dozens of animals of all kinds, take their skin, and leave the meat to rot in the forest. One day, he had even seen a hunter cut the antlers of a wounded stag while the animal was still alive and was belling its death tones. That day, Hogar understood that Man is an animal unlike any other, and one not to be trusted. And since that time, Hogar had avoided these strange creatures that, for him, always brought misfortune.

He hadn't been wrong because now his family had become the game and it was Hogar's job to protect them. The noises seemed fairly close and an increasing tide of forest animals was accompanying the three Ogres in their flight. The ground became less and less solid. They were approaching the marshes and soon they would be in safe territory. The farther along they got, the higher the water, and now they were sloshing through calf-high mud which slowed their progress. Hogar walked ahead to find the more solid areas and avoid quicksand. His instinct guided him and he remembered that his father had brought him here as a child to hunt the giant carp and the gray cranes with such tender and flavorful flesh. The noises were still following them. The Ogres had water up to their waists now. Hogar went ahead at a steady pace, his wife following without a word. They continued like this for long hours, until night had fallen, and still the other side of the marsh was not in view. They were beginning to get tired and a bit cold, but the humans hadn't stopped their pursuit. Hogar reflected with his Ogre intelligence. If he had water up to his chest, how could the little humans, no taller than three boars, keep walking with their heads above water—and above all, so quickly? Their pursuers sounded ever closer. Looking in their direction, Hogar could see glowing lights dancing on the water. Looking left and right, he saw the same flickering lights. The sound grew louder and the lights bigger. He inhaled sharply through his large nostrils and grew nervous.

'The fire, the fire's getting closer, let's go, quickly, quickly.'

Ogres, like all other forest creatures, are afraid of fire. Fear makes them lose their way, they can't think straight, and only the instinct to flee comes out clearly. Men know this and they make use of it. The earth beneath the water grew firmer again; they were able to make swifter progress, and that also meant that they were also closer to the other side of the swamp. The noise from the hunters was now deafening. There must have been very many of them, and very close behind. Loganda turned around and let out a wail. Right away, Hogar turned his head and saw behind them, just ten stones' throws away, dozens of hunters seated on long hollowed-out tree trunks, gliding rapidly along the water behind them. He took his wife by the hand and increased his pace, still heading toward dry land. The water level was quickly falling now; it reached only up to their thighs. Loganda kept glancing back furtively to see where the hunters were and what they were doing.

'They're five stones' throws away and still getting closer.'

Then the water was down to their calves and they could once again run. Despite the danger, Ogrino was mesmerized by the myriad lights dancing on the water. Scarcely had Hogar set his wide foot on dry ground, when a multitude of little noises rang out, nearly in unison. Little bits of glowing wood flew through the sky and fell just in front of the three Ogres. As soon as the projectiles reached the ground, a line of fire sprang up and consumed the tall grass. Hogar roared, but courageously took hold his wife and threw himself across the wall of flames, and they disappeared into the darkness.

Commander Erasmus, who had remained on the front lines since the beginning of the hunt, told the oarsmen to row faster. The boats were barely ashore when he took charge of a twelve-man commando intended to race along the fugitives' path. Four deep footprints confirmed the presence of a pair of Ogres, the ones Erasmus had seen in the half-light of the swamp. The male surely led the way, followed by the female. The trail was easy to follow, thanks to their torches; however, they couldn't allow themselves to fall behind because in general, Ogres are very fast. The long walk through muddy waters and the presence of a female were good news, since both would slow the Ogres' flight, while Erasmus and his men had been able to rest as they crossed the swamp in boats. The ground rose in a gentle slope. According to his map, the trail led to an area full of caves, and they had to stop the Ogres from reaching it, or they risked losing the trail and having to spend days searching out the fugitives. So the Militians sped up their running despite their heavy equipment.

Ogrino tugged on his father's thick hair.

'Papa, I'm tired and hungry,' he said in his little voice.

'I know, my son. I'm very hungry too, but we're in great danger, so we'll eat when we're somewhere safe. That should be very soon.'

Loganda dug into her dress pockets and found three quails and two partridges that she had saved to snack on before all the business with the hunters began. She gave them to her son, whose eyes lit up in delight.

'OOOH! Mama, you're the best Mama ever!'

And in an instant, he devoured the providential provisions. Hogar smiled tenderly at Loganda, then quickened his stride. The ground became more and more sloped, meaning that they were getting close to hills or mountains. They would surely find a way to hide there. Little by little, the vegetation grew thicker. Tall grasses gave way to bushes and then shrubs. Hogar and Loganda felt new hope. But as joy grew in their hearts, Loganda automatically turned back, as if to check that all was well and, there she saw about a dozen lights moving rapidly, still in pursuit. So the humans would never stop. Why were they chasing the Ogres like this? This determination was no good omen. They would have to escape the humans or fight to the death; now she was sure of it. She looked at her husband in the eyes again and knew that he was thinking the same thing. They picked up their pace once again, heading toward the boulders that they could now make out in the moonlight.

The full moon had just risen as predicted by the Docts' calendar. The task would only get easier as the prey could now be spotted with the naked eye. The Militians extinguished their torches, put them back into their backpacks, and began to run even harder. The silhouette of the bigger Ogre stood out against the night and climbed ever higher toward the mountain's peak. Although his men were fast, Erasmus wasn't sure they would be able to catch the fugitives before they reached the caves, where they would be protected. He made a decision. He stopped his men, took out his backpack, opened it, and took out a little cage. He tore a bit of paper from a notepad and scrawled a few words. Then he took a sextant, made some adjustments to calculate the Ogres' exact location and began to write again. He took a dove out of the cage. He slipped the piece of paper into a little leather pouch attached to the bird's breast, then threw the bird in the air, toward the South. The bird took off without hesitation, speeding away to its destination.

'There is no wind tonight, so my order should be carried out approximately five minutes from now,' said Erasmus to his troops. 'We'll keep going to keep the Ogres in sight, but one thing is sure. The end of this hunt is near.'

Ogrino was glad to see a familiar landscape, full of boulders and big trees. The long journey across the water in the cold and damp had chilled his bones. He was shivering.

'Mama, I'm cold,' he whimpered, for although he was a robust little Ogre, he was barely seven summers old.

Still running, his mother tried to comfort him. 'We'll be there soon, and then we'll make you a soft cozy bed with moss and grass that will keep you nice and warm.' She meant for her voice to be calming but there was a sliver of anxiety in it.

They advanced for another long while before they were finally able to make out the top of the mountain they were climbing. Soon they would pass the summit and be hidden from their pursuers. There, they would be safe and sound and would surely find a deep cave where they could hide and wait for the hunt to be over. However, before they could reach their goal, they suddenly heard a loud explosion in the distance.

They turned around and saw three huge jets of light in the sky, descending upon them at full speed. A moment later, all was chaos. The balls of light struck the ground very near them, cutting off their route to the summit. Hogar roared in rage and bitterness. This time an immense wall of flames barred their path. The grass, the bushes, and the trees were all on fire. The unbearable heat left them no hope of being able to cross this obstacle. Hogar saw the men running their fastest behind them. They whooped with joy. The clash was imminent and might be extremely violent. Hogar looked at his wife for a long moment and whispered something in her ear. As she listened, her eyes filled with tears. She took her child in her arms, clasped him to her chest, and kissed him on the head. She passed him to his father, who kissed him as well. Hogar held his son in his large hand and said, 'We're going to play birdie—you're going to fly over that wall of fire. You see the big tree there? I'm going to throw you up into the air, you'll land in its branches, and you'll latch onto them like a little squirrel. You'll wait there while Mama and I teach these ridiculous puppets a lesson. All right?'

Ogrino didn't know whether to be excited or sad about this new game as he vaguely felt that it wasn't as simple as his father was making it out to be.

'All right, I want to be a birdie, but afterwards you'll come and get me. Right?'

'Of course, as soon as we've finished. It won't be long,' said his father with a forced smile.

Then Hogar leaned to the left, released his arm, and with one abrupt movement threw his son into the air. The little Ogre felt like he was flying in slow motion. Then he saw the fir tree getting closer, and at full speed came the impact. He had hit the tree trunk head-on and he was a little dazed but not hurt. He had slid down the side of it and now found himself astride a big branch. His head was spinning a bit but he twisted his neck to look behind him and see what was becoming of his parents on the other side of the big wall of flames. From his viewpoint, perched up high, he could see the whole scene. His father and mother had bravely hurtled down the slope to meet the humans. Hogar had an enormous branch that he was whirling around above his head, and his mother had several big stones in each hand. They must have seemed very impressive to these puny, little creatures dressed in black that didn't even reach up to the Ogres' chests, Ogrino thought to himself proudly. For that matter, he wondered why they had had to flee when his father looked so powerful. One did have to remember, though, that these hunters' curious weapons were unknown and dangerous. The child rejoiced in seeing his father descend upon the attackers. However, before the confrontation took place, just before his father reached his enemies, they aimed their strange bows at him and shot out a barrage of arrows. Hogar slammed his heavy branch into five soldiers who fell backwards, their legs broken, and then he cried out in pain, covering his eyes. Loganda threw her stones, hitting three men. She broke the first one's arm, the second's ribcage, and the third's jaw. The four remaining unhurt soldiers threw several nets onto Loganda, who got tangled in them and lost her balance. In short order, she had torn through one and freed her head. During this time, Hogar, blinded by the sticky substance that hindered him and hurt his eyes, staggered and waved his massive arms in the air. Two soldiers slipped in front of him silently and took aim with their crossbows.

Loganda shouted, 'Look out, Hogar! In front of you!'

The Ogre squatted suddenly and dove forward at the level of the humans' legs, mowing down two Militians. They rolled onto their sides, knelt, and were once again ready to shoot. Loganda, out of her net, ran toward her husband. The other two soldiers, who were watching her, shot almost simultaneously and hit her straight in the face. She teetered an instant and then fell in a heap.

'Noooo!' Ogrino screamed.

But the loud crackle of the spreading flames covered his cry. Next, he saw the soldiers aim at his still-blinded father, who was staggering about without knowing where he was going. The four soldiers took their time and adjusted their weapons, creeping as close as possible to their target. They shot for the head. Hogar, hit straight on, spun slowly like a top and fell heavily to the ground.

'NOOOO! NOOOOO!' the child cried again.

The soldiers turned their heads toward the tree where Ogrino was hiding, but they saw nothing because the fire was now immense, devouring the great fir trees all around. The heat was becoming intolerable and the little Ogre hurried to climb down the tree and distance himself from the furnace. The nearby pines were crackling, their sap boiling. Shards of flaming bark flew off toward neighboring trees. Explosions of sap bombarded the forest with flaming pinecones. The very top of Ogrino's tree had caught fire and blazing twigs were now falling onto his back. He climbed down faster and just as he set foot on the ground, a thick branch full of embers fell in front of his face. Terrified, he backed into a stump, then found himself sitting on a pile of burning pinecones. He screamed with pain, stood up as fast as he could, and patted his breeches to put out the fire that was gnawing at them.

Then he began to bolt like a rabbit to escape this hell since now the blaze was everywhere. He extricated himself from the furnace as quickly as possible and soon found himself in the dark of night.

Now he was safe and sound; the fire could no longer reach him. He caught his breath and tried to calm down. He realized that for the first time in his life he was alone, without his parents, who were dead now, all alone in a big black forest with no one to protect him. He sat crying for a long time. Never again would he feel his mother's warmth or her great soft chubby hands on his head. No one would tell him stories before bedtime. No one would come console him if he had nightmares. His father would never again bring him hunting, carrying him on his shoulders. He would never tickle him or make him fly through the air, tossing him up with strong arms and laughing. Ogrino cried harder, sobbed, his eyes streaming fat drops that warmed his cheeks in the ever-colder night. Now that he had escaped the fiery furnace, he noticed, with even more bitterness, how chilly the night air was. It wasn't really that it was so cold, since it was the middle of springtime, but the weighty absence of his parents chilled him from head to toe. Despite his heavy heart, he had to find somewhere to spend the night, a dry and sheltered place to rest a little. Although the moon was full, the thick woods offered almost no visibility, and Ogrino was forced to feel his way along. More and more holes and ditches were scattered across the terrain. He had to pay attention to each step, stay focused. A sudden crackling of the brush behind him made him jump. He had just turned around when he was knocked over by an imposing mass of hair, claws, and fingers. A Troll's hand! His father had told him that these creatures were ferocious but clumsy and, that if you could take them by surprise, they were easy to escape from. But here he was too late; the giant hand encircled him in a vise-grip from which only his head emerged. The Troll, who was a good four meters tall, looked at Ogrino with glassy and myopic eyes and emitted a series of grunts that sounded like 'GROOMPF, GROOMPF.'

In Troll language this meant:

'You are on my territory and the punishment for this crime is death!'

Of course, Ogrino could not understand Troll language. He was terrified by the size of this monstrous creature and by its foul-smelling breath. The little Ogre wished with all his might that his father could be there to fight this deformed, hairy giant. Alas, the child was alone and weak and the Troll knew it. There was no easier prey in the world. Ogrino bit down as best he could on the enormous index finger encircling him. His bite was deep enough that the Troll, feeling the sharp pain of the gash, loosened his grip a bit. The child immediately took advantage of this to slip his right arm out of the beast's fist and, since he found himself near the face of the Troll, who was sniffing him, he jabbed two fingers into the monster's left eye. The Troll let out a terrifying howl, shaking the forest, then let go of Ogrino to bring his hands to his face. The child fell on the soft dirt without the slightest harm, free at last, and began to run.

After the pain came a craving for revenge, and the monster, all the while covering his wounded eye, pursued the fugitive, beating the air with his right arm. In a few strides, he was upon his target and swept it across the ground like a piece of straw, scratching it with his steel-sharp nails. On first impact, the child was sent rolling into the undergrowth ten meters away. Only slightly dazed, he stood up right away. He might have been small, but he had learnt from his father how to face down an old lone wolf or make a solo attack on a young, impetuous boar.

Here, he was fighting for his life. Fear, mixed with the excitement of battle, galvanized him, and he felt a fierce energy building within him, despite his wounds where the Troll's nails had slashed him. After all, he was an Ogre. He too was a predator, feared by the creatures of the forest. And so, he let out a loud war cry. The Troll paused in surprise. Ogrino seized the moment to dive between the monster's legs and bite deeply into the hollow behind his left knee. Once again the Troll howled in pain. Lightning-quick, he caught the perpetrator, but as he tried to take a step, his foot would not respond. The tendon had been severed by Ogrino's bite. Off-balance, the Troll fell from his great height. The impact was all the worse because the Troll was very large and full-bellied. Concentrating on breaking his fall, the Troll let go of Ogrino again and the child rolled to the ground, then jumped up quickly.

The Troll, too, succeeded in standing up again, though with difficulty. Dawn was beginning to break, but neither of the two combatants paid any attention. The Troll wanted to be done with the little morsel of prey taunting him, and the child was concentrating only on the Troll's movements. The monster blocked his path, and Ogrino suddenly realized that his back was to a precipice and any false move could be fatal. The Troll raked one arm through the air to prevent any attempts at escape, while with the other hand he picked up a big rock that he lifted above his head. Despite their usual nearsightedness, Trolls are formidable foes as far as the accuracy of their throws is concerned. The little Ogre knew this from his father. The Troll had begun to cock his arm back to throw the rock when something strange happened.

The first ray of sun illuminated the two fighters at the exact moment that the enormous projectile came soaring toward Ogrino. As swiftly as a cat, he dodged to avoid the impact. Blinded by the rising sun, he realized too late that he had one foot in the void behind him. He lost his balance and felt himself falling backwards. Before falling, he had time to see the Troll, still frozen in the same position, arm raised. The light of day had irrevocably and eternally transformed that creature of darkness into a statue.

And for the child—the void! It was a moment set apart from time in which everything seemed to be in slow motion.

Fear mixed with all sorts of thoughts raced through his mind. And then the impact, sudden and heavy, onto a sort of thorny bush! The child didn't feel hurt, only numb. He contemplated the starry vault hanging over the cliff from which he had just fallen. How beautiful! His eyes began to want to close, he fought it off a bit, and then very soon all was dark and silent.

When he awoke, it was the middle of the day. The sun shone brightly, already high in the sky. He got up and felt hungry, very hungry indeed. He looked about; he was surrounded by a thick bush, full of thorns, that were scratching him. Examining his body, he saw that he was scraped and cut up all over. The bush could not have been the only cause of so many wounds. Whatever had happened to him, he did not remember. He extricated himself without too much damage from the spiny plant and immediately set about finding food. He was tired and a bit stiff; his legs felt as if they were made of jelly. His progress was slow as he lifted leaves and stones in search of some berries, fruits, or insects—anything, as long as it was edible. Seeing an anthill, he plunged a stick into it. The stick was instantly covered with hundreds of ants, which he eagerly licked off. They crackled between his teeth and tasted slightly sweet. After having plunged the stick in another twenty times or so, he discovered that he was still hungry and decided, therefore, to look for snails hidden in the tall grass. When he found one here or there, he devoured it immediately, shell and all. After about a hundred, he stopped. He already felt better, but he was hungry for something else, something more substantial and juicier. It was at that moment that he heard a hare, digging in the earth in search of some root or tuber. He slowly picked up a nice stone and threw it as hard as he could at the animal, hitting it right in the head. He was happy to discover that his aim was better than he had ever suspected. With a bound, he was upon his prey and swallowed it in a single mouthful. How delicious that hot meat was, that fragrant blood and those little bones that cracked between his teeth. What a feast! It was so good that he needed another one.

He walked a fairly long way before catching a glimpse of a large, black and white shape scurrying along among the ferns. He positioned himself directly behind the animal and began to run as fast as he could. The beast, surprised, bolted, but too slowly to escape its predator, who caught it by the tail. The little Ogre spun around, whirling his prey around him until the animal's head hit the trunk of a tree, breaking its neck. The child threw himself on his lunch, which was in fact an old badger, big and quite fat. He reveled in the musky meat as well as the fat melting beneath his tongue. A real delicacy! When he had finished his frugal meal, he felt much better but was still a little hungry, so he kept walking in the woods in search of other game. He was very thirsty as well. A spring or a river would be a welcome find. Lifting his nose, he sniffed to see if he could smell water. How did he know how to hunt game? How could he detect a smell as subtle as water? He didn't know. It was instinctive in his nature − of that he was sure.

Still walking, he heard a rustling behind the trees and squeezed himself between the rocks. A lovely and large river was outstretched before his delighted eyes. He plunged his hands into the clear, fast-flowing water, brought them to his mouth, and drank greedily. He drank and drank and drank whole liters. What happiness, to no longer have a burning throat, a cottony mouth, the disagreeable sensation of being all dried out. Despite this, he was still hungry. To appease the rumbling in his stomach, he would have still needed a little deer or a dozen rabbits. He set himself to his quest, listening carefully for the faintest sound as he walked along the river. After a good hour of walking, during which he had gorged himself on tons of berries, he saw ahead of him, four plump young boars gamboling along against the wind. He licked his lips with delight, already savoring these little roasts on hooves. He approached on tiptoe, hidden by the high brush. The boars were very busy digging in the earth with their snouts and didn't even lift their heads to survey their surroundings. The little Ogre was upon the four of them in an instant, encircling them with his arms and squeezing with all his might. The young boars began to squeal, high strident cries that pained the ears. The child ate one of his prisoners in a single swallow, but the noise was still insufferable. He was getting ready to devour a second one for a little bit of peace when the sound of galloping behind him made him turn his head. An enormous sow was charging upon him. He instinctively let go of the three miserable little boars to prepare for combat, but the closer the animal got, the larger it looked.

The impact would be violent, so the child dug his feet into the soil and bent his knees slightly, waiting for the assault. The female boar's head crashed into his stomach with extreme violence, lifted him into the air, and sent him flying several yards away. As he twirled in the air, the child prepared himself for the impact of his fall. How surprised he was, then, to feel himself land not on hard ground but in water. He disappeared in a cloud of spray, right in the middle of the river.

After his relief came anxiety because he couldn't touch the bottom and he didn't know how to swim. He fluttered wildly, trying to stay on the surface, all the while aiming for the still faraway riverbank. He used a ridiculous amount of energy as the current was growing ever stronger. His head was now above, now below the surface, and he kept getting water up his nose. The torrents' fury was increasing every minute and all hope of reaching the bank seemed lost. The little Ogre heard a hollow rumble from downstream. It sounded like an angry giant's continuous grumbling. As time went on, the rapids bubbled and foamed all the more and the child was exhausting himself trying to keep his head above water.

The rumbling was now deafening, and the trees and boulders on the bank were flying past. The little Ogre couldn't tell what was happening for all the water in his eyes. He found himself surrounded by water and yet he was falling, still falling. The fall seemed quite long and then he was once again plunged underwater, under tons of swirling water that dragged him ever deeper. Little by little, he floated back to the surface like a cork. As soon as his head poked out of a wave, he breathed in a huge mouthful of oxygen, so forcefully that it seemed his lungs would burst. He was alive. He had survived a long drop from the top of the waterfall that he could now see high above him.

The current was calmer now, but the child struggled to keep himself barely afloat, and certainly could not aim for any particular direction. As he was flailing awkwardly, trying not to sink, his left arm struck something hard behind him. He turned around and saw that something big was floating on the surface. One might have guessed it to be an immense, rough-skinned crocodilian but luckily, it was nothing but a thick tree-trunk. The child quickly latched onto the prominent bark and began to scale this heaven-sent raft. He sat with one leg on each side of the trunk, feet dipping into the water.

He lifted his chest and leaned back his head, letting loose a big, joyous, 'YAHOOOO! I'M ALIVE! I MADE IT!'

His powerful glad cry echoed for a long time in the forest, sounding like this:

'GRAHOOOO . . . GRO GRONO GRIGO . . . GRO O GRIUGITO . . .'

For that was how the language of the Ogres went. He was so glad to have escaped all those dangers and now felt as if he were king of this imposing skiff in the middle of the river that had frightened him so much until just now. He could rest while waiting for the current to bring him to the riverbank and there, he could take up his path again. But actually, where should he go? And where was he coming from? What was he doing all alone in this immense forest? Why was he wounded? What had happened to him? He had no answers to any of these questions. Despite all his efforts to dig through his memory, he didn't remember anything. It was as if his life had begun when he awoke in the bush full of thorns. And then, too, what was his name? What was he called? He had racked his brains, but nothing, nothing came to mind. He didn't even know if he had a name. So he began to cry, lying down on his stomach and resting his head on the rough trunk. He cried tears of distress because not only did he feel frighteningly alone, but worse, he had the impression of being nobody. Having neither a past nor a name, what would become of him?

He cried for a long time, then, worn out, fell asleep with his face against the bark. Nightmares followed one after another. Sometimes he was battling wild boars with sharp tusks, sometimes he was falling down a dizzying waterfall, unable to resurface. His anguished dreams lasted for hours even as his heaven-sent vessel glided peacefully on the calm waves, under the dense canopies of hundred-year-old trees.

PANTALEONE & SLEVANIA

Shivering, the little Ogre awoke with a start. It was night. The trunk had gotten stuck in the rocks along the bank, making a long bridge to dry land. In the blink of an eye, the child had stood up, skipped down the trunk, and jumped onto the shore. Then he walked along the curve of the bank for a little while, and there appeared a multitude of colorful lights that trembled in the night. The little Ogre, fascinated, couldn't tear his eyes from the sight and approached it, hypnotized. With each step, the lights grew larger and a joyful tune began to reach his ears. When he was very close, he saw a great many colorful wooden cabins on wheels, lit torches attached to their walls. Behind the cabins, a huge, brightly colored tent presided over the scene. Inside it were many dancing lights. That was where the music was coming from, a loud and lively melody full of BOM BOM BOM and LA-DA LA-DA DADA DADA. It was both peculiar and fascinating.

Although he was a bit afraid of all these oddities, since he had never seen anything like them, he gathered up his courage and entered this bizarre universe. Upon reaching the edge of the big tent, he tried to lift it up, but it was stuck to the ground, so he quickly burrowed into the earth so that he could slip inside.

When the hole was big enough, he put his head through and found himself underneath wooden steps full of legs, dozens and dozens of legs, and also full of laughter, laughs that were braying and sharp and deep but mainly joyful, very joyful indeed. He wanted to know what the source of all this commotion was, and he slipped under the benches to the center of the tent. There, a creature with an all-white face, an enormous red mouth, and orange hair was holding between its arms a sort of giant square caterpillar that made music each time it breathed. During this time, a big monkey went to get some kind of fluffy, soft white fruits to throw at the musician, each time producing great peals of laughter, particularly among the children. Looking more closely, the little Ogre saw that the closest row of seats encircling the stage was filled with radiant-faced children. He didn't understand much about all this, but the friendly atmosphere here was intoxicating, especially after all he had been through in those long recent hours. He would have liked to stay there forever to laugh with these children who resembled him, except that they had parents who would take them onto their laps or buy them multicolored sweets. His stomach began to growl; he was hungry again, feeling a ferocious appetite that could not wait. He left the way he had come in and wove between the wagons in search of food, lifting his nose to sniff the air. An appetizing odor of fresh meat tickled his nostrils, so he ran up to a long cage in the shadows, where he was able to make out an imposing hunk of meat in one corner. He held onto the cage's bars, gracefully slipped inside, caught hold of the bone, and began to devour the carcass noisily. At that moment, a big reddish shape moved at the end of the wagon and threw itself like a lightning bolt onto the little Ogre.

'HELP, HELP, quick, come here. He's going to get himself eaten!'

The adolescent shouted as he ran between the wagons but didn't come across anyone. So he went hurtling off toward the big tent, stopping only in the middle of the ring.

'Help, a child is getting eaten in the lion's cage. Come quickly!' he cried.

Immediately the music stopped, silence settled over the circus, and Pantaleone, the director, took his whip and ran toward the beast's cage. When he got there, he saw with horror that a little child was struggling between the growling lion's powerful paws.

'Back, Royal, back,' he shouted, whipping the cage.

The lion didn't even lift its head but continued to lunge at the child, who was kicking it in the belly. Its open mouth was near the child's throat. Then Pantaleone opened the cage and went in. He whipped the lion with all his might, several times. The lion roared softly in pain and suddenly stopped fighting, going to lie down contritely at the end of its den. The little Ogre stood up and looked, astonished, at the tall, robust, mustachioed man who had frightened the lion.

'Come here, my boy, it's all over. You're safe now. I'll bring you back to my wagon to take care of your wounds, and your parents will meet us there.'

The child couldn't decode these words, but he could tell that they were friendly. What he couldn't understand most of all was why the man had interrupted his game with the lion, who was so kind and was just as lonely as he. He had been surprised at his own ability to understand, or rather to perceive, the feelings of this solitary old lion, who was badly in need of a friend. He had been happy to have found someone who was a bit like him and whom he could play with.

The man had taken the child in his muscled arms, which vaguely reminded him of something he had experienced before. It was as if in a faraway past, someone big and strong had carried and protected him, but he had no recollection of who that could be. They arrived in front of a colored wooden wagon decorated with a lovely painted wheel surrounded by funny marks that the child did not understand. They went in. There, they saw a variety of odds and ends: boots, pots and pans, fruits, clothing, hoops, stools, and hats. At the top of a ladder, Ogrino saw the big monkey waddling about, the one that had been throwing cream pies at the accordionist clown's face during the show.

'Here's Gumbo, my chimpanzee,' Pantaleone said joyfully. 'And in back there, that's the apple of my eye, Slevania Orlanova.'

The little Ogre, who had not gotten a single word of all that gobbledygook, understood by the mustachioed man's tilted chin that he should look to the back of the wagon, where in the low light a white shape was shining. A woman came out of the corner. She was pretty, with a delicate face, big gray eyes, and silvered hair but elegant features. A broad smile lit up her face. She was wearing a long white dress topped with a beige fur that snugly warmed her neck. She approached and carefully observed the child with a curious, yet amused air. When she saw his wounds, she cried out:

'OHH! My goodness, what happened to him?'

'Royal scratched him. His wounds are deep. He needs your herbal salves.'

'Undress him. He must be washed first. Take the hot water from the big pan and pour it into the tub. We'll dip him in it and I'll be able to tend to his wounds. I will get my ointments.'

The man with the mustache tried to take off the child's clothes, but the latter protested with wild gestures and pulled his shirt down. Sullenly, he shook his head left and right. The big man tried again to pull the garment off, but the child suddenly opened a wide mouth and bit him. The adult stifled a wail; the child didn't loosen his hold, which was cutting into the man's hand.

'Stop, stop—I mean you no harm! Can't you see that we just want to wash you and take care of your wounds?'

The child did not respond, but he let up and freed the man's hand, which was bleeding abundantly from a semicircular wound. The woman had come back, laden with jars of all sizes.

'What's going on? My goodness, you're really bleeding!'

'Yes, this little terror bit me hard. It seems he does not understand our language,' said Pantaleone angrily. 'Slevania! Take care of him. Maybe you will have better luck than I did. I've got to go bandage my hand right away.'

The woman approached the child, smiling, making slow and subtle movements. She gazed intensely at his big bright eyes, a torrent of affection flowing from her pupils. The little Ogre felt himself melt. He had endured so many trials, had been so cold and so hungry before arriving in this warm shelter, that he now felt like letting go, letting himself be cared for, and this woman seemed trustworthy. When she delicately removed his garments one by one, he finally gave up. She then picked him up tenderly, holding him against herself, and placed him into the tub of hot water. It felt so good to be in this perfumed liquid that warmed both body and spirit. Slevania Orlanova, wife of Pantaleone, had never been able to have a child, and so she felt close to all the children in the world. This one, however, was different in both appearance and behavior. As she sponged him clean, she noticed the details of his body type—the thick short hands, the stocky arms and legs, the broad shoulders, the thick neck, the round face with its robust bones, the straight black hair. The teeth most of all attracted her attention, for they were extremely pointed, which gave him a strange smile, like a toothed saw. After having thoroughly soaped up each part of the child's chubby body, she took him out of the tub and sat him on a thick towel in which she then wrapped him, drying him off from head to toe. The child, tickled, erupted in laughter. So Slevania, too, began to laugh heartily.

Pantaleone, who had finished dressing his wound, came back and admired the scene with great joy. It had been years since he had seen Slevania so jubilant. Slevania took the child tightly in her arms and kissed him affectionately again and again. The little Ogre found this very agreeable, as if this too recalled very distant memories. So he, too, wrapped his stubby arms around the woman and pulled himself close to her. Slevania was still; she was savoring this happy moment. Pantaleone's eyes grew moist with emotion, and a tear began to bead on his cheek. For him as well, it had been a long time since his old wagon had last been blessed with the warm and enchanting presence of a child. For years, he had been traveling the world, going from city to city to bring joy to the hearts of children and adults. He realized suddenly that his devotion to this pursuit was due to a hole in his own heart that he was trying to fill. He gave to everyone since he had no one to give to in particular. And this wild child had burst into his life all of a sudden, and now he felt a violent affection toward the little dear, who intrigued Pantaleone although he knew nothing about him. Slevania coated the child's wounds with various ointments, taking care not to hurt him. When he was completely swaddled in bandages like a little mummy, she put one of her pullovers on him, rolling up the sleeves which were two times too long. Only the child's feet peeked out from the bottom of the thick, warm woolen sweater. Pantaleone placed a large, steaming pot on the table and spooned a large portion of stew onto a plate that sat before the little boy. The child threw himself upon the food and devoured the big piece of beef in one bite. Seeing this, Slevania and Pantaleone were frozen in astonishment. The child then climbed up on a chair to be able to look into the pot. Seeing that it was full of other delicious morsels of meat, he lifted the pot and poured it into his mouth, crunching on and drinking down the whole family's meal in only a few seconds. Having finished, he set the pot down with a satisfied air and a wide smile lit up his face. Pantaleone and Slevania, who had remained still this whole time, looked at each other, stupefied. Decidedly, this child was very strange. They whispered into each others' ears and Slevania went to get something from the cabinet. She came back with an enormous cream cake that she placed in front of the child. Barely had it been set down when the little Ogre pounced upon it and, seizing the cake with bare hands, he gobbled it up as quick as a wink. He rejoiced in it; he had never eaten something so delicious. It was sugary, unctuous on the tongue, sweet on the palate. A real delicacy! Jumping up from his chair, he ran to hug Slevania, who was bowled over, torn between delight and worry. This was no ordinary child—and in fact, was he really a child after all? The little Ogre sat down again and felt very tired now. His eyelids began to droop. Slevania noticed this, took him in her slender arms, and delicately laid him down in her large bed. She drew a thick blanket up to his chin and hummed a lullaby. The child, enveloped by the soft melody, fell gently into a comfortable sleep.

Scarcely had he closed his eyes than Pantaleone said, 'Slevania, we cannot keep this child. Anyway it isn't a child, and you know that as well as I do.'

'Precisely,' Slevania responded, 'he has no family. He is lost. If we do not keep him, what will become of him? He will wander the streets, loot trash cans for food.'

'Or else he will go back to the forest where he belongs!' Pantaleone flung back coldly.

'I do not believe that to be the solution,' retorted Slevania. 'I will consult the cards.'

She took out a tarot deck and laid out twelve cards in three lines in front of her. She turned over the first card from the top left. *The King of Swords: a bad omen, a meticulous man representing repression and harm,* she thought. Then she lifted the card diagonal from the first, on the bottom right, and saw the Knave of Cups, who is passionate and far from loved ones. Undoubtedly this one referred to the child. She flipped over the Knight of Cups, a sentimental man who defended love, as well as the Queen of Coins, a sensual woman, the both of whom undoubtedly represented his parents. Then she drew the Two of Swords, which signifies an adversary or a devastating illness. Slevania trembled because the child seemed to be in real danger. Her unsteady hand came to rest next upon the Knight of Swords, a helpful and enterprising character who represents an unexpected source of support. She couldn't see what this might mean as of now. Continuing on the same diagonal toward the right, on the bottom line she turned over the Nine of Swords, which brings the illness or death of a loved one. She moved down a rung and took the card to the left of the last one; it was the King of Spears, that is, an intelligent man paving the way for success. Then she turned the card to its left and saw the Queen of Cups, who is an affectionate and devoted mother, who gives courage. Clearly these two cards represented Pantaleone and Slevania. Then she turned over the one just above the last, the Nine of Cups, then the one immediately to the right, number 21. This configuration promised joy and happiness in one's private life. The last card turned up was number 20, that is, the judgment that represents an important change. It was all so clear now! The child's mother and father were in death's grip and the child had been threatened. Slevania was sure now that she and Pantaleone had a role to play in protecting the child; it was their duty, even.

'We must keep him—this is proof!' Slevania declared. 'The cards have spoken. He needs us to protect him from some threat, and his destiny seems linked to ours.'

These words eliminated the last of Pantaleone's reluctance, since deep down he had really wanted to keep the charming, boisterous little man, though his reason had told him not to do it. So the adoption of the little Ogre was decided and a long, passionate kiss between Pantaleone and Slevania sealed the precious moment.

The next morning, after an almost sleepless night because of all their excitement over what had just happened, Pantaleone gathered the whole troupe beneath the big tent to announce the news.

Standing next to Slevania, who held in her arms a little boy all wrapped up, he declared, 'Destiny put this child, whom you see here, in our path, and after consulting the signs, we have decided to keep him since he is in fact an orphan and seemingly alone in the world. Soon we will officially induct him into the community, but for now, we simply want you all to know that from this day on, he must be considered as our son and a full member of our circus. I ask you to welcome him warmly and to watch over him.'

The sole response was a thunderous applause from all assembled and then everyone came to kiss the child's forehead. Ogrino was smiling blissfully at this spontaneous demonstration of so much affection toward him. In the days that followed, he came to know the different members of the circus, one by one. The mime Pianissimo, who, although he was a deaf mute, understood everything people were saying. The clown Cordicello, the accordionist, was lanky as a vine and always with a trick up his sleeve. The Messeyer twins, flying trapezists whom you could never keep straight as the brothers were like two peas in a pod. Othello, the juggler, who could keep ninety balls in the air at once. Pantaleone himself, apart from being the circus director, was also the animal trainer and he put on fantastic shows with Royal the lion, Colossus the Clydesdale horse, Herculium the elephant, and Gumbo the chimpanzee. Each day, the child would poke his nose into everything, curious as he was to understand this new world he now belonged to. From his own past, he remembered hardly anything, except that he had suffered in a hostile world before coming to this peaceful haven, full of warmth and attention.

A year passed in this way, punctuated by schooling provided by Slevania, games with other circus children, and diligent observation of the artists' practicing. The clowns particularly pleased the little Ogre. So through a mixture of simple pleasures and encounters with people of peculiar talents, he had little by little settled into the human world. He had learned their language and even how to read and write. What's more, the child knew how to count as well, and he very much liked to do so. He did sums in his head all day as he walked around. He even amused himself occasionally with multiplication, from the number of poles in the big tent to the cents on the receipts that Slevania entered each night into the circus's account books. But to really become a little boy almost like the others, something important was still missing. And that was why, early in the morning on the day of the winter solstice, Slevania gathered all the circus people together, as the event was an important one. That day, when the light begins to little by little overtake night's darkness, was the day of her adopted son's baptism. One and all, of course, had accepted the invitation, out of friendship for their employers as well as affection for this strangely charming little boy. It took place in the main ring of the circus, in the big tent. Even Colossus, Gumbo, and Herculium were present, their eyes wide at the unusual decor for the event. In the middle, a fire smoldered; then, near a big barrel filled with water, a plate of salt sat on a stool; and finally, a ceremonial cup full of incense rested atop a stepladder. Slevania said a few words in a tone that was both serious and joyful.

'We are gathered here for a solemn moment. Today not only do we, Pantaleone and I, adopt this child, but we also give him a name. In this way, he will formally enter into the circus community, and through that, into the community of the Wind People. We will practice a rite as old as time itself. This rite is truly an initiation; it deeply transforms the being, and after this ceremony, the child will not be the same at all.

The little Ogre listened attentively and was very moved since he knew that after this special day, things would no longer be as before. At the same time, he was a little afraid. He did not like the sound of the process Slevania had described one bit, not one bit—for some unknown reason, it even terrified him.

Slevania spoke in the slow tones of an enchantment.

'Each of the four elements we have here is a symbol − the fire is death, the water, life, the rock salt, earth, and the incense, air. For the rite to be complete, the child must experience each of the four elements, beginning with fire, for he must die to be reborn into his new life.'

Cordicello, the musician, began to beat a drumroll that increased in volume until Gumbo took over, beating on the tom-toms under Pantaleone's direction. Excitement took hold of the audience and the child. The young Ogre began to feel a furious need to dance, little by little forgetting the visceral fear that the blaze's remains inspired in him. Slevania murmured something in his ear, and he took off his shoes and resolutely aimed himself at the glowing coals.

'Fire,' Slevania continued, 'represents the force of destruction, death, but also the painful trials of life that every man is called upon to battle. So beginning at this moment, our future son will forge his ability to overcome even the most terrible hardships.'

The rhythm of the drums, now spellbinding, had taken possession of the boy, who was already taking his first steps onto the glowing coals as if they were only pebbles. The leathery soles of his little Ogre-feet could not, on their own, explain why he felt no pain. Certainly something was going on. Perhaps it was the music that put him in a sort of trance, soothed him like a protective balm, healing his burns. If the smoke emanating from his feet and the foul odor of roasted pig in the air were to be believed, the little man was well and truly burning. As soon as he had arrived at the end of the coals, Pantaleone took him in his arms and sat him on the edge of the barrel, feet dangling in the cool water.

The director then proclaimed, 'You have emerged victorious from the most difficult part of the rite. Here you are, a new being, ready to begin a new life, but for that, you must pass the second trial − water. Water represents the force of regeneration, fertility, life. Submerging yourself in water, you will truly achieve your rebirth.'

A flute's soft, joyous melody streamed into the midst of the assembly on a refreshing breeze. The child felt serene. He quite liked taking baths, and he knew that this one would be different, that it would cleanse him on the inside, and his heart leapt at the thought. Pantaleone carefully lifted him above the barrel, and when the flute stopped, a weighty silence took hold, and the little Ogre was entirely plunged into the water. He came out soaking wet, a smile on his lips, then disappeared below the surface again, emerging only to be immersed a third and final time. When the rite was finished, Slevania wrapped him up in a white towel from which only his face emerged. Pantaleone held him up with outstretched arms, turning around to present him to all assembled.

He announced in a loud voice, 'This boy is now our son. From this moment on, his name will be OGRINO in honor of his insatiable appetite, which brings to mind that of the forest creatures we call Ogres!'

All applauded. Some threw their hats in the air, and Herculium, the elephant, trumpeted loudly, his trunk held high. The child was thrilled to have a name at last. He had an identity now. Without his really knowing why, the name seemed familiar to him. Certainly, Slevania had not revealed that before the ceremony, she had consulted the tarot cards to find out what name to give him. As always, unseen threads had woven a tapestry that contained messages available to those who were ready to decode them, but hidden from those with closed hearts. Guided by her love for the child and her desire not to hurt him, Slevania had been able to divine the name that had already belonged to the little Ogre, in the past. Ogrino was now a person in his own right, and what's more, he was now part of a real family and a happy community. All of this delighted him and made him feel deeply secure. Still, for some unknown reason, in the depths of his heart a veil of sadness and melancholy managed to cover the most wonderful moments of his life, even a day like today.

Before the boy was dragged too far into his inner thoughts, Pantaleone declared, 'The ceremony is not over—two more elements remain. First of all, the earth represented by the salt, taken from the depths of mines. The earth represents density, stability; it is incarnation. We are the children of the earth, and our presence here must have some meaning. We find ourselves here for a precise reason: we must do our bit to further the evolution of the world. Our lives must have flavor. In eating a bit of this salt, Ogrino will take on the flavor of the earth, so that he in his turn may flavor his own life and those of others.'

Another solemn moment followed. Several men began to blow into long, wide tubes of wood resembling big hollow reeds, one end of which rested on the ground. A very low and insistent sound arose, vibrating the assembled bodies like so many resonant drums. Ogrino felt irresistibly pulled downwards, as if he would be forever rooted to the spot where he now stood. He felt energy flowing beneath his feet, and he transformed into a kind of obelisk planted deeply into the ground, vibrating in unison with Mother Earth. The sensation proved so pleasant, pulled you so far down into yourself, that it took the child a bit of time to come back to the reality surrounding him.

'The time has come to taste the salt and take on the essence of the earth,' Pantaleone continued.

Once again silence reigned, and Slevania brought the plate up to Ogrino's face. The boy opened his mouth instinctively, stuck out his tongue, and closed his eyes. A bit of powder fell onto his tongue, and a salty, sharp, and slightly bitter flavor with a hint of earthiness spread delicately toward the back of his throat. He swallowed, and strangely, the taste became a flood of milk and honey in his mouth. Ogrino's jaw dropped in surprise. This was all incomprehensible. This baptism had certainly turned out to be an extraordinary and wondrous experience. He was grinning from ear to ear. Slevania, Pantaleone, and all those in attendance smiled as well, in chorus with the child's delight.

'We have now reached the critical point of the celebration,' Pantaleone declared, 'because the incense symbolizes the being's elevation.'

He took Ogrino in his arms and sat him on the top rung of the stepladder, a cup of incense between the child's feet. Then Slevania brought up a candle and lit the incense. A heavy ochre smoke rose up, forming a veil that caressed Ogrino's face. At the same time, the strings of a harp began to quiver with a light and peaceful melody. After having felt anchored to the earth, now Ogrino felt pulled by some invisible hand toward the sky. The more he breathed in these heady vapors, the lighter he felt—so light that he felt the slightest breeze could carry him away. He became a musical note rising into the air, an effervescent vibration, a sound that did not die, but perpetuated infinitely in space. The harp continued to unwind its melody and Ogrino was each one of its notes, jumping from Do to Mi, from Sol to Ti. He climbed octave by octave toward ever-more-crystalline sounds. It seemed to him that this would never stop, that he would rise ever higher. Intoxicated by the curls of perfumed smoke, he felt his head spin slightly. It was as if he were drunk. The harp had stopped but the child continued to hear delicious, fascinating, enchanting sounds from a celestial orchestra. Suddenly he had an extraordinary vision. He saw two large, robust figures sleeping. A woman and a man floated in a clear blue liquid. It seemed that he knew them, and yet he could not remember ever having met them. Who, then, could they be if he felt this deep affection toward them? The vision was gone as quickly as it had appeared. The child, deeply moved, lost his balance and fell from the stepladder. Pantaleone barely had the time to catch him in midair. Ogrino, who had scarcely realized that he was falling, found that he was wracked with sobs, his eyes haggard and tearful.

'He is a very sensitive being. He must have been shaken up by this rite, which by its nature touches your very core. It will pass, but he needs calm,' Slevania murmured. 'We will celebrate later this evening,' she added.

At these words, everyone fell silent, and some began to leave quietly already. In a short time, Slevania, Pantaleone, and Ogrino were alone.

'My child, my son, how did it go? What emotions are you feeling?'

Ogrino did not answer, but stared off into space. He was still haunted by his strange, incomprehensible vision, which had filled him with great sorrow, like the feeling of a parting.

'Leave him be,' advised Pantaleone. 'Don't you see that he's not entirely himself yet? He must have risen very far, high up into spheres known only to him. Maybe even beyond that and that's why he seems so upset.'

Ogrino was inconsolable for most of the afternoon, and it wasn't until the evening, when the paper lanterns were lit, when a big cheerful fire crackled in the middle of the tables set up for the banquet, that his eyes once again burned bright with mischief.

'Where was I? What happened to me? I remember a bottomless sadness and I don't know why,' the little Ogre wondered plaintively.

'You took a very long trip within yourself, to shores that only you can reach and perhaps you found something there, some event or memory that hurt you,' Slevania answered. Then she murmured, 'Maybe it has to do with your parents from before.'

'My parents from before?'

'Yes, you know that we found you in the circus one evening. To know where you came from, I consulted the tarot cards and your parents from before appeared to me.'

'Where are they?' Ogrino interrupted feverishly.

'Do you think that we would have kept you here if we could have returned you to your parents, my child?'

'NOOO, I don't want to hear any more. Leave me alone, leave me alone!'

And he ran between the wagons and into the night.

The child had not reappeared after a good hour, and so Slevania was preparing to send the whole circus out to look for him.

Pantaleone stopped her, saying, 'I know where to find him.'

He left the wagon and strode confidently toward the back of the tent. He wasn't surprised to see Ogrino snuggled against Royal, who was listening patiently and growling softly in approval as Ogrino confided all his woes.

'Come along, everyone is waiting for you. Don't forget that tonight was organized in your honor. We will talk about all of this again tomorrow. Tonight is the time for joy, music, dance, a wonderful meal where we'll roast a whole cow over a wood-burning fire . . .'

'A whole cow?' Ogrino cried.

He got up, kissed Royal right between the eyes, and scampered off lightning-fast toward the inferno dancing in the distance. A succulent odor of grilled meat tickled his nostrils. He took a long kitchen knife and cut off a large slice of flesh, dripping with fat, from the animal's haunch. Despite the intense heat that slightly burned his tongue and palate, Ogrino thoroughly enjoyed this tender, musky meat. The whole circus community had gathered again before the heartwarming sight of this little man who had regained his good spirits and legendary appetite.

Tambourines began to quiver, then to rattle, to an upbeat melody. The women performed dances that were now lively and staccato, now slow and sensual, while the men formed a big circle around them, clapping their hands. When Ogrino was full, which is to say when he had eaten half of the cow, Slevania took him by the hand and brought him to the center of the circle, where she began to dance dreamily. Ogrino was hypnotized by the sensual movements of her body, of her arms and especially of her hands, which seemed to attempt to comb through the air. He lost himself in this dance, a strong yet fluid expression that inspired contemplation, as if before something sacred. Ogrino remained frozen, stunned, and overcome by his adoptive mother's talent, which he had never suspected. When she finished her dance, the spectators remained silent for a moment in reflection, then the music continued in a joyful burst of cymbals, drums, trumpets, and violins. Couples formed instantaneously and entered into a boisterous dance. Pantaleone kissed Slevania and led her into the middle of the other dancers, where the couple disappeared, absorbed by the frenetic centipede of dancers. The festivities lasted all night, and the members of the circus did not return to their wagons until dawn's first rays.

The Magnus Legifer watched the break of day from his office window. It was exactly six twelve and twenty-three seconds. Very often, unable to sleep, he awoke before sunrise, which allowed him to start the day with a grandiose show, worthy of someone of his rank. His insomnia was caused by both excitement and anxiety about the task at hand, the staggering heap of problems to be solved. The goal was immense and the obstacles were in scale with the ambition. Despite the worries gnawing away at him, Primus remained fixed on his plan's ultimate success since the stakes were too high for him to allow failure.

He took down his bullhorn and requested four couriers. One minute later, they were knocking on the heavy door.

'Come in immediately,' he said peremptorily. 'I want you to set out immediately for the North, South, East, and West to recruit mercenaries to help our Militians on the lines, to fulfill their mission of capturing prisoners and collecting information. Time is of the essence and I will not tolerate any delay, so I have decided to allot part of Legiferius's riches to hire four thousand strong, courageous men, men who won't be fazed by anything. Go to taverns, inns, to the seediest parts of little villages. Do not be too concerned about their morality; in fact, take the most uncouth and boorish because what we need them to do is no task for choirboys. Each man will receive one hundred silver coins for one month of work and a bonus of a gold crown for each creature captured. You will each leave along with twenty Militians and a carriage with a trunk full of coins. A month from now at the latest, I want to see that the one hundred and eighty legendary creatures on this list have been captured and brought here to be interrogated by the Docts of Legiferius. To be safe, in case some of them will not cooperate with the interrogation and have to be imprisoned, bring me at least three specimens of each kind. Is that clear?'

'Very clear, Magnus Legifer,' the four messengers answered in unison.

'We will go as swiftly as the wind and will keep you informed on proceedings by post,' added one.

'I want a daily report from each of you,' Primus interrupted, 'and whoever completes the mission first will receive one hundred gold crowns. Now go!'

They immediately turned on their heels and disappeared into the hallway. As soon as they were gone, Primus pressed a button and a secretary immediately appeared in the half-open doorway.

'You rang, Magnus Legifer?'

'Yes, I want to see the Magnus Scrutator as soon as possible. Get him for me,' Primus said curtly.

The man turned and bolted. It was only a few short minutes before Tertius arrived in the office.

'Ah, my dear Tertius! You're awake then? I thought I would be pulling you out of bed.'

'You know, I do not sleep much, Primus. Does not a Scrutator need to know all that is happening in the kingdom, night as well as day? Here is my report of last night's events. I'll sum it up for you. A Sprite captured by the Militia just as he was about to set fire to an abandoned barn. Pixies imprisoned for making a racket in a hotel. A Gnome caught red-handed climbing into a cottage window, apparently in order to steal a baby. Last but not least, an old, nearly blind Troll captured for knocking into and destroying a statue in a neighboring village.'

'That's all small fry,' interrupted Primus, 'but they will serve to begin our sampling of creatures of the Legendary World and become laboratory specimen for our medical Docts. Haven't we really done something admirable with this policy? Not only are we ridding our cities and country of these harmful pests, but also every day we will learn a little more about them and, so, enrich our Encyclopedia Legendari Mundi on course to our final goal.

'As this great event approaches, I have a special mission for you. I wish for you to personally take care of a matter of utmost importance. I want you to go meet the Baron of Swordscar, as he has information very precious to our cause. We need someone diplomatic and convincing, two qualities that come naturally to you. Along with your cunning, they should work wonders for obtaining his works on the Legendary World. It seems the Baron has put together a collection of detailed notes that we absolutely must obtain. Go as soon as you can to meet him at his manor at the edge of the forest and come back with his notes. If he does not cooperate, if he resists, you are to use any means necessary to obtain them, whatever the cost. Have I made myself clear?'

'Crystal clear, Magnus Legifer,' said Tertius with a hint of irony. 'You shall have your notes in no time at all. Goodbye for now, Primus.'

With this, he turned gracefully and left with a dignified air.

As soon as he had gone, Primus was already calling for his secretary.

'What may I do for you?' the man asked, having arrived at the office lightning-fast.

'Get for me the Commander of Infantry. I must speak to him at once.'

The Commander took about fifteen minutes to reach Primus, who met him coldly.

'I hope your men are quicker than their leader, Quintus, or else we shall have trouble in accomplishing our task.'

'I have been on maneuvers for the past week and we returned late last night, so I had a lot to take care of this morning . . . .'

'Enough! Excuses are for the weak. Whining is not worthy of a soldier and even less so of a Commander,' Primus interrupted brusquely. 'Our troops need practice. I want you to lead a major operation to give them a chance to stretch their legs and to test our capacity to attack, should conflict break out. By the way, where are we in the development of the Tetrabomb?'

'Our last expedition to the mines at Serangotch came back with a sufficient amount of fuel to allow us to try out the first prototypes. The expedition cost the lives of a dozen of my men since working conditions are so dangerous in that far-flung region of the kingdom.'

'The Order's greatness requires sacrifices, and your men should be proud to have perished in the noble service of Legiferius. We'll have a ceremony in their honor this week, where the chief of staff will meet with the families of the deceased. That said, when do you think you will be able to carry out the first tests? Before the end of the month?'

'I wish we could, but I think that we will need another forty days or so to work on the mechanism, and we won't be able to start tests until two months from now.'

'Two months! That is infinitely too long. I want everything to be in order a month from now, maximum. Use all necessary means. If the tests are conclusive and my calculations are exact, it will take nearly another two years until the Tetrabomb is really operational. Every day of delay could compromise our plan. You ought to be very aware of this and remind yourself of it each day, of course!'

'Absolutely. Please be assured, Primus, that I serve the Order unceasingly and that this project is particularly close to my own heart, as its completion could revolutionize everything.'

'So go, do not waste a second!'

Quintus left quickly, hiding his face so he would not show how much Primus's unreasonable demands had upset him. Primus, for his part, had already turned his thoughts to another subject. He was frantically ringing for his secretary in order to deal with the next matter.

Aristophanes had not appreciated the contents of the letter with Legiferius's coat of arms on it, not one bit. It announced to him the Magnus Scrutator's arrival that very same day. That did not bode well. The Baron's status as a noble and especially his passion for biological research made him an indispensible ally for an Order that claimed to be the perfect embodiment of scientific reasoning. He had already come into contact with the Docts from time to time, but he did not care for their attitude, which he thought was not respectful enough of the natural world. He believed, perhaps naively, that scientific research should serve to benefit life, not power. This fundamental difference in approach made him uncomfortable and prompted him not to cooperate with the Order, which he considered narrow-minded. Nevertheless, to oppose Legiferius too openly could cause him endless trouble. He had to make a good impression and seem to want to collaborate, all the while strictly limiting his contribution to projects he deemed dangerous.

Tertius arrived in the midmorning. Despite his triumphant air, he complimented the Baron profusely, as he had read the man's latest texts on the morphological similarities of Trolls and Sprites.

'You are a credit to the scientific community, thanks to the depth and quality of your research,' said Tertius in a honeyed voice.

'Oh, I am a mere enthusiast, and my methods are certainly less rigorous than the Docts'

'Do not be so modest; your conclusions on the behavior and customs of Pixies were drawn from the most careful and minute kind of study there is.'

'Indeed, but my resources are of significantly lesser scope than the Order's.'

'Sometimes one can achieve great things without great means. In fact, you are the perfect example. I happened to learn that you have assembled quite a collection of data on magical creatures, more specifically on marine creatures as well as on Elves. I consider this quite a feat, as Elves are difficult to find and even more so to study. Standing before a man such as yourself, whom I consider to be a leading expert in the field of the Magical World, I simply must invite you to attend the next Docts' colloquium. The kingdom's most eminent scientists will be present. There, you will be able to present your work, debate studies and theories, and expand your knowledge through fruitful exchanges with other researchers of your caliber. What do you think?'

'Your proposal honors me greatly. The opportunity to meet the most brilliant minds in the world is very appealing indeed. When is the colloquium?'

'In three days, which is why I came in person to inform you.'

'Three days! That's no time at all. I'll never be ready . . . I don't think it will be possible.'

'Do not be concerned—even if you are not able to prepare a paper for the occasion, it will be quite sufficient to bring your collection of notes to Legiferius, and you can present a summary of your work to the Docts. You will have access to your documents as needed, in order to develop any point more precisely. Don't you find that to be a nice solution?'

'I do not know. This is so sudden. I need to think about it.'

'I think perhaps you have not understood. There is no time to think about it. This colloquium is an incredible opportunity for you. Not only will you perfect your knowledge, but you will also become known and renowned throughout the kingdom. Do not dawdle! Say 'yes' and I can assure you that the Order will support you in your future undertakings.'

'The offer is incredibly tempting, and it is very difficult for me to refuse . . . So be it! Though I hardly think myself ready, I will attend. I suppose I will not sleep much over the next two nights, as I still have a quite a few little things to refine before my work will be coherent and presentable enough for an audience.'

'Well done! I am so very pleased with your wise decision, one befitting a true man of science. I shall have an escort prepared to bring you and your work to Legiferius, where you will stay for the four days of the colloquium.'

'You are too kind. However, I prefer to sleep in an inn that I know of not far from the fortress. I am comfortable in that intimate environment.'

'Come, come. Let's not make a fuss. You are my guest, and what's more, you are the guest of the Magnus Legifer, who wishes to have you at his table each night of the colloquium. There, you shall dine with such illustrious personages as Segundus.'

'The Magnus Doct in person?'

'Himself! What do you say then?'

'In that case, I agree to stay at Legiferius.'

'Let us shake hands as a sign of friendship and to seal our fruitful collaboration. You will not regret your decision. Your discussions will be so intense that you will enjoy every moment there.'

'I do not doubt it. And thank you for reaching out to me,' responded Aristophanes, trying to sound sincere.

'It's settled then—I shall send you an escort in three days.'

'Indeed. I will have my bags ready so that we can leave immediately.'

'Perfect! I must go now as I have other business to attend to. Until our next meeting, I bid you good day.'

'I will see you out as my butler is unwell.'

When they reached the threshold, the Magnus Scrutator left quickly, mounted his horse with ease, and set off at a gallop. As he disappeared in the distance, Aristophanes, filled with mixed emotions, did not move. He was repelled by the Order and all that it stood for, but on the other hand, he was tempted by the prospect of meeting people with whom he could have real scientific exchanges: a rare chance in this kingdom. That was why he had yielded to Tertius, but he would be on his guard and try to obtain as much information as possible for his own research without revealing more than necessary to the members of Legiferius. The colloquium would prove to be an exciting challenge, like a game of chess against the Order.

Far from these power struggles and ignorant of the trouble brewing, Ogrino was living a peaceful circus life. He felt affection for every member of the troupe, man or beast. Thanks to his Ogrean origins, he was always conniving with Royal, Gumbo, and Colossus, but this didn't hinder him in forming deep friendships with humans. In the company there were some, such as Camillo, who truly impressed Ogrino. The child was fascinated by Camillo's hands because they seemed to know how to make, tinker with, fix, and arrange everything. The circus people said that he had golden hands since they were so ingenious and surprisingly nimble. Ogrino watched them in hard labor like beating one of the big tent's poles in order to straighten it out, as well as in the most meticulous tasks, such as repairing the mechanism of a pocket watch.

Camillo also filled another role and a rather important one. He was one of the circus's crowning glories: the Human Cannonball. He appeared in the ring to a wild drumroll, dressed in immaculate white, with his cape floating behind him like an angel's wing. He had an elegant face, beautiful hazel eyes, and wavy jet-black hair. He was alluring, seductive. Compared to Pantaleone he was not very large; however, he was none the weaker for his slight frame, for his muscles were lanky and powerful. In short, he was built for the job. He had to be thin to be able to fit into the cannon's barrel and also quite toned, in order to shoot out like a rocket and be able to grasp the trapeze hung from the top of the tent. It was really something to see the eyes of children and adults alike, filled with fear and amazement, when this flying man suddenly burst into the air. Shortly after the clown had lit the cannon's fuse, he would explode out, seemingly carried by a cloud of thick white smoke and a thunderous roar. Camillo delighted in defying the danger nightly, dangling above the crowd on his trapeze with a broad smile, waves of applause washing over him. Ogrino froze up like a statue every time he saw the performance. He would have given anything to be able to experience something like that.

Camillo was married to Angelina, the cook. Angelina was her husband's complement: rather large, stocky, and quite plump, as she had a weakness for big, sauce-drenched dishes. Baby-faced, with mid-length, chestnut-brown hair and dark brown eyes that were as round as marbles behind her thick glasses, she could not see very well, but she could read your heart like an open book. The whole circus troupe rallied around her, as she took much care in preparing great quantities of delicious food. Three times a day, she set up a feast, the table adorned with a thousand-and-one flourishes, such as fruitcakes with maple syrup, goat sausages, or ginger-roasted bear. No one would have missed her meals for the world, as all rejoiced in the convivial atmosphere where they all shared their problems, triumphs, and hopes, and exchanged news of the Wind People.

Angelina was Ogrino's closest friend, or at least the one he loved the best. It must be said that she spoiled him particularly, serving him five or ten times the normal amount of food. She so loved to seeing this little man enthusiastically clean any plate she set before him. Ogrino, for his part, delighted in devouring all these dishes, but mostly, he loved for Angelina to tell him all kinds of stories from all over the world. As the cook, she went to market everyday to buy her own ingredients. She enjoyed talking to people, so she always had the latest news through her encounters with shopkeepers, traveling salesmen, voyagers, and vagabonds. It was she who first told Ogrino about Legiferius, the Order that ruled the kingdom and its inhabitants with their laws and militia. She explained that the Order was the supreme authority in the kingdom, that its power grew a little every day, and most importantly, that the Order hunted the creatures of the Legendary World.

'The Legendary World? What is that?' Ogrino questioned.

'It is the world of the magical creatures that live all around us, especially in the great forest. Some are kind and some are not, for example Trolls, who are stupid, violent half-giants.'

For some unknown reason, a shiver immediately ran down Ogrino's back.

'And then there are the Sprites, little gnomes who set fire to barns and terrify children. And so Legiferius is trying to re-establish order and peace in the kingdom. Still, I cannot help but feel a bit sick when I run into their soldiers, the Militians. Sometimes the cure can be worse than the disease.'

Ogrino didn't understand all that Angelina was saying; Nevertheless, he saw in her a mix of fear and revulsion, which he shared without knowing why.

'Try to avoid them as much as possible, my child. If you run into them, do all you can to go unnoticed. Never provoke them—they might bring you to their fortress, over in the middle of the city.'

'But I'm not a magical creature!' Ogrino said. 'Why should I be afraid?'

'You can never be too careful!' Angelina concluded. 'And now what would you say to a nice huckleberry pastry? I picked the berries myself in the forest this morning.'

'Yumm!' Ogrino licked his lips at the mere thought of a big pie, full of creamy butter and sweet huckleberries dripping through his fingers. 'You'll take me to the forest one day, won't you? So I can pick tons of wild strawberries and raspberries too?'

'When you're older,' said Angelina, 'because the forest can be dangerous for those who do not know it, and it is nowhere to take little children.'

Ogrino wanted to say that he did know the forest because that's where he had come from the night he arrived at the circus. But Angelina cut short his reflections, saying cheerfully,

'Come on, then! Our snack awaits!'

And that is how Ogrino forgot the cook's worrisome comments and returned to his carefree youth, made up of simple joys and immediate pleasures.

TIBOURSIO

Two years passed like that, dotted with school lessons from Slevania, games with other circus children, gargantuan snacks, and performances in which Ogrino participated more and more. Wherever the circus stopped—whether in villages, hamlets, or cities—it brought joy and liveliness, which warmed Ogrino's heart every time. He was glad to be part of bringing happiness to the people of the kingdom. Pantaleone and his friends played a truly useful role in this drab world, where poverty and poor living conditions could make everyone so mournful sometimes.

One day, the morning after a performance where Ogrino had made waves as a gluttonous clown, a man knocked softly on the door of Pantaleone's wagon. Pantaleone, who at this hour was washing up, took a while to open the door and appeared in a large red robe and with shaving soap all over his face.

'Hello! Who are you and what do you want?' he said in his big, deep voice.

'Allow me to introduce myself, sir. I am Aristophanes, the Baron of Swordscar, at your service!'

'My service? Great God, what service could you be of to me?'

'It's just an expression we use in my field, but it is entirely possible that I could be of service to help you discover something, something concerning the little boy named Ogrino, who works in your circus—he is named Ogrino, is he not? Is he your child?'

'Ogrino is indeed my son, yes, but how does that concern you?' Pantaleone asked suspiciously.

'It so happens that I am a great observer and that I have long studied all sorts of fields, especially genealogy. Do you know of it? The study of origins, lineage, descendants, ancestors, that sort of thing. This leads me sometimes to be a paleontologist as well, which is to say to study the living things that have existed throughout the ages.'

'Do you work for Legiferius?' Pantaleone asked with a hint of anxiety.

'No, and may God keep me from it! I could never serve a cause I do not support. You see, Legiferius fights whatever it believes to be uncontrollable, rather than trying to understand and communicate intelligently with those beings. There lies the big difference between Legiferius's approach and mine, and why its so-called Order is destined for failure. No! My motivation is an interest, a fascination I would have to say, for the magnificence of all creation and its varied life forms, each one more complex and ingenious than the last. Isn't all this diversity marvelous? Far from being a nuisance, as Legiferius sees it, it is a song of praise to the glorious perpetuation of Life! By trying so hard for order, Legiferius's system is running itself into the ground. Anyway, their methods are despicable. Did you know that several years ago, the Docts tried to steal my research when I was their invited guest? They are vile and deceitful people. But I digress, excuse me! I came to speak to you about Ogrino. Perhaps we would be more comfortable discussing this inside if you do not mind inviting me in for a cup of tea.'

Pantaleone felt sympathetic toward this noble who had taken the liberty of 'mixing' with the people by coming to see him in person, without great ceremony. He was also, it must be said, intrigued by the man's discourse. What insight could he have about Ogrino that Pantaleone had not already discovered?

'Of course, please come in,' he said cordially. 'Excuse the mess. We did not expect visitors at such an early hour. If you don't mind, I will finish washing up while my wife makes you a nice cup of tea. Slevania, dear, would you come here? We have a distinguished guest, the Baron of Swordscar, first name Aristophanes,' he called. 'May my wife call you Aristophanes? That would not displease you?'

'Not at all! Indeed she ought to as I sense that we will become the best of friends.'

As he was saying that, Slevania appeared in the door to the room, wearing her white dressing gown that made her look like a fairy.

'Good morning, my lord. Or Aristophanes, if you prefer?'

'My utmost respects, fair lady. Aristophanes will do very nicely.'

'Would you like purple tea or orange?'

'I see that Madam is a connoisseur! Purple, if you please, and splashed with a little cloud of milk,' he said, eyes sparkling. 'So I am here for a reason of utmost importance, as in studying the natural world, I have taken an interest in the Legendary World and its representatives. In short, I've begun to create an immense catalog with classifications of all the creatures I have taken it upon myself to study. Throughout all these years, I've made quite a lot of progress in my work, and I can say with all modesty that I've created a significant scientific document, as I've catalogued no fewer than four hundred kinds of creatures, such as Elves, Gnomes, Dryads, Pixies, Trolls, etc., etc. I've been able to classify them in a three-level genealogical chart, which is really phenomenal!'

The Baron had enunciated all this in a trembling voice full of passion and reverence, so excited was he by his research.

'Pardon me, but I'm not so familiar with this sort of thing. Could you tell me in simpler terms what your research is about?' said Slevania.

'Oh, how silly I am! Please forgive me. I am incorrigible. Always ready to flare up for my cause, without thinking for a moment that I might bore my listener with my technical terms. I'll start over. It's quite simple. When you want to know about your origins, you draw a genealogical chart or family tree in which, beginning from yourself, you go back to your parents, then your grandparents, then to your great-grandparents . . . You continue like this as far back in time as you can go. And well, for the classification of living things, it's exactly the same! One can discover blood relation between creatures that at first glance seem very different. Man and monkey, or even man and pig, are distant cousins, for example—they come from a common ancestor very long ago.

'Goodness!' said Pantaleone, who was coming back from the washroom, clean-shaven now. 'That's quite a discovery!'

'And that's not all!' Aristophanes continued, now on a roll. 'The beings of the Legendary World, although they are also extremely diverse, come from the same stock. And I believe I know what that is—it comes from a plant originally.

Except, there's just one specimen of it on the whole Earth, and it's called the Gigantum. I know that Legiferius's Docts are pursuing the same type of research but with a very different goal : to destroy!'

'But what does this all have to do with our son?' wondered Slevania, placing the steaming teapot on the table.

'I'm coming around to that! Out of all the creatures that I have studied, one kind particularly held my attention − Ogres. They're not too difficult to find and study. It is enough to go walking in the forest, concealing yourself, and you're able to approach them. Over the course of various missions, I've been able to collect a considerable chunk of information about their way of life, their habits, and their family ties. So I am qualified to state not only that your son is an Ogre, but also that I know his family!'

His declaration hit like a ton of bricks. Stunned by the Baron's seeming confidence and sureness, Slevania and Pantaleone didn't dare move.

'The child's parents are dead! He has no family—we are his family!' Pantaleone finally said, in a voice full of emotion.

'Perhaps, you are right. Still, the little one must know that he isn't human and remember his parents.'

'No, he has amnesia. He has no memory from before his arrival in our home,' Slevania said curtly.

'Sooner or later he will discover the truth, and he will suffer,' Aristophanes continued. 'It would be best to help him uncover that memory. It won't change his love for you at all since you are his family now.'

Slevania and Pantaleone looked at each other silently. Should they listen to the Baron, who was trying to be reassuring, or would it be better to end this discussion as quickly as possible?

'I would like to try an experiment if you don't mind. Not far from here, to the northeast, in the forest, there is an old Ogre named Tiboursio, who according to my research, happens to be Ogrino's great-uncle. A meeting between them could provoke a sort of electroshock that would reactivate your child's memory. Then he would know where he came from, without disconnecting from his current life in the least.'

'How can you assert such things?' Slevania exclaimed. 'You assure us that Ogrino is the grandnephew of some Ogre when we do not even know who his original mother and father are. And then you want us to participate in an "experiment" that risks our family's stability and might bring us great pain. And all this for what?'

'Then you don't understand,' said the Baron immediately, 'your son's well-being is at stake. Already, he is realizing that he's different from other boys. Who else can gulp down so much food in one performance without being sick? What's more, I imagine that he, like all Ogres, has a gift for communicating with certain animals, such as perhaps your elephant, or even your monkey.'

There, the Baron had hit home because undeniably, all that he had said was true. Since the child's arrival at the circus, Pantaleone had noted his camaraderie with the menagerie, the dogs, and especially with Royal.

'Anyway though!' Pantaleone countered, 'what use would it be for him to learn the truth so soon? If it is the truth!'

'The truth is always a good thing to say, and it is never too early. He will be very grateful to you and love you all the more. And most importantly, you must realize that if I have discovered that he is, in fact, a little Ogre, others will discover that too, and have other motives—and there it will be useful for him to know what he really is if you see what I mean!'

Upon hearing these words, Slevania's face fell because she realized that the danger hanging over her son's head could make itself known any day now as Legiferius's patrols were becoming more common.

'Let's say you are right,' continued Pantaleone, 'what will knowing about his origins do for him?'

'It will give him an explanation for his difference and give him reassurance, self-confidence. He'll know about his lineage and be able to confront the future knowing what resources he can count on. Should he be, unfortunately, discovered and persecuted, he'll be able to defend himself knowing why.'

'I am ready to try the experiment,' Slevania declared brightly, much to Pantaleone's surprise.

'You want him to meet this uncle? This creature that, perhaps, knows neither good nor evil? What good could that do our child? We're lucky that he does not remember his life from before, and you want to spoil it all and traumatize him by suddenly bringing back his memories? If he remembers everything, he will be torn between his old life and ours together.'

'We cannot build a relationship with him based on lies,' Slevania cut in. 'He has the right to know, especially if he's threatened. And we know what he is. The cards have spoken, do not forget!'

'All right!' Pantaleone said wearily. 'We'll go to the forest to meet this Tiboursio, this "worthy" representative of what is left of Ogrino's old family. I'll agree on one condition. If nothing happens in this meeting, if Ogrino doesn't remember all on his own, we won't argue with destiny and keep forcing things. We'll have done our part, following your advice, but life might decide otherwise, and then we will wait for another, more appropriate moment to tell him the truth.'

'A wonderful decision! You won't regret it, I promise you—a good deed is never wasted!' Aristophanes joyously proclaimed. 'It's a beautiful day. The morning's just begun—to the field! That is . . . as soon as the child is awake.'

His timing was impeccable, for a few moments later, a little tousled head with sleepy eyes appeared in the doorway.

'Ogrino, my son!' Pantaleone boomed. 'Welcome! Today is a special day because we have an important visitor, Baron Aristophanes, who is very fond of you!'

'Good morning, sir,' Ogrino said cheerfully, looking with interest at the face and fancy clothing of this stranger at the table.

His graying hair was pulled back and fell lightly to his shoulders. He wore a white button-down shirt with an upturned collar that closed with a silken mauve frill. His riding pants, of beige linen, ended in long, well-polished brown leather boots. He wore a beige woolen jacket, which gave the ensemble a certain class. *This man was rather refined*, Ogrino thought.

'First of all, you'll have breakfast while we tell you about the day,' Slevania told him.

'Oh goody, breakfast! I'm very hungry this morning. Dreaming always makes me hungry, and especially because I had a nightmare. I dreamed I was being chased by bad people who wanted to kill me. I was stuck against the wall at the end of an alley, and they were going to get me. I was about to have to fight them off and I didn't know how, and then suddenly I woke up. It was all a dream, and now you're here, my dear old parents!'

He jumped up to Slevania's neck and kissed her loudly, then did the same to Pantaleone, under the gaze of the Baron, who was touched. While Ogrino scarfed down a dozen chocolate muffins, two dozen pancakes, and plenty of jam and bread, Pantaleone explained to him that today they—he, the boy, and Aristophanes—were going into the forest to hunt.

'Hunting! What a great idea! I've been wanting to go to the forest for a long time now. I think I'm going to be very good at this, even though you've never taught me about how to track and catch game.'

Slevania took three kerchiefs and put in each one a piece of bread, some cheese, some biscuits, a bottle of water, and a metal plate and utensils. In Pantaleone's bundle, she also put a bottle of red wine. Then she knotted each kerchief to make bundles, she threaded onto sticks, which the three 'hunters' carried over their shoulders. As they left the wagon, Pantaleone hung back to kiss Slevania for a long moment and to grab his blunderbuss, a type of old gun where the end of the barrel is flared out like a trumpet.

Ogrino, already outside, was jumping up and down, impatient to go out and bring home game for dinner. Knowing that he would get to feel like a predator in search of prey was terribly exciting although he didn't really know why.

So the three of them set off for the nearby forest with lightness in their step. The circus was camping, that day, at the edge of a rural town. They walked for four hours, passing from clearings to undergrowth and from valleys to hills, plunging deeper into the forest, which grew ever denser. The trees seemed thousands of years old, so majestic were those oaks and elms.

'I'm hungry,' Ogrino declared loudly, 'and a little tired. Can we stop and eat?'

'Absolutely!' Pantaleone answered. 'But it would be better to catch some big game before we do that. Don't you think?

I'm sure the food in your bundle is not enough to fill you up, right?'

'Huh, that's true! There's nothing but little snacks in there, and I'm really, really hungry!'

'So let's catch something! I think I see fresh wild goat tracks here,' Aristophanes said nervously, pointing at the ground with his index finger.

'Yes! There are at least eight of them!' Ogrino rejoiced. 'We'll feast! There will be just enough for the three of us.'

And he was off, skipping gleefully in the direction of the tracks. They had to put in another twenty minutes of forced march until they found the little herd of goats grazing in a clearing by a pond. The three hunters separated. Pantaleone loaded his blunderbuss, and Aristophanes got out his musket, which looked like a pirate's pistol, and took off the safety, ready to fire. They approached the unsuspecting beasts on tiptoe as close as they could get. They were only a few yards away, and Pantaleone was already taking aim, when the goats suddenly began to run, to everyone's surprise. Aristophanes took a shot, and Pantaleone, not wanting to miss such easy targets, followed suit.

A dead branch cracked loudly on the left, and a half-naked giant appeared in a fury. His hair was sparse, his features rough, and his ears large and sticking out from his head. What really struck the viewer at first glance, though, was the single eye in the middle of his forehead. *A Cyclops*, Pantaleone immediately thought. He had never expected to see one in his life, let alone today.

The woodsman was annoyed that these little two-pawed creatures had made him lose his chance at so much choice game. Only bloody vengeance could appease his anger. So he searched with his one eye for where the cursed bipeds could be hiding. In fact, as soon as they had seen the huge monster in the shadowy undergrowth, Pantaleone and Aristophanes had hidden in the foliage of a shrub. They needed these precious few moments of respite to reload their weapons. *Where could Ogrino be?* Pantaleone wondered to himself, even as he tamped down powder in the barrel of his blunderbuss. From his hiding place, he couldn't see the area where the child had been. He imagined the boy crouching under a bush, frozen and dying of fear. This was completely wrong. Ogrino had chased after a fat goat, determined not to let lunch escape. In a few agile bounds, he had reached his prey and broken its neck with his powerful jaws. Ignoring the gunshots and other noise, he hadn't even noticed the Cyclops's arrival on the scene. Too hungry to take his catch back toward Pantaleone, and certainly to wait and cook it, he devoured the tender and juicy, musky meat raw.

The monster lifted his nose to sniff the air and try to determine where the bothersome creatures could be holed up. He could smell 'yellow belly' with a hint of sweetness—no doubt, one of the bipeds was two stones' throws to his right. He went over to find out, letting out a great groaning war cry and running, waving his arms in all directions. It was quite a sight, scary even to watch. Pantaleone, despite the stress, was trying to stay calm in the face of this giant, who in another few big steps would be upon him. He was about to pull the trigger when he heard:

'NO! Don't shoot!'

Pantaleone paused in surprise. What a mistake! During that moment, the Cyclops ran into him with all his weight, sending him through the air and crashing into a tree behind him. Though he was stunned, Pantaleone hadn't let go of his gun. The giant was getting ready to smash his head with both hands when the shot rang out. The Cyclops, frightened, took several steps backwards, just enough time for Pantaleone to get his wits back and stand up. Aristophanes arrived next to him and then he shot above the monster's head. The bullet cut off a large branch, which landed on the Cyclops's forehead and left him reeling. The two men took advantage of his confusion to run away as fast as they could. When they were far enough away, they stopped to catch their breaths.

'Whew! Nice work. That was a close one,' said Pantaleone, relieved. 'But why on earth did you tell me not to shoot?'

'We couldn't very well shoot the creature we came to find.'

'What! You're saying that that monster is Ogrino's great-uncle? Why didn't you tell me right away?'

'From where I was hiding, I couldn't see him perfectly. It was too dark. It took me a little time to recognize him. But now I'm sure that is definitely Tiboursio!'

'You really mean to say that this Cyclops is related to my son? That's impossible, you must be mistaken—they have nothing in common.'

'Much more than you realize! Physical appearance isn't everything. The same blood runs in their veins. It's just that Ogrino has taken more traits from his mother, who belonged to a more evolved branch of Ogres than Tiboursio does. Is that clear?'

'Not really! I still have a hard time believing that my child could be family to that hideous, boorish, violent savage.'

'I am sorry to disappoint you, but it's definite. I took a census of nearly all the Ogres in the kingdom, and I can assure you that these two are on the same branch of the family tree.

In fact, I witnessed many encounters between Tiboursio and Ogrino's father over the course of these last years. I'm almost sure that Tiboursio would have known Ogrino when he was a baby.'

While the two men were talking, Ogrino had finished his meal, though he was still very hungry because even a very fat goat is a rather lean meal for a little Ogre. He had to find something else. He didn't really want to go back to Pantaleone and the Baron right away, especially as he knew they weren't very far off and his sense of direction was excellent. He followed other tracks that led a little deeper into the thick birch forest. These were certainly bucks, judging by the prints. Once more he was surprised by his own hunting knowledge. He trotted a few dozen yards before arriving in a ferny area strewn with large rocks. He found himself walking up a hill in the middle of a narrow canyon formed by two long and tall walls of rock. All of a sudden, a dark mass appeared, silhouetted in front of him. Ogrino had to squint into the sun and he had trouble making out the sort of half-giant that stood before him. Strangely, he wasn't at all afraid of the imposing shape advancing upon him.

'GRRRRUUUAOO! KRIMO TRAO DRUVOA? AOU CRONOU VRITUU GRIGAO GROU O MAUGIUO?' slurred the titan, approaching slowly.

To his great surprise, Ogrino had the vague impression of understanding what this gibberish meant — something about himself and his clothing.

'Who are you?' asked Ogrino.

The great being was now very close, and Ogrino jumped a little as he realized that he had only one eye. The Cyclops looked at him fondly from up high and breathed in his odor with enjoyment. Delicately, he bent toward the child and took him in his large hands. Ogrino, sensing that he was in no danger, did not struggle. The Ogre slowly and tenderly articulated the following:

'GRIROO TRINAO TIBOURSIO CRWA GRUTA BROGUA KRASOU ORUTIO DRANUO IRUVOA HOGAR, SRAOU PRASOUNIU.'

Which meant: 'I recognize your odor. You are my nephew Hogar's boy.'

Then he went off on a long tirade of rumblings, each one more incomprehensible than the last. Still, Ogrino managed to get the general sense of what he was saying. Apparently the Ogre was called Tiboursio and had known Ogrino a long time ago. The rest was hazier and involved family relationships and another Ogre named Hogar.

As the child was wide-eyed and looked very stunned, Tiboursio sat down, set the child on his knee, and patted his hair gently, murmuring, 'Groulmiou rancoa triwai cromnia massuiaau vriimnuo grwareu lesriu trunio grotra numio Loganda. Ho crandrou fromo lassu braclou kreuduao grumsio.'

Although Ogrino only vaguely understood, this meant something like:

'It's a great joy to find the son of my nephew, who we lost along with his wife Loganda. If you wish, I will bring you to the tribe.'

Seeing that the boy showed very little reaction to his invitation, he stood up and took the child's hand to help him out of the canyon. Ogrino followed him willingly, as he felt that Tiboursio wanted to show him something interesting. All his senses were on alert as he found this situation both worrisome and exciting. He should have been frightened of this huge, sinister-looking titan, but instead he felt a natural affinity for him. And hadn't Tiboursio said that they'd met before? Despite his lack of memories, he was convinced that he was no stranger to the world of the forest and its inhabitants, bizarre as they might seem.

So Ogrino let himself be led through a labyrinth of shrubs, groves, streams, and rocks, until they came upon a large clearing in front of a deep cave. There, Ogrino was surprised to see a group of about fifty Ogres, busy with various tasks. They could have been villagers at a makeshift campsite if not for the population's unusual size and appearance. Children were running about and playing, while women carved up small game and men sharpened their weapons.

Once Tiboursio was clearly visible, everyone stopped and turned to face the two new arrivals. The little Ogres rushed over and began to touch Ogrino and look at him questioningly. They asked, 'Groumouniou transoiou greu krialou?' and heaps of other questions that Ogrino couldn't quite understand. Seemingly, it was again his clothing that was provoking so much curiosity.

Tiboursio began to speak loudly, and once again emitted a very, very long series of rumblings, in which Ogrino recognized the names Hogar and Loganda. The little Ogres stopped questioning him, and the members of the tribe stood aside to allow their slow passage toward the cave. From the respect that the Ogres showed Tiboursio, Ogrino deduced that he was someone important and respected in the tribe, perhaps even the chief?

They entered the cave, where two old Ogresses were tending a big fire. Tiboursio spoke to them briefly, and they welcomed Ogrino warmly, giving him big toothless smiles. Although they appeared very ugly, with their puffy faces and the tufts of hair on their chins, Ogrino found them to be quite friendly and affectionate. They showered him with words and seemed very happy to see him. He returned their smiles and even shared a laugh with them when he stumbled, unbalanced by a flurry of kisses and hugs from one of the old matrons.

During this time, Tiboursio had gone to look for some dried herbs at the back of the cave, and now he returned with an armful of long sheaves. He signaled Ogrino to come over to him and they sat down near the fire. Tiboursio threw the vegetation onto the blaze and murmured a sort of incantation in a low voice. Ogrino and the Ogresses were quiet, sensing that this was an important moment.

In the dancing flames, a thick orange and blue smoke rose up like a flowing curtain. Little by little as Tiboursio spoke what must have been a magic spell, subtle images emerged slowly, becoming ever more clear. Ogrino was on tenterhooks, as he knew that what Tiboursio was doing must have very much to do with his presence. Would he discover some secret?

Finally one could discern human figures in the smoke—a couple holding hands affectionately. Actually they weren't, strictly speaking, humans, for their features were larger and they were hairier . . . no doubt about it, they were Ogres! A pair of Ogres! It took Ogrino a few moments to realize that they might be his real parents. The idea was shocking. What was comforting, though, was the similarity between these figures and the vision he had had during his baptism. Twice now, he had been able to look these two beings in the face, and his questions now gave way to deep certainty.

He was in the home of what humans considered to be 'primitive creatures,' but by their magic, he was seeing an image of his mother and father. All sorts of feelings were swirling inside of him: gratitude for Tiboursio, the joy of finally being able to put a face to his parents, and a deep sadness, as he felt that this touching image signified that his parents were dead. He dove into Tiboursio's arms and wept for many minutes, during which the three Ogres were silent out of respect for the sobbing little one's grief.

When the right moment came along, Tiboursio took the child's face in his hands and looked into his eyes. There was no need for words. They belonged to the same family, the same blood ran in their veins. Ogrino was certain now. Images were flying through his mind. He saw a strong Ogre with a tender gaze carrying him on his shoulders. His mother, a slender figure, smiled warmly at him. He heard laughter mixing together, representing light-hearted moments. Then all was erased and he was left alone with Tiboursio's single eye, which was watching him with compassion.

Sudden shouts from outside the cave broke the spell. Four male Ogres entered the cave, looking anxious. They spoke quickly and in short sentences, and Ogrino understood that some danger was very near. Tiboursio exited the cave promptly, giving brief orders. Immediately, the Ogres formed little groups that left to go deep into the forest in different directions, while the Ogresses and their children stayed in the cave. Ten or so Ogres stood at the entrance to the cave in protection.

Ogrino wondered what was going on. Who would be able to threaten a whole village of Ogres in the middle of nowhere in a forest? It was at that moment that he realized that Pantaleone and Aristophanes must be looking for him. He hadn't noticed the time passing, but it must have been late in the afternoon, judging by the angled sunlight.

He wanted to tell Tiboursio. He used many gestures and charades to explain that some friends of his were outside and that they must not be harmed. Tiboursio observed the child's gestures and, despite the strange language the boy was using, understood that there was something outside that needed protection. So he lifted the boy up by the armpits, set him on his shoulders, then left hurriedly, and broke into a long-strided run. In the blink of an eye, they were under the cover of trees, skillfully threading through bushes and rocks. Ogrino was astonished by how light on his feet the giant was, when he could easily seem clumsy at first look.

From time to time, Tiboursio stopped to listen. His hearing was so acute that he could hear a twig breaking thirty yards away. After having turned his head like a weathervane, he ran off even faster, hopping rivers like they were only gutters. At one point, he stopped short and lifted his nose to sniff. No doubt, there were humans coming slowly toward them. They hid, side by side, behind a big oak, waiting and holding their breath in order to hear better. The muffled sound of footsteps on the moss became clearer every moment. Ogrino dared to peek out to try to identify who was coming. Tiboursio pulled him back violently and signaled him to be quiet. The steps were still coming nearer.

'We can't be very far now.'

The voice was like a thunderbolt to Ogrino, who despite Tiboursio's warnings had expected to find Pantaleone. This voice was completely unknown to him.

'Their tribe, or what's left of it after our last attack, should be a mile from here. From now on, absolute silence,' said Commander Erasmus.

Tiboursio put Ogrino back on his shoulders and fast as lightning, jumped on the man who reached his height. Before the soldier knew what was happening, he was lying motionless on the ground.

'Shoot him!' cried Erasmus.

He couldn't say anything more because Tiboursio had already knocked him down with a punch to the jaw. As he fell, Erasmus managed to reflexively fire off an arrow, which buried itself deeply in Tiboursio's left arm. Despite the searing pain tearing up his muscle, Tiboursio promptly dashed behind a rampart of trees for safety. The Militians launched all sorts of things at him with their crossbows. Some projectiles exploded, others lodged themselves into the trees' bark. Luckily, none of them reached Tiboursio, who nimbly dodged all the attacks.

Shortly, they were out of range, and the Ogre was able to catch his breath. Ogrino saw that he was very worried. His village was going to be attacked, his companions, and he had to be there to head up the troops and orchestrate the battle. Ogrino had the terrible feeling that he must be a burden to Tiboursio, an unhelpful constraint. Tiboursio had to be free of outside concerns to lead the battle well. He couldn't be encumbered by a little child who'd suddenly come out of left field. Although it made him very sad, Ogrino decided to communicate to Tiboursio that he should leave him there and go back to his tribe.

The old Ogre didn't want to abandon his grandnephew, whom he'd just rediscovered. He understood the meaning of Ogrino's awkward gestures, but he refused to obey them. They returned together to the cave, taking a long detour to avoid the patrol. Tiboursio was wrapped up with planning when suddenly, the crack of a branch once again perked up his ears. Footsteps, human footsteps! He was sure of it! He flattened himself against a huge elm, put a hand over Ogrino's mouth, and held his breath so as to listen better. On his left, a rustling of dry grass indicated that they were no more than a stride away. He spun around and in the blink of an eye, his enormous hand was around the first man's neck. He was about to throw him onto the second man when Ogrino cried, 'No, let him go!'

Tiboursio, not understanding the child's entreaty, lifted his prisoner higher. So Ogrino covered his single eye with both hands. Tiboursio let go of his hostage to free himself. Ogrino jumped to the ground and, with much recourse to gesticulation, communicated that they must not hurt the man because it was his adopted father. Pantaleone and Aristophanes, after much wandering, had ended up crossing paths with Tiboursio once again, due to random chance rather than to any of the Baron's logical deductions. Once everyone involved had recovered from their respective surprises, Ogrino tried to explain that he had to leave with Pantaleone so that Tiboursio could go back to his tribe. Tiboursio didn't want to hear it because in fact, the little one was rightfully a part of the tribe. Still, he could tell that the child was turning out rather differently than the average little Ogre as he had lived with humans and been influenced by their world. The boy also seemed to feel strongly toward the human with the mustache.

With a very heavy heart, Tiboursio decided to yield to Ogrino's wish to depart with his friends. He did, however, make him promise to come back and visit once peace was restored. The child promised, on the memory of his previous parents, that as soon as he could, he would spend some time among the Ogres, renewing his connection to his roots. Tiboursio lifted him up to his face and Ogrino hugged his great-uncle tightly, kissing him on both cheeks. After the touching goodbyes in which Pantaleone and Aristophanes shook hands with the Ogre, fearing for their fingers, Tiboursio bounded into the foliage without turning back, feeling the need to be with his tribe on this tragic day.

The three companions set off on the path home in silence as they were all shaken by what they had seen that day. Ogrino, in particular, was wondering whether Tiboursio would reach his tribe in time to lead the battle against Legiferius. He hoped with all his heart that his great-uncle and his people would be victorious in the clash and that the wound on Tiboursio's arm would heal quickly. He swore to himself to go back, as soon as possible, to the Ogre village as he had memorized the route there. His rancor toward Legiferius kept growing. Although he couldn't understand the Order's motives, he considered them to be evil because Legiferius brought nothing but pain and destruction wherever it went.

THE BARON OF SWORDSCAR

Destiny wasted no time in crossing Legiferius's path with Ogrino's once more. It happened one night during a circus performance, for the little Ogre was now an integral part of the circus, even playing a central role to the clown portion of the show. In the wings, flanked by Gumbo and Colossus, Slevania finished putting on his make-up and adjusting his costume. He was disguised in a yellow and orange checkerboard suit that was too big for him. A large orange wig sat on his head under a tall, pointed red hat. His face, entirely covered in white, showcased his oversized, fluorescent red mouth. His hands were covered with enormous white gloves and his shoes, also red, were enormous, with their upward-curving tips. The entrance music began. It was time to go on and Ogrino, as always, felt his heart beating wildly in his chest. They called it stage fright and apparently everyone had it, but it was still very disagreeable and exciting at the same time.

The Magnus Scrutator detested nomads, these so-called 'travelers' who came and went in the kingdom and required a control system all to themselves to be located and tracked. Tertius, one of the most important members of the Order, had come to observe one of these strange societies in person. After all, wasn't he the Order's eyes and ears? Certainly, he had not come alone—a man of his rank would never travel without an escort—but he had mixed into the crowd with a dozen of his soldiers, leaving behind anything that would give away his association with the Order. He was tall and skinny with straight black hair that framed his sharp face. He had a nose like a hawk's and a solemn, severe gaze. Despite his natural disgust for the circus people, whom the Docts had labeled misfits because they were so difficult to classify, he had wanted to come here to confirm the rumor that was going around about one of the circus members. This evening, although he was quite amused by the offerings, he was here in the professional capacity of inspecting. Some of the performers rather impressed him, and he wondered if he could get them to enroll in the Militians of the Order, such as the acrobats, who would be excellent at capturing the quick and furtive Will-o'-the-wisps. He was lost in thought when the clown act began. Four very different clowns came out into the ring. One, holding an accordion, was tall and skinny as a pole; another was smaller, stocky, and sturdy. The third had a mustache and an imposing allure, and the fourth, judging by his size, must have been a child. At the beginning, the show went along as one might expect, with silly music, gags, falls, and to finish, a cream pie fight.

Legiferius's spies were at highest attention when the clown with the mustache introduced the child clown as the 'Little Gargantuan,' capable of eating a disproportionately large amount. His interest in the boy increased as the child gobbled down astronomical quantities of food. The other clowns took turns at pouring full cauldrons directly into his mouth. He wolfed down pounds and pounds of cookies, brownies, pies, and cakes, under the envious eyes of the children in the audience and the incredulous looks of their parents. When all the cauldrons were empty, the little clown got up and chased after the others as if he were still hungry and wanted to eat them up to finish his dinner. The three clowns ran away as fast as they could, but quite clumsily, to laughs and applause.

Tertius did not move, did not take his eyes off the child who was left alone in the ring, and who was fully enjoying all the attention and applause. Before the little clown left the stage, Tertius gave a signal to his men, who were already discreetly making their way down to the exit of the tent. In a few moments, they were all outside and headed backstage. There they found Ogrino, being congratulated by Pantaleone and Slevania.

'Seize the child!' Tertius cried.

The Militians rushed at the child, but Pantaleone, the Messeyer twins, Cordicello, Camillo, and even Angelina blocked their way as Slevania led the boy out of the tent.

'You dare to contradict the Order? Do you know what you are doing and what you're bringing upon yourselves? Nothing can go against Legiferius's decisions! Everyone has to obey the Law!' Tertius pronounced this imperiously and with finality. Anyone would have been shaking in his boots before such an imposing representative of the Order's authority, but Pantaleone and his friends weren't just anyone. The soldiers saw this as they had to push rather forcefully to clear themselves a path. There were so many of them that they succeeded without much difficulty as Pantaleone didn't want to use violence. Still, they had lost precious seconds, and when they made it out of the tent, Ogrino and Slevania were already on the other side of the camp, slipping between the wagons.

'Catch them! Don't lose sight of them. Unit 4, take the right. Unit 5, go left, and we'll trap them.'

Slevania felt her heart beating out of her chest. It was a long time since she had run so hard and so far. Fear and exertion combined to keep her heart racing and she felt a horrible pain in her chest. Her legs became heavy and her breath shortened.

'I can't go on,' she murmured, out of breath, leaning against a wagon. 'You've got to go on alone. Go to the Baron of Swordscar. He'll protect you. He knows you and is fond of you. Don't worry about us. Everything will be fine and we'll be reunited soon. Go, go!' she managed to say, with the hint of a sob in her voice. Before Ogrino could decide whether to obey her or not, one of the Militians appeared at the end of the alley of wagons. He sounded the alarm and rushed toward them. Slevania slipped into the darkness between two barrels as Ogrino began to run again as hard as he could. Other soldiers appeared in front of him. He had to turn off course and slalom between the piles of utensils and circus equipment. When he got out into the open, he was horrified to see that they were already there. He was totally surrounded and in a few seconds, they would have him.

Galvanized by fear, he scanned his surroundings and noticed two things that seemed very important. In a bound, he seized a torch hung on the side of a wagon, then in the blink of an eye, he was atop a pile of accessories stored right by the cannon. The Militians had already reached the base of his refuge and one of them was halfway up the pile. As fast as lightning, the child lit the fuse and slid into the barrel of the cannon. Before the soldier reached the top, there was a violent explosion. Thick, acrid smoke spewed out, blinding the pursuers. The cloud dissipated slowly. The Militians' eyes were teary, but the first one was still able to peer into the cannon to dislodge the child. To his great surprise, it was empty! Ogrino, in fact, was clinging to the top of the main tent's central pole. He had adored flying through the air like Camillo, feeling the wind on his face and seeing the circus and the city zoom past below him. Where he was now, he was no longer afraid of his pursuers, and he was enjoying the view. A large structure caught his attention. It seemed to be an austere and imposing fortress that dominated the city from its position atop a hill. Something unsettling, even threatening, emanated from the building. At least, that was what Ogrino was thinking before he was torn from contemplation by shouts from below.

'There he is, on top of the tent! Let's go, quickly now!'

The voices sent a shiver up his spine. He knew them only too well. It was Camillo, the cannon man and the Messeyer brothers. They were already setting up a trampoline at the edge of the tent.

'Slide down the top of the tent as if you were on a sled. Use your hands to keep yourself heading straight at us, the trampoline is right below where we are.'

Without hesitating, Ogrino let himself fall onto the tent and slid down it as if tobogganing down a snowy hill. He picked up speed all the way to the edge of the tent before landing on the material stretched out for him. He bounced back up three or four times before landing steadily on his feet as if he had just finished a gymnastic act.

'If it weren't due to such awful circumstances, I'd say you gave an exceptional performance tonight—the public would be on cloud nine!' Camillo declared happily.

Several sharp noises rung out at the same time, and before anyone knew what was happening, the four friends were struggling, tangled in flying nets.

'Get them under control!' shouted the now unfortunately familiar voice of Tertius.

The two units threw themselves on the prisoners, who were immediately immobilized, except for the child, who had managed to cut through the mesh of the nets with his teeth and was already halfway free. When one of the soldiers tried to grab him, a wave of anger rose up in Ogrino and he shouted at the man.

'You don't know, you don't know, you don't know WHO I AM!'

He was suddenly filled with a strange confidence, as if a long buried memory had awakened in him and his true Ogre nature was coming to light. And in a fit of rage, he bit the man's arm so hard that he broke it. The soldier, his bones crushed, cried out in pain and began to sway. The others, terrified at the sight, hesitated, and Ogrino made use of the opportunity. He was able to jump out of the trap and run off at full speed. Weaving between equipment, wagons, and other structures, Ogrino popped out into the street near where the circus had set up and found himself in the middle of a religious procession. At this late evening hour, a mass of hooded penitents was marching through the city's streets, carrying icons and statues of saints. Thousands of pious people had gathered to see the long line of priests, monks, and penitents as well as to pray, themselves. Although the crowd was mostly composed of adults, no one paid any attention to the child, thanks to his short stature. Ogrino had no trouble blazing himself a trail in this forest of robes and cassocks. Tertius, having arrived on the scene, cursed in rage, knowing that finding the child here was like searching for a needle in a haystack. For all his power, he couldn't interrupt the procession without provoking the anger and indignation of the whole population, which was politically undesirable. So he gave his men the order to discreetly spread themselves throughout the crowd and sent one of his messengers off for reinforcements. Himself, he returned to the circus tent, where Pantaleone, Slevania, and the rest of the troupe were still prisoners.

'Where could the child have gone?' he asked brusquely.

Slevania drew in a breath, then in a calm and measured voice, said, 'How do you expect us to know? The child was frightened and ran off blindly into the city. God only knows where he's thought to hide.'

'Sooner or later, he will come back here looking for safety and comfort from his family. If that's what you call yourselves! You abominations! To hide an Ogre in the very breast of the kingdom of Legiferius! Not only are you fools, but also outlaws and that's punishable by very harsh sanctions. You will come with me to Legiferius for a proper interrogation. Then you'll have a little time in our jails to think about what you've done so that your circus will be here for the little monster to come back to and for us to grab him.' And then, Tertius said to his soldiers, 'Get to it! Take them away, the traitors, and don't worry about being gentle!'

At these words, Pantaleone couldn't restrain himself from rebellion. Lifting his arm, he was ready to knock Tertius senseless, but the latter nimbly sidestepped so that two billy clubs could come crashing down on the back of Pantaleone's neck. The blows were so brutal that it took him a few minutes to return to his usual, robust self. With their wrists in cuffs behind their backs and closely flanked by the guards, the prisoners walked in single file to the movable dungeon that awaited them at the edge of the circus. The soldiers pushed them inside violently, even Slevania, whose shoulder was painfully knocked against the doorpost. The wagon departed, pulled by horses, and had to take a long detour to bypass the crowd of utterly oblivious bystanders, for their attention was turned elsewhere.

'Bread and circuses, or rather, bread and rituals, that's what it takes to pacify the people,' Tertius muttered to himself, looking at the crowd from above, from his seat by the coachman.

Ogrino ran until he was panting. It seemed to him that his pursuers were always hot on his heels, ready to grab him by the collar. But now he had to admit that there were only joyful or reverential people around, unless it was another one of the Order's tricks. He couldn't see any sign of the soldiers' presence, though. No uniforms on the horizon, no recognized faces, no Tertius (who was proving to be a truly and deeply cruel man). He had better not hurt Ogrino's family or friends, or he'd really regret it. All that had just happened had shown the child that he had more courage and skill in battle than he'd known. How had such power come to him that he, a mere child, had been able to knock down an adult soldier? He pondered the question, then had the idea that the Baron might be able to help him answer it. So gathering up his energy, he set out again, now aiming south of the city, where the Swordscar castle lay.

During this time, the Militia's reinforcements had been deployed in the city at all the key points: bridges, city squares, the main streets going both North-South and East-West. For the moment, there was nothing to report, no sign of a little

Ogre, despite the clear description they'd received. Valius, a simple soldier, did not like these surveillance missions; he much preferred battles where the danger raised his adrenaline and got his blood pumping. He was nearly sleeping when he saw, for a fraction of a second, a little brown head peek out from between two robes. Convinced that he hadn't been dreaming, he felt an electric charge run down his spine and without thinking, he began to run. Finally a little action, and who knew, maybe an easily won reward. His progress was slow because of all the people pressing against one other for a better look at the procession. Valius had to use his elbows to jostle a way through. His large, muscled frame wasn't even much help in this sea of humanity, which carried you with it despite your best efforts. Valius thought he was losing precious minutes being dragged around by the crowd like this, when surely the little boy could easily slip through, ducking between the spectators' legs if necessary.

In fact, Ogrino had managed to escape from this mass of people as if from the jungle. He made his way into the clear air and open fields of the surrounding countryside. Nothing was left but to head due south and in a little over two hours, he would reach his destination, if he was remembering correctly from when Pantaleone had brought him to the castle. Valius had the idea to walk between the crowd and the penitents, ignoring the protestations that brought. He moved ten times faster this way and he, too, finally reached the edge of the city. He was able to see, in the distance, a traveling salesman stop to let a little boy climb onto his cart, then set off at a quick pace.

'What's your name?' asked Vertin, a peddler by trade.

'I am Ogrino, son of Pantaleone,' the boy said proudly. 'Our traveling circus goes from town to town so that everyone can enjoy it.'

'I enjoy the circus, too, although I don't often have the luxury of going. My work keeps me on the road and I don't have much time for amusements. I brought my children a few times, though, and they really loved it. There was a big lion that jumped through a flaming hoop and a monkey that knew how to play music.'

'But that's my circus!' Ogrino exclaimed. 'That was my good friends Royal and Gumbo that you saw. We play together all the time because they understand me better than humans do.'

'What a funny little chap you are! And tell me, why are you going into the countryside so late?'

'My father had to send me to stay with a friend, the Baron of Swordscar, and he can't come with me because he's sick. He must have eaten something that didn't agree with his stomach,' the little Ogre lied brazenly.

'And he's letting you go all alone? No one to accompany you?'

'No. In a circus, there's always so much to do, especially after the show, you know. So much to put away, to clean up, all that! And anyway, I'm big now! I'm not afraid of the dark, and I can take care of myself!'

'Well, that's certain!' Vertin rejoined. 'With me you've got nothing to fear. I know plenty about bandits, I can spot them from fifty fathoms away! If you want to take a little nap, you can lie down between the crates with a blanket. I'll wake you up when we've arrived. It'll be about an hour.'

'Yes, please,' the child responded. 'I'm a little tired. I've had a long journey today.'

Ogrino snuggled up in an old woolen blanket that was a bit scratchy. Rocked by the cart's movement on the uneven road, he soon fell asleep. Vertin wondered who this little boy with mysterious motives and a strange air about him could be as he hadn't believed a word of Ogrino's story. He would know more when they arrived as he had vowed to get to the bottom of it.

'Requisition, requisition!' Valius shouted. 'I need your horse!'

'But I need it to go home. I can't lend it to you!' the farmer retorted.

'Do you dispute the orders of a representative of the Order? Do you know who you are dealing with? Give me that horse immediately. It will be returned to you tomorrow along with some hard currency in compensation. Unless you refuse, in which case you'll be privileged to meet some of Legiferius's harshest officers if you know what I mean!'

'All right, all right,' said the poor man, resigned, 'but how will I bring my family home?'

'What do I care for your problems? Come to Legiferius early tomorrow to reclaim your mount. And now, to the open road! I have an urgent mission to complete.'

He hastily mounted the old mare, which bolted off in a clatter of hooves, racing across the cobblestones, and disappeared into the night. The animal wasn't used to being ridden at this hellish pace, as its master was peaceful and respectful, but this rider was demanding herculean efforts. Valius cracked the whip on the useless old nag. This was just his luck. He'd come across the most wretched ride in the kingdom just when he most needed a battle steed. But he knew how to get the most out of this mare. Although they were never going fast enough, they were making very rapid progress. He felt that the distance to his target was ever diminishing since the cart he had caught a glimpse of earlier had seemed heavily loaded. He was lost in thought when, just as they were about to take a bend in the road, the mare got slightly off-balance, swayed, then swerved to the right, and fell into the ditch there. Valius reflexively jumped into the air and landed, rolling, on the soft shoulder of the road. As soon as he got up, he realized that he was uninjured. He turned around and saw the animal lying on its side. He took its bridle and pulled on it to lift the mare to its feet. It let out a long, pained whinny. Its two front hooves were crushed.

'Cursed beast! I knew you would fail me, but I didn't think it would be this soon! There's nothing for you but to stay here and suffer—that's all you deserve!'

He turned away from the animal, whose eyes were pleading for help and began once again to run down the road.

At the same moment, Vertin saw in the distance the Swordscar castle's towers, illuminated by the rising moon. It was an old manor, a little decrepit, but with a certain elegance to match its proprietor: a wealthy old fool interested in nature's mysteries, or so they said. Vertin had never met him, though he'd passed the home on more than one occasion. It was now or never. He would kill two birds with one stone, learning more about this strange child as well as making the acquaintance of an eminent person in the region. *A good deed is never wasted,* he thought as he turned onto the dirt road, lined by beech trees on either side, leading up to the castle.

Valius was a little out of breath, despite his soldier's training. The road looked flat but was actually pitched slightly uphill over the course of several miles, which was tiring him out, especially with his backpack that seemed to weigh a ton. He stopped, took off his pack, opened one of the side pockets, and took out a little pigeon cage. He wrote something quickly, sending it by carrier pigeon to Legiferius. He knew that this time the reinforcements would be swift, and thanks to him, the mission would be a success.

At the end of the drive, Vertin looked to his left and discovered an immense park, enclosed by a very long white fence. Between the scattered trees were all sorts of animals: dwarf horses and wooly cows, ostriches, hippopotami, kangaroos, tapirs, anteaters, and many others that he wouldn't have known what to call. Apparently the Baron's reputation was accurate! On the right, there was an immense aviary, at least forty feet tall. You could see all kinds and colors of birds in there, toucans, parakeets, bald eagles, vultures, condors, and whole populations of ducks and wild geese. In the trees you could make out sloths hanging from the branches, but also gibbons, orangutans, and a whole tribe of baboons; not to speak of the growls of the beasts that lurked in the darkness. He woke the child, who was sleeping peacefully. Ogrino opened his puffy eyes and smiled upon seeing the manor.

'We're here! Come, I'll walk you up to meet the owner. Let's hope he's not asleep or off on one of his expeditions,' Vertin said amusedly.

The child leaped joyfully to the ground. The nap had done him good, and the idea of finding refuge here eased his heart.

Vertin energetically tugged three times on the rope of the large bell that served as a ringer. The signal resonated for a long time in the dark silence of the night. They waited. Nothing happened, not the smallest hint of a sound that might have suggested that someone was moving inside. Still, the second floor was lit up, a sign that someone was there. After a while, they decided to walk around the building. They still saw nothing, no trace of life. The back door, too, was shut and locked. Ogrino was drawn in by an old barn at the back of the garden, whose the door looked to be ajar, with a dim light escaping from it. They hurried over and opened the door wider with a great creaking. They were stunned by what they saw. A man with wild hair and a white coat was standing in a tub with water up to his waist, rushing around a submerged figure, also white. They timidly approached to try to understand what was going on. The man pulled something forcefully toward him. He backed into the side of the tub and lifted his arms to the sky as blood and water ran down them and cried, 'I've done it, I've done it! It worked. This is a first! A day that will go down in history! A giant leap toward preservation for all biodiversity!'

'Ahem,' coughed Vertin. 'Excuse us, sir.'

The man, surprised, jumped and immediately began to interrogate these strangers standing in the shadows.

'What are you doing here? This is private property! You're disturbing my work!'

'We're sorry, Baron,' said Ogrino, 'we didn't mean to disturb you, but my father, Pantaleone, sent me to stay with you because there's a lot of trouble right now.'

'Pantaleone? So you must be Ogrino? Come into the light so I can see you better.'

Ogrino stepped forward and saw that the Baron was holding a sort of deformed baby Mermaid in his hands. Seeing the child's surprise, the Baron explained:

'Do not be afraid of what you have just seen. On the contrary, rejoice at it! You have just been present at a birth, and oh what a birth! This is a newborn Manatee, which is the common name for river Mermaids since they have a tail like a fish but are mammals like you and me. They're an endangered species, almost gone in this area, as certain of the Docts of the Order's experiments poison our waterways, slaughtering these peaceful aquatic animals by the hundreds. I was able to create one here, in captivity, by artificial insemination. This is a big first in the kingdom, I can promise you that.'

He put the baby down into the water delicately, next to its mother, who hastened to lick its snout tenderly.

'So here you are! Ogrino! And how long I've waited to see you again! Still, if you're coming alone, without your parents, it must be serious indeed. And you sir, who are you? A friend of the family, no doubt?'

'No, alas, no. A simple traveling salesman who found this young man on the side of the road tonight and gave him a ride.'

'Aha! I see. A good Samaritan of sorts. It's late, so I won't keep you here any longer. Your journey must be long. I'll accompany you to the door.'

'If it's not too much to ask, my lord, could I take advantage of your hospitality for the night? As you remarked, it's rather late and a good night's sleep would allow me to leave early tomorrow, refreshed and ready.'

'In that case, both of you come with me. My butler will take care of you.'

He brought them to the castle's back door, which he opened with an enormous wrought iron key. As soon as they had entered, an upright, elderly man dressed in livery and with a dignified air approached them.

'If these good sirs would let me relieve them of their coats, they might be more at ease.'

'Very good, Gaston, would you prepare their rooms for them? The blue one for Mr—what was it again?'

'Vertin! Vertin Barrich,' the peddler rushed to answer.

'The blue one, then, for Mr Barrich, and the green for our friend Ogrino, who will stay in the parlor with me for a moment while you show Vertin to his room. You don't mind if I call you Vertin, do you?'

'But of course not!' the peddler responded.

'If you would follow me, sir, the blue room is already ready,' said Gaston.

And they went up the stairs together.

'Alone at last!' Aristophanes hastened to say.

'It has been a long time since we have seen each other since our journey into the forest with my uncle. I didn't think our next meeting would be in such dramatic circumstances. They're after me, but I think I've lost them, and my father told me I would be safe here.'

'You've done well to come. Always together against adversity, eh? But who's after you?'

'Legiferius, of course!'

'How silly of me, what was I thinking? They've discovered your identity and want to capture you for their vile collection.'

'What collection?'

'You cannot imagine the evil things they do. They are insane and cruel and will stop at nothing to further their so-called 'science' of the Order, led by the Docts. You know, their prisoners—if they're kept alive, which is rare—are tortured to make them talk so as to obtain information on the Legendary World. Then the Docts use them in experiments, all in the name of learning more about the creatures of the Legendary World. Finally they're kept in jars in lethargic states, like common laboratory animals.'

'So is it possible that my parents from before are prisoners?'

'I doubt it. As I said, they take very few prisoners, and most of them die under torture.'

'My father from before was very strong, I'm sure of it, and could have resisted their techniques, and my mother too. I have to go release them! Where are they, where do they put the prisoners?'

'My poor boy, you don't know what you're up against. Legiferius is very strong and they know how to protect themselves. Their fortress, which is also the prison, is even more heavily protected.'

'The fortress, is that the big building that towers over the city?'

'It is.'

'I saw it before I ran away. It was surrounded by a big wall. It must not be easy to get inside.'

'Not only is it impossible, but even if you do get inside, you'll be captured before you can say boo, there are so many guards and soldiers. Forget that idea, it won't get you anywhere. The important thing for now is that you stay here, hidden, while things calm down.'

Valius, out of breath and tired out by his long run, was relieved to see the silhouette of a castle in the distance. Surely there he could find a horse and a good meal to keep him on his way. He headed straight for it without hesitation. Imagine his surprise when, at the end of the manor's driveway, he discovered the peddler's cart he had seen the child climb into. He had to stifle a cry of joy. His work had paid off. Now it was only a matter of time. All he had to do was guard the house to make sure the fugitive didn't escape him once again. He opened his backpack, took out a second carrier pigeon, and sent off a message. Watching the bird fly away, he was already anticipating the promotion that he'd surely be awarded for such a skillful capture.

Vertin came out of his room to rejoin them, the stairs creaking under his every step.

'Shh!' murmured the Baron, 'not another word, your secret must stay safe. Ah, dear Vertin, would you care for a glass of port?'

'Ooh, how could I refuse when it's so cold out tonight?'

The Baron poured the garnet-colored mulled wine into a tall glass. The reflections on the glass looked like rubies. He then brought his guests to his table, where a feast fit for a king was laid out.

'Please excuse this frugal meal, but I didn't expect to host anyone tonight. I had had this prepared to sustain me after a day of working on birthing, which is generally exhausting and gives me a good appetite.'

'My dear Baron, there is nothing to excuse. All this is marvelous. I've never seen so much food on a single table in my life, not even for my own wedding! You're spoiling us.'

Ogrino didn't bother to ask, but jumped onto a chair and began to fill his plate. Vertin sat down next, followed by Aristophanes, who was still amused by the little Ogre's legendary appetite. The boy was swallowing whole chickens, patés, and sausages at an astonishing rate. The salesman was stupefied by this spectacle, and ever more intrigued by this really very strange little boy. However, seeing that the Baron was so casual about it, he didn't dare say anything. The meal was wonderful, the atmosphere friendly and vivacious. It must be said that a delicious wine, one from the Baron's own vineyards, flowed continuously into Vertin's glass.

During this time, the reinforcements Valius had called for had finally arrived. A squadron of thirty Militians had joined him silently assembling in the low light under the cover of trees.

'He's there!' Valius announced triumphantly to Rector Mortengus. 'He's in the castle and no one has come out since I've been here.'

'Perfect!' responded Mortengus. My men will surround the manor, then you and I will go inside. If the Ogre tries to escape, he won't get far. Let's go!'

He made a wide gesture with his arm and his troops dispersed to encircle the house, hiding behind one tree-trunk, then another. They stayed low to the ground so as not to be spotted by any guard who might be on the lookout from the big second-floor windows. The Militians stationed themselves at strategic points, where they could watch all the exits to the castle: doors, windows, cellar doors. Two soldiers even hid in the shed, and two others in the stables to prevent any attempt at escape on horseback. Valius walked close by the Rector, feeling more confident than he had in a long time.

'Sir,' said Gaston, coming down from the second floor, 'if I may permit myself to interrupt, I believe you will have to cut short this lovely conversation among friends to take a stroll under the moonlight. It seems we will be receiving old acquaintances, who strongly suggest a promenade.'

Aristophanes understood immediately what he meant and said to Vertin, 'If you do not object, Ogrino and I will take a little digestive stroll as you get ready for bed.'

'Certainly. I'm exhausted. In fact, I can hardly sit up straight. The long day and the wine have gotten the better of me.'

Gaston wrapped his arms around Vertin and pulled him toward the stairs. At that moment, the doorbell rang frenetically and the door shook under the force of three violent knocks.

'I believe our friends have arrived,' Gaston said calmly, setting down Vertin, who had fallen asleep, on the settee in the entryway. 'Here I am. I'm coming, just a moment!'

He had barely turned the key in the lock when the door burst open and the massive silhouette of a man in uniform appeared.

'We want to see the Baron immediately, along with everyone currently in the castle,' Mortengus ordered.

'The Baron is not here. He is out hunting rock partridge. He ought to be back tomorrow morning.'

'Where is the child?'

'There is no child here!'

'What are you playing at? Do you dare try to deceive Legiferius?' Mortengus grabbed Gaston by the collar and lifted him from the ground.

The butler, feet dangling, stammered, 'I have no idea what you are asking about.'

'You'll pay with your head,' added Valius. 'I followed the child and the peddler here from the city and you say that the child is not here, when I see the selfsame peddler sprawled out on the sofa there! You are trying to buy time!'

Turning back, he shouted to the Militians outside the door to come in and search the house at this moment.

'This is an intrusion, an assault on private life!' Gaston protested.

In response, Mortengus threw him to the ground and headed for Vertin, whom he began to shake violently.

'Wha -? What's going on? A thief, an assassin! He's hitting me, he's assaulting me! Help, help me!'

'You will shut your mouth, you cursed brat,' Mortengus bellowed. 'Where is the child?'

'What child? What are you talking about? Oh the child! I don't know, he must be asleep in his room upstairs.'

'Valius, stay here and watch them. I'm going to inspect the second floor.'

Mortengus took the stairs four at a time and was in the upstairs hallway in the blink of an eye. He surveyed the rooms one by one, methodically, to make sure no one was hidden there, all the while keeping an eye out for any secret passageway. Finding nothing suspect, he went up to the third floor and did the same. Neither he nor his men found a living soul.

'The cellar! Quick, they must be in the cellar!' he shouted to his men.

They tore down the stairs like a pack of wild animals chasing their prey, finding themselves stuck at the door leading to the cellar.

'It's closed! Shut and locked!' howled Mortengus. 'Butler, where is the key?'

'It should be hanging with the other keys in the utility room.'

'Too far. It will take too long to go get it. Get out of the way. I have a better way to open this damned door!'

He took an explosive out of his belt and loaded it into his crossbow, aiming at the lock. Ogrino, who was following in Aristophanes's steps in the darkness, heard a large explosion that echoed down the tunnel.

'They must have blown up the cellar door. We'll have to hurry. In no time they'll be on our heels,' the Baron said calmly.

He quickened his pace, the way lit by a torch that flickered in the subterranean air.

'We should be out in the open soon, but the hardest part is yet to come.'

Indeed, the air grew colder as they went along. After some time, they reached a cul-de-sac, where a sort of pool lay under the bottom of a long chimney, from which you could see the starry sky.

'The well, finally! Here we are. This passage was dug by my ingenious ancestor Theodorium, in case of invasion. We have never needed it until today, and I salute his presence of mind, which is saving us now. All right, into the bucket.'

The child didn't need any more encouragement and jumped into the container, immediately followed by the Baron. There was just enough space for them to stand.

'Take this rope, and when I tell you, pull as hard as you can. Careful, we have to pull at the same time if we don't want to exhaust ourselves and also waste a lot of time, because the well is thirty meters deep.'

So they pulled together and the rope slid through the pulley far away, at the top of the well. The bucket began to rise into the air.

Valius was spurred on by the rage and greed of a predator who cannot allow the idea that his prey might escape him. He ran into the dark, having long since passed Mortengus. He felt that the fugitives were ahead. He could feel the air coming in from there, where the tunnel's exit must be. He redoubled his efforts and very soon found himself at the foot of the well. He lifted his head, and to his great delight he saw, balancing upright in some container, the two runaways. Without the slightest sound, he loaded his crossbow and shot. The impact shook Ogrino and Aristophanes, who clung even tighter to the rope and pulled as hard as they could, to hasten their ascent.

'They must be below us. They've found us and we're within range of their weapons,' the Baron said sadly. 'We're less than two meters from the surface, we can get there! That's it, my boy!' he added, meeting Ogrino's eyes to reassure him.

Still, although they braced themselves, they couldn't move another inch upwards.

'Something must be holding the bucket back, but I don't see anything,' Aristophanes said nervously. He threw his lit torch out into the open. It briefly illuminated the shaft of the well before it went out in the pool of water. Still, they had time to see the grapping hook that was deeply planted in the bucket, which was attached by a rope to a soldier who was very solidly grounded. He, too, was pulling with all his might on the rope.

'Attention! Attention! They're in the well!'

Valius hoped that the sentries stationed behind the castle could hear him despite the well's depth. Driven by despair, Aristophanes pushed the child up with one hand to help him climb the wall of the well. He was less than a half-meter from freedom. Ogrino was finally able to jump into the garden, where he was immediately seized by strong hands. Three Militians had thrown themselves upon him.

'No! NO! You won't get me, not now!'

Powerful arms gripped him tighter and tighter, and the guards were yelling out. Fear and rebellion mingled in Ogrino's mind, slowly transforming into great anger, which led him to say, 'You don't know, you don't know, you don't know WHO I AM!'

Suddenly, he was ten times as strong, and all at once, the soldiers had trouble keeping hold of him. He got free, and before one of the soldiers could hit him, he bit down on the man's leg and broke it. Another leapt onto Ogrino from behind. Without turning around, the boy grabbed him by the neck and threw him over his head into the third man, who was advancing upon him with a dagger. Before the two men had the time to stand up, Ogrino was already upon them, arms flying in all directions, fists clenched. The poor soldiers were hit with a whirlwind of punches that deformed their faces and left them wailing in a heap on the grass. Aristophanes had just come out of the well and looked upon the happy scene. The child was radiant with victory while the three Militians lay wretchedly at his feet.

'Come along, let's not stay here. Others might be coming.'

The Baron took him by the hand and they began to run into the woods. As they ran, the Baron asked, 'How did you do that? You were alone against three of them!'

'I got very angry and then it was all so simple. It was as if they turned into wisps of hay in my hands, so light and breakable. Is that strength coming to me from my parents from before?

The Baron was about to answer when a suspicious noise rung out behind them. He turned around and saw that they were being followed by about fifteen soldiers, who were approaching at top speed.

'Hurry, faster! They're nearly upon us, they'll catch us.'

In a few more strides, they were in the woodland. A shower of arrows whistled by, tearing through leaves and planting themselves in trees.

'Don't slow down, keep straight ahead, but zigzag a bit.'

And then they came upon a river.

'We're done for,'said Ogrino. 'I can't really swim, and the river is far too wide to be able to jump.'

'Don't worry, come this way,' said the Baron, running to the right.

He stopped short and, with both hands, lifted some branches that were lying on the ground. Despite the dark night, Ogrino could see an elongated shape. *A boat*, he thought. They were going to escape in a boat. He promptly helped Aristophanes put it in the water, and they jumped inside. The little river was fast, and the current quickly got hold of the boat. They found two oars and paddled so as to steer their skiff. It was at that moment that the first soldier saw them and shot at the boat, below the water line. Immediately, a rivulet of water began to stream into the boat through a hole in the hull. A second shot, and another hole appeared in the boat. Three more Militians arrived and began to shoot at the boat as well. Throughout all this, the current continued to carry the fugitives ever farther away, and chasing them became difficult because the vegetation was so dense and the ground hilly. The soldiers ran and jumped along the riverside, shooting all the while. They knew that the river would soon take a bend and the fugitives would be out of their range. At the last volley of shots, five or six more holes appeared in the hull and Ogrino wondered if they weren't going to sink. He turned to the Baron to ask, and that was when he saw him leaning slightly forward, a red mark on his chest.

'What's wrong? Are you injured?'

'It's nothing, nothing serious. Merely a little pellet that's lodged itself in my abdomen. It's certainly a surface wound. It should not slow our progress.'

Despite Aristophanes's reassuring words, Ogrino remained worried as the bloodstain on the Baron's shirt seemed to be getting bigger. He paddled on alone as his friend lay down in the bottom of the boat, plugging the holes with rags. Their pursuers were now far behind; at least they had nothing to fear from them.

'Where are we going?'

'To see one of my old friends. We'll be safe staying there, and he has much knowledge and will be able to heal me.'

'How will we get there? You can't walk very far in your state.'

'No need to walk, you'll see.'

They traveled the rest of the way without incident, although the Baron's wound continued to bleed abundantly. Aristophanes took a mirror out of his pocket and, despite his pain and the meandering river, persisted in keeping it pointed toward the full moon.

PROFESSOR LOVESTONE

From the top floor of his windmill, where he was looking at the stars with his telescope, Professor Lovestone saw something glint on the river. Looking more closely, he was able to make out a boat. He pointed the apparatus at the source of the signals and was quite surprised to recognize his old friend Aristophanes, along with a child. Their boat was now only a few dozen meters from his house, so he raced downstairs and pressed a lever.

The Baron realized that his friend had spotted them when he saw the river lock opening before them. The boat was pulled into the little branch of the river that led to the wheel of the windmill. Ogrino was not very comfortable with heading straight toward this big, turning wheel.

'We're going to be cut into pieces, we have to get out of here!' he called to the Baron.

At that moment, the hull struck one of the blades of the windmill, which stopped turning. Aristophanes hoisted himself up, with difficulty onto the nearest blade, and motioned to Ogrino to join him. As soon as the boy had climbed up, the wheel began to turn again and in an instant, they were at its zenith. A door opened in front of them and they saw a little stooped man with wild white hair that looked like rays of sun radiating from his head. Ogrino jumped to his feet and the Baron followed suit, slowly.

'My poor Aristophanes, what happened to you?'

'Legiferius is tightening its hold on us. They're after this child here.'

'We'll see about that! Let's not waste time, come along. I'll examine your wounds,' said the professor in response.

Generosity and intelligence emanated from his face. He had little sparkling blue eyes, framed by silvered oval glasses. His nose was round, his cheekbones high, and his lips very thin but smiling. He wasn't very tall and was rather tubby, but he still seemed to be energetic and eager to help. He took the Baron under the arms and helped him over to the sofa, where he laid him down. He unbuttoned his shirt to examine the injury.

'The wound is deep, but your days are not numbered, my friend,' Lovestone quipped. 'I'm going to give you an injection and remove the bullet.'

Ogrino's eyes opened wide at the sight of the big syringe and long needle that was piercing the skin of the Baron's arm. In a few moments the Baron was asleep. The professor cleaned the wound with a bit of cotton and disinfectant. He then took out some knives and made an incision below the injury. Finally, with tweezers, he plucked a little metal object from the bottom of the wound.

'And the work is done,' he stated proudly. 'There's nothing left but for him to rest. In a few more days, he won't feel anything. We'll have time to get to know each other better, my boy,' he added, turning toward Ogrino. 'Now tell me, you aren't a child like all the others. Come into the light and give me a smile.'

Ogrino felt comfortable with this impressive little man, who must have been a doctor, seeing how easily he operated on the Baron. So he had no problem smiling widely at him.

'I knew it!' the professor said, noticing the boy's pointed teeth. 'And how did a little Ogre come to be traveling with my friend Aristophanes?'

So once more, Ogrino told his story, under the old man's compassionate eye.

'I understand now why my friend took such risks. It's becoming really intolerable. The men of the Order think they are spreading the truth and are ready to sacrifice anything on the altar of their doctrine. It's an insult to human intelligence and an insult to life itself! But enough philosophizing. You must be hungry. We can certainly find you something in my pantry. Come upstairs.'

They climbed an old wooden spiral staircase that opened onto a big rectangular room with a long table piled high with all sorts of devices. There were complicated machines whose function Ogrino couldn't even imagine. Lovestone made a little space by brushing aside all his utensils. He took some vegetables from a basket and put them into a bowl atop a metal tube, then pushed a lever. There was a shrill noise. Ogrino was stunned to discover that the vegetables had been liquefied when he saw Lovestone pour a warm green mixture into two bowls. Then the professor gathered a dozen oranges, which he placed into a filtered funnel. They fell, one by one, onto a turning wheel, where a piston crushed them. The juice streamed into a transparent glass. This whole process was both fascinating and appetizing. Atop a purring, wood-burning oven, the lid of a big pot was whistling and shooting out steam. Alongside it, there was a long coffer covered in frost—hard to believe since the room was hot. Lovestone went out onto the balcony, where he took a huge amount of food out of a cupboard. Ogrino was already licking his lips at the sight of all those treats. They had barely been set upon the table when he was upon the hams, the roast beeves, the sausages, and the fowls. Although he knew the child's nature, the professor was nonetheless impressed by his appetite, even wondering if there would be enough food. After the meats, the child devoured the boiled potatoes, entire loaves of bread, then the soup, and finally the fruit and desserts. Only after having wolfed down a large punch bowl of chocolate mousse did the child pause to rest.

'Ah, I think you must be feeling better now?' the professor ventured.

'Couldn't be better if only I wasn't so tired.'

'Oh yes,' Lovestone agreed. 'All today's events and emotions must have tired you out. Come, I'll show you your bed.'

They went up one more floor, where there were large rooms that were nevertheless packed full of big wood and metal machines. The walls were covered with large sheets of parchment filled with sketches, graphics, and indecipherable formulas. Ogrino was able to recognize a drawing of the moon between two other circles, one blue and the other big and yellow.

'This way! This room is the least filled up with all my jumble of equipment. You'll sleep like a king.'

The child took off his boots and clothes and immediately got under the covers. He was deeply asleep the moment his head hit the soft pillow. The old man, for his part, couldn't sleep because of all the troubling recent events. Surely it wouldn't end there. His friend would recover from his wound, but would he be able to return to his castle? Legiferius did not take kindly to anyone who resisted their authority, and aiding a fugitive was a heavily punishable crime. The Baron had taken huge risks for this child. And for what reason? Defending the weak and oppressed? An independent spirit? Resistance to a barbaric government? He reflected on all of this and its possible consequences for hours. The first light of dawn caught him still lost in thought. At that moment, he heard a knock on the front door. He went out to the balcony and saw three soldiers below, and about twenty others surrounding the mill. His heart skipped a beat when he realized that one of the soldiers had spotted him.

'Hey, you! Come down and let us in!' a soldier ordered.

'On my way! I'm just going to get dressed and I'll be right there,' the professor responded compliantly.

Lovestone ran furiously into Ogrino's room and shook him awake. The child jumped up, and before he could say anything, the man was handing him his clothes so frantically and frightened that the child knew what was happening. He got dressed in a flash and put on his boots, hopping toward the terrace. The cool air finished the job of waking him up. He was taken aback by what he saw. A huge bird made of wood and fabric lay before him. The professor squatted down and lifted him easily.

'May I introduce my most ingenious invention: the Icarius. It's a marvelous flying engine and today, it will allow us to escape the hand of tyranny. Below, the soldiers' voices became howls.

'Open up, open up immediately, or we'll break the door in!' the old man and the child could hear, although they were at the very top of the windmill.

'Aren't you worried? They broke through the Baron's door and they'll do it here too.'

'Don't be afraid, I've taken care of everything. Don't forget I'm a brilliant inventor!'

At that moment an enormous shot rang out and the door gave way. Mortengus and Valius jumped over the threshold, only to see a heavy metal gate clang down just before their feet.

'Curse this professor!' Valius roared. 'It'll take us hours to destroy this lattice! We've got to find another way to get into the place.'

'No problem. My men know what they must do,' responded Mortengus. Then he stepped back through the door and yelled 'ATTACK!'

Ogrino heard a loud noise on the edge of the balcony and leaned over to find out what was going on. To his horror, he saw a grappling hook, then two, then three, attach themselves to the stone guardrail. Four more impacts further confirmed that an attack was underway. The soldiers were already beginning to climb the cords.

'They're coming up, they'll be here in a second,' he called to the professor.

Lovestone, perched on a tall stepladder, had attached the Icarius to the back of a J-shaped launch ramp.

'Don't be afraid, join me up here. It's all right! See these pedals? You're going to put your feet on them and pedal with all your might when I tell you to, okay? And now get into the Icarius so I can strap you in.

Ogrino lay down under the airplane, or whatever it was, and let the professor buckle him in horizontally, his feet up against the pedals and his hands gripping the framework. Lovestone then crawled under the apparatus, buckled himself in, and told Ogrino, 'Now I'm going to count to three, and when I say three, start to pedal as hard as you can! Use all your strength! One, two, three!'

The two companions pedaled forcefully. The movements of their legs were perfectly synchronized. Ogrino noticed some movement on his right, and when he turned his head, he saw that the Icarius's wing was moving up and down like a bird's, and when he turned to the left the other wing was doing the same. Little by little, the flapping intensified. Suddenly a soldier jumped onto the balcony. Seeing what was happening, he ran toward the engine. Lovestone redoubled his efforts, shouting, 'Faster, faster!'

Then Lovestone pulled on a latch and the Icarius began to slide down the ramp, accelerating. It was halfway off the terrace when the Militian grabbed onto the stretched material that made up the Icarius's tail, just as it was flying out into open air. Holding tightly onto his prey, the soldier was swept away and he, too, fell. The Icarius, unbalanced by this extra weight, went from a level horizontal flight to a vertical fall. The fabric of the tail tore under the intruder's weight, and the Militian fell like a rock, liberating the Icarius. The professor and Ogrino, despairing, pedaled like madmen, and when they were only about three meters above the ground, the apparatus finally regained its balance and leveled out. At that moment, Mortengus took aim at the engine and fired. A cloud of bullets tore through the material and the wooden framework of the apparatus, but nothing crucial was hit. Before the Militians could reload their guns, the wind and the frenetic movement of its wings had the Icarius sailing majestically through the air.

As it passed the top of the windmill, its silhouette disappeared against the sun.

'Curse those rebels,' Valius grumbled. 'They've escaped us once again. But sooner or later, they'll pay. They've won the battle but not the war. Legiferius will be the victor there. Come here, everyone. Let us go help our friend, Salatius, who courageously defended the honor of the Order—if there's still time! Afterwards we will see to the Baron, who must still be inside.'

As they approached the body of the fallen soldier, Ogrino could barely make them out, they were so small. They seemed like ants. Feeling the wind in his hair and on his face, watching magnificent and foreign landscapes passing by, Ogrino was overcome by an intense sensation of freedom. The Icarius was proving to be a remarkable machine, as it glided along with the wind at an astounding speed, then spiraled like a bird of prey over a hill or a field of wheat and so gained even more altitude. Ogrino was certain that the professor could do as he wished with the engine. They seemed to be not two distinct entities, but one. Lovestone only had to tilt his head slightly to one side for the Icarius to turn in unison.

'Can we fly like this forever?' Ogrino asked.

'As long as we have the strength, or the wind will carry us, we'll stay in the air. The weather is wonderful for flying. A little breeze will take us wherever we want to go.'

'I would like to go back to the circus and see my parents,' Ogrino said, full of emotion.

'Isn't that dangerous? If you are a fugitive, you and your family are considered enemies of the Order. I seriously doubt that they are still at the circus.'

'Exactly! If they've been taken prisoner, I have to set them free.'

'You are admirably courageous, but what can one young, unarmed boy, even an Ogre, do before an entire army? And anyway, if your parents had been taken prisoner, they would surely be in Legiferius's prison, which is the best guarded in the world.'

'I absolutely have to go to their fortress because maybe everyone I love is locked up in there! We'll go to the circus first to find out news about my parents and then we'll construct a plan to get into the citadel, if we have to. Even if it's protected by the devil himself, I know we can get inside!'

'I'm not sure that that's the best plan as the Militians are probably monitoring the area around the circus. As soon as you arrive there, they'll catch you.'

'I've already escaped from them a few times, and anyway they don't scare me. I'll find a way. Besides, even if the circus is under surveillance, the soldiers there don't know you, and we'll be there before they have time to give the alert. What do you think?'

'Why, you're right! The Order often communicates by carrier pigeon, while we're benefiting from a tailwind that's pushing us along at at least fifty knots. None of those birds can reach that speed. If conditions stay favorable, we should reach Legiferius City from here in fifteen minutes.'

'Yahooo!' Ogrino cried. 'They'll never catch us, and they won't have time to sound the alarm. My plan's going to work!'

And as they shot through the blue skies, as fast as a cannonball, Ogrino explained to Lovestone what he wanted him to do. While they were talking, a dark mass appeared in the distance, standing out from the green of the countryside.

As the Icarius got closer, Ogrino was better able to make out the shapes, and what he saw sent a shiver down his spine. Legiferius City! The city, as he had never seen it before, suddenly appeared to him in all its horror. In the center, there was an immense fortress made up of four square towers linked by a thick wall at least thirty meters tall. Right in the middle of this rectangle there was an immense L-shaped structure. Seen from above, the fortress formed the emblem of Legiferius, which could be seen everywhere on the Order's flags, chests, weapons, and vessels: a big black 'L' inside of a red circle, itself inside of a black square. Eight avenues led out from the fortress: four diagonal ones leading out from the corners, and four perpendicular streets leading out from the sides. These avenues were linked by streets which formed wide concentric squares around the citadel. From Ogrino's position, he could finally see the true face of Legiferius City: a network forming a hideous and immense spider web! So thanks to the Icarius, it was all becoming clear. Even the city reflected the Order's influence on society and on the world. A vile tarantula spun its web, day after day, to imprison it all. A feeling of disgust rose up in Ogrino and he nearly vomited, but the fresh air and the beauty of the rest of the countryside calmed him and his nausea slowly passed.

'Here we are,' the professor declared.

'But not at all!' Ogrino replied. 'We're only at the edge of the city. My circus is more on the right. Look there, you can see the top of the big tent. We've got to keep going. Our time is precious if we want to keep the element of surprise on our side.'

'We're going to stop here, on the top of this lightly wooded hill. This will be perfect,' Lovestone said.

'Can you explain to me why, Professor?' the child asked in frustration.

'It's very simple. The Icarius, in order to take off, needs altitude. So a hill, if a mountain is not available, will do the trick nicely. The trees here will also hide us, allowing me to find the Icarius safe and sound when I need it again. Now you understand.'

'I'm sorry, Professor. I was so impatient to get there!'

'Impatience and impetuosity are common traits of youth, and I cannot blame you, considering all that Legiferius has put you through. But enough talk! The time has come to focus on landing.'

While Lovestone was concentrating, Ogrino observed all of his movements, trying to understand how he steered this extraordinary machine. The Icarius swooped around in the sky, coming to fly against the wind. They lost altitude and speed. A clearing appeared ahead of them, rapidly growing larger as they approached. Ogrino closed his eyes, dreading the impact. To his great surprise, he felt only a gliding motion and the smell of fresh grass. He instantly unclenched his eyes and saw that they were delicately perched on daisy-strewn ground.

'One of my best landings! You saw it! They call that an "angel's kiss." We landed like a feather! I don't mean to brag, but it's quite an art!'

'Bravo, bravo!' Ogrino sang out, clapping his hands. 'Let's go now.'

They unbuckled themselves, pulled the Icarius under the trees, and threw some branches over it to camouflage it better. Then they bolted, running down the side of the hill, and skipping over tall grasses, headed for the city. Breathing in the fresh air fragrant with herbs, Ogrino thought of Aristophanes, wounded and maybe now prisoner of the Militians. He secretly hoped that they hadn't found him. The Baron had sacrificed himself to save Ogrino; he would never forget that. If only for his sake, Ogrino had to keep fighting the Order.

Evening had just fallen when they reached the dark and narrow alleyways outside the city walls.

'You'll stay here, hidden in the confessional of that little church, while I go look for news. You'll be safe. No one will think to look for you there. But first, I'll buy you a big loaf of bread for your wait.'

Shortly after having left the child in the booth with his snack, Lovestone wandered down roads, passages, bridges, and alleys until the big tent of the circus appeared before him, lit up weakly.

'Doesn't look like there's a show tonight,' Lovestone said to a poor devil slumped on a barrel. The man's face held all the sadness in the world.

'Our director, his wife, and part of the troupe were arrested a few days ago. We don't know what's become of them, or when they'll come back, so the circus is dead now. Our leader is the spirit of the circus! You understand? Without him and his wife it's not the same, there's no spirit, no get-up-and-go . . . We have no motivation now.'

'And if I were to propose to free them?' the professor replied in a half-serious, half-amused tone. 'But allow me to introduce myself. My name is Lovestone. I am an inventor, and it so happens that I know Ogrino and where he is right now.'

'Shhhhh! Don't say that name! The Militians have taken over the circus. They're always patrolling. There are even two of them in Pantaleone's wagon.'

'Then here's what you'll do . . . ' Lovestone whispered in his ear.

The chapel was completely quiet and empty at this late evening hour, and Ogrino was contemplating the beautiful golden candlelight from his hiding spot. Comfortably seated on a thick cushion, he could look through the grill of the confessional and see magnificent paintings of fantastic scenes with people flying in the sky. He quite admired them.

Despite the place's small size, there was an impressive abundance of gold objects: vases, candlesticks, cups, plates, and crucifixes. Ogrino had never seen so many treasures in his life. The people who lived here must be very rich and also very trusting since the door was always open and they didn't seem to be afraid of having things stolen.

At that moment, a creaking near the door caught his attention, and Ogrino saw an old, stooped man enter, leaning on a cane. His hair, long and white, looked like a waterfall tumbling to his waist. His face was filled with deep wrinkles, although his blue eyes sparkled with an indefinable light that radiated majesty and inspired respect. The man, who advanced with a slight limp, was dressed in a beige cassock, from which only his gnarled hands and feet emerged. He looked so old that Ogrino wouldn't have even been able to guess at his age. Intrigued, Ogrino followed with his eyes as the man approached the altar. He saw him kneel and pull something out of his pouch, then draw on the ground with large gestures. Pushed on by curiosity, the child furtively slipped out of his hiding spot without making the least noise. Standing behind one column, then another, he soon found himself at the old man's left, close enough to finally see what was going on. He leaned his head out from behind the column slightly and saw mysterious designs chalked in purple on the white church flagstones. A five-sided shape enclosed a circle, which enclosed a cross. The man was kneeling at the intersection of the two axes and looked as if he were reciting a poem.

"Ho! You, Father on High
Deign to listen to your servant
Hear the humble cry
Coming from his heart
Now, when times are trying
May your good will fall
On all creatures great and small
So that a new cycle may start."

Barely had he finished his invocation, when a ray of moonlight shone through a stained-glass window and illuminated him from head to toe, so that he gleamed with an immaculate white light. Then a gentle breeze, from who knows where, rushed through the chapel's nave, extinguishing a few candles as it passed. Engrossed by this strange sight, Ogrino did not notice that the man had turned his head and was now staring directly at him. The man rose slowly and turned to Ogrino, saying, 'Gromniou creuduao vromiu srincoa grawuiau prissaou tresriu braoclou gronio dratro krecma grismu?'

Which meant, in Ogre language, 'What is a little Ogre doing alone in a city and dressed like a human child?' Ogrino understood from these rumblings that the old man spoke the language of his ancestors.

'I don't understand what you're saying. I only speak human language,' Ogrino answered simply.

The old man started. He hadn't expected such a miracle.

'So you really exist! The one the breeze whispers about, the one the leaves murmur rumors of. As you can see, I am a hermit who has lived in the forest for such a long time that I know all its secrets. The creatures that live there hold no mystery for me. As time went by, I sank into this marvelous nature, so rich with lessons, so much that I became one with it. So I knew of your existence long before I had the pleasure of making your acquaintance this evening, in such an unexpected, yet predictable way! You've arrived at just the right moment, as I was saying a prayer for the coming springtime. Springtime is a renewal, you see. And here you are, you've appeared—it's a sign!'

'I don't understand,' said Ogrino, stunned. 'How can you know who I am when you are meeting me for the first time?'

'There are details that do not lie. In the first place, a little Ogre would never venture into a city, much less a chapel. Second, you speak human language and don't understand Ogre language, which reveals that you were found and raised by humans. And third, it is written in the great book of life that someone who is between two worlds will play an important role in what is to come. From this, naturally I deduced that it had to be you. Don't you come from the Legendary World? And aren't you just as much part of the human world?'

'Hah! Certainly not! Or at least, not the entire human world, because some of them are cruel and vile! Legiferius killed my parents, and now it's me they're hunting. Actually I am hiding here, waiting for a friend.'

'You have nothing to fear from me. I won't betray your secret. I cannot accept the murderous tyranny that the Order has developed toward magical creatures. I am far too close to the animals to allow it because of the life I've lived, far from the teeming anthill of humanity. But I haven't introduced myself! My name is Theophilas, and I am a solitary hermit-monk who has left the world in order to better listen to it and serve it.'

'My name is Ogrino, and I am the adopted son of Pantaleone and Slevania, the circus people.'

At that moment, the door squeaked, and Ogrino instinctively concealed himself behind the hermit, who did not move. Already, a man was quickly moving toward the side aisle of the church. He brusquely opened the little door of the confessional and saw that it was empty.

'What are you looking for, my son?' Theophilas asked.

'Nothing, Father, or rather, yes. I lost a gold chain in this chapel this afternoon, and I thought that I might find it tonight. Apparently I was mistaken.'

'Lovestone!' Ogrino cried out, having recognized his voice. 'Here I am!'

'Hah! There you are. Come quickly as time is short!' said the professor, without any more attention to the monk. 'Let's go!'

Ogrino would have liked to run up to join him, but he couldn't in good conscience abandon this strange and fascinating hermit so suddenly.

'Come along! We can't dawdle!'

'I may be able to help you,' offered the hermit.

'Thank you for your offer, but I think that's impossible. What we need to do is a private concern.'

'Freeing Legiferius's prisoners could be considered a private affair, to be sure,' the monk continued. 'However, standing up to tyranny is a public affair, and it concerns us all. There are many for whom this resistance is vital, and I am one of them.'

Lovestone was silent, wondering who this man could be, who seemed to be able to read minds, unless Ogrino had told him everything. So then either the child had been very imprudent, or he must have had blind faith in this monk.

'Theophilas is on our side,' Ogrino finally said. He, too, was astonished by the hermit's deductions. 'But how did you figure out what we are going to do?' he asked, turning to the old man.

'I learned to read other's hearts, you see. Your sad story, your zeal, and now the arrival of your friend – all of that leaves no doubt as to your intentions. I think that our paths have crossed so that I can help you. You know, Legiferius consults me for anything having to do with simples.'

'Simples? You mean the simpleminded?' Ogrino questioned.

'No, of course not!' Lovestone butted in. 'He means the medicinal herbs that are commonly called simples.'

'Yes, the Docts are very interested in the benefits of plants. They have an entire library where they are dried, classified, and catalogued, with all their properties. They are always looking for new species, and as I live in the forest, they know I can help them discover even more. In fact, my donkey is tied up outside the chapel with a full load of herbs that I have to deliver to them tomorrow morning. That gives me an idea. This is what we'll do. Ogrino, you'll hide in one of the herb sacks and we'll go into the fortress like that. Then you'll slip away to search the place and find out where your parents are.'

'I already have another plan,' Lovestone interrupted. 'Everything has been set up for Ogrino to enter Legiferius's fortress easily, and go as far as possible into the grounds.'

He pulled the child close and whispered something in his ear. After listening to everything, Ogrino exclaimed, 'I think

I'll use Theophilas's strategy, and if somehow it doesn't work, we'll have your plan to fall back on.'

Lovestone was a bit vexed, but he grouchily accepted the child's proposition. They then set out on the path toward the inn where Theophilas was staying, and where they might be able to find a room. The place would surely prove safer than the circus, which was still under strict surveillance. As soon as they arrived at the inn, they ate a meager meal, except for Ogrino, who gulped down four fat hams and then all three went to sleep as they were quite tired.

In the middle of the night, Trentus, who tended the pigeon-house, started, as a bird had come into its alcove and set off its little bell on the chart on the office wall. A simple system of rope and pulleys, linked to each one of the nests, allowed Trentus to see when the carrier pigeons had returned home.

'Go, see what message R728 has brought,' he told a soldier.

Two minutes later, Trentus was already decoding the message from Mortengus. He forwarded the information to the Magnus Scrutator's personal secretary so that he would receive it upon awakening.

THE DOCTS' CASTE

There's nothing better than a good night's sleep to restore you to top form and appetite. Ogrino merrily leapt up from his bed, ready to face the coming day with energy and determination. Today was an important day, for it would be that of his reunion with Pantaleone and Slevania—at least, he very much hoped so. He tugged on Lovestone's sleeve to wake him and went to knock on Theophilas's door so that everyone would be at breakfast together in the inn's salon.

After a light meal, at Ogrino's urging—the boy had only allowed himself ten glasses of milk and fifty pieces of toast—they set off swiftly toward the fortress. Despite the early hour, the streets were already congested with merchants carrying their products, artisans pulling their carts laden with tools, and the many people going to market or to work. Our three friends made their way, sometimes better than others, through all of this bric-a-brac, finally arriving at the foot of Fort Legiferius. The fortress was truly imposing. The disgust that Ogrino had felt before was now mixed with a crushing sense of smallness. The architects designing the citadel had wanted to express the Order's power and domination, and they had absolutely succeeded. Anyone approaching the place found himself suddenly feeling small and pitiful in the face of this grand, austere monument and all that it represented. After this initial sensation had passed, Ogrino regained his enthusiasm and irrepressible will to infiltrate the place successfully, impressive though it was.

Still, entering the fortress would not prove easy. Theophilas noted that the guard posted in front of the massive main door had been doubled; security was tighter than usual.

'Maybe we'd do well to go with the second plan straightaway,' he said. 'The sentries seem unusually tense.'

'Stay here, hidden in the crowd,' Lovestone ordered them. 'I'll go take care of what we talked about.'

He disappeared, caught up in the human magma that was swarming about like ants on an anthill. The child and the old man waited until nearly noon before they saw their friend appear in the distance and give the agreed-upon sign. So they quietly began to walk toward the tall door. Ogrino stopped suddenly and slipped underneath a cart that was stopped near the outer wall. Theophilas continued on calmly, as if nothing was afoot, and took his place in the long queue leading up to the fortress, where people were let in one or two at a time. After a long while, he found himself face-to-face with the guards.

'What is your business here?' the head guard demanded.

'Good day, gentlemen. I'm bringing my trimestrial offering to the medical Docts. I have here some very interesting new plants.'

'Where is your pass?' the soldier asked brusquely.

'Right here,' the monk answered calmly.

'Everything is in order, you may go in.'

Theophilas was pulling on the rope to get his donkey to come along when suddenly the guard stopped him.

'First let us see what you have in those sacks.'

Two Militians pushed him aside unceremoniously and opened the bags to inspect them.

'Nothing suspect, Sergeant,' one of them declared. 'Just herbs and dried leaves.'

'All right, you may go. Next!'

At that exact moment, a cacophony of cries broke out from the end of the plaza, and a frightened crowd was moving every which way, waving their arms frantically.

'Help, help! Please! Militia, come quick! Help us!'

The moving mass of humans was advancing inexorably toward the entrance of Fort Legiferius. Seeing this, the guards called in reinforcements, and soon a double row of security had formed, while other Militians were pouring out of the fortress, charging toward what seemed to be the cause of all this panic. The soldiers couldn't make effective progress against the current of the crowd, and only four of them reached their goal. They were surprised by what they saw, but being dutiful military professionals, they got into position for combat. A full-grown beast with bulging muscles was roaring ferociously and giving them a belligerent look. He jumped on the first of the soldiers on his right and struck him to the ground. A second soldier tried to shoot him in the back with his crossbow, but the animal did an about-face and not only avoided the arrow, but also knocked the Militian over with a single bound. The last two shot simultaneously just as the beast was attacking the third. A bullet pierced its mane, but it was nevertheless able to knock one of the soldiers senseless. As copious reinforcements arrived, the animal turned and fled lightning-fast, with majestic ease. The crowd flowed back into his path and the soldiers were ensnared in the sea of people, fighting to advance.

During all of this commotion, taking advantage of the jostling and the guards' relative inattention, Ogrino had left his hiding place and slipped between their legs.

Brave Royal, he thought. *He did exactly as we planned. I just hope he wasn't injured by the shots I heard.*

Theophilas had set one of his sacks on the ground as planned. The child had only to jump into it, and once it was sealed up again, voila, they'd done it. The hardest part for the old man was lifting the heavy bag onto his donkey's back again. Theophilas then began to walk slowly toward Fort Legiferius's court. During this time, a second cordon of guards had materialized in a half-circle, barring the way.

'Your pass!'

'I've just shown it to your colleagues.'

'Your pass! Now!'

Theophilas handed them the paper uneasily.

'What are you carrying?'

'Medicinal plants.'

The soldier walked around the donkey with an air of suspicion. He tapped on the sacks, then stopped. In one sudden movement, he undid the tie to one of the pouches and plunged his hand inside it. The monk's heart stopped. He grew very pale.

The Militian turned toward him, looking him straight in the eyes, and said, 'Everything is in order, you may go ahead.'

Stunned, Theophilas did not move for a moment. He had just realized that Ogrino was in the other sack. Regaining his spirits, he crossed the line of guards, forcing himself to look at a point on the horizon so that his face wouldn't betray the emotions swirling inside of him. When he arrived at the stable at the back of the citadel, he sat down on a bale of hay to catch his breath. He was just beginning to feel better when a groom arrived.

'I'll curry your mount, Father, but first let me help you unload him.'

'No! Don't worry about it. I'm used to it, and besides I'm carrying fragile things that must be handled carefully.'

'I may be as husky and strong as a blacksmith, but I know how to be gentle with animals. I think I can take care of your bags.'

Saying this, he unloaded the first one easily. When he went to take the second one, he was surprised by its weight.

'What have you got in here, rocks?'

'No, they're tins of ointment made with medicinal plants.'

'Ooh, I'd quite like to see that. I have joint pain and I'm sure that using a nice cream every night would do me a lot of good.'

He detached the big bag with difficulty and set it on the ground.

'May I take a peek, Father?'

'I don't think the Docts would approve, my boy. Remember, this is a special order they had me bring.'

'Oh please Father! Have pity on a poor, suffering fellow.'

'No, I am adamant. I cannot, and in any case . . .'

At that moment, a shadow appeared in the stable door.

'Theophilas! The Docts sent us to look for you,' said the soldier.

Saved by the bell, thought the hermit.

'Here I am. I'm on my way. I just need your help to carry my bags because I am old and tired.'

'Guards! Take these bags!'

Four Militians carried out the order, then set out all together, in step, toward the fortress, leaving the groom grumbling in his corner. They passed a new line of sentries guarding the door to the citadel, then continued into an immense room that led to an impressive number of hallways and staircases. Five Docts arrived, pushing a small, wheeled table.

'Dear Theophilas,' one of them said in a honeyed voice, 'here you are at last! What a joy to see you again! Have you made any new discoveries?'

'My good Trentimus,' responded the hermit sincerely, 'It is always a pleasure to meet with you and discuss botany and medicine. In fact, I have new extracts that I believe will interest you, especially those concerning skin diseases.'

'We'll continue in my office, in the laboratory,' Trentimus replied. 'Let us go now.'

They loaded the sacks onto the rolling cart and took a long hallway that led to a spiral staircase. There, four Docts lifted the table and climbed to the top floor. They entered a big room that was white from floor to ceiling, where many Docts were occupied with colored jars, half-dissected animals, measuring and weighing instruments, and chemistry equipment. Theophilas never tired of watching this spectacle, although he was very familiar with it, having been here many times. All this research, all this accumulated knowledge! He felt a spasm of joy thinking of all the good this could bring to humanity. What relief of illnesses, wounds, and pain! He was glad to contribute to all of that. Alone, he wouldn't have been able to help as many suffering souls, but thanks to the help of the Order, which expanded upon his feeble means tenfold. Still, he was not deceived. He knew very well that the Docts had very little esteem for him. They thought only of their own glory, of being able to announce to the Magnus Legifer that the Order had made even more scientific progress. Theophilas had no use for all that, as only the well-being of the masses mattered to him. The Docts distributed their medicine abundantly in the bosom of the kingdom, and that was all that counted in the monk's eyes.

'Now, let's open these bags. I can't wait to see the marvels you've brought,' said Trentimus eagerly.

'Right away, my dear Doct,' Theophilas responded immediately. 'However, first we must go into the shadows because my preparations cannot withstand bright light.'

'Let's go into the storeroom, then.'

Once they had arrived in the little room, the Docts pushed the cart toward the back and the monk ordered, 'Go and get me a candle, please as we need a dim light.'

The four Docts disappeared and Theophilas was alone with Trentimus, who showered him with questions. When they were finally able to light up the room, the monk opened his bags and took out his treasures before Trentimus's shining, eager eyes. They spent a good four hours this way, analyzing, evaluating, comparing, and studying the different plants he had collected. Then the old man interrupted the discussion on the pretext that he was tired and needed something to eat.

'You are quite right. What was I thinking? It's nearly noon and you have travelled a long way to see us, even if you did sleep a little at the inn.'

Theophilas's blood froze in his veins for an instant. The Doct knew a lot. Was it possible, then, that he had been followed? So Trentimus must have known that a child had been with him. Had their plan been discovered? Did Legiferius suspect something?

'Do you feel unwell? You're deathly pale. I'll go prepare you a mixture that will get you back on your feet.'

'No, thank you, I have what I need in this flask,' he said, taking two swallows. 'There, that'll do it,' he said in a quavering voice.

'You seem upset.'

'No, it's nothing. Just a little queasiness that will be gone in a moment.'

'All right, let's go to the dining hall for a bite to eat.'

'Gladly! I feel better already and that's given me an appetite.'

They joined a stream of people, who were apparently all going to the same place. They reached a very large rectangular room with long rows of tables where many people were eating in total, almost militaristic, silence. Even the utensils didn't make a sound as they struck the bowls. They sat at a table on a platform overlooking the assembly. It could hold only a dozen people, all of whom turned out to be Docts.

Before the first plate was served, a soldier burst loudly into the dining room, shouting, 'Trentimus! A spy has infiltrated Legiferius and Theophilas is his accomplice. Arrest him!'

Immediately, the Docts seized the poor hermit and held him down him securely before pushing him to one of the interrogation rooms. During this time, Ogrino was running as fast as he could, furiously cursing himself for having allowed the Docts to discover him in such an idiotic way. As he fled, he couldn't help but remember the scene. After the monk's and the Doct's departure, he had left his hiding spot behind the low shelf of jars. He had then opened the door just a little, noiselessly, to peek out and had seen Docts facing away from him, concentrating on their work. So he had slipped behind a very nearby workbench. However, his eyes, still a bit bleary from his hours in the darkness, had betrayed him: he had not seen the set of vials on the floor. He had stumbled on this pile of glass, which broke with a crystalline crash as Ogrino found himself flat on the ground. The Docts had all turned around, seen the intruder, and thrown themselves upon him. He had barely had the time to jump up and rush toward the entryway, narrowly escaping them.

Now he was being pursued not only by the Docts, but also by soldiers armed with crossbows. He had dashed down a big white marble staircase, pushing past ascending Docts and servant, who were left dazed in the wake of this little man shooting by like a rocket. Before anyone had had time to react, he had reached the lower floor and turned down a large hallway made of ebony marble. On his right, a large, half-open door caught his eye. Without thinking, he entered surreptitiously, ducking down, and sliding under a table. From there, he could see dozens of Docts, who were writing or handling large books. He made his way through the room quietly, hiding under one desk, then another, until he succeeded in approaching the enormous desk in the center of the room. At that moment, the door opened wide and some Militians entered loudly.

'We are looking for a fugitive. Have you seen anything?' their leader asked.

The Doct-scribes responded in one voice that they hadn't seen anyone. This answer, far from reassuring the rector, only increased his worry, and he ordered his men to search every inch of the room. The soldiers methodically examined the shelves, the trunks, and the undersides of the tables. Unavoidably, they approached Ogrino, whose mind was running at top speed in search of an escape route. It was a precarious situation. From his hiding place, he couldn't see whether there was an emergency exit at the back of the room. Not far from him, a roaring fire was burning in a large chimney. Not seeing any feet near him, he got out from under the desk and found an enormous book before him. On his far left, a door opened and a Doct entered, carrying an armful of parchments. When he saw the child, he let out a little cry, which was enough to mobilize the soldiers. In an astonishingly short time, two groups had lined up on either side of the room, and a third was rushing up the central aisle. Feeling trapped, Ogrino, galvanized by fear, jumped onto the table and seized the formidable tome, which was as wide and thick as ten dictionaries. He lifted it and opened it unto a 'V' just as a volley of arrows planted themselves in its massive leather cover. Then, in a desperate move, Ogrino jumped to the ground and threw the book into the fire.

'NOOO!' shouted the Docts. 'The Encyclopedia! Save the Encyclopedia!'

Another shower of shots rained down on the child, who at the last minute turned and took shelter behind the burning book. Then, without wasting a moment, he ran to his left and threw the great work onto the Militians, like a firebomb. While the soldiers were retreating to avoid the book, Ogrino found the exit, closed the door behind him, and miracle of miracles, saw a big key in the keyhole! He locked them in. The boy was already halfway up a sort of attic ladder when he heard the soldiers banging against the door, trying to knock it down. When he got to the top, he pulled up the ladder, then closed the trapdoor leading to the attic. At that exact moment, the door gave way under the Militians' shots. Ogrino had some time to spare before they realized where he had gone. He saw a small window on the wall near the roof, and with the help of the ladder, he reached it easily. The lock was rusty, and he had to go back down and get a piece of iron to use as a lever.

After four or five tries, the lock gave way suddenly, and the metal bar slipped out of Ogrino's hands, falling loudly to the ground.

'He's above us! Bring a stepladder, quickly!'

Hearing these words, he clambered out of the little window and found himself on the roofs of Legiferius. If he hadn't been so anxious, he could have admired an unparalleled view of the city from its tallest building. He ran along the central ridge of the roof looking for a window that might somehow have been left ajar. Finally, nearly at the end of the roof, he saw a half-open skylight. He was approaching it carefully, trying not to slip on the shingles, when suddenly a swarm of arrows planted themselves near his feet. To avoid the shots coming from one of the towers on the surrounding wall, Ogrino began to jump around and zigzag. Having escaped a few more waves of arrows, he arrived at the little window and lifted the pane. A cabinet stood a good three meters below. He was gathering up his courage to jump when the force of an explosion sent him tumbling into the room with a crash of broken glass. He had fallen onto the cabinet, but his momentum carried him further, and he dropped onto a workbench below and broke all the glass jars sitting on top of it. A little dazed, and with his hands cut, he sat up and discovered a horrible scene.

The shattered containers were releasing the blue-tinted bodies of a half-dozen magical creatures suspended in a viscous green substance. A nauseating odor was escaping from the jars, and Ogrino was dejected, seeing the atrocity of the Order's experiments. Lifting his eyes, he discovered that the room was filled with thousands of receptacles of all sizes, some as tall as pillars, in which forbidding creatures floated, suspended between two greenish fluids. A huge male and female caught his eye. They had to be adolescent Trolls, judging by their size. Although he couldn't see their faces clearly, they looked vaguely familiar and had a majestic bearing. He wondered if they were really Trolls or if they were actually . . .

His ponderings were interrupted by the sound of rapid footsteps at the other end of the room. *The Militians*, he thought, ducking down and slipping behind a wall of jars containing Pixies, Gnomes, and Sprites, who looked to be in a deep, melancholy sleep.

'Search every corner, he can't be far away,' ordered an authoritarian voice, one that Ogrino recognized.

Valius had obtained command of a small unit in order to finish the hunt that he'd begun. Now it was personal. This little boy had been taunting him for too long.

'Something moved on the right!' called a soldier.

Part of the squadron went in that direction. One of the Militians saw feet sticking out from behind a large container. Then they disappeared; the fugitive must have been crawling. So jumping to the side, the soldier got a better angle and released his bowstring. A scream broke the heavy silence, and the squadron pounced on their victim. It was a stampede. Clothing was bursting into flames as some soldiers collapsed and others froze in place. The second squadron, which had stayed behind, ran up on the left and, seeing the disaster, began to let loose a flurry of arrows. The poor magical creatures that had come back to life when Ogrino inadvertently liberated them were now dying under the soldiers' fire. Taking advantage of the confusion, Ogrino had slipped between the jars and reached the back door. He found himself in a little cellar, which he quickly crossed, finding a door that led to one of Legiferius's great hallways. Opening it slightly, he saw that it was packed with people moving in both directions. He heard the soldiers behind him and, having no choice, threw himself into the crowd. Aside from the Docts, who backed away, screaming, when they saw him, a passing platoon of guards spotted him and was quickly hot on his heels. Once again Ogrino was dashing through Legiferius's long corridors, pursued by guards and soldiers. He was looking for an exit, but all of the windows were barred. Suddenly, he saw another troop of guards coming toward him from the other end of the hall. His heart jumped. He was terrified. They were going to get him, imprison him, and torture him to make him talk, to make him reveal some terrible secret that he did not even understand. On his right, a massive black wooden door was embossed with Legiferius's crest. Without thinking, he opened the door slightly and slipped inside before the guards were upon him.

He had barely reclosed the door when he regretted having entered this large, frightful room, as tall as a cathedral, where at least three thousand people dressed in black were assembled. They were reciting, or rather proclaiming, strange words. It took him a moment to realize that they were in fact Docts in ceremonial dress. The Docts were concentrating so intently—some almost had their eyes closed—that no one noticed the presence of the little Ogre, who stayed crouched behind the last row of congregants. To his great surprise, the guards hadn't followed him in. Perhaps they hadn't seen him, but it couldn't be long before they realized he wasn't hidden behind a suit of armor or a curtain, and very soon they would come in. He couldn't lose a second in finding an exit. There had to be another one, behind the ten-foot-tall pulpit sort of thing that dominated the room. On the pulpit, facing the crowd, a man, also dressed in black and wearing a tall, brimless, cylindrical hat with two long flaps that fell on his ears and cheeks. On the front of the hat, there was a brilliant capital 'D.' Ogrino noticed that all the other participants were dressed the same way, except that the 'D' on their hats was smaller. The man at the pulpit made a horizontal sweeping movement with his right arm and the room fell silent. Ogrino didn't dare move or even breathe. The man with the big 'D' began to speak in a booming voice.

'My friends, after our customary opening recitation in the ancestral language of Legiferius, I would like us to joyfully proclaim the Hymn of the Docts of the Order to celebrate the dawning of such a great day.'

He had just finished these words when all the participants recited together:

'We are the Caste of the Docts, the elite of the kingdom. Upon us rests the Order. We are its only base, past, present, and future. Without us, the Order would disintegrate and perish. Without the Order, we are nothing, and without us, all is nothing. We are the guardians of Legiferius. We collect, we catalogue, we classify, we study, we analyze, we decode, and we ORDER for the greatest glory of the Order!'

Ogrino was most impressed. Three thousand resonant, eager voices had chorused out in unison as if one giant had spoken authoritatively. There was a sense of superiority in the room, of absolute certainty in all that they said, but Ogrino felt instinctively that it all rang false. The man with the big 'D' spoke up again, in an impassioned voice.

'Today is a great and glorious day. The advent of the Order's supremacy over every living being. The Encyclopedia Legendari Mundi, our encyclopedia that catalogues the totality of legendary peoples, those evildoing magical creatures, is finally complete. All these creatures, all these anomalies of nature, are now known, and all their characteristics compiled. In this way, we will finally know how to destroy them all. Three years ago on St. John's Day, the day when this vile world shows itself most openly to the eyes of men, we struck a great blow, won a great victory. We killed thousands of them and captured some who allowed us to complete our classification. Now, the time has come to use all of our knowledge to wipe these evildoing creatures from the face of the earth. They are an insult to the Order. They are the expression of the uncontrollable chaos. They are a threat to the order we've established, to the logical progression of organized thought that we defend. If chaos is not wiped out, the Order will remain in danger, and that we cannot accept. Men are volatile creatures, always ready to be seduced by the imagination promoted by the Legendary World's malicious and bewitching creatures. But we, the Docts, know the dangers of this fascination. As long as rational thought is not the only way, certain rebellious souls will be able to fight the Order's doctrine. We need great, merciless demonstrations so that humans frail consciences will be forever marked and none will dare, or even think, to call the Order's laws into question ever again. Three weeks from now, the Magnus Legifer will deploy all the Militians of the Order throughout the entire kingdom for the greatest military operation of all time so that not a single magical creature will ever again disturb the world's order. This mission will be a success. I am convinced of it and, that is thanks to you, my friends—thanks to your long and devoted work, which not only allowed us to collect an impressive amount of precious information about our enemies but also gave us the means to fight and defeat them.'

Ogrino couldn't stand to hear any more of this. He felt like screaming and like making the man with the big 'D' eat his vile words. He felt he was dealing with madmen, all the more dangerous because they believed that they embodied the law, the Truth. But most of all, he felt an anger rising in him, an anger the likes of which he had never felt before, for now he understood that if his parents were dead, it was Legiferius's fault. Ogres were surely part of the Legendary World, and so without even knowing it, they were enemies of the Order. It must have been about three years that he had been living with Pantaleone. Three years since his parents had disappeared—killed by the Militians of the Order, he was now certain. From this moment on, the Order embodied for Ogrino all his misfortune, the deep wound inflicted on him by his tragic separation from the ones he loved most in the world. And all of that to preserve the power of a so-called Order of idiots, blind men, whose pride was equaled only by their cruelty and the coldness of their hearts. He couldn't stifle the hoarse cry that rose from the depths of his being, a deep and terrifying howl that made everyone look back in shock and fear. The Docts were terrified. They had never heard such a cry, a cry that tore through the air of the enormous room. After an interminable pause, during which the Docts were like statues, the Magnus Doct—he of the big 'D'—shouted, 'Seize him!'

And all the Docts nearest to Ogrino pounced on him. His anger became even more violent, his eyes reddened, and Ogrino shouted, 'You don't know, you don't know, you don't know WHO I AM!'

And he threw himself on the two nearest Docts, and with Herculean force, seized each by his clothing, lifted them off the ground, and threw them against each other. Their heads collided violently, made a dull cracking noise, and they fell limply to the floor. The other Docts backed away, horrified.

The Magnus Doct said, 'Go, get the guards, and don't let him out of your sight.'

Ogrino sprinted across the immense room, toward the pulpit where Magnus Doct was seated. He stared him in the eyes as his anger continued to grow. The ease with which he had knocked down the two Docts gave him renewed energy, more self-confidence than he had felt in a long time. But his rage was still intact, and his thirst for vengeance grew and grew. He would not be calm until the Magnus Doct was dead. The sound of many footsteps from the other side of the room indicated that the guards were rapidly pouring through the big door. Ogrino gained speed as he charged up the pulpit stairs, but before he reached the last step, he found himself face-to-face with a crossbow pointed at his nose. There was a loud snap, as if a big rubber band had been released, and then some sort of green liquid spread over his face, and he couldn't breathe and then everything went fuzzy and then there was nothing.

When Ogrino awoke, he was held tightly by large metal rings, his hands and feet closely fastened to a thick metal table that had been propped upright. His face was enclosed in an iron mask with three little holes for his eyes and mouth. He couldn't see much because it was hard to turn his head with the leather collar holding his neck to the table. He heard a voice on his left, but he was unable to see who was talking.

'I want to punish them before everyone as an example. To be fooled by a child, even an Ogre-child, and most of all to allow a Conference of the Order to be disturbed, especially this conference, the one announcing the beginning of our supremacy . . . it's the most unforgivable act there is. Those guards are incompetents. They will be whipped tomorrow at dawn in Legiferius Square, in front of as many Militians of the Order as the place will hold. I'll make an example of them. We are so close to our goal that I don't want to allow any failures. The Order must be strong if we are to be victorious. If the importance of their noble task does not motivate our men, fear will. Executioner, you will give each of the condemned one thousand lashes.'

Another voice chimed in, weaker but determined, and Ogrino felt his anger rising again, for it belonged to the Magnus Doct.

'Magnus Legifer, don't you think that a thousand lashes might be excessive? They will die. I quite agree that you should make examples of them. Those guards proved themselves to be unusually incompetent and lacking initiative. They ought to have chased the little Ogre relentlessly and not have waited patiently behind the door for the Docts to call them. But perhaps they were afraid? So a punishment, of course, but to kill them . . .'

'Segundus, my friend,' Primus responded in a harsh voice, 'we are at war, and war cannot afford any errors. Today, we have nearly lost two of the Order's most prominent members. Tomorrow dozens, maybe hundreds, could be endangered by the negligence of a few, and I cannot tolerate that. The Order cannot afford it. What is a handful of men sacrificed on the altar of the Order's victory? I can assure you that on the eve of our great battle, this execution will have an invigorating effect on the troops, and they will unceasingly and efficiently strive to fulfill their missions. There is nothing more to say. Our conversation is over.'

He had pronounced these words imperiously, in a manner that did not allow for any further questions or discussion. The Magnus Doct understood this and did not say another word. The Magnus Legifer had called him by his first name, Segundus, which was a sign of friendship. At the same time, it was clear that such orders, harsh though they might be, had to be carried out to the letter for the greater good of Legiferius. Segundus exited, leaving his superior with the captive.

'Executioner, bring the elixir the Docts have prepared.'

A very tall, frail man appeared in Ogrino's field of vision. It seemed that he hadn't eaten in ages as he was so lean and pallid. He looked like a corpse. His black hair framed a severe face whose most prominent feature was a narrow, hooked nose like a beak. His eyes, also black, were the darkest of any in the Order. He approached Ogrino with a smile that did not bode well. In his right hand, he held a little vial containing a viscous green liquid. It was the same color that Ogrino had seen on his face just before he fell into a troubled and tormented sleep, only to awaken in this filthy room that stank of suffering and death. The executioner set the vial on a little table near Ogrino, then left. When he returned, he was carrying a funnel and a vise. He put the vise around Ogrino's right hand and began to tighten it. The child felt a twinge of pain in his palm and fingers. Little by little, the pain grew, grew until it was unbearable. It became so intense that Ogrino began to shout.

'He is ready,' Primus said.

At that moment, the executioner put the funnel into the hole in the mask, so that it dangled before Ogrino's mouth. The boy instinctively pressed his lips together.

'Tighten the vise,' Primus commanded again.

The executioner grinned sadistically and gave the vise another turn, which made Ogrino's hand feel like it was on fire. He wanted to cry out, his lips parted, and the funnel poked into his mouth. He closed his teeth so tightly that he crushed the end of the funnel until it was flat like a whistle. The executioner, believing himself successful, poured the viscous liquid into the funnel, but to his puzzlement, the elixir did not disappear into Ogrino's mouth. Ogrino blew out very hard and the funnel and elixir shot out toward the executioner's face, hitting him in the eyes.

'My eyes! My eyes are burning! Aaaaaah! Help me, help me, do something!'

The Magnus Legifer took a bowl of water and threw it at the executioner's face. The green liquid dripped off, freeing the man's face. His eyes were very red.

'It hurts so much! I can't see. I've been blinded!'

'Calm yourself. It will pass. Tomorrow you will be able to see. Sit down for a moment and catch your breath.'

Primus opened the door and called to two of the guards on duty. One, he asked to accompany the executioner to his quarters, and the other, to fetch three medical Docts. Five minutes later, the Docts had arrived.

'Inject him with truth serum. I want to know what he knows. I want to hear the story of one of the last of his kind, one who for once knows our language. Mostly I want to confirm the routes of access to the Gigantum. Any Ogre, however young, must know the secrets of the forest, and that information is crucial to our plan. To work, Docts! Drag it all out of him, down to the soul! I will be back in two hours. Work efficiently!'

Then he left, and the Docts filled four syringes with green liquid and stuck them in Ogrino's arms and legs. The boy yelled in pain. Immediately, he felt dizzy, felt a great coldness invading his body, and then, once more, nothing.

'Go back . . . memories . . . forest . . . ' Little by little, words were reaching Ogrino. It seemed that someone was talking to him from very far away. This disagreeable voice pulled him out of his agitated sleep. He was nauseous, but he felt that he had to answer this voice.

'Go back in your mind and find memories of when you lived in the forest with your parents.'

Then the voice stopped and Ogrino felt very nostalgic. A great sadness surfaced. His parents, could he really recall his parents after having lost all those memories? The only thing he had a clear impression of was the moving image of two faces that Tiboursio had called up in the magic fire. But he could only vaguely recall his life from before, the shared moments from those happy, at least, he imagined they were happy days.

A strong image came to mind, of when he was playing with other children among the circus wagons.

'A circus? What does that have to do with Ogres and their life in the forest? Is the child mocking us? Does he have some unusual resistance to the serum? We'll double the dose,' ordered the Doct named Seisius.

Another Doct intervened. 'Isn't that dangerous? What if he isn't trying to resist? What if we lose him? The Magnus Legifer will never forgive us. Maybe there is another explanation. Didn't the Magnus Scrutator's report of the child say that he was a sideshow act, with his insatiable appetite? Without a doubt, he spent several years among the circus people, who taught him our language. Let's have him talk about the circus and maybe we will discover the key to these locked-away memories.'

'Perhaps!' said Seisius. 'Who were your friends in the circus?'

'Pantaleone and Slevania, Camillo, Angelina,' Ogrino listed, 'and also Royal, Gumbo, Herculium, and . . .'

'All right, all right,' the Doct interrupted, 'what did they tell you about your parents?'

'That they were captured, well, killed, by the Militians of the Order,' the child answered sadly.

'Is it possible?' the Doct wondered. 'Is it possible that this is the child that we catalogued and who should have been captured three years ago, on the St. John's day operation? Oh oh oh, no one escapes the Order! We are always triumphant, sooner or later. Perfect! And after that little family reunion, let us continue the interrogation.'

'Before you were in the circus, where did you live?'

'I was in the forest. The first image I have is of crawling out of a spiny bush with red leaves. I don't remember anything before that.'

'A red bush? VintOctavus, go get the Encyclopedia Legandari Mundi. I'd like to check something.'

The Doct exited and came back several minutes later, followed by four guards carrying an enormous, apparently very heavy book, which they very delicately and carefully set on the table. The book itself looked fragile because it was partly damaged and burned in spots.

'What happened?' Seisius asked, irritated.

'The Encyclopedia ended up in the fire during the pursuit of this Ogre,' he said, pointing at Ogrino.

'What? You mean to say that this child committed the sacrilege of endangering the most concentrated collection of human knowledge there is, and nobody was able to stop him!'

'The guards and the Militians were chasing him, but it seems that he's gifted with superhuman strength and was able to use the Encyclopedia as a firebomb.'

'Does the Magnus Legifer know about this?'

'I do not know. Perhaps not yet as he was in a meeting and has probably just returned to his office.'

'When he finds out, he'll fly into a rage, and certain people will be brutally punished, starting with this little prisoner. For the moment, what matters to me is to understand the cause-and-effect link between the Ogre's memory loss and this bush.'

Seisius opened the book to the plant section. Everything was in alphabetical order with explanations for each plant, a drawing, and a sort of genealogical chart that situated it in the plant kingdom.

'Here it is!' Seisius exclaimed, triumphant. 'It's a Tormentine. A spiny plant whose venom enters the body through the scratches it inflicts. It causes heaviness of the limbs, loss of consciousness, and then a deep sleep. But the most interesting thing is that it causes amnesia in the subject, who, upon wakening, remembers nothing of what happened before. Hah! Good sirs, we have here a living example of a Tormentine victim. What an opportunity! We can experiment with all sorts of substances, antidotes to recover this little Ogre's memory for the glory of the Order. We'll not only be advancing the path of knowledge, but in addition we shall have precious information to bring to the Magnus Legifer. So to work! Bring in the nine Docts who specialize in medicinal plants.'

When the Docts arrived, they met and discussed for at least an hour, after which they left in several groups to concoct a mixture. Some crushed plants in large wooden bowls to make a mash. Others dipped flower petals into pots of hot water. Still others made some kind of cream out of pollen. The last group was mixing the juices of different plants to make a jelly. After half an hour, everything seemed ready, and each of the four elixirs was poured into a vial. Seisius took the vial of plant mash and poured it into Ogrino's mouth. This time the boy showed no resistance. The liquid flowed slowly down his throat. He breathed out a taste that was both sweet and bitter. Ogrino began to shake. He fought it, but the metallic cuffs kept him solidly attached to the table. Fleeting images crossed his mind. Fear, even terror, invaded him. He heard threatening voices, shouts, footsteps approaching, gunshots, hoarse cries. His parents, it was his parents wailing. No! It wasn't possible, his parents couldn't be dead!

'Papa, Mama, help me, I'm frightened . . . come, get me. Where are you? Who are these hunters? Why are you running? Mama, Mama . . . Papa . . . Wait for me.'

'We have succeeded,' announced Seisius joyfully. 'This memory is from before the contact with Tormentine. Bring that cream of pollen. I believe that is what's best suited to this.'

Seisius daubed the cream onto Ogrino's lips with a spatula. It tasted like marzipan. It was delicious, and Ogrino licked his lips and swallowed all of the cream. New images appeared. He was picking fruit from trees with his mother. She was smiling. She was beautiful. She had big almond-shaped eyes. He climbed up to the very top of a tree and then fell into her arms. Another image arrived. He was sitting on his father's shoulders, one leg on each side of his powerful neck. He had black curly hair and a thick beard that smelled wonderful, like mushrooms. He was very tall, reaching nearly ten feet as big and robust as a young oak tree. His arms were muscled and thick as branches. His chest was large and hairy. He was wearing shorts made of red foxskin, gleaming in the sun. Despite his massive body, he was incredibly agile as he navigated bushes, shrubs, and ditches. He was advancing steadily and quickly as if there were no obstacles at all before him. He was the embodiment of gentle power; nothing could stop him. They had gone on a long trek in the middle of the forest, which became more and more dense, until they arrived at the foot of some gray boulders that glistened silver where the sun came through the branches. It looked like the wall of a castle. The ground seemed to have decided to make it difficult for anyone to pass through. His father walked along the wall for a long while before they arrived at a large natural arch, tall and wide enough for three carriages to pass through side by side. His father stopped and set the child on the ground.

'Look, my son. This door leads to the Kingdom of the Elves. No one is allowed to pass through the arch. It is a sacred place that must be respected. You see there are no guards, not even a gate. Every creature in the forest knows the law and no one tries to break it. Everyone respects the Elves and their Queen, for they are the guardians of our world. You are still small, but you're big enough to understand this. Actually, deep down inside, you have always known it, like every forest creature, every creature of the Legendary World.'

The sound of his words died out, silence reigned again, and then nothing, blackness, and once again sleep.

'We have succeeded!' cried Seisius. 'With this information and our detailed map of the forest where we've catalogued all the known terrain, we can find this wall and the arch that leads to the Elf world. Our attack will be much easier then. We can ambush them on multiple fronts and not one will escape!'

At that exact moment, the door to the room swung open. Magnus Legifer was back. The two hours had already passed.

'So?' he said impatiently.

'Glory to Legiferius, glory to the Order! Our potions were able to tear some information from the snippets of the little Ogre's memory, crucial information for our plan to conquer the kingdom!' Seisius responded excitedly.

'And? Be brief and precise,' said Primus curtly.

'Give us one more hour and we will give you the precise route leading to the Elf world. We only need to make some calculations and consult the maps to be sure.'

'Good. So it's all turned out to be very satisfactory. I expected nothing less from you, my dear Docts. This is one more factor in favor of a victorious conclusion to our quest. Thank you, sirs. I await your conclusions in one hour. I will be in my office.'

'Magnus Legifer, we also discovered that the Ogre child has committed the sacrilege of damaging the Encyclopedia Legendari Mundi.'

'What? What are you saying? The Encyclopedia!'

'You can see for yourself.'

Primus looked around and his eyes stopped, shocked and pained, on the partially burned tome. He paused, his mouth open. Not a sound escaped his lips. He closed his mouth and his face hardened. His cheeks grew red. His eyes fairly shot lightning bolts as he turned toward the sleeping child.

'The blasphemer will pay for his crimes. We'll subject him to the same treatment as the Encyclopedia. He will burn at the stake tomorrow at dawn. I put the execution in your hands. Have I made myself clear? And how was it that I wasn't informed of this? I must speak to my Commanders immediately. Heads will roll! To hide something so important from me!'

He walked up to the Encyclopedia and caressed it as if he were touching a beloved face.

'Call the librarian, Docts, to restore it. May they do their best . . . I want it restored like new. Most importantly as much information as possible must be saved. I will come back myself to survey the extent of the damage and the reparatory measures. For the moment, I must go. I have other business to attend to.'

'What should we do with the prisoner?' asked Seisius.

'Put him in the dungeon under Legiferius and post two guards at his cell. I do not want him escaping again! Now!'

Primus left quickly. The Docts made sure that Ogrino was deeply asleep, then unlocked his cuffs. The guards brought him to the cellar, where he was unceremoniously thrown on the ground. Still under the influence of the drugs, his body stayed slumped on the floor where he had fallen, totally limp.

RAZENBRUCK

When Ogrino opened his heavy eyelids, he saw a dark room—too dark and cold and moist. He was lying on a thick, bad-smelling mattress. A single, sad ray of light fell in the center of the room. Ogrino lifted his head with difficulty and saw a tiny skylight at least a whole stone's throw above the floor, dreadfully inaccessible. A massive wooden and metal door irrevocably enclosed him in this grimy room with sweating walls. A coarse-cut wooden cup filled with some enigmatic liquid was lying in front of him. Starving, he took the cup and greedily drank down the substance, which turned out to be a thick soup. Despite the rancid, putrid taste of this meager fare, the act of eating brought him some semblance of comfort.

He tried to stand and the pain made itself known again, with atrocious rapidity. His right hand, which he had used to push himself up, felt like it was being pierced by a thousand needles, and his bruised legs could barely support him. He sat down and tears began to flood his eyes. His tears made the jail door look warped, and the straw on the floor looked like it was dancing. He dried his eyes with his left hand and, to his great surprise, the straw continued to move. Some rat or mouse must have been struggling in the thatch. Ogrino, forgetting his pain for a moment, pounced on the animal in one nimble jump. He was delighted at the thought of an extra snack to go with his meager meal.

'You vile pig! How dare you put your dirty paws on my illustrious person? Aren't you afraid? I'll turn you into a common slug.'

Ogrino, caught completely off guard, released his grip, and saw, to his great surprise, a very strange creature of his own size. The being had a monkeylike face, pointy ears, baleful eyes, and long, hooked hands. The two long horns that sprouted from his forehead gave him an impish look, which was accentuated by his red, jingle-belled hat. His clothing looked like something a clown would wear, a frilly outfit with rumpled leggings and pointy shoes that were full of holes. After the shock wore off, Ogrino was rather amused by this unexpected meeting with such a strange character.

'Excuse me. I took you for a field mouse.'

'I should tear out your tongue for such an insult to my status!' the stranger retorted. 'I am Razenbruck, former court jester to Delphoros, the king of the seas, who reigns over the vast and rich depths. You owe me honor and respect, for my powers are great. Since I hardly go out but in the dead of night, everyone fears me. I can change shape at will. I can even become invisible.'

As he said this, he disappeared before Ogrino's eyes. A 'clack' and a tinkling of bells made Ogrino turn his head to the left, and there he saw Razenbruck clinging to a stone slightly sticking out from the wall. Once again invisible, he reappeared near the door to the cell, then he disappeared again and turned up right next to Ogrino who jumped.

'I am quite impressed and admiring, and I sincerely regret having confused you with an ordinary rodent.'

'You have seen nothing yet! I can turn myself into any living creature. Look!'

In the blink of an eye, a menacing, drooling dog was baring its teeth aggressively at Ogrino. A moment later, a cat meowed in the opposite corner of the cell and ran over to rub itself against Ogrino's legs. A second after that, a big wooly ram pushed its horns against the little Ogre's back playfully.

'That's, ah, that's all very impressive. But if you have all these powers, how is it that you are a prisoner here, like me?'

'My young friend, I am the prisoner of no man and never could be. I'm far too nimble, intelligent, and clever to ever be caught, for you see of all my gifts, the most precious one is the ability to walk through walls. Yes, indeed! I can pass through any wall, so no earthly prison can contain me!'

With these words, as if to illustrate what he had said, he walked through the heavy jail door as if there was nothing there at all. Ogrino was speechless. He waited for Razenbruck to return, then seeing that he had not reappeared after a long moment, he cried, 'Come back, come back! Please don't leave me here. I have something important to tell you!'

Nothing. There was no response, no sign of Razenbruck. Ogrino turned around, anguished, and slumped on his straw bed. As soon as he had sat down, he felt something bump him gently. A kitten was licking his forehead.

'Razenbruck?'

'Did you really think I would risk losing an admirer?'

With a jingling of bells, the kitten became an Imp again.

'Whew! Razenbruck, I was so afraid you wouldn't come back. I absolutely have to get out of here because I have to tell my father, Pantaleone, about what Legiferius is planning. In a few days, they're going to attack, send out their whole army against the Legendary World, and destroy it. We have to do something to stop them. It's so horrible!'

'Hah! Legiferius. Curse them a thousand times! I've already given the evil puppets a fair amount of trouble. I've burned quite a few of their chariots, spooked their horses, and dried up their wells, but they seem to get stronger every day. And even though they can see me when I'm invisible, they haven't been able to capture me yet. Come on, we'll get out of this filthy place!'

As soon as he had finished saying this, they heard loud footsteps and the clinking of weapons in the corridor.

'The guards! They're coming, let's hurry! I don't want to deal with them any more,' whispered Ogrino fearfully.

'Quick! Get in that corner and don't move!'

The guards were now at the cell door. Ogrino's heart was beating out of his chest. Razenbruck had disappeared again, and Ogrino was already imagining big, brutal hands seizing him to bring him back to the torture room. Lost in his gloomy thoughts, Ogrino hadn't noticed the strange phenomenon occurring at his feet. One of the flagstones of the cell floor had come loose, revealing a little tunnel. The door opened loudly and Ogrino, seeing two big silhouettes against the light, jumped into the hole.

'Get him! He's trying to escape!' said the head guard.

They immediately pounced toward the prisoner. To his horror, Ogrino discovered that the opening was too narrow or that his stomach was too fat. He was stuck, unable to slip through. The guards were upon him, pulling him upwards from the shoulders. In a last-ditch effort, Ogrino began to bite. One of the guards lost a finger and let go. The other one had a firm grip on the child's armpits, and Ogrino couldn't reach him with his razor-sharp teeth. At that moment, a beastly growl filled the cell, practically bursting the eardrums of Ogrino and his assailants. Behind them stood an impressively tall dark-furred, long-clawed, big-jawed adult grizzly bear. It swatted at the air with its large paws and sent the wounded guard crashing into the wall. He fell loudly and limply on the ground. The other guard, terrified, let go of Ogrino and made a run for the door. The bear jumped onto his back and the man, unbalanced, ran into the edge of the door and was knocked out by the impact.

'Come on, slide through the hole,' said the bear.

Ogrino was shaking from fear and relief. He realized he was still stuck halfway into the tunnel. The bear pressed down on the child's head gently and Ogrino succeeded in wriggling the rest of the way through the opening. As soon as he had reached the bottom of the tunnel, he heard a scratching from the cell above, like someone writing on a chalkboard. Then there was a dull noise of a heavy object landing and then total darkness. Soon afterwards, something jumped right near Ogrino, with a jingling of bells.

'We have to hurry!' said Razenbruck. 'They'll regain consciousness soon and give the alert. God only knows what evil schemes they might use to keep us from our goal.'

'Are we going to see Pantaleone, my father?'

'No, it's too dangerous, for us and for your parents. No, we have other plans—we have to try to relay your vital message as fast as possible. And I think I know someone who will be very interested in meeting you. Come along!'

'But I can't see anything! I don't have cat's eyes, here . . .'

'Ah yes, I forgot. Anzimir Coutimir, let there be light!'

Instantly, a little ball of fire burst into being and floated in the air ahead of the two fugitives. Ogrino was astounded by this feat and very impressed with Razenbruck himself, who was certainly a very powerful magician. It was better to have him as a friend than as an enemy, judging by the pitiful state in which he had left the guards. So they set off in what proved to be a narrow tunnel where they had to duck their heads, though they did have enough room to jog. Ogrino hobbled along, as his legs still hurt, but he was reassured and comforted by Razenbruck's presence. After a long while, they reached an intersection where five tunnels branched out in different directions.

'Where are we, and who dug these passageways?'

'It's a very long and fascinating story. I'll tell you while we walk.'

They veered off to the left, heading North in a tunnel with a much higher ceiling.

'These tunnels actually date from a very, very long time ago, when the Giants still ruled.

'Giants!' Ogrino exclaimed.

'Yes, immense titans who could move mountains and dig riverbeds, even scoop out seas in the middle of continents. They were incredibly strong. They wandered the earth wildly, building here, destroying there, and most of all fighting fire-breathing dragons, which would attack the Little Folk whom the Giants had promised to protect. For, this is something you really must know, the first intelligent creatures created on Earth were tiny beings with huge amounts of wisdom so that they could tell good from evil and know what each part of creation was destined for.'

'But who were these tiny creatures?'

'Well, I have the honor and the privilege of serving their current ruler, the thirty-seventh Precelestine King. After Delphoros chased me from the kingdom of the seas, I was able to use my prodigious talents to serve noble people. Their king, in his great wisdom, immediately detected my value and named me the Emissary of the Empire. So for many years now, I have walked the infinite labyrinth of tunnels, caves, pits, chasms, caverns, cellars, dungeons, and crypts, in order to bring information about his innumerable people to my lord, and so allow him to rule better. That is not my only task; however, I am also the ambassador of the Little Folk to other tribes of the Legendary World, except to the Elves who have a separate one since only a few select beings can enter their domain.

'So what is this society you serve, and is that where you're taking me?'

At that exact moment, a very strong heat wave hit their backs like a violent, stifling wind. They turned quickly, in unison, and saw something that was hardly believable. An enormous fireball that filled the entire tunnel was rolling toward them at the speed of a galloping horse. Ogrino began to run as fast as he could, limping all the while. Although his limbs were still in such pain, fear gave him wings. Razenbruck, for his part, didn't seem to be very afraid, despite the stifling temperature and the pursuant flames. Ogrino, too absorbed in saving himself, had not even noticed his friend's transformation. He was surprised to suddenly see a noble steed trotting along happily by his side.

'Get on! We'll be out of this man-made hell of flaming petrol all the faster.'

Ogrino grabbed the horse's mane with his good hand, and the animal bent down so that the little Ogre could mount more easily. The short time they stopped was enough for the fire to nearly reach them, and they could feel its intolerable heat. As soon as the child was situated, Razenbruck bolted with a large bound, plucking them from the flames licking at the hair on his back legs. As quick as a wink, they would have been far from the furnace. However, Ogrino, exhausted from his wounds, lack of food, and the ordeals of the past few days, lost his grip as the horse was leaping over a large crevasse.

'Noooo!' the child screamed as he fell into the dark abyss.

Razenbruck stopped short, turned 180°, and jumped into the precipice. A long fall, followed by one SPLASHHH, then another. The two companions found themselves floating in a subterranean river. They looked upwards and saw, about fifty feet above the water, the bright light of the fire, which had reached the edge of the crevasse and was falling down along the wall.

'We're not in danger any more, here. The current will bring us to the sea, and by and by, their fire will die out.'

Ogrino, who had learned to swim from Pantaleone, appreciated the cool water after the stiflingly hot air.

'Come, hang onto me,' Razenbruck offered kindly.

Ogrino turned around and saw that he had turned into a big dog with thick black fur and a gentle look.

'I am a Newfoundland, a rescue dog that swims incredibly well, and which sailors use to retrieve men who have fallen into the sea. That cursed fire ruined all of my plans. I was going to bring you to the Gnome King, my master, and he would have known what to do about your valuable information on Legiferius, but now our path is cut off . . . and even if we wanted to, in your state you wouldn't be able to climb up this steep cliff. The river will take us very far south, too far for us to be able to quickly reach our original destination on the northern border. There's only one thing left to do. I'm not at all fond of the idea, but we have no other choice since we are short on time.'

For the first time, Ogrino saw through Ravenbruck's smile and noticed his sad, moody eyes. They floated downriver for hours, finally emerging from underground into blinding daylight, by way of a cave that opened onto the ocean. The Newfoundland swam nimbly over to a little cove where they could rest up next to a warm fire, ablaze thanks to some dry stumps gathered from the shore and a little bit of Razenbruck's magic.

'I'm going to get you something to eat, and afterwards we'll take care of your wounds.'

He began to run across the pebbly beach, so fast that it looked like he was flying. After about fifteen minutes, he came back with a dozen gulls, holding their necks in his mouth. Their bodies swung back and forth like a metronome. Ogrino jumped for joy when he saw the delicious feast. As soon as Razenbruck had dropped the game, Ogrino seized the birds with both hands and devoured eight.

'Well, I believe I'll go hunting again! You've got quite the appetite!'

And he disappeared once more.

'Ogrino, Ogrino, come here!' he shouted a little later.

The child tottered awkwardly along the rocks until he reached a marvelous scene. An old, dead seal had recently washed up on the beach. Razenbruck had already hacked off a large piece of it to fry, but, excited at the prospect of finally satisfying his hunger, Ogrino couldn't restrain himself. He began with the animal's tail, and in less than ten minutes, only its skin, bones, and entrails remained. Razenbruck had just had the time to build a fire and grill the piece that he'd saved from his young friend's insatiable appetite.

'I should have guessed that such a delicacy, despite its size, would just be enough for a gourmet like you,' Razenbruck said mischievously, with a twinkle in his eye as he watched Ogrino greedily lick his fingers.

'All right, now that we've gotten our strength back, we'll continue our journey. First, though, I've got to take care of your wounds. Let me see, now.'

He carefully examined the hand which had been crushed, then the injuries the executioner had inflicted on the boy's arms and legs.

'It's not too serious. In a little while, you won't feel it any more,' he said confidently.

Then he closed his eyes and began to mutter incomprehensible phrases as if he were talking to himself. He put his hands on top of Ogrino's legs. The boy looked into his eyes, literally hypnotized. The wounded spots on his thighs began to feel warm. Little by little, the warmth radiated throughout his limbs, erasing the pain. Then Razenbruck took the boy's wounded hand in his own and the same thing happened again, with warmth chasing the pain away. And to finish, he healed the child's arm. Ogrino was both grateful to his friend and floored by the power of his magic.

'How do you do such amazing feats? I'm totally healed! I don't even have any scars, it's incredible!' the child exclaimed.

'In my opinion, it's the most beautiful kind of magic!' Razenbruck assented joyfully. 'And the most noble, actually, because it comes from the heart!'

Ogrino was delighted. Not only had he met a very powerful magician, but also, behind his rather brusque manner, his friend shone with generosity, a bit like Pantaleone and Slevania. *When will I see them again?* the little boy wondered sadly.

'So! Let's not waste another minute,' Razenbruck declared. 'We've still got a long way to go, and we have to find a good way to travel.'

'Where are we going? This cove doesn't lead anywhere, and the rock walls are too steep and fragile to climb,' Ogrino lamented. 'Unless we use one of your tricks!' he added gaily.

By way of answer, Razenbruck simply told him to come and huddle up against him, and he began a new incantation. This time in an intelligibly loud voice.

'ANZOUSTRADIM POTENTAS SUMMER GICTERE, protect us with the unbreakable sphere!'

To Ogrino's astonishment, nothing seemed to happen. No explosion, no balls of fire, no Razenbruck becoming some strange animal. Nothing, seemingly nothing, unless . . . ?

'Perfect! Now we can go,' Razenbruck announced amusedly. 'From now on, walk exactly in step with me, in the same direction,' he gently ordered Ogrino, who had no idea why.

They headed to the beach like Siamese twins. Right when they stepped into the water, something unexpected caught Ogrino by surprise: the water parted before them. The farther along they walked, the stranger it got. The water made a wall around them as if it didn't want to get them wet, nor engulf them. They descended the slightly sloped beach, and now the water surrounded them from head to toe, even higher than that in fact. It was at that moment that Ogrino understood that they were walking in an invisible, protective bubble that Razenbruck had created with his magic. The child was all excited, realizing that he was now entering a foreign and fascinating world. As they progressed, the sand gave way to a seafloor of brown rocks, and fields of algae appeared, replete with thousands of little purple and yellow fish. Ogrino's eyes widened at the scene before him, illuminated and shimmering in the sun's rays.

'All right! I think that we're far enough away from the shore now, that should do it,' Razenbruck announced, taking out a short little flute. He began to play a lilting and repetitive tune. Ogrino wondered what he was doing and didn't really understand the appeal of the flute. Still, he had absolute confidence in his friend's powers. Something very strange pulled him out of his thoughts. The sun seemed to be blocked as if during an eclipse. He raised his head and couldn't believe his eyes. A giant was floating above them. Ogrino shivered in fear.

Razenbruck, seeing this, said to him, 'Don't worry, he is harmless. His name is Welchar. He must be the largest fish in the world. He weighs some impressive number of tons but he's as gentle as a lamb. That's why I've called him to help us.'

The animal came down and faced them. Ogrino wasn't even slightly reassured, for the fish was enormous. His oval mouth, large enough to swallow up three carriages, was full of dozens and dozens of little, razor-sharp teeth that reminded Ogrino of his own. Only his gentle gaze and the designs on his blue skin—small rectangles with yellow dots in the centers—made him seem friendly.

Razenbruck played another air on the flute, slower and more serious this time, and the whale shark opened his mouth as if to swallow the two friends.

'He's going to eat us up!' cried Ogrino.

'No, he isn't! He's a friend, and anyway our protective sphere is unbreakable, so relax.'

The shark wedged Razenbruck's bubble between his teeth and with a swish of his big tail, headed for the deep. Now they were going along at a dizzying speed, sometimes coming across schools of sardines or anchovies, which the shark swallowed whole. The water passed through the vertical slats on his cheeks. Ogrino began to appreciate this mode of transportation, whose gargantuan appetite was not unlike his own. As they descended into the depths, the light became fainter and duskier and their surroundings transformed. The seafloor changed from plains to vast prairies to mountains covered in pink and purple corals. Then came the deep, midnight-blue pits, and finally the plateaus carpeted with giant, translucent orange tubes of sea squirts. Ogrino would never have imagined that there could be so many different panoramas under the sea. Actually, he had never seen the ocean until today, and here he was, flying along as if on a magic carpet. He let out a whoop, exhilarated by the beauty all around him. Welchar tilted his head, surprised, then set off faster than ever, whipping through the water with his enormous fins. Ogrino was thrown against the back of their bubble by the sharp acceleration. The feeling reminded him of when he would play 'human cannonball' with Gumbo. He was on cloud nine. He slipped through the sea at an incredible speed, nestled in a living submarine, brushing past mountain walls covered in lacy, red, and green sea fan corals.

Only Razenbruck didn't seem to share in this euphoria. His face remained serious and dark. *Maybe this fascinating world held no more secrets for him,* Ogrino thought. Maybe this explosion of colors and seascapes seemed banal to him now, if once upon a time he had lived here for many years, or perhaps it was something else entirely. Ogrino's reflections were stopped short as they came to a pass and the shark dove sharply into a very deep crevasse, where Ogrino was dumbfounded by another fascinating scene. At such depths everything should have been dark, and yet a thousand lights glimmered at the base of the majestic mountain that rose before them.

Is this where the sun goes home when it sets? Ogrino wondered.

The vision was disconcerting. The farther they descended, the brighter the glinting lights, until they had to close their eyes to avoid being blinded. Little by little, they got accustomed to the brilliance and were able to make out its source.

'A troglodyte city,' Razenbruck announced neutrally. 'The palace of King Delphoros, master of the seas.'

'But didn't you tell me that that king banned you, once upon a time?' Ogrino asked sadly.

'Yes, but destiny has decided that our paths will cross once again, thanks to your entry into my solitary life. It's the first time I feel I've had a friend, someone to hold onto.'

Ogrino was very touched by Razenbruck's words and was preparing to say something in response when he noticed, surrounding them on all sides, the stunning, chaotic dance of thousands and thousands of aquatic creatures in motion. There were all kinds of animals of all shapes and sizes and colors, which Ogrino had neither seen nor ever imagined.

'A Grand Council!' Razenbruck exclaimed. 'What could be so important that Delphoros would call together so many representatives of the undersea world?'

Looking upwards, one could admire an immense spiral that converged on the palace. It was made up of a multitude of lobsters, octopi, jellyfish, seabream, tarpons, grouper, tuna, parrotfish, moray eels, manatees, seals, penguins, walruses, sharks, belugas, orcas, and dolphins. Then came the impressive giant squid, gigantic blue whales, and innumerably many other large fish. Ogrino felt minuscule in the face of such a profusion of life, and these excessively huge creatures. Until now, he'd thought that Herculium was as big as any animal on earth, but now he was forced to admit that all his reference points were positively dwarfed. The sea concealed wonders beyond his wildest imagination.

Joining these marine animals were many creatures of the Legendary World, of whom the Sirens, Naiads, Ondines, and other Nymphs were incontestably the most elegant. They were followed by robust Tritons, horrible Bosches with tentacled feet, and Tud-Gomons with suction-cup mouths. There were also Hooks with a head like a lime and a left hand like a crab's pincer, scowling little Ellylldans, with their pointy ears and thick hair, and many more magical beings. The whole crowd was solemnly parading toward the door to the palace, which Ogrino now recognized as the source of the blinding light. The cliff wall was carpeted with millions of mother-of-pearl abalone shells, which shone with silver and majesty.

As they slowly approached the wall, they saw that large round alcoves were carved out of it. The whale shark slowed down and stopped just above one. It was a better point of view for Ogrino to see the bewildering scene play out. A whole mass of various animals had gathered in the alcove. On the left, about fifteen dolphins, belugas, and orcas were continually emitting sharp noises and clicking their jaws. On the right, several Tritons were strumming the stretched tentacles of giant jellyfish, producing harp-like harmonies, while others blew tunes from conical seashells. In front, a multitude of crabs were clacking their claws, accompanied by scallops, which were frenetically opening and closing their shells like castanets, marking the tempo. In back, other Tritons used clubs to beat on giant clams, which served as makeshift drums. The whole ensemble formed a philharmonic orchestra whose intoxicating melodies thrilled the soul as well as the ears. Ogrino discovered creative dimensions he'd never dreamed of, thanks to these aquatic musicians in perfect accord.

The shark was already moving away, passing another alcove. This one was filled with manta rays, turbots, plaice, flounder, and soles. All these fish, each one flatter than the last, glided like birds in a graceful dance, forming complex and ephemeral shapes. Ogrino was once again enthralled by this fluid, graceful choreography. Razenbruck, seeing his friend in a stupor, commented softly,

'Delphoros is the patron of the arts. His kingdom's power and influence is more due to art and creativity than to military power. He has always encouraged all sorts of talent. Anyone in the kingdom can take a post as an artist in his court as he has no prejudice. Even the smallest mollusk has his chance as little as he may value his artistic talents. So in each cavern of the palace, companies form by affinity. Orchestras are born here, choirs there, and then there are groups of poets or sculptors, theater or dance troupes like the captivating one here, with the manta rays.'

Welchar slowly began to move downwards again, toward the titanic main alcove, a sun-like circle from which sixteen enormous rays extended. Other grottos were lined up in a single file along each of the rays. As they passed, Ogrino snuck a peek into one, a sculpture studio where sawfish, swordfish, and great white sharks were carving stone into incredibly lifelike sea horses.

A little farther down, Tritons and Nymphs filled a painting studio, where they were creating living canvases of mosses, lichens, sponges, corals, anemone, and multicolored algae. These monumental frescos adorned the grotto's walls. The effect was a luxuriant, vividly colored vision that pulled the spectator into the very heart of the painting and into another dimension. As Welchar continued on his way, Ogrino was torn from the paintings' hypnotic effects, but he kept the beatific smile of one filled with subtle yet powerful emotions.

A melody reached his ears when they pulled up parallel to another grotto. A whole classful of Sirens, Naiads, and Ondines was assembled in a sublime, enthusiastic choir. Ogrino had of course heard of the legend of the Sirens, whose voices enchanted sailors, but the reality of it was even more fascinating. First their crystal clear voices enveloped you from top to bottom, then installed themselves in every one of your cells, making you quiver with quiet joy. You stopped thinking and drank in this sweet chant like life-giving nectar. The choir's grace transported you, transcended you, and magnified you. You felt bigger, stronger, braver, and more talented. You were filled with an irresistible desire to begin a project, outdo yourself, and you knew for certain you could move mountains. Ogrino, gorged on this reassurance, felt a rarely matched enthusiasm. He was astonished; his gaze remained fixed on these slender, superbly beautiful creatures. As Welchar continued his descent, Ogrino's neck twisted around so he wouldn't miss an instant of the enchanting spectacle.

The intense brightness made them squint; they had arrived at the top of the gigantic main grotto. Its dimensions were entirely indescribable. No human creation—not even one of Legiferius's—could rival what Ogrino saw here. It seemed like they were standing in front of the earth's very mouth, open wide to reveal a glimmering world beneath. The ground, which was made of mother-of-pearl, gleamed with iridescent color. The walls and ceiling were covered with thousands and thousands of pearls, shining like diamonds.

DELPHOROS

The shark came to rest on the sandy seafloor just in front of the entryway, which was guarded by twelve Tritons with impressive muscles and sparkling helmets. Razenbruck was very stressed, as impervious to the castle's sumptuous beauty as he had been to the Sirens' melodies. Welchar opened his mouth delicately and the sphere rolled gently out onto the sand. As fast as lightning, six guards suddenly surrounded our two heroes, stopping the sphere with their trident-shaped lances. The bubble's perimeter unexpectedly heated up and began to glow. One of the Tritons interrogated Razenbruck.

'What are you doing here? You know very well that you were banned and condemned to death if you ever came back.'

'I am here as an ambassador from the Little Folk, and I am accompanied by a messenger carrying crucial information.'

He meant to speak authoritatively, but Ogrino could hear a tiny bit of uncertainty in his voice.

'Therefore I request an audience with Delphoros!'

Razenbruck extended his right hand, where on one finger he wore a ring with the seal of Precelestine XXXVII. The guard, electrified, shouted to one of his sentries to go and inform the king immediately. A moment dragged on under the imposing guards' harsh stares as they looked Razenbruck up and down. *What terrible thing could he have done to merit death?* the little Ogre wondered. Finally the great Chamberlain, a tall, thin Triton dressed in a long purple coat, came out of the grotto to meet the two prisoners.

'You must have some nerve or else you are completely oblivious if you've come back to taunt us! Razenbruck, I hope for your sake that for once you are telling the truth and not up to another of your tricks. So what is this message so important that you've risked your life to come here to deliver it to the ones you so offended?'

'Please be assured that I take no pleasure in returning here. Circumstances have forced us to come, for time is short. We do not have a minute to spare. The security of the kingdom is at risk.'

'Your words ring true to my ears and seem to be corroborated by rumors at the Grand Council. A threat is crystallizing, but we don't know why or how dangerous it is or when it will come.'

'Bring us to Delphoros immediately!' Razenbruck insisted.

'You know no one interrupts a Grand Council like this. You will wait quietly until it is over.'

'But the information we have will benefit everyone and could influence the Council's decisions,' Razenbruck asserted forcefully.

The Chamberlain looked pensive for a moment, then asked Razenbruck, 'Who is the little boy?'

'He's a young Ogre named Ogrino, and he's part of the Legendary World of the Empire Above. He's bravely battled a very powerful enemy who will soon be a threat to us all, and that's why he wants to let you know what he learned at the very heart of the enemy city.'

'So this is what we'll do, Razenbruck. Can you duplicate your protective bubble, so that you and your friend will each have one?'

'Yes, of course, it's quite simple.'

'Then do so at once,' the Chamberlain ordered.

Razenbruck closed his eyes, concentrated, recited his incantation loudly, and once more worked his magic. Another bubble formed, this time around only Ogrino.

'This way, follow me,' the Chamberlain told him kindly.

As Ogrino timidly stepped forward, he saw that his bubble detached from Razenbruck's and his friend remained immobile, prisoner of the guards and their tridents. Still affected by the Sirens' energizing song, Ogrino felt no fear. He passed through the long corridor of sentries at the doorway and beyond them, discovered an immense gathering of wildly diverse creatures. Looking closely, he realized that the Grand Council was made up of one representative from each living species in the undersea world. So one saw amusing juxtapositions in which all sorts of tiny fish sat side-by-side with gigantic beings like a blue or sperm whale. An elephant seal was seated next to a grouper, a moray eel with a manatee, an emperor penguin with a catfish, and so on and so on, infinitely, it seemed, since there were so many of them.

The general atmosphere of the assembly was solemn and serious. Ogrino felt proud to be part of such a meeting although he wasn't even part of this world. But was that really true? Despite their differences, these beings constituted a single people devoted to the same king. They even shared the will to live in peace but also defend their domain, and perhaps he would be able to help them.

Walking behind the Grand Chamberlain, he advanced slowly and ceremoniously to the middle of the big center alley, like an official ambassador. Everyone's head turned slowly toward him, and Ogrino recognized the old feeling of stage fright, which reminded him of when he used to come out into the circus ring as one of Pantaleone's troupe.

In front of him sat a colossal throne made of the enormous, half-open shell of a giant clam. It was immaculately white and looked to be embedded in the very rock of the ocean floor. At the center of this monumental seat resided a very impressive being. Delphoros, there was no doubt about it, had the dignified appearance befitting a monarch. Not only was he blessed with an imposing stature—Ogrino judged that he must have been twelve feet tall—but most of all, everything in him emanated the quiet power of an uncontested natural authority. The lower part of his body, black and white, looked excessively large and seemed almost to be a part of the shell. His torso and arms were those of a muscular human, and his head was a dolphin's, topped with long white hair and a large golden crown.

The more Ogrino advanced, the more Delphoros's majesty intimidated him. The Chamberlain finally stopped in front of the throne, at the center of the council that united all the representatives of the Legendary World around the sovereign. There were Dolphin-men, Ondines, Triton-Sharks, Naiads, Octopus-men, Nymphs, Hooks, Jellyfish-women whose hair and legs were tentacles, Bosches, Hermit-Imps who carried their homes on their backs, and all sorts of other beings, each one stranger than the last.

Seeing his Grand Chamberlain, Delphoros interrupted the discussions by merely raising the huge trident he held in his hand. A respectful silence fell over all the council-members and the innumerable representatives of the peoples of the sea.

'Who is this messenger, then? What has he to tell us that is so important at this solemn hour?'

Delphoros's voice resounded like thunder in the room, but his tone was benevolent.

'Ho, my sovereign! If your majesty will permit me to introduce his grace Ogrino, an emissary of the Empire Above, who has come down here to bring us crucial information about our enemies.'

Ogrino felt very flattered to be presented so formally. All of a sudden he had become someone very important, and what's more, all the eyes in the immense crowd were now upon him.

'Come forward, my young subject, and deliver your precious message.'

The king's voice, though soft, was absolutely authoritative. Ogrino thought to himself that no one could have disobeyed such an order, and he felt his stage fright growing within him. He recalled the choir of Sirens once more and began.

'Legiferius has declared war on the Legendary World. They are set on destroying all magical beings – no one is safe. Three years ago, the Order's soldiers began a preliminary offensive, in which they captured and killed many creatures. Thanks to all the information at their disposal, and to their sophisticated weapons, they intend to destroy the whole kingdom this time, less than three weeks from now.'

An indignant exclamation passed through the immense assembly. With an inquiring look at Ogrino, Delphoros unrolled a long parchment made of algae on which a large, unusual-looking vehicle was drawn.

Ogrino, stunned, declared, 'The sign of Legiferius!' Turning to the king, he asked, 'What does this mean? And why do you have drawings of Legiferius's machines?'

'We don't know what threat this large vehicle represents, but it came into our world several weeks ago, from the western shore, and since then has relentlessly traveled on the seafloor toward my palace. My painters have depicted it according to my sentries' descriptions. What you're telling us about an imminent attack by soldiers confirms our fears. Actually, humans have always made timid forays into the fringes of our world. Their boats run across the surface of our seas. Their nets, ever more numerous, capture entire shoals of fish. Sometimes turtles, sharks, even dolphins die in them, although that has remained limited. However, for the last few years, their actions have become more and more threatening, since they're not only looking for food, but also aiming to capture and murder some of my most prominent subjects. I've suffered the loss of more Tritons, Bosches, and Naiads recently than in all the time since the dawn of humanity! The river Ondines have given us incriminating eyewitness reports on soldiers' atrocities toward the magical creatures of the rivers and forests. Men are cruel and destructive creatures who do not respect the balance of the universe. Before, they were slowly pillaging our world, but now they are openly and ruthlessly attacking us. We cannot stand for this!'

Delphoros's voice resonated in the palace's great hall.

'Not all humans are destructive. Some are bighearted and have honest souls. Only Legiferius and its Militians want to end the Legendary World because they're afraid of what they don't understand, and what could challenge the spread of their power.'

Ogrino himself was shocked by the truth of the words coming out of his mouth.

'Still, be careful of their weapons, which are terrifying. Their Docts have developed a whole arsenal of destructive tools that magical creatures should be wary of because they have studied our weak points. This L-shaped underwater vehicle, I'm sure it's full of bombs, cannons, and other tricks meant to reduce your palace to ashes, Your Majesty.'

'ENOUGH! That will suffice. I will not stand for being taunted by these warmongering runts much longer. I'll send them a troupe of sperm whales from my royal army.'

He picked up a long, twisted, trumpet-shaped shell and blew on it powerfully. A low sound escaped it, and not long after, an imposing chariot, frosted with silver, entered the cave. A proud-looking Triton was seated in it, being pulled by four robust sea horses with Mermaids' tails. Five hotheaded sperm whales, ridden and reined in by helmeted Tritons, surrounded the chariot.

'Go, destroy this submarine,' said the king, handing over the drawing of Legiferius's amphibious vehicle as well as a map of the area.

Ogrino couldn't resist the desire to participate in the mission, and he heard himself say, almost against his will:

'Your Majesty, I ask that you please allow me go along on this expedition, as I could prove very useful, seeing as how I've already fought this enemy.'

The king rubbed his neck, thinking, and then said, 'Triton Major, you will take the child with you, at the head of the squadron, and listen to his advice. May victory be yours! GO!'

His voice shook the cave's walls, and Ogrino barely had the time to climb into the chariot as everyone simultaneously pushed toward the palace porch. In an instant, they were in the open sea and the palace was shrinking rapidly behind them. Ogrino was disoriented. He had thought that Welchar was the fastest thing under the sea, but now he was forced to admit that the chariot was flying along like a shooting star, so fast that the sperm whales were having trouble keeping up. He was exhilarated by the fluid sensation of this kind of travel, by the beautiful scenery, by the honor the king had bestowed upon him, and by the excitement of battle. Finally he was going to be able to take revenge on the Order who has stolen his parents from him and caused him so much suffering. He felt a wave of joy, mixed with anger at those he was about to encounter. Full of all these emotions, there wasn't a thought in his head for Razenbruck.

Commander Edwimus was both unnerved by the thought of the many tons of water above his head and excited to have been chosen for the mission. Being in command of one of the Order's most powerful machines made him feel incomparably omnipotent. Never before had he felt so imbued with the Order's supremacy. At the controls of this magnificent vessel, he and he alone represented Legiferius, whose power covered not only above-ground land, but now, thanks to him, also the ocean floors. In just a few days, his mission would be complete, for the greatest glory of the Order. He was commanding one of the Docts' most prodigious inventions. This Aquanef, a sort of tracked engine, was the embodiment of the Magnus Legifer's intelligence and ingenuity. Only he had had the brilliant idea to expand the Order's conquest to a stronghold that might have seemed unattainable: the palace of King Delphoros. By capturing Tritons, Mermaids, and other creatures, the Order had been able to discern the precise location of the palace where the little water-king was trapped. With his destruction, the whole undersea Legendary World would be thrown into chaos, perhaps even destroyed, and in any case, left powerless. Along with the acquisition of new territories, this would assure the Order's expansion throughout the whole world. The Aquanef's military arsenal was a delight for a ship captain. Here, Edwimus had access to some extraordinary firepower: thousands of repulsive grenades, harpoon arrows, nets that froze, blinding rockets, and other deterrent weapons. But most of all, he had *the* weapon: the Tetrabomb, whose detonation would decimate a city in the blink of an eye. Far from frightening him, being in charge of such a terrifying force electrified him, sent him soaring to the level of a vengeful god capable of unleashing apocalyptic wrath on trembling, cowering creatures.

'Abnormal sperm whale movements, starboard!'

This declaration from the soldier on watch tore Edwimus from his glorious reverie. He grimaced in discontent, then quickly slipped back into his role as Commander. He carefully scanned the bluish ocean to his right, and his experienced eye immediately picked out five sperm whales approaching quickly, following after a pearly carriage pulled by horses. *Magical creatures*, he thought. He shouted into the bullhorn by the rudder.

'To your battle stations! At the ready! Enemy at two o'clock! Arm the machine guns! Grenades and shrapnel shells!'

His orders were crisp, and the elite soldiers executed them with military precision and speed.

'Confirmation?'

The four watchmen responded almost in unison that everything was in place.

'They'll see what happens to those who dare attack the Order. I'll teach them a lesson that will go down in history.'

As he was saying these words, the five sperm whales had gone off in different directions. The chariot itself remained far off.

'Threat port and starboard!'

The soldier standing watch opened his eyes wide, trying to follow the giant mammals.

'We have visual contact with four of them, the fifth seems to have disappeared,' he reported to Edwimus.

'Redouble surveillance efforts!' he spat once more into his bullhorn, which linked all the control rooms and the armory of the Aquanef.

Triaos was known as a strategist. That was why he had been awarded the rank of Triton Major, allowing him to take part in the kingdom's most important and influential missions. This intrusion, of implacable enemies into the heart of their well-loved undersea world, was surely the occasion to demonstrate his ingenious tactics. He was reassured by his Tritons' courage, and too much was at stake for them to fail. Looking at the little stub of a man in a bubble at his side, Triaos saw in him the same determination to crush this evil insect creeping slowly along the ocean floor like a big, poisonous inchworm.

After having carefully observed the machine, Ogrino had alerted Triaos to the existence of the little cannons surrounding the whole submersible. These might have a long shooting range, so they had to be especially vigilant. Triaos had thus opted for a massive, multidirectional attack, so as to divide the enemy's attention and resources. His point of view was optimal, offering a wide perspective on the whole scene, and everything was playing out as planned. In a few moments, the monstrous inchworm would be still forever more. He moved his trident and already, eight giant squid began to turn around the Aquanef at a dizzying speed, leaving large and dense jets of black ink around the cabin. A thick darkness engulfed the submersible, hardly disturbed by the enormous air bubbles its chimney was emitting. So Triaos was very surprised to see unexpected rays of light burst through the night, enveloping the big metal larva.

Edwimus smiled at his enemies' pitiful attack. Undoubtedly, they had underestimated the Order's capacity to defend itself. A mere dozen wide-spectrum floodlights had sufficed to reestablish the necessary visibility for a counter-attack. Still, the sperm whales' ballet was inexorably unfurling, each one in its place, attacking one side of this horrible, gigantic sea cucumber.

Edwimus said coldly, with clock-like precision, 'Four attackers at 300 feet, one at twelve o'clock, one at three, one at six and one at nine o'clock. Speed, thirty knots, impact in seven seconds. FIRE!'

The cannons on the front, back, and sides of the ship spat out their deathly shots in unison. The grenades exploded in four dense clouds into the dark water and hit the sperm whales' heads, tearing deep and painful wounds into their flesh. The four colossuses reared their heads, veered off course, and missed their target, too bruised and tormented by their injuries. The Triton riders were no longer master of their mounts, who were writhing about like earthworms. Edwimus rejoiced; his grenades had worked miracles, and in very little time, the scene would be still more infernal.

Suddenly, an incredibly violent impact rocked the Aquanef. The shockwave smacked the soldiers against the walls or floor. The doors clattered, the shelves went flying, the glass dials exploded, and water began to pour into the submersible. Edwimus collided violently with the main cabin window, and there, he saw the enormous mass of a sperm whale brush against the roof of the Aquanef. *The fifth one, that's where the fifth got off to,* he thought, enraged. He got up, his lip split, and bleeding abundantly. He wiped his face with the back of his sleeve and called into the bullhorn:

'Launch the sonic emitter. Helmets on, everyone.'

A few seconds later, a strident noise rang out through the Aquanef and the last few soldiers, who hadn't equipped themselves leapt upon their helmets. The Tritons, for their part, began to feel a great pain in their eardrums.

Then an excruciating migraine took control of their heads. Their suffering was unbearable. There was only one thing to do: flee, flee as far away as possible. They rushed toward Triaos, abandoning their wounded whales. Dozens and dozens of gray sharks, leopard sharks, and great whites were already gathering, drawn by the odor of blood. Soon hundreds of them were upon their enormous, distressed prey, whose minds were dulled by pain. The great whites attacked first, tearing into the whales' already-gaping grenade wounds. Very quickly, the other sharks joined in this colossal *danse macabre* and were voraciously ripping off large strips of flesh. The whales twisted in all directions, trying to free themselves from their aggressors. Under the impact of so many monstrous, cutting jaws, the once proud sperm whales were no longer anything but a big, bloody mass rapidly losing life force. They fell helplessly onto the ocean floor, unable to struggle, too weak to react. Their tails still beat lightly against the sand and then nothing; it was over. Then the sharks went after them all the more forcefully and the ocean turned blood red. Edwimus reveled in this killing. Everything had gone according to his plan. In the future, this King Delphoros would think twice before launching another attack. Now nothing could stop him from reaching his goal. The Aquanef just had to hold together until then. Once more he cried into the bullhorn:

'Ship conditions immediately! All watchmen report!'

Two minutes later, the ten watchmen stood before him, each detailing the losses. Overall, it actually hadn't been too catastrophic. The Aquanef, the Docts' technological marvel, had admirably resisted the thirty-ton whale's attack. Not too much damage, then, despite the mass that had plunged vertically toward them, hitting the very middle of the Aquanef's roof at top speed.

Edwimus shouted, 'Neutralize the top corridor and cut off rooms 8 and 9.'

The soldiers, drenched and frozen to the bone, were glad to leave the half flooded rooms, carefully closing the watertight hatches behind them. Edwimus judged that the situation was generally under control. Neither of the two tracks, nor either of the axles, was damaged, which was the important thing. The amount of water that had entered the ship when the roof failed didn't seem all that overwhelming, and the extra weight would hardly slow the Aquanef's crossing. It had all come out all right; they just had to be extra vigilant and keep the radar plugged in to warn them of any hint of another attack.

Edwimus was impatient to report to the Magnus Legifer in person. He called the soldier in charge of transmissions.

'Please take down this very important message. "Have escaped our first attack with success and minimal damages. Stop. Taught the enemy a lesson. Stop. Little chance of another attack. Stop. Goal will be reached on schedule. Stop. Long live the Order, glory to Legiferius. Stop."' He paused, satisfied, and then said, 'Translate that into Morse and send it by telegraph immediately.'

No less than two minutes later, the precious message was running along the telegraphic wire that extended from the back of the Aquanef and rose to the surface, following the slope of the undersea floor.

Triaos saw his Tritons pass above him furtively. They were fleeing toward Delphoros' palace at full speed. His sea horses had gone mad; each one was pulling in a different direction, so it was impossible for him to drive his chariot. His headache was still getting worse, and now he had to plug his ears to slightly ease the deafening ringing in his skull. The sea horses jumped, danced, ran into each other so chaotically and violently that all of a sudden, the harness tore, freeing the four steeds, which ran off in their respective directions. The chariot began to sink downward and Triaos, whose head was now threatening to explode, propelled himself desperately away from the submarine, which had to be the origin of this murderous sound. Ogrino saw himself falling with the chariot and felt as if a magnetic force was pulling him toward the sea floor. He curled up in preparation for the impact. When the sphere hit the rock of the ocean floor, he only felt a gentle shake because the bubble had absorbed the shock. Thank goodness for Razenbruck! His magic was really powerful. Actually, when everyone had seemed to be going mad in pain, he had only heard a soft, sharp noise like a woman's cry, nothing more. Apparently the sphere also protected him from certain external noises. Suddenly, everything went black as if someone had blown out the only candle in the room at night. Ogrino realized that the chariot had fallen on top of him, upside-down, forming a kind of shell. He tried to free himself, gathering his strength to push the sphere forward with his shoulder, but nothing doing; the chariot proved to be very heavy, and the bubble stuck in place. So he shouted as loud as he could, he yelled and yelled some more, but who would be able to hear him, lost in the middle of nowhere on the ocean floor? Aah! If only Razenbruck were here, he would know what to do. But once more, Ogrino was alone, so he began to shout again, louder than before.

After having swum as fast as he could, Triaos found himself a good ten leagues away from the submersible and finally noticed that the sound and his headache had disappeared. He got hold of himself. Ogrino! The little man—he must have been left on the battlefield. How to go back and look for him? He had to find a defense against that destructive sound. Perhaps Delphoros, or else the Grand Council, would find a solution. So he shot off like an arrow toward the palace. When he arrived at the cavern entrance, he saw that the Tritons were all there before Delphoros, seemingly in the middle of making their report. He crossed the vast room and heard the king address him wrathfully:

'Triaos, you, in whom I had such confidence, have betrayed me. You allowed this humiliating affront from a ridiculous enemy, who is not even of this world. You had the advantage of being in your element, of great mobility, and you let yourself be destroyed in the very first battle. I lost four of my precious sperm whale fighters, mounts that I myself trained. Luckily, none of my Tritons were affected. You deserve to be stripped of your title of Major. Now you need to make up for your failure. What do you propose?'

'Sire, although they were not in their own world, they have powerful and deadly weapons, and above all—above all!—they can emit a devastating sound that no one is immune to. In fact, I had to abandon the little man in the middle of the battle, that's how unbearable the sound was.'

'We'll deal with the child later! Our kingdom is in danger and we must find a way to eradicate this dangerous insect, and lose no time in doing so. Let the Grand Council meet again in the council room as we must make a serious decision that will affect our future. I have a difficult proposition for you. I am thinking of a solution that could prove very painful, even if we succeed,' Delphoros said gravely to the gathered attendees.

Ogrino had lost his voice from crying out into the night; he was almost mute. All of a sudden, he felt a shockwave. The chariot moved. A second impact, and the sarcophagus trapping him turned over. In the darkness, he saw an enormous mass loom over him and a big mouth open. He was terrified because even if the sphere were very solid, he wasn't sure it would be able to withstand the sperm whales' teeth, which he had seen during the battle. Moments after he was lodged in the animal's mouth, he recognized the oval shape of Welchar's smile. Kind Welchar had come looking for him, this time without Razenbruck, who was almost certainly still being held prisoner by the guards. His heart leapt with joy and gratitude toward the giant fish. He was safe and sound, and what's more, in a short while they arrived at the entry to the palace, where Welchar delicately deposited Ogrino onto the ground. The boy made as if to caress the shark on the cheek, through the bubble as a sign of gratitude. Then an escort of guards accompanied Ogrino to Triaos.

'How happy I am to see you again, my child!' Triaos said, a bit sheepishly. 'I felt guilty for abandoning you but that sound was tearing through my ears and I couldn't have stayed a second longer. I hope that you understand and that you are not too angry with me.'

'I was the one who wanted to join you in the battle, so I accept the consequences. I might have died if Welchar had not come and saved me.'

'We would surely have thought of something, in fact the Grand Council is deliberating to determine what course of action to take. Come! Let's approach, quietly.'

A grouper-man was speaking vehemently.

'Wake the Metanor? But Sire, you can't be thinking of that! He lives by his own laws, his own rhythms. He can't be woken from hibernation without his consent.'

'The circumstances require it,' Delphoros cut in imperiously. 'What other solution do you propose? Who else in the undersea world is powerful enough to fight such a strange enemy?'

'The Metanor could turn against us,' a Jelly woman added uneasily, her hair waving in all directions.

'I've thought about that at length, but it's a risk I have decided to take, for the safety of our kingdom. If we do nothing, that human submarine will be here a few sunrises from now, and who knows what it will do then. My life is at stake, as I cannot flee the palace. I am one with it. Our world's structure is in danger, so there is no other choice. We need Metanor's help, even if we'll have to pay a price. I submit this decision to the Grand Council's vote, as it concerns us all,' Delphoros proclaimed.

There were long whispers in the crowd of representatives from the Legendary World. Then the crucial moment of the vote arrived, marked by a loud gong ring. Lifting a hand, a fin, or a paw, everyone voted unanimously for Delphoros' proposition, though they were hardly reassured.

'Wonderful! A wise decision,' the king announced triumphantly. 'Triaos, come forth! You failed at your first mission. Now I offer you the chance to redeem yourself. I charge you with the mission of waking the Metanor. You will explain the situation to him and convince him to ally himself with us to fight our common enemy.'

'Very good Sire, it will be done as you wish, but the very act of waking him will take some time. Remember that he lives in the frozen depths of the abysses. To rouse the beast from hibernation, we will need to bring to him a powerful heat source, nearing the temperature of the ocean-floor magma, and that will take a long time, far too long even, seeing how fast the men's tank is progressing,' Triaos announced wearily.

Delphoros was silent for a moment, taken aback. He realized that he had been too preoccupied with finding a definitive solution to the threat of Legiferius and had completely forgotten that time was not on his side.

'I think I have a solution!' Ogrino said excitedly.

'What is this? How can you allow yourself to speak up when no one has authorized you to do so?' the Grand Chamberlain interjected wrathfully.

'Let him speak. He might well have some good advice,' Delphoros cut in.

'I know someone who could help you since his magic is very powerful. That person is Razenbruck,' Ogrino announced proudly.

'RAZENBRUCK?' Delphoros thundered, 'the traitor, the deserter! Where is he now?'

Ogrino regretted having said his friend's name. Seemingly, the king would tolerate no delay or equivocation in answer to his question. So Ogrino hastened to announce that his friend was being held outside of the palace.

'Send for him at once!' Delphoros ordered.

In an instant, still closely flanked by six guards, Razenbruck appeared before the enraged sovereign, looking submissive.

'So you dare to appear before me like this, vile pig, after insulting my daughter so despicably. Your thoughtlessness has doomed you. My wrath is unleashed! You shall die under my trident.' Delphoros raised his powerful arm, his lance pointed downwards menacingly.

'NOOO! I beg you, do not do that. He could be useful!'

It had been unstoppable. Ogrino hadn't been able to help but intervene and now, under Delphoros' terrifying regard, he felt so minuscule he wanted to crawl underground.

'How dare you speak out against MY decision? Who are you to oppose the king of the seas?'

'Your Majesty, I'm nothing but a small child, but I can promise you that without Razenbruck, I would never have made it to you. Now he's the only one who can succeed at the difficult mission of saving your kingdom, and so make up his long-ago offense to you.'

The whole assembly could feel the anger boiling deep within the sovereign.

Despite this, after a moment that seemed to last an eternity, the king lowered his trident and said in a restrained voice, 'Your words are wise, and your advice judicious. So you will accompany Triaos and your friend, to whom you seem so attached. But if you come back empty-handed, if you fail at your task, if you don't come back with the Metanor three sunsets from now, then all three of you will die by my trident, and no one and nothing will be able to save you. Is that clear?'

Triaos, Ogrino, and Razenbruck nodded their heads slightly in acceptance and then turned and walked promptly to the terrace of the palace, where the carriage and its spirited sea horses were already waiting. They had barely climbed into the carrier when the steeds bolted off, to the standing ovation of the enthusiastic crowd, all so hopeful about this mission. Despite himself, Ogrino waved to the mass of creatures, smiling, feeling close to this strange society in spite of all the differences separating them. So fast were the sea horses that soon the palace was nothing more than a small, glowing dot in the distance. Since the journey might nonetheless be a long one, Ogrino began to explain all that had happened to Razenbruck, who had regained his natural enthusiasm, so happy to be free once more.

The ride went on for hours and hours, so Ogrino had the luxury of savoring thirteen grouper all to himself, out of the fifteen or so that Triaos had caught for them. Finally, the carriage arrived, gliding over a fault so deep that it looked to be bottomless.

'The Deep Abyss, the lair of the Metanor,' declared Triaos. 'We will enter into his domain, a domain left undisturbed for centuries, ever since he went to sleep.'

'To sleep?' Ogrino asked.

'Yes, the Metanor is a creature of the Legendary World, and of course a subject of King Delphoros, but he's the most independent of marine animals, thanks to his incredible age. In fact, legend has it that he was born before Delphoros, and that's why he just barely tolerates his authority as king. Actually, he wasn't at the Grand Council because not only did he not deign to answer the call, but none of us, not even the king himself, had the courage to come force him to wake up. He has been sleeping for so long!'

'But why is he sleeping?' asked Ogrino.

'It's a long and complicated story, but you should know that before the end of the war in another age, before the Giants disappeared, he made the decision to retreat, to live apart from the tumults of the world, swearing not to reappear until the time had arrived. The hour seems to have come round for him, to be born into life again, and to play a crucial role in the survival of the kingdom. So let us go, and complete what we have been appointed to do.'

This rather imperious order was nevertheless spoken in uneasy tones. So the chariot tipped to almost vertical and headed into the deep blackness of the abyss. The farther they descended, the fewer fish they saw, and the stranger, losing their beautiful colors to become only gray or white. Some of them had faces like monsters, with even little lanterns atop of their heads to light their way.

All of a sudden, Ogrino saw an enormous white mass at the bottom of the pit. It looked like a gigantic jellyfish lying on the ground. It was as big around as Legiferius's huge plaza, and as tall as a cathedral. The farther down they went, the more impressive it seemed. The chariot stopped halfway down, near the surface of the thing. Then Ogrino understood that this motionless giant was nothing more than an immense dome of ice. Razenbruck immediately began his incantations and Triaos looked on, dumbfounded, as one, then five, then ten, then fifty, a hundred, a thousand, five hundred thousand balls of fire formed and settled all over the frozen surface. They waited while, slowly but surely, the ice melted, revealing an incredible scene. Dozens of boats of all sorts—galleons, battle galleys, merchant vessels, and even canal boats and barges, for the most part gutted—were lying on the ground. Underneath this tangle were golden and sparkling reflections. *Treasure*, Ogrino said to himself. Coins and jewelry in such numbers that it seemed impossible. Right in the middle of all this finery, one could make out the hazy form of a fantastic creature with white skin and the titanic head of a resting iguana, eyes half-closed.

The chariot stopped just in front of the Metanor's mouth, and Triaos launched into a soft melody, blowing into a seashell. The monster opened its steel-gray eyes and lifted its head, which proved to be sitting at the end of a giraffe-like neck, only longer. He straightened up and Ogrino realized that this outsized creature was in fact an aquatic dragon. It looked like the ones that Slevania had shown him in picture books, but although he was, naturally, the same size as winged dragons, he couldn't have been more than a distant cousin. There were no batlike wings on his back, but rather a fine membrane that linked his front legs to his back ones. It reminded Ogrino of certain flying squirrels that he had seen gliding from tree to tree, spreading their limbs. His body was monstrously enormous and full of rippling muscles. His incredibly long tail resembled a kind of whip, sweeping slowly back and forth on the ground like a serpent.

Suddenly, the Metanor reached out one foot with startling speed. His long, razor-sharp claws brushed by the three messengers' heads, crashing down onto the sea horses, which barely had the time to whimper. The enormous paw closed instantly on its prey, which was thrown into the dragon's gaping mouth and swallowed up in a second. Ogrino was as terrified as his unfortunate companions. They would be the next victims before they could even deliver their message. And yet Triaos wasn't moving. Perhaps he was paralyzed by fear.

'We hope that this present was to your liking. In the name of Delphoros, we brought you the plumpest and most succulent sea horses in the kingdom as we know your refined taste for the finest meat. Delphoros hoped to be able to speak with you about a very grave matter that affects the kingdom, which is why we have taken the liberty of coming to you.'

A husky, deep, and glacial voice arose.

'The liberty? The liberty of coming to disturb my sleep! Who do you think you are to be able to make decisions for me? You are nothing but insignificant pill bugs that I could crush with a single breath. I am nearly as old as time itself. You are nothing but passing shadows, as soon forgotten as born, and you have the presumptuousness to tear me from my dreams—me, the Metanor! You have no idea of the sacrilege you have just committed, and for that, you deserve death.'

He stretched out his neck and his head rose up very high, threateningly before the three visitors, who were having trouble containing their trembling. Triaos inhaled deeply and spoke.

'Legend says that you will awake from your deep sleep to take part in the battle at the end of time. That time has come, and you can destroy us, certainly, but you cannot escape your destiny. Your place is at Delphoros's side, in defense of the kingdom, and you know it. We are nothing but passing souls, but the kingdom—that must remain eternal, like you!' He concluded in a voice full of certitude and authority.

The Metanor stared at him for a very long moment, then said, 'You are full of courage and self-sacrifice. You were able to overcome your fear for a cause greater than you and that touches me. The world's fate rests in the hands of beings like you. I myself am one of the principal guardians of that fate, and after probing your soul, I see that you speak the truth, so I will reflect on Delphoros's request.'

At this, with a rapid fluttering of membranes, he flew off, creating a violent current that sent the three minuscule creatures tumbling, enveloped in a thick cloud of heavy dust. It took a very long time for the fog to dissipate enough for Ogrino to once again see anything. The Metanor had left without their knowing if he was going to help the king or not, and now they had to make it back to the castle without horses. Triaos and Razenbruck exchanged several comments, and Ogrino saw the latter transform into a magnificent Triton and both of them leave in great haste. They came back a few seconds later, carrying long algae, which they were plaiting together like a fishnet. They pushed Ogrino's sphere forward into the center of the net and the two Tritons each grabbed one end, forming a sort of hammock. They advanced with their precious cargo. Rocked by the movement, Ogrino quickly fell asleep, tired from all these adventures.

The Metanor entered the palace as slowly as possible, filling a large part of the grotto with his imposing figure. Delphoros awaited him, looking impassive. The dragon stopped before him, floating in midair, fixing him with his bright eyes in order to read his soul. Delphoros spoke first, in order to maintain the superiority of a king over his subject, but the relationship remained unequal since for one thing, his authority over the Metanor had always been, in a word, relative, and for another, today he was asking a great favor.

'I have permitted myself to pull you out of your retreat not for my own amusement, but because I am forced to do so.' His tone was both solemn and conciliatory. 'Grave things are afoot. The underwater world is threatened, and all of us must take part in its defense. That's why I am asking for your support.'

The Metanor's cavernous, bone-chilling voice boomed out. 'You fear for your kingdom. You fear for your life! You say that you merely want me to intervene, but in actuality, you have no other choice. Without me, your little world would crumble and you along with it.'

A long shiver traveled up the king's back. He contained himself so as not to let anything show through.

The Metanor continued in a metallic tone, 'What would happen if you disappeared? There would have to be another king of the undersea world, and who but me could fill that role, with all the authority that goes along with such a task? In fact, if I do not help you, it would be equivalent to putting the royal crown on my head, myself. A very interesting prospect indeed . . . . ,' he added sarcastically.

These comments were devastating to the king, who had never felt so helpless in any situation. Was his power so frail? Then he pulled himself together and spoke.

'You know very well that power has never interested you. If it did, then you would have challenged me long ago. What's more, you are well aware that I am connected to the Gigantum and that my presence here assures the balance of the undersea world,' said Delphoros, regaining his confidence, for everything he had said was evident and incontestable.

'Everyone is connected to the Gigantum, myself included!' the Metanor cut in. 'Therefore I might equally act as an intermediary, as you do, as the ancient forces of the Legendary World would be able to compensate for the 'regrettable' loss of an important link in the chain.'

'You are rambling,' Delphoros retorted. 'One does not decide to be an essential link. One deserves it, by being born worthy, which is the case for me and not for you.'

'The preservation of the Great Balance is more important than its members, however worthy they may be,' the dragon responded. 'What's more, Felicia Regina would be eternally pleased to rule this part of the world if destiny led that way.'

'Only a heart that hopes for the good of its kingdom could find favor with Felicia Regina. You, your worries are entirely different. You think of nothing but your own power, and you would rule by fear and not by respect, and so your rule would be one of terror.'

'A lovely flight of fancy, however it is not sufficient to convince me. Still, more than power, I covet something else entirely concerning your kingdom. What would you be prepared to give me if I were to accept to help you?'

'To give you? How dare you haggle over the security of our world?' Delphoros flared up in irritation.

'You are not in a position to impose anything upon me, nor to lecture me on morality. I want an answer. What would you give me?'

The king reflected for a moment, calming himself, and said, 'I could offer you the most beautiful galleons, precious stones, works of art, or even . . .'

'That's enough,' said the Metanor. 'None of that has anything to do with you. What I want belongs to you personally.'

'I don't see . . . Other than my crown, my trident, my palace.'

The Metanor took his time in responding, savoring in advance the pleasure of wounding his old rival.

'The one and only present that would be sufficiently precious in my eyes for me to deign to help you is . . .'

Once more he paused, then after a long while began again.

'That being who occupies an essential place in your kingdom.'

The king mentally reviewed all his subjects with important posts in his kingdom: the Grand Chamberlain, the Triton Majors, the ambassadors, even the artists. Which of them could the Metanor be referring to?

'Do you swear to me that if I conquer your enemy, you will keep your promise and give me the creature I specify?' the dragon said.

'How can I swear if I don't know the price to pay?' the king retorted, sickened by this unjust demand.

'The price to pay, as you say, is the gift of . . . your daughter.'

'MY DAUGHTER! You dare to insult me, demanding MY DAUGHTER! This filthy haggling says much about your morality. You're nothing but a despicable beast, taking advantage of an extreme situation to murder the highest representative of the kingdom.'

'Know that my proposition is the only one I will offer. Either you will accept, or you will perish, and in that case, you will never see your daughter again. If you agree to my request, you save yourself and your world, in exchange for one single being. Think about it!'

'I save my kingdom, perhaps, but I would mortify myself for all eternity in losing my only daughter.'

'And there is the difficult task of a king, whose feelings must be placed after the well-being of the kingdom.'

A sadistic smile spread insidiously across the dragon's face. He reveled in the situation. Delphoros remained silent for a long time, a very long time, going through all the alternatives before finally deciding that he had no other choice but to deliver his gentle daughter into the claws of this cold, cruel monster.

'I accept,' he finally said, sounding like a man destroyed. 'I will give you my daughter, Delphania, in exchange for your victory over the enemy. As soon as they are defeated, she will accompany you to your lair. If you fail, she will remain at the palace with me.'

The dragon exulted; he had trouble containing his joy.

'Swear to it on this piece of parchment, writing in your own blood.'

He gave Delphoros a cormorant feather and a papyrus made of algae. The king stabbed the quill into a vein and, with a grimace, began to write. As soon as he had finished, the Metanor snatched the document from his hands, reread it, and began to laugh.

'The long-awaited moment has arrived. I have wanted your daughter for centuries and finally she will be mine, on this memorable day. I'll make a mouthful of your pathetic enemies and tonight, Delphania will be with me. Her melodious voice will brighten my dark nights for eternity. Now show me these pesky insects so that I can crush them.'

The king gave him the map showing the Aquanef's location. Everything about him reeked of sadness. His face was drawn, his eyes melancholy, even his mouth was pulled into a tense pout. The Metanor studied the map carefully, turned, and with one swipe of his paws, shot off lightning-fast. When the king raised his somber eyes, the dragon had already disappeared. All the members of the Grand Council, who had witnessed in silence the scene between the two titans, now expressed their compassion toward the poor king, who had had to sacrifice his daughter for the survival of the kingdom.

The Metanor flew through the water like a rocket, his impressive mass zooming with surprising agility through the currents and past the seascapes. He stopped short, all of a sudden, behind a rocky peak. His sharp eyes had detected, nearly a half-mile away, a big metal tank spitting enormous bubbles. The adversary was there, crawling along like an insult to the aquatic world. Still, he had to be prudent as they possessed unknown and surprising weapons. The dragon reflected for a moment and suddenly shot off at a dizzying speed toward the objective, taking care to zig and zag quickly. Then he began to make concentric circles around the Aquanef, getting a little closer to his target with each orbit.

'Enemy portside—no, starboard—no, at six o'clock! He keeps moving, and very rapidly!'

The watch-soldier's alert had the effect of a thunderclap in the submarine. Not only had the enemy not been thrown into chaos by their crushing defeat, but also it had dared to launch a new offensive, and this time, apparently, with a much more formidable attack. Edwimus, seated at the control panel, kept his eyes trained on the enormous animal that was twirling around them, taunting them with his irregular yet swift trajectory. Concentrating hard, he quickly studied the monster's movements. The men were on edge. Their adrenaline levels were rising, for the beast looked so frightening, like a monster from a nightmare. Everyone stood at his post, ready for orders.

'Arm the cannons. Number 27 explosives.'

The Militians executed the order, knowing that that type of ammunition could easily pulverize an elephant.

'FIRE.' The order dropped like a cleaver. A dozen missiles discharged, exploding about a hundred yards from the dragon, who suddenly accelerated his movements to dodge the detonations.

Not must he be immune to the infrasound since he's always getting closer, but he's even playing around with our shots, Edwimus said to himself. 'Number 35 tracking bombs,' he called to the machine gunners.

The monster kept gaining ground. The Commander waited patiently, studying the animal's movements more and more carefully. The beast was only fifty yards away when he opened his mouth wide.

'FIRE now!' Edwimus shouted. A half-dozen torpedoes sped off simultaneously toward the target, just as the Metanor spit a huge waterfall of ice onto the Aquanef. The two opposing attacks reached their objectives at the same moment. An explosion tore at the dragon's underbelly, and he let out a strident cry that frightened all the crewmembers, despite their helmets. Then they saw nothing; all the Aquanef's windows and portholes had become opaque. It was as if shutters had been closed on them. A thick coat of ice now covered the submarine, like a cocoon. The vehicle's tracks seized up and the Aquanef's forward progress stopped entirely. A heavy silence settled over them. Legiferius's most powerful weapon was now paralyzed more than a thousand meters deep, incapable of either carrying out its mission or returning to open air.

Such a situation was inconceivable; they absolutely had to find a way out, a defense, a counter-offensive. The Militians had to be victorious. Edwimus took a new tack. Didn't he have access to a whole battery of inventions, each one more perfected than the last? He could certainly make it out of this sarcophagus; in any case, they had to, or else they would all die the slow death of asphyxiation. Horror washed over him at the mere thought of that prospect. A race against time had just begun; each second would count. Not just their mission, but even their survival depended on their determination and temerity.

The Metanor's right flank hurt dreadfully. The explosion of that cursed human projectile had torn at his scales, skin, flesh, and organs. The pain was so sharp that he was frenetically batting his tail and paws, causing him to flail around chaotically in all directions. Despite his gaping wound, which was bleeding abundantly, no sharks or other predators appeared on the horizon, thanks to his deafening shouts. He wished he could spit more ice onto his evil adversary so as to forever seal them into an eternal tomb. He didn't have the strength, though, and perhaps wouldn't for a long time as he knew his wound was very deep. He left his defenseless prey where it sat and oriented himself, more or less, toward the palace, despite the insistent pain. The thought of returning to the king injured but victorious, and most of all to be able to rightfully claim Delphania's hand, was a comfort to his heart and so eased some tiny portion of his pain. On the way, he brushed up against tufts of medicinal algae known only to him, which deposited a thin film of strands, making a healing dressing for his wound. He chuckled in contentment over the nearly immediate relief. The injury would take days and days to scar over, but at least the pain was now moderated. He redoubled his speed, and this time his trajectory was direct, so focused was he on his single and ultimate goal: Delphania.

The scout Tritons who had watched the battle from very far away had given the alert with their shell-trumpets. The Metanor had conquered the enemy.

'He is coming back to claim his due,' the Grand Chamberlain announced to Delphoros.

The king, far from being relieved at the destruction of the menacing enemy, stayed stone-still, mute, crushed by the weight of the promise he had made. He broke from his torpor and murmured, 'Call for my daughter at once.'

The Chamberlain disappeared and came back a moment later with one of the most elegant Sirens there ever was. Her delicate face was a pale color and her long green hair fell onto her bare shoulders. Translucent fairy-wings ornamented her back with colorful touches, and the scales of her slender tail shone with rainbow iridescence. In the most melodious voice, Delphania addressed the king.

'Father, you called me. What is it? What can I do to serve you?'

'My beautiful child, my poor child. Today is a day of mourning. I ought to be rejoicing as the leader of a liberated kingdom. Alas, my heart is a father's, and it cannot begin to feel except to express its unspeakable sadness. My spirit bleeds, on this cursed day when I have sacrificed my only daughter on the altar of liberty.'

'But what is this all about? What are you saying?' the princess asked, disconcerted.

'I had no other choice, believe me. I was forced to choose between two equally horrifying evils, and to save the kingdom, I have handed you over to the Metanor.'

He finished this sentence in a murmur as if he were exhaling his last breath.

'To the Metanor!' Delphania said, terrorized. 'You offered me to that dreadful creature in exchange for the liberation of the kingdom. That's it, isn't it? There wasn't another solution? Are you really certain? Did you look into every possibility?' she said fervidly, her tone full of reproach.

'There was truly no other solution. The enemy had proven to be too powerful, and only the Metanor was up to the task to not only fight, but also most of all beat them.'

'I would rather die than be joined to that repugnant monster. Can't I run away, exile myself in an unknown place where no one will be able to find me?'

You could hear the anxiety and a supplicating plea in her voice. Once so harmonious, it was now strangled in an invisible vise.

'I signed with my own blood. I can't renege, and what's more, where could you hide that the Metanor wouldn't be able to flush you out? No, unfortunately, we cannot escape our destiny. Our fate is sealed, both of us, for the greatest unhappiness.'

Delphania, wracked with a sudden sob, took off brusquely, beating her butterfly wings. She was getting ready to leave the palace when, through reddened eyes, she saw with horror that she could not take another step. The Metanor rose up before her like an immense wall, insurmountable for the fear he created.

'Delphania, oh sweet dreamy creature, what a pleasure to see you here again!'

The Metanor tried to make his expression amiable, warm, charming even.

'Has your noble father told you the news?'

His tone slowly became that of a conqueror, sure of his victory.

'We established an irrevocable pact and I have fulfilled my part of the contract. I defeated the enemy at the risk of my life. My wound testifies to that. I risked death for the kingdom's well-being. Now I have come to take what rightfully belongs to me.'

'NO! You can't force me. I am an independent being and I won't follow you against my will,' Delphania asserted vehemently.

'Your will! Your will means nothing to me. You belong to the people of the seas, and you owe your king, who is also your father, complete obedience. You must follow the laws of the kingdom. Your father signed a statement with his own blood, and he cannot allow his own daughter to make him a perjurer.'

'He speaks the truth!'

The voice had rung out with force and authority. Delphoros, upset as he was, nevertheless confirmed that his daughter could not possibly escape such a solemn agreement.

'You will become an outlaw if you do not leave with him. My own guards will be forced to chase you until the promise is fulfilled. Go now, this moment is too unbearable for it to be drawn out even instant more. Metanor! Promise me that I will see my daughter again.'

'I accept. When we have become more intimate, when she has pledged friendship to me, then she will be able to come back to see her father from time to time—but not before then. Is that clear?'

He had added this question as he turned to Delphania, lifting her pretty head with the tip of his tail so as to gaze deep into her eyes.

'Yes,' the sweet Siren replied timidly, wounded to the depths of her soul. So the Metanor took her gently in one of his clawed paws and deposited her, with infinite tenderness astride his neck. Turning his head to her, he murmured, 'You will learn to love me. And now, sing a song of farewell for our departure.'

Delphania looked at her father one last time, desolately. He looked stooped, prematurely aged. He no longer gave the impression of a powerful king, but rather that of an almost-senile old man. So digging deep within herself, Delphania began to sing a melody of infinite sadness. The song was at once rapturously beautiful and poignantly melancholy. All those present felt that their hearts were tearing, that a terrible depression had settled on top of them and that they were all infused with a frightening bitterness and complete discouragement.

Everyone was grief-stricken. Still, he who suffered the most was not the king, but poor Razenbruck, who, barely arrived, had to watch his love walk away from him, with no hope of return. Because of her, he had been banned; he had wanted to tip fate in his favor by putting a love potion in Delphania's cup. He had so little confidence in himself at that time that he thought that such a graceful and sensitive creature could never deign to set eyes upon such a miserable fiend. He was wrong, but didn't know it. Delphania had long been drawn to this man, so different from her world. She was amused by his facetiousness and irreverence, seduced by his vivacity and intelligence. Her strict education stopped her from conveying her feelings, however, especially as they might have been against the wishes of her father, who had other plans for her. Today, everything in Razenbruck was crumbling, and he had been the architect of his own discontent. He himself had awakened the one who was now before his very eyes, forever carrying away his reason to live. He fell to his knees and cried all the tears his body could contain. When he came back to the reality of the surrounding world, he saw that Triaos was standing squarely before him.

'The king wishes to see you and the child immediately.'

He joined Ogrino before the throne.

'Although this day is the gloomiest of my long existence, it will go down in history as the day the kingdom was liberated. Razenbruck! You were a part of the plan that brought us victory. I have thus decided to pardon you and cease your banishment, on one condition. You must accompany the child to Felicia. She needs to be updated on what is happening, for though we may have won the battle, we have not won the war. Who knows what else the humans are capable of inventing, or where they will strike next. So I give you the mission of bringing the child to the doors of the Kingdom of the Elves. To aid you along the way, I have chosen Triaos as well as two Ondines, Loreline, and Auraline, who you see here. They will accompany you as far as the rivers can bring them. In fact, they know of all the rivers, canals, and floodplains that will bring you to your destination. And now, you must go immediately. I have rigged up a chariot with spirited horses.'

He had barely finished his sentence when a sparkling red chariot pulled up in front of them. All five jumped nimbly into the carrier. Auraline cracked a long whip, and the horses bolted off lightning-fast. Ogrino, intoxicated by the speed, saw the monumental palace shrink and disappear and knew that he would surely never see it again. He felt a twinge of regret as he thought that he would never more experience the enchanting beauty this fascinating world had to offer.

PRECELESTINE

Once more, the underwater voyage seemed to take place in fast-forward, so swift were the steeds. In a flash, the team found themselves in the estuary of a river that sent green waves washing back to where these roiling waters crashed into the ocean's blue. Without slowing down in the least, the chariot traveled up the powerful current. The more they progressed, the worse their visibility, as the impetuous river was dragging along an impressive mass of silt, leaves, and garbage. Nevertheless, the speedy steeds continued to gallop along, imperturbable. Little by little, as they went farther upstream, the current lost its intensity. The powerful river became a mere stream.

The vigorous horses, which had pulled the chariot with such speed up to that point saw their progress slowed by the stream's decreasing depth, and especially by the algae tangling around their feet. It required more and more energy to advance only a few paces, jolting the passengers around uncomfortably.

'We'd do better to leave the chariot here,' Triaos called out, sounding a little annoyed. 'Our progression will be much faster if we swim from here on out.'

'Let's take the net,' Auraline proposed. 'Triaos, you'll pull from above, and Loreline and I will pull from the sides.

And you, Razenbruck, what would you say to transforming yourself into a nice Triton to help us out? You'll take the net from below, and that way we'll be able to easily pull along Ogrino's bubble. We'll be fishing for the fisherman, in a way,' she said with amusement.

Everyone smiled and got to work, then Triaos sent the horses to wait at the mouth of the river, thinking ahead for their return journey. Once more, Ogrino was very comfortable as he sat peacefully in his bubble, towed behind as his four friends swam vigorously. The water had become clear again as the stream was flowing more slowly here; they had entered into a sort of little lake. Ogrino admired the fluvial vegetation: the algae that looked like long hair, the water lilies, of which he could see only the roots, but whose pink flowers were reflected on the surface. Ogrino couldn't tear his eyes from this aquatic ceiling, with its moving colors that formed ephemeral paintings. He noticed a black shape that must have been a charred tree, with a pale flower atop it. When one of the branches abruptly began to wave around, Ogrino understood that something wasn't right.

'Soldiers!' he cried. 'Up top! They've seen us!'

'About-face!' Triaos called. 'We'll have to retrace our path before they shoot arrows or something else at us.'

Suddenly, before they could turn back, fat balls of dark glass fell into the stream, barring their passage. A moment later, dull explosions rang out, and the shockwave traveled rapidly through the water. Everyone was stunned by the detonations. The Tritons and the Ondines, scattered and half-deaf, managed to float just below the surface but were no longer in any state to fight. Ogrino, protected by his bubble, had only barely felt the impact of the explosion. He rolled his sphere onto the lake-bed to approach Razenbruck, whose head was lowered like a groggy boxer's.

'Pull yourself together! We have to leave as quickly as possible!'

While he was speaking, he spotted a broad movement above their heads. A big shadow filled the sky, followed by a little disturbance on the surface. *A net,* Ogrino thought immediately. *It was a trap.*

'Wake up, Razenbruck! We'll be prisoners if we don't react!'

He shook him violently, and Razenbruck's head bobbed up and down enough for him to see the open mesh above their heads. Instantaneously, he transformed into an enormous crocodile. Ogrino recoiled in shock and also in fear as the animal was really quite intimidating.

The net had barely fallen upon their heads and already it was closing from the bottom to gather them into a bundle. Triaos, regaining his spirits, struggled with his trident, trying to cut through the wide stitches. Razenbruck opened his large mouth and closed it violently on the net, easily cutting through the thick cords. While this was happening, other balls were falling around them. This time, no explosions, but they were emanating a dark green liquid that, carried by the current, was drifting toward them. Razenbruck took another bite, and a large passage opened up. He dove through it with Ogrino's sphere solidly wedged in his large mouth, and Triaos and the Ondines followed swiftly.

Despite their escape, the cloud was already enveloping them. They became sluggish. They felt as if they had drunk some kind of strong alcohol and had trouble staying on course. Ogrino shouted to keep them all alert. Razenbruck whipped his tail through the water so as not to fall asleep, and little by little he began to outdistance the others. Ammunition was tearing through the water all around them, and something that must have been an arrow planted itself in the crocodile's lower back. Far from weakening him, this only spurred him on, and he began traveling at a phenomenal speed. The soldiers ran along the bank in order to stay even with the animal. The crocodile kept diving further into the basin of the lake, so much so that soon, the Militians lost sight of him, in the cloud of mud he was stirring up as he passed.

Triaos, half-conscious, had pulled the two Ondines up beside him, and together they were clutching his trident as he murmured a magic formula. The river began to move, forming a spiral around the three aquatic creatures. The whirlpool intensified, and the mass of water moved outwards as if in a centrifuge. Everything around them was bared. No more green poison to intoxicate them. Now, once again, they were in their right minds, with all their facilities. Triaos pointed his trident above the heads of the enemies he could see, and invoking Delphoros, he concentrated. A discharge resembling electricity escaped from the three points, making an arc which left the water and traveled through the air. The Militians hit by the bolt leaped backwards before falling into the tall grass.

After a long moment, when he thought they must be safe, Razenbruck began heading for the surface, finding rays of sun in the water, which was becoming clear again. When they had arrived in the open air, Ogrino was once again able to admire the sky and the sun's light glancing off the bank, reddening in the late afternoon. His rapture was cut short as on the north bank, a whole line of soldiers were standing guard, blocking their way.

'We'll have to take a long detour if we don't want to face Legiferius's henchmen again,' Ogrino said distastefully.

'Ayha ah besher ihea,' Razenbruck tried to say, his mouth blocked by the bubble.

'What?'

Before Razenbruck could answer, they washed up on a little island covered with verdant shrubs. With one sweeping movement of his head, Razenbruck balanced the sphere on the shore and then, in turn, climbed up onto solid ground. When the reptile's long body was entirely out of the water, Razenbruck became himself again and put his hands on the bubble, reciting an incantation. The sphere disappeared as if by magic. Ogrino took a deep breath of fresh air, happy to feel the wind on his skin again after that long aquatic saga.

'I hope Triaos and the Ondines were able to escape,' Ogrino murmured hopefully.

'Triaos has more than one trick up his sleeve, and don't forget that he is one of Delphoros' body guards, which is a sign of fierceness and cunning. Don't worry too much for him. I'm sure he's safe and sound, and already far away.'

'What will we do now?'

'As I told you a minute ago, I have an idea. We'll go to meet Precelestine XXXVII!'

'But the Militians?'

'What do the soldiers matter to us? They're stupid and slow. And most of all they don't know anything about the World Below.'

While he was talking, Ogrino couldn't help but scan the bank of the lake, where the seemingly omnipresent enemy was standing. He noticed a certain agitation amongst the Militians and saw several of them slipping something into the water.

'Boats! They're putting boats in the water. They've surely seen us and they're coming to capture us. This will never end!' Ogrino lamented.

'Come!' was Razenbruck's only response.

He led Ogrino to the center of the little island, across the tangled bushes. Little by little, a gray form rose up before them, until Ogrino could make out an old, dilapidated, miniature temple, largely covered over by moss and climbing plants. Who could have guessed that a building like this would be found in such a desolate place? This structure must have been erected many years ago since it was so damaged. Still, it had an air of nobility, with its pyramidal roof, round columns, and thick walls made of gray blocks of granite with decorative plants carved in relief.

'What is this?' Ogrino asked?

'You'll see what my abilities allow me to accomplish.'

Razenbruck went around the temple, knelt, and placed his right hand on a very precise location high on the wall, to the left of a little portico. Pushing forcefully with his thumb and index finger, he moved one of the stones. With a dull sound, a heavy door began to open, slowly, gently, out from the wall. A descending staircase appeared, little by little, out of the darkness as the door opened all the way now. The putrid scent of mold rushed into their noses, making Ogrino cough and feel a bit nauseated.

They heard a little impact and some splashes behind them, followed by the sounds of twigs breaking. Razenbruck looked at his friend, and grabbing his sleeve, pulled him unceremoniously into the tunnel. He ran his hand along the wall, looking for a specific location. The half-light didn't make his task any easier, and he was losing precious time. Finally, he found the place he was looking for and pushed decisively on a crevice in the rock. The door began to move once more, closing off the passage. It was halfway through its path when a shadow appeared in the opening. A tall soldier was pointing his crossbow at the two friends. In the blink of an eye, Razenbruck transformed himself into a majestic cobra and in a flash, struck at the Militian's face and bit deeply into his cheek. The man doubled over in pain, all the while trying to strangle the reptile with his two hands closed on its throat. But very shortly he was overcome with shaking; the fatal poison coursed quickly through his system. Soon he released his grip and the snake easily escaped. The man fell forward and landed flat, his body half in and half outside of the tunnel. The door, having arrived at the end of its trajectory, hit the dying man's haunches. He let out a short cry as the heavy door crushed his pelvis. He was dead, but in a final act of defiance, his body was blocking the closure of the stairway.

'We absolutely must clear the opening,' Razenbruck ordered.

Before they could make the slightest movement, many more noises of sticks breaking sounded outside.

'They're arriving, they're all ready,' Ogrino whispered.

'Oh well, come on! Let's go!'

And they hurtled down the stairs at full speed, despite the growing shadows. The staircase led downwards in a seemingly interminable straight line. Gradually the darkness became complete.

'Couldn't you do a bit of magic and light the path for us?' Ogrino whispered, huffing and puffing.

'Later! For the moment, the darkness is our dear ally.'

In fact, they could hear rapid footsteps resonating on the flagstones behind them. This staccato noise seemed to be growing closer, motivating Razenbruck to increase his pace. Ogrino had had enough of always having to flee these soldiers, who hunted him down so mercilessly. For the moment, however, he oughtn't to ruminate, but only to sprint down these neverending stairs like an automaton. Suddenly the ground became flat and Ogrino stopped short.

'Keep going!' Razenbruck cried.

'But I can't see anything!'

'There's nothing to fear, there are no obstacles here. We're in a market room.'

'A market room. What does that mean?' Ogrino asked as he began to run again.

'We've entered the kingdom of Precelestine XXXVII. The World Below is full of a multitude of rooms and tunnels dug by the Little Folk, who reign over it. Soon we'll be safe. Don't slow down!'

It seemed that nothing could stop their progress, and Ogrino, becoming more confident, was continually picking up speed. All of a sudden, a flash of light tore through the darkness and a bright, phosphorescent ball rolled alongside them. The two friends turned around to discover that a good thirty soldiers were following them, brandishing torches, their weapons pointed directly at the fugitives.

'Zigzag, quickly!' Razenbruck shouted.

They began to run in a disorganized fashion in the great dome that now appeared to them, thanks to the Militians' lights. In the distance, Ogrino could make out wide columns whose tops disappeared into the shadows. He immediately veered toward these unexpected ramparts, with Razenbruck following right behind—and quite fortunately too, since a volley of flaming arrows struck the first columns at the height of a man just as they disappeared behind them. At that moment, Ogrino heard some kind of movement in the darkness. Something was dragging itself along the floor.

'Stay close to me,' Razenbruck ordered. 'And do not move!'

In the next moment, Ogrino saw, or rather, perceived, in the darkness, what the source of the sound had been: dragons, enormous Komodo dragons, larger than alligators and faster too. There must have been at least a hundred of them, waddling along toward the light. They passed in front of the two friends, who stood motionless like statues, their backs flat against a column. The dragons, indifferent to their presence, continued on their way toward the soldiers and their dancing torches.

As soon as the Militians saw these hideous monsters pouring out toward them, they opened fire. Arrows rained down and the first ones dropped like flies, twisting in agony and yowling with pain. Far from frightening the other dragons, this distressing scene made them only more excited and aggressive so that they sped up and descended upon their attackers en masse before the latter had time to reload their weapons. It was a bloodbath, as the monsters were slaughtering the soldiers, upending them with their tails, and then tearing them apart with their large, clawed feet or their razor-sharp fangs.

It was all over in a matter of minutes; only a few of the Militians were able to save themselves and retreat to the staircase, while the dragons were feasting on their victims.

During this time, Razenbruck had made a ball of light magically appear and was back on the trail, without waiting for the outcome of the frightful battle. Ogrino was at once relieved to know that their pursuers had been rendered harmless and afraid of what else they might find in the depths of these dark caverns.

'Have you been here before?' Ogrino asked, to reassure himself.

'Of course. Although it has been a long time. Those dragons didn't live here then. The market room was most often full of the Little Folk's shopkeepers, who came here regularly to trade their finds from the World Above. You must know that the Pixies make furtive excursions to the surface and bring back little treasures like spoons, little barrels, balls of wool, books, saucepans, and all sorts of various objects they pinch from humans. Once this place was a hotspot for commerce, and magical creatures came from very far away, for the quality of trade here had made a name for itself. But since Legiferius has been relentlessly tracking the Legendary World's representatives, the Pixies have gone out less and less, and nearly all commerce has disappeared.'

As they spoke, they arrived before an underground river, passing under a bridge that was marvelously worked in stone and decorated with magnificent sculptures.

'Wowee, how beautiful!' Ogrino exclaimed. 'That bridge was made by Pixies.'

'Clearly! The kings of the Little Folk have always loved beautiful crafts, whether in architecture or blacksmithing. Remember that these are masters of metals and gems, and that they can create incomparable weapons and jewelry of inestimable value.'

They climbed onto the bridge, which loomed high over the river, and saw where the dragons were coming from. Many females and their offspring were frolicking about in the water. The males were hurrying back with the leftovers of their meals held in their mouths, which they deposited for the nourishment of the rest of the herd. As they ate, they cast their glassy eyes at Razenbruck's ball of light.

'Let's go ahead! I don't want to see this!' Ogrino declared of the scene. 'I've had enough for today. Actually, it must be time for us to eat too. What can we find around here?'

'It's no problem as long as you like dragon!'

'Hah! No, I'd prefer something more appetizing.'

'You know, here under the ground, life has taken very different forms from what you're familiar with. You might not find it very appealing.'

'If I have no choice, I'll eat dragon, but is there really nothing else in the area?'

'Follow me!'

They walked upstream for a while, crossing through a series of sumptuous ochre, yellow, and orange grottos. In this way, they arrived at a large subterranean lake. The water was so still it looked like a mirror. An eternal peace and silence reigned. Everything seemed frozen, beyond time, and Ogrino would have felt he was in another dimension if his stomach had not begun to growl so loudly.

'I'm hungry!' he exclaimed suddenly. 'I can't stand it any more!'

'A little patience. Here we are, and the time has come for fishing. You see this lake? It's a treasure trove of underground life. A multitude of animals are gathered here, from the smallest, like snails, shrimp, salamanders, crayfish, and cave-dwelling fish, up to the largest, which are bats and guacharos.'

'Guacharos? What are those?'

'They're birds. They look a bit like falcons, but bigger.'

'There are birds here?'

'Yes, but they often go out to feed, although they find food here too. Look up there, on top of that wall – see all those nests?'

Ogrino sensed, rather than saw, as Razenbruck's ball of light, even reflected on the surface of the lake, barely penetrated the surrounding darkness. During this time, Razenbruck had submerged himself in the lake to his waist, and begun to recite a low incantation, keeping his arms parallel to the surface. A ripple appeared, as if the water were imbued with its own life-force, and very quickly the lake began to roil where hundreds and hundreds of fish had amassed and were swimming straight toward Razenbruck. As soon as the fish were within arm's reach, he began to scoop them out of the water, using his hands as strainers. Ogrino ran to the lake, jumped in, and began to do the same. In the space of twenty minutes, this miraculous catch had yielded a small hill's worth of fish, heaped on the bank. When the two friends judged that they had enough, they let plenty of escapees slip through their fingers. They got out and Razenbruck conjured up a large fire, which warmed them up immediately.

A predatory cry tore through the air as several birds of prey took flight and glided over the water toward them. With a swift movement of its talons, one of the birds snatched a large fish, still alive and wriggling, from the top of their pile. At that moment, Razenbruck threw a stone which hit the guacharo right in the head. The bird, carried by its momentum, traveled a few more meters before falling down not far from them. Ogrino dashed off and quickly returned with the game.

'Bravo!' he applauded. 'That's a nice catch, but for two it's a bit of a stretch, especially since I could eat a dozen of these!'

While he was speaking, other guacharos had begun to swoop down onto the heap of fish. Ogrino, in turn, gathered up stones and began throwing them adroitly at the birds, with such skill that in just a few moments, he and the Imp had tallied up some twenty birds.

'Now that's better!' Ogrino said. 'We've got a real meal here, with meat and fish.'

They put their catches on twigs to roast them over the fire and enjoyed the ample meal. After satisfaction came exhaustion: the exertions and emotions of the last few days had tired Ogrino out that he was yawning over and over. He quickly fell asleep, stretched out on a flat rock. Razenbruck, who didn't have the heart to wake him, curled up against him gently so as to keep the boy warm and get a little rest himself. He soon fell into a deep sleep, where he relived recent events, his hopes and fears. Would he ever see Delphania again, or would she remain the Metanor's prisoner forever? Lost in these dark thoughts, he slept fitfully.

They were rudely awakened by a noisy aerial commotion. They got up and discovered a roiling black cloud looming over them.

'Get down! Get on the ground and cover your hair!'

Ogrino didn't have the time to complete Razenbruck's order before a half-dozen creatures had fiercely latched on to his hair. He felt claws scraping his skull and pointed teeth persistently attempting to bite him. Razenbruck began an incantation and a kind of sound wave extended around Ogrino. The creatures, which he discovered were enormous bats, let go of him immediately and fell senseless at his feet. The others, stopped by an invisible wall, could not come any closer, and so turned and left.

'Are you all right? Nothing serious? Let me see your wounds,' Razenbruck said, examining Ogrino. 'It's just a scrape. In three days, it will be completely healed. Well, at least you got breakfast out of this. There are at least eight of them! I'll take one and the rest are for you.'

Recovered from the excitement, Ogrino wasted no more time in devouring the plump, tasty flyers. Then they rinsed of their faces in the lake and took up the path again. They had a long day of walking ahead of them in this sunless place, taking labyrinths of tunnels, creeping along precipices and climbing underground mountains. Finally they reached a valley whose only exit was an immense cave so tall that they couldn't see its ceiling despite the brilliant light shining from inside it.

'Those crystals are so bright they're blinding. They look like diamonds!' Ogrino said excitedly.

'Precisely, they are indeed diamonds, and among the purest as we are now at the heart of Precelestine XXXVII's kingdom.'

'Oh! But we haven't seen anyone yet.'

'That shows you aren't familiar with Pixies. They have been watching us for an hour and escorted us here. Their guards are exceptionally gifted at the art of camouflage. They can mimic anything they wish, and I challenge you to pick them out. In fact, you've got one right behind you.'

Ogrino turned quickly, looked around, and then inspected the rock more carefully. It wasn't until he was practically glued to the wall that he made out a face wearing a pointed hat.

'A Pixie!' he exclaimed.

'My name is Djill. At your service,' the sentry said, amused. 'I certainly recognized Lord Razenbruck, although it had been a long time since he has visited us. Not knowing you at all, young man, I nevertheless had to assure that no human trickery was afoot, that might harm our Little Folk, and besides it is always interesting to practice mimicry. I will lead you to our city.'

And he began to trot along happily before them, practically melting into the walls, the rocks, and the stalagmites adorning their path. He turned around periodically to wink at them. Very soon, the path opened onto a large cavern.

'Here you are,' said Djill. 'I will go take up my post again. I leave you to meet our good king. Razenbruck knows the way. See you soon! I wish you all the best.' As he disappeared, he called gaily, 'Until we meet again!'

Ogrino's eyes habituated once again to the extreme brightness here, after their journey through darkness, and now he could make out all the details of Precelestine XXXVII's cave. A whole population lived here, in what appeared to be an immense troglodytic city. The cave's walls were full of holes, making it look like a gigantic piece of Swiss cheese. The millions of openings were actually the windows of apartments, some of which opened onto little balconies that looked like swallows' nests. From time to time, one could see silhouettes pop up in the distance, in these openings that radiated golden light. On the ground, it was very different. Giant mushrooms of all different colors made up a kind of city with alleys, streets, and avenues. On each stem there was a door, and on each cap, the house's windows. The Little Folk used the entire space for shelter. A soft and industrious joy radiated from these little and, for the most part, bearded beings, who were tending to their thousand-and-one everyday tasks. Ogrino wondered if they weren't all identical, as they were dressed the same in a pointed red hat, a large white shirt, green pants, and boots.

As the two friends progressed into the crowd, only some of the Pixies greeted them, recognizing Razenbruck as most were very busy. Everywhere Ogrino looked, he saw smiths working with molten metal, armorers assembling shields and helmets, cutlers honing axes and brilliant swords. Further on, diamond cutters shaped precious stones with a thousand sparkling facets, and jewelers made infinitely elegant rings, necklaces, and earrings of silver and gold. The women, too, were very busy knitting coats of mail, or sewing legendarily tough boots. Looking at all the activity, Ogrino couldn't say whether so much work was just part of their way of life, or whether it was all due to the troubling recent events. Did they already know what was going on above the surface? He would soon discover the answer to that, for in moving through the winding alleyways, they had crossed the whole village and climbed the little hill beyond the houses, without even realizing it.

Precelestine XXXVII's throne now stood right before them. Eight tall, translucent columns with gold highlights ran up to the cave's ceiling, encircling the throne and forming little Greek temple of sorts around the ruler. Only two large statues, which looked like large lizards standing upright, bordered the entryway. Here, unlike in Delphoros's palace, there were no guards, no chamberlain. A simple, short stairway led to a gleaming chair made of pure diamond, both transparent and dense, shining with some interior light. Ogrino was fascinated. Precelestine XXXVII looked to be as old as the earth itself, with his wild white hair and long, long, immaculate beard, which was unrolled like a carpet down the steps of his throne. Deep wrinkles marked his forehead and the corners of his eyes, making them look like two little suns. Peace emanated from his deep-blue gaze, and reached into the depths of your soul. Glittering jewels arranged in spirals and flourishes adorned his pointed red hat. He wore green pants tucked into tall brown boots. On his torso, he wore a tunic of silver mail and a red coat with a thick, gray fur collar. In his right hand, he held a golden scepter, whose spiraled upper end encased a diamond.

'Razenbruck! My dear jester and Ambassador, what a joy to see you again! But what have you brought me here, a being from the World Above? I'd even say a little Ogre, from his looks.'

'O Sire! O light of the underworld! Your wisdom is without equal, and your eye sees through all! May you live to eternity! I am accompanied by a young Ogre, who despite his age has quite an unusual story. He was raised by humans and so speaks their language. Although he lived among them, he was chased by Legiferius's forces as he has become a danger to them. I will leave the rest to him as he can tell you better what he knows.'

'Well then, my child, speak with complete confidence, for if you are Razenbruck's friend, then you are equally one of ours.'

'Your Highness, I thank you for your words of confidence, and I must say that I am astonished by your kingdom's beauty and grace, and by the skill of the Little Folk. My name is Ogrino. My parents are dead, killed by the Order, and I owe my life to Razenbruck, who plucked me from Legiferius's claws. I know that they are making a plan to destroy all the peoples of the Legendary World, including yours. In less than fifteen days, they will strike as hard as they can, with dreadful weapons. Their cruelty is unrivalled, and their determination complete. It is the worst danger that the earth has ever faced, for their leader is both cunning and mad.'

While Ogrino was speaking to the king, the Little Folk had gradually approached as they could tell that important things were being said. Hundreds of uneasy and questioning faces were now observing the scene.

'Your words ring true. My people have lived among, observed, and studied humans for as long as they have been on earth, and we know them well. We know that the so-called Order of Legiferius wishes to control everything and cannot accept the existence of things it does not understand. I also know that they covet all the riches of my kingdom, whether from sheer greed, for love of money, or to grow their power with this unlimited means of financing wars and conquests. So what you have said tonight only confirms what we already knew. The important part, however, is the date. We did not know when the Order's armies would attack, and now we do. We must make haste to prepare ourselves for combat, for the Little Folk are endowed with more courage than most men.'

'Your Highness, an idea is coming to me. You are the king of the depths – the tunnels, caverns, and other catacombs. So you can show up anywhere your passages go. And if I draw the plan of the fortress for you, you could easily reach key points for Legiferius, and do them great damage.'

'That's true. We are quite familiar with Legiferius City and its damned heart, there where the Magnus Legifer lives as we have visited them from below more than once. However, we have never really been able to reach them as all of our explorers were taken with terrible headaches and had to double back quickly. The fortress is well protected, by the Docts' technology as well as by soldiers.'

'Your Highness, I might have a plan to propose . . .'

And so Ogrino talked to King Precelestine XXXVII for hours. Apart from the threat of Legiferius, they spoke of the time before humans, the Titans' wars, and of all the trials the Little Folk had faced. Through Precelestine's tales, Ogrino discovered the strength, resilience, and ingenuity of the people of the Empire Below. Such wisdom and serenity emanated from Precelestine, thanks to all his experience, which itself was due to the great length of his life. Not only did he and Ogrino exchange perspectives and ideas, but also most of all they discovered something kindred in their spirits, all under Razenbruck's mischievous eye. After their long conversation, Precelestine paused, then said to Ogrino seriously, 'Now, come! Follow me.'

The child fell in behind the old man, who continued past the throne. Precelestine lifted a thick, immaculately white curtain, which Ogrino had not noticed until then. They slipped under it, leaving Razenbruck sitting at the foot of the throne, a little frustrated at not being included. As soon as the curtain had fallen again, Ogrino discovered a dark room, weakly lit by a dozen torches. At its center stood a large stone flower, whose petals made a basin. Approaching, the child noticed that he could see his reflection in the dark water filling the bowl.

'The Mirror of Time,' Precelestine announced reverently. 'This water comes from the depths of the earth. It goes back to the origin of the world. Its power is immense, for it reaches beyond time. Any being that looks into it will see his destiny. You are courageous, despite your young age. What's more, you carry a lot of responsibility on your shoulders. So you have the right, at least, to know if you wish to. Are you ready to see your future?'

Ogrino heard himself say 'Yes' in a wavering voice. Precelestine recited a short incantation, in a language from the beginning of time. Then he moved behind Ogrino, took him by the shoulders, and placed him behind the basin. Next, he gently pushed the boy's head until his face was ten centimeters from the surface. Suddenly the water began to tremble and Ogrino's reflection was blurred. Horrible scenes appeared before the child's widened eyes. He was moving through forests on fire, cities engulfed in flames. He was taking part in bloody battles, fleeing with defeated armies, seeing magical creatures locked up in heavy chains. Everywhere he looked, there was suffering and desolation. Fear and sadness filled this vision of a people crushed by Man's brutal force. Another scene took its place and Ogrino saw himself standing before his parents, who were floating in the air, their faces blank and pale, and eyes shut. Then the Magnus Legifer appeared, smiling grotesquely.

In a voice filled with hate, he shouted at the child, 'I will destroy you before you destroy my work!'

At this, Ogrino took a step backwards in shock, and the image disappeared immediately. Still stunned by the vision, feeling revulsion and sorrow, Ogrino was deaf to Precelestine's appeals as the king whispered in his ear, 'Come back! Come back to reality!'

After a long moment, Ogrino regained his spirits, though a strong feeling of bitterness remained in him.

'It was horrible. There were dead and dying creatures everywhere. So much pain and suffering, it was disgusting. Legiferius is really abominable! We absolutely have to stop them, even if I have to personally confront the Magnus Legifer as I saw in my dream.'

'The Mirror of Time gives you a vision of what might be. What appeared there isn't necessarily what will happen as we all have free will. We have choices. Either we can act, or we can stay still, but whatever we do will affect our future. We must be the masters of our destiny . . . at least as much as is possible,' Precelestine concluded.

'I'm more determined than ever. I would do anything to stop Legiferius's evil plans. I swear it, by my parents from before!'

Full of this conviction, he looked Precelestine straight in the eyes and said warmly, 'Thank you for showing me this future because now I will never stop fighting to make sure that it doesn't happen.'

'Let us go now. All those emotions must have stirred up an appetite in you.'

'It's true. I'm starving!' Ogrino responded cheerily. The prospect of a good meal was already beginning to erase the awful dream's hold on him.

They left the room, and Ogrino once more laid eyes on the blinding light in the cave, as well as Razenbruck, who seemed surprised by the child's still-pale face.

'We're going to have a feast!' Ogrino said, to cut short any questions his friend might have wanted to ask.

He had no desire to speak of the horrors he had seen, and the thought of tasting whatever surprises Precelestine had for him was far more exciting. Then the king spoke.

'You will continue on your journey to the kingdom of the Elves, as planned, but first we will make merry in honor of our meeting. All are invited. Let the table be set and the festivities commence!'

In the blink of an eye, tables and chairs appeared before them, and magnificent tablecloths, plates, and silver covers over them. Splendid crystal glasses gleamed in the light of the big fire, lit for the occasion. As soon as Precelestine sat down, all the guests did the same. So began the banquet, a joyful gathering of at least five thousand people. Ogrino was seated to the ruler's right and Razenbruck to his left. Precelestine stood, and everyone followed his lead. He lifted his silver cup, which held a gold liquid.

'I would like to propose a toast in honor of our friends, specifically to this brave young Ogre whose destiny is leading him to face a force threatening us all. May the spirit of the Great Balance be with him, so that his perilous quest might be a success.'

When he had finished, the whole assembly proclaimed in unison, 'Long live the king, long live Razenbruck, long live Ogrino, and may the ancient spirit show him the way!'

With a single motion, everyone drank of the excellent beverage, which was sweet as honey but burned like fire.

'This is so good! What is it?' Ogrino asked Razenbruck.

'Mead. It's made from honeydew from ants. It is invigorating, but you mustn't drink too much, or else it will make your head spin.'

Then the Pixie women brought out all sorts of succulent-looking things. There were platters of fried lizard, ragout of bat, scalloped mice, and roasted rat. For vegetables, they had beetroot fries, carrots, stewed onions, and sautéed turnips. Dessert was apple cakes topped with cream of termites.

The king leaned toward Ogrino and explained, 'We are the guardians of the World Below, and we take care of the seeds of everything that lives underground. Thanks to our work, nature is reborn every spring. Flowers bloom again and trees regain their leaves. So this meal has been prepared from meats and vegetables found in the depths. It's delicious, you'll see.'

The king gestured with his arm and everyone sat down again. Merrily they pounced upon the food. Ogrino was overjoyed at the quantity and paid respect to his host by gobbling up an incredible amount of lizards, moles, fries, cakes, and cups of mead, which made him a bit tipsy and quite jolly. Peals of laughter erupted all over as apparently everyone had been drinking a little too much alcohol.

At the end of the meal, Precelestine turned to Ogrino and said, 'The time has come for your departure, Ogrino, and of course, Razenbruck will go with you. I will have two mounts prepared for you so that you can save precious time on the journey.'

He clapped twice and said loudly, 'Send for two workers!'

Immediately, a little Pixie in the crowd ran toward the edge of the cave and returned a few moments later holding two sets of reins, which were attached to two giant ants as large as workhorses. Ogrino had never imagined that such insects could exist.

Seeing his surprise, Precelestine said, 'Remember that you're in the Kingdom Below now. This world existed long before yours, and the beings which live here are descended from the beginning of the earth. Some of them have kept the mark of their ancestors. That's what's happened with these two workers, whose descendants are much smaller today. They aren't the only creatures here who are much larger that you're familiar with, for example moles, which help us dig our tunnels. Or snails, which also make good mounts – actually here comes my Royal Snail.'

Razenbruck and Ogrino turned their heads and saw before them a superb escargot a meter and a half tall, with a silver body and gold shell. A red fur blanket sat on top of the shell, serving as the base for a magnificent, finely wrought, and sparkling seat. The king walked slowly toward his mount and, with deliberate gestures, began to climb up. When he was comfortably in his seat, he spoke.

'We will accompany you to the Main Hall, where you will enter the primitive forest that borders the Elves' kingdom. There, Razenbruck, you will find my friend Themistomene, who rules over the World Above. You will tell him the news so that he, too, can prepare. Then you will ask his help in accompanying you to the edge of the Kingdom of the Elves.'

Turning to Ogrino, he added, 'As an Ambassador, Razenbruck knows Themistomene well and will introduce you to him. And now let us depart!'

A few moments later, Razenbruck and Ogrino were sitting astride the ants' necks, falling in line behind the king. A joyous little parade was on its way. The snail was advancing so quickly that the other members of the procession had to trot along to keep up. He left a glistening trail on the earth, like a thread through the labyrinth of the underground world. They passed through long tunnels and various rooms, all the while singing a seemingly endless series of merry tunes. Ogrino's heart swelled to hear the peaceful Little Folk express such sweet, simple joy. Almost despite himself, he began to sing along, not realizing that they must have been written in some age-old language. The trip passed happily in this way, and they finally reached a very large room full of stalactites and stalagmites, some of which formed thick ochre-colored columns. The ceiling was orange and the ground red. At the other end of the room, a single tunnel was the only exit.

'Here we are,' Precelestine declared. 'Soon you will reach Themistomene's world and then Felicia's. All our good wishes go with you, and we will do what we have told you.'

He dismounted and kissed Ogrino's forehead affectionately. Everything was clear now; each person knew what he had to do. Then he took Razenbruck in his arms.

'Come back to us soon as I'm eager to hear what happened to you in Delphoros's kingdom.'

Razenbruck nodded in agreement and turned to Ogrino, saying, 'So let us go! For even if this detour has been very useful, it's made us lose precious time.'

'Goodbye, everyone!' Ogrino cried. 'May the Great Balance watch over you all!'

With these words, they set off for the tunnel, the little crowd, cheering and throwing a bevy of pointed bonnets into the air. They travelled many kilometers through the darkness, their only light Razenbruck's luminous sphere since the walls were no longer made of crystal. After a long time, a feeble light appeared in front of them. Ogrino immediately recognized that glow. It was unmistakable: sunlight. Finally! Although all the underground landscapes were magnificent, they had also been a bit stifling, even oppressive. That kind of confined life, in enclosed spaces, was definitely not for him; he was undeniably an outdoor type. So when they made it to the open air, he inhaled deeply and savored the fragrances on the wind, which caressed his face for the first time in a long time.

'And now, how about a meal? I'm a good hunter. I'll take care of the game and you can make a fire, okay?'

'No problem!' Razenbruck answered.

Ogrino came back a half-hour later, pulling three fat boars behind him by their tails.

'They're so plump! There's one for you and two for me.'

'As I suspected,' was all Razenbruck said, amused.

After having roasted the beasts, they lunched, finishing with a delectable fruit salad made of berries that Razenbruck had gathered.

'Ahh, that's better,' said Ogrino, with a small burp. 'We'll be able to continue on after a little nap. What do you think?'

'I would quite like to, but we haven't the time at all. We must reach Themistomene's territory before nightfall.'

So they set off again. Ogrino's heart wasn't entirely in the journey as he could feel that the hour of their separation was approaching. It seemed that Razenbruck saw this, or even felt the same thing. In order to distract himself the Imp redoubled his efforts, so then he was tearing along at full speed down these paths that only he knew. Ogrino tried to follow him, stepping over thick roots and tall ferns, up slopes, and across streams. His heart was beating wildly and he was short of breath, but he didn't want to lose sight of his bobbing and skipping guide at any cost. So he focused all his energy on following Razenbruck's frenzied footsteps.

THEMISTOMENE

They arrived at the top of a dune overlooking a wide clearing. From their perch, they could see a stunning panorama. The clearing was surrounded by an open-air circular structure composed of twelve menhirs supporting twelve dolmens with runes engraved on them. All together they formed an imposing, awe-inspiring Megalithic temple of sorts. A spiral pathway was drawn on the ground in the middle of the monument. Looking more closely, they could see that the low walls outlining the paths were made of a multitude of vegetables. There was a profusion of carrots, rutabagas, eggplants, broccolis, squash, potatoes, cauliflower, green beans, tomatoes, pumpkins, and all sorts of strange vegetables that Ogrino had never seen before. The most shocking thing was that as you approached the middle of the spiral, the larger and more outsized the vegetables became. The zucchinis were the size of clubs, and the pumpkins as big as wardrobes. In the center, a magnificent twisted tree rose up above the gargantuan accumulation of plants. In an alcove under the tree sat a large-bellied Sprite. His face was comical, with tiny little round eyes, a pug nose, a very large mouth, and a thick black beard. His hairy belly button poked out from under his too-short blue shirt, and his pants, which were also blue, stopped at the knees, revealing his skinny calves. His feet were shod in short, brown boots that curved up at their pointed ends. He was surrounded by a dozen little maidens with goat's feet, who were playing the flute. As our friends approached, the music stopped and the portly Sprite spoke.

'Welcome to the Kingdom Above, welcome to the divine forest, welcome to my home. I am Themistomene, the ancient guardian of the woodlands. All the creatures who live here make up my people, from the Alfs, Gnomes, Sprites, Akkas, Will-o'-the-Wisps, to the Imps and Leprechauns. In this place, only the Trolls do not recognize my authority, or any other, for that matter. Here are my muses, my dear Floreannes who inspire the plants, the guardians of the grains and flora. They spread abundance and beauty wherever they go. But enough talk of us. I see that Razenbruck is here. Would my distant cousin Precelestine perhaps be in need for something, sending me his ambassador along with a little Ogre?

'Sire!' said Razenbruck. 'We thank you for your welcome. As you've guessed, we were sent by his majesty Precelestine XXXVII to notify you of a very serious situation.'

'Do you think we are blind?' Themistomene interrupted. 'The peoples Above are in closer contact with men and their barbaric practices than the Pixies Below are. We are perfectly well-informed about their actions, and I doubt you can teach us anything that we don't already know.'

'In fact, Sire, I have nothing new to report, but perhaps this child, named Ogrino, can lift the veil on some grave events to come.'

'Your Majesty, if I may allow myself,' Ogrino piped up, 'I have had the misfortune, or perhaps I should say the fortune, of a stay in the very heart of Legiferius, where I discovered their terrible plans.'

He told his whole, sad story, and when he had finished, he noticed that once more, many little creatures had gathered around him, and that each had listened attentively to his tale. Everyone was silent, and Themistomene looked to be deep in thought. Finally he spoke.

'Legiferius does not realize its folly. They are running toward their own destruction. Destroying us means destroying themselves, for we are part of the Great Balance. If you do not understand already, I'll tell you. Without us, nature would go to sleep forever. She would become barren. Everything would die and disappear. No more flowers, no more fruits, no more vegetables, and so no more animals, and then humans would die too. See what power we have! Floreasis, come here! Show our young friend the gifts we possess.'

The beautiful young lady opened a little bag that hung from her waist and pulled out a tiny yellow seed. She blew on it and the seed opened, a tender little green shoot sprang up, and began to grow very quickly, sprouting leaves that expanded before Ogrino's eyes. The stalk grew wider and taller until it had become a leafy little tree. Then lemons appeared and grew large and ripe in just a few moments.

'This is an example of our role in nature. My people do this every day. They help seeds to sprout, heal damaged trees, and rejuvenate dried-up plants. We know the earth's secrets. We are the masters of terrestrial energy. We know how to play with the flow of the earth and the cosmos. So we are the guardians of the forces of nature. If we disappear, all will become nothing. We cannot stand for that − too much is at stake. Although we are a wily people, we are not warlike. We do not know how to fight. '

Having said this, Themistomene signaled to the Floreannes, and each one quickly skipped off to stand in front of one of the pillars of the megalith. They closed their eyes and began a low murmur through closed lips. They stayed this way for a long while, suspended in time. Little by little, Ogrino began to feel a growing vibration beneath his feet. He sensed, rather than realized, that the vibration was coming from the dolmens, which formed resonance chambers for the Floreannes's humming. Now his feet and legs were quivering and the feeling began to climb up his spine. It was a strange yet pleasant sensation. Ogrino realized that Razenbruck was also experiencing the same thing. He felt good now, very good; it reminded him of his baptism at the circus. Was it possible that his parents knew such powerful secrets? He was lost in thought when the low sound and the vibrations suddenly stopped. The magic was gone. Still, he remained very calm and lucid. Ogrino's mind was clear and his thoughts precise. He felt that he had become more intelligent. He could think faster, more efficiently. It was all very remarkable.

'What did you do to us?' he asked Themistomene.

'Nothing. We only awakened your potential, the gifts that are dormant within you. If things seem a little simpler now, more obvious, it's only that you are a little more open now than before.'

'More open? You mean to say that doors have opened inside of me?'

'Yes, in a way. You now have access to as-yet unexplored corners of your being.'

'Will I regain my memories someday, the memories of my life before?'

'So you've got amnesia! Resewing the thread of memory is not easy even for me. There may be a solution, but that would require much preparation, and it doesn't always work. Alas, we haven't the time. Our priority is to counter Legiferius's plans. Faced with such a serious situation, such imminent danger, we hardly have a choice. I will call all the heads of families, hoards, and tribes so that we can organize ourselves. Our intelligence, artistry, and spells will all be of great use, but without Felicia's help, it will still be very difficult. We absolutely must warn her! She will know what to do, and her magic is so powerful!'

'Sire! We are on our way to Felicia Regina, however we had to warn you, first,' Ogrino explained.

'You have done very well! Now you must be on your way as fast as you can. I will prepare some food and a mount for you. Ogrino, you must come back and see me when peace is restored, so I can see what I can do for your amnesia.'

He made another signal toward the assembly, and a few seconds later a pair of Follets, dressed somewhat similarly to their king, brought two full knapsacks. A third arrived, sitting on an enormous caterpillar with the head of a man.

'A Processionaire!' Razenbruck exclaimed. 'I've heard tell of them but never seen one! They come from the dawn of time . . . it was born from a Pixie and a Nymph who had to flee since their relationship was not allowed. As they were chased, they hid their child in a cocoon, where he became half-man, half-caterpillar. He will be very useful on our journey, especially for travelling at night.'

'I am Bernicol,' said the Processionaire. 'I am the fastest creature in the forest, or nearly, so it won't take us long to arrive at the kingdom of the Elves. If you would kindly climb onto my back, we shall be leaving immediately.'

Ogrino and Razenbruck didn't wait for him to say this twice: they put on their knapsacks and climbed up to sit astride the Processionaire, just behind his head. As soon as they sat down, their mount stretched out his whole body, becoming incredibly long. His body seemed to reach through the whole forest. Themistomene barely had the time to say his goodbyes, and the Little Folk theirs, before Bernicol squeezed himself together again, shooting away from the clearing and toward the undergrowth. His tail passed by the laughing assembly at full speed, and he disappeared into the trees. They were, in fact, making very quick progress, but Ogrino was a little nauseous, as Bernicol pitched his riders back and forth as he moved, like a ship on a stormy sea. They also had to be careful not to get hit in the face by low branches as the Processionaire was pushing forward single-mindedly, head down, paying no attention to obstacles. After several hours on this roller coaster, Ogrino did not feel especially well and asked to get down. Bernicol stopped and the child jumped to the ground, feeling a strong urge to vomit. Razenbruck saw what was happening, uncorked his gourd, and made the child drink. The liquid was delicious, like fresh fruit juice, and very quickly Ogrino's nausea disappeared.

'Ahh, that was wonderful! I never want to drink anything else. It tasted so good, and most of all it works!'

'Let's stop for lunch,' proposed Razenbruck.

They took out hard wheat cakes which they dunked in a jar of cream. Not only did the taste surprise Ogrino, as it was like nothing he'd ever tasted before, but also he was especially shocked to notice that after a dozen or so bites, he wasn't hungry any more. It was absolutely incredible. What kind of magic was this?

'The forest-dwellers are masters at the culinary arts as they know the secrets of the plants and herbs. They are able to use plants' subtle properties to extract the essence of their power and so make nourishment that's more than mere food. You've experienced that today. You've just eaten concentrated energy. That corresponds to, shall we say, a cow and four wild boars, in your case.

'Wowee! All that! Well, all right! I never would have thought you could fit a whole cow into such a little cake!'

'Themistomene is the best cook in the world, as he, too, is very old. He is about Precelestine's age, and he knows recipes that no one has even heard of. He has great power. Some say that he can make a dish so revitalizing it makes you nearly immortal.'

'What would happen if that secret fell into Legiferius's hands?' Ogrino asked immediately.

'That would be a catastrophe, as it would give the Order unmatched power, allowing them to devote even more energy to causing trouble, and indefinitely into the future.'

A Machiavellian plan was being laid out in Ogrino's mind. Precelestine's treasure, the Mirror of Time, Delphoros's riches, and now Themistomene's immortality. And if all this persecution and this coming war were entirely based on getting ahold of all the Legendary World's treasures? It was becoming clear now. Legiferius wanted to destroy the Legendary World in order to control all its riches.

'Let's hurry!' Ogrino said right away. He couldn't stand the idea that such an outrage might be allowed to happen.

They climbed back up on Bernicol, who again took up his dazzling speed. Our friends would have made incredibly quick progress had they not finally run into a swampy area layered with fog.

'We're going to be slowed down here,' Bernicol announced. 'I have to make sure that the ground is stable enough to hold my weight.'

So a strange ballet began, in which the Processionaire lifted his head diagonally like an inchworm, then bent down to brush the ground. He tapped the earth delicately with his feet before relaxing his body, squeezing up once again, and setting off in search of another patch of solid ground. At the height of each diagonal foray, Ogrino tried to make out something despite the fog. The place was completely deserted. Who could have lived here? They heard a splash to their right. Razenbruck immediately created a ball of fire which zoomed over to the source of the noise. The flame was bright enough for Ogrino to make out human forms.

'Militians!' he whispered.

At that moment, several shots rang out and Bernicol twisted violently. His body contracted and with jerky movements bent toward the sky. Unbalanced, Ogrino and Razenbruck both fell into the muddy water. Luckily it was deep enough that they could swim. The shots continued and Bernicol struggled wildly. They could hear bodies falling into the water and cries of distress. The Militians were certainly paying for their attack on the Processionaire. The two friends were nearly to shore when they noticed a long, massive form gliding very quickly over the water toward them. Ogrino just had the time to hoist himself onto a rock and jump as far as possible onto solid ground before he heard the sound of jaws snapping shut behind him. He turned around and saw before him the enormous, hideous mouth of a water snake eagerly biting at Razenbruck's legs, which were still in the water. Razenbruck had successfully avoided being crushed by the monster twice now, but he was sliding in silt and couldn't get out of the swamp. The snake lifted its head at least three meters out of the water and pounced on its prey. At the moment, its steely teeth closed around Razenbruck, Ogrino closed his eyes so as not to faint in horror. When he opened them again, the snake was shaking its head violently. It would certainly take his best efforts to successfully swallow his victim. Ogrino was distraught. To lose his best friend so violently, in such awful circumstances! Suddenly the monster began to shake even more, writhing from left to right, anxiously coiling itself up. Finally, looking toward the sky, it opened its wide mouth, then dove down once more into the depths of the swamp, causing a forceful wave that knocked Ogrino to the ground. He stayed there, lying in the mud, crying. Life was throwing him one thing after another. He had the responsibility of a difficult task on his shoulders, and everyone closest to him had been taken away, one after another. Why? Whatever could he have done to deserve so much misfortune?

A deafening buzz shook him from his dark thoughts. He lifted his eyes and saw, hovering in the air in front of him, an enormous wasp, which was staring at him. Ogrino recoiled, looking on the ground for a branch he could use as a weapon against this belligerent-looking insect. Before he could find anything, the wasp disappeared in a tinkling of bells, leaving only Razenbruck, smiling with pleasure at his trick.

'Dry your eyes, I'm safe and sound. You didn't really think I would let myself be defeated by that brainless monster!'

'You gave me quite a scare!'

'You shouldn't have worried. The snake didn't know who it was dealing with. I've got more than one trick up my sleeve! All I had to do was transform at the moment it closed its mouth, and I was in the perfect position to make it pay for its stupidity and nerve. I had the pleasure of stinging its palate and gums and the inside of its throat. My venom will have the monster in pain for quite a while. It will not cause us any problems.'

'Oh Razenbruck, you really are the best. I'm so glad nothing happened to you.'

The two friends hugged and Ogrino quickly forgot his sadness. The sounds of explosions, shouts, crashes, and falls from the water interrupted their outpouring of emotion. The Militians must have been engaged in a relentless battle not far away.

Perhaps because of the fighting, the layers of fog had somewhat dissipated, and Ogrino could make out what was happening before them. The snake was coiled around the soldiers' boat and had one of them, screaming, in its mouth. It dropped him and lunged toward another one, seizing him by the head. The others tried to shoot it with their crossbows, but that proved difficult as the boat was shaking wildly. The snake spit out its lifeless prey in order to attack the survivors. One shot reached the beast's left eye, and it clenched his muscles. As its coils tightened, the boat broke in half. The Militians fell into the water and the monster, too, disappeared into the depths. As the soldiers swam toward the little island where our heroes sat, Razenbruck noticed a black shape underwater, heading toward the first survivors. One after another they disappeared, swallowed up by the monster, and not one reached the shore.

'Well, that's over with,' said Razenbruck with relief. 'The snake must be full now and the Militians won't be giving us any trouble. We have to find Bernicol. Wait here for me. I'm going to take a look.

He immediately transformed into a bald eagle, whose piercing vision would allow him to find the Processionaire. He took to the air majestically, letting out a strident cry. No more than five minutes later, he landed on the island again. Returning to his normal form, he told Ogrino sadly, 'Bernicol is injured. The Militians opened up his side and broke four of his feet. He's in pain.'

'He's not going to die, is he?'

'The wound is fairly deep, but he's not in mortal danger. It's just that his movement will be considerably slower. Well, look, there he is.'

His wide head appeared in the fog. He tried to put on a smile but ended up with a grimace.

'These damned soldiers of Legiferius are only here to bring death. This time, however, they've paid dearly. It's only justice—look at my wounds.'

Razenbruck leaned in and observed the gash on his side, which was oozing blood and water. He put his right hand on the wound, closed his eyes, and began to chant a spell.

He continued this for a good fifteen minutes, then stepped back and said, 'There, you're practically healed. You'll still have to be careful as it will be very sensitive for several days. As for your feet, if you do not walk on them for one moon-cycle, they will heal on their own.'

Bernicol looked wide-eyed at the place where only a few moments before there had been a gaping hole and saw nothing more than a pale scar.

'Goodness, thank you, a million times thank you! You are a great magician, perhaps stronger than Themistomene as far as healing is concerned. Do not tell him that, though, or he will be upset.'

'I don't think that's true. Themistomene knows secrets I couldn't even dream of. I know because once, when I was already Precelestine's ambassador, he showed me the extent of his powers. It was a particularly harsh winter, following a dry summer. Food was short and many of the villagers were suffering from the famine. Pushed on by hunger, they were venturing ever deeper into the forest in search of game, chestnuts, acorns, or tubers. One day, a group of about twenty men went so far in that they were on Themistomene's territory. The king and I were having a conversation at the World Above's entrance to one of the tunnels, at the bottom of a crevasse. We heard voices coming from the top of the cliff. We could make out what they were saying. They were discussing whether to cross the fault using a fallen tree that had formed a natural bridge. The first of the men advanced cautiously, testing the trunk's stability. He was halfway across the bridge when the tree started to turn to the side. The poor man lost his balance and fell off. However, he was able to catch a branch. Some other brave souls came to help him, but by the time they arrived, he had unfortunately lost his grip and fallen to the bottom of the abyss.

'We had seen this all play out, powerless as everything had happened so fast. The man was lying not far from us while his companions were shouting and gesticulating on top of the cliff. Then they disappeared and there was silence. We approached the victim, who was lying on his stomach and bleeding from the head. Themistomene leaned over, then looked at me, and said, 'He's still breathing. Help me put him on his back.'

'We turned him over very carefully and were horrified to see that his abdomen had been torn open, so his organs were visible. His caved-in ribcage looked like a W. On his forehead was a wide gash running from his right eye to his left ear. He was frightful to look at and hadn't long to live. Even with magic, I would only have been able to ease his suffering, to give him a peaceful death. That's when Themistomene took a vial from his pocket and let about thirty drops fall through the man's parted lips. Despite being quite used to magic, I was stunned to see the man's torso immediately regain its shape, his stomach close up, and the scar disappear from his face. His breathing became stronger and more regular, and the victim opened his eyes. He looked at us, seemingly unafraid, and smiled.

'Where am I? I had the strangest dream. I was flying through the air when suddenly I felt a sharp pain and fell into a black, bottomless well. Finally a bright light appeared at the end of a silver tunnel. Elves and Pixies were dancing around me when one of them, who looked exactly like you, whispered to me, saying 'Come back. It's not your time. Gather your strength and come back.' And that's when I opened my eyes and saw you two.'

'Welcome to the world of men and Pixies. You washed up on the shores of the beyond, but here you are, come back to your own life and friends. Actually, they will be here any minute now. Sit up.'

'Even as the man began to push himself to a sitting position, his friends ran up and began to shout in joy.

'Are you all right? What did you break? Where are you hurt?'

'I'm all right, I'm not hurt. It's completely miraculous, but I'm unharmed!'

'Unharmed! After a fall like that? It's impossible!'

'Then ask these people, the two here behind me.'

'But there's no one behind you. What are you talking about?'

'What!' he said, turning around.

'In fact, Themistomene and I had made ourselves invisible as the Legendary World has to keep a certain distance from humans.

'What! But where did they go? They were just there! I'm certain that a stout Pixie helped me. He's the one who saved me.'

'A Pixie! Now you're seeing Pixies! No doubt it's shock. Your fall must have been broken by the plants growing along the wall, but you must have hit your head, and it's making you hallucinate. You've been lucky! You ought to have died after a fall like that. We'll light a candle for Saint Rita, the patron saint of lost causes.'

'I would like to say a thankful prayer here and now as it was the beings of this forest who saved me.'

'So everyone took the same humble posture and began to pray silently but fervently. Themistomene became visible again and waited, stationary, in the middle of the group. When they opened their eyes, they were quite surprised to discover this bizarre, yet very kindly looking creature among them.

'It's him. It's the one who helped me!' the man who had fallen said fervently. 'I told you so! I didn't dream it!'

'My dear friends. We, the beings of this forest, rarely appear to humans as the Legendary World has its own laws. We often help you without your knowledge as we are protectors of all forms of life. Today I've done a little more than is usual but for a good reason. My name is Themistomene, and now you know

I exist as I have permitted you to see me. To seal our friendship, I propose that you make a pilgrimage each year, on the winter solstice, to the heart of my Dolmen. You will find it on your left as you leave southward. I will teach you some of my craft there so that you will be able to heal yourselves as well.

'Thank you, a million times thank you!' said the man, falling at Themistomene's feet.

'Stand up. I saved you because you have a good soul, and I know that you will accomplish great and good things over the course of your long life. Before we part company, tell me, what is your name?'

'Pantaleone."

Hearing this name, Ogrino jumped.

'Pantaleone is my adopted father!' he declared.

'Oh goodness!' Razenbruck exclaimed. 'What a small world. So they weren't villagers, but rather the Wind People. That is why they know secrets that other humans do not. They are more open to nature's mysteries, and they practice magic.'

'All right,' said Bernicol. 'That's all very well, but we must be moving along. This place gives me goosebumps.'

So the two friends jumped up onto the Processionaire's neck, and he squeezed himself up, ready to set off into the mist once again. In that way, they traveled very far as the marshes stretched over a great distance. Finally they arrived on more solid, although somewhat spongy, ground.

'What lies ahead is hardly more pleasant than the marshes,' said Razenbruck. 'Soon we will be in a place filled with noxious gases.'

'Yes,' said Bernicol, 'and actually, I won't be accompanying you much farther.'

With that, they arrived at a thick wall of brambles. Bernicol traveled along it, not getting too close as the spines were large and pointy. Just brushing against them would have caused a painful wound, especially because of the thick, poisonous sap oozing from the thorns.

'The bramble labyrinth,' Razenbruck announced. 'This place is extremely dangerous. You can easily get lost or pricked by poisonous thorns. It serves as a kind of protection for the Elf world, as crossing it is quite a trial and even the most tenacious of men think thrice before venturing into its corridors.'

A violent explosion ripped through the air and Bernicol contorted in pain, bleeding from his side. Ogrino, unbalanced by the Processionaire's jolting, fell to the ground just as a new volley of projectiles rained down upon them. Razenbruck had thrown himself down to avoid the bullets. Bernicol twitched once more, this time because of a shot to the neck. Waves of blood spilled from his wound, and shortly he stopped moving. His face was ghostly white. His expression, however, was no longer one of pain, but rather serenity. He looked like he was sleeping. A troop of soldiers was already advancing toward them. Where were they coming from? Were they the same ones from the marshes? Had one boat been able to escape the snake? Protected by their deceased friend's imposing body, Ogrino and Razenbruck wept as they looked at their former companion. How many more victims would the Order leave in its wake? How many more friends would be sacrificed before Ogrino's quest could be achieved?

However, they couldn't grieve freely at the moment, as another explosion right near them sent dirt clods flying. Luckily, they were unhurt but for a few scratches. Through the thick but dissipating smoke, Ogrino saw a hole in the wall of brambles. Without a second thought, he pulled his friend by the sleeve and they dove into the passageway. Before the tufts of smoke had dissipated completely, the fugitives had evaporated. The Militians found only footprints in the muddy earth, leading toward the center of the labyrinth.

'One squadron take the right with Rector Nolius and the other come with me,' Commander Pavius boomed imperiously.

The men were creeping carefully between the labyrinth's walls when one of them cried out, 'They're here. I see one!'

So Pavius's group retraced its path to join the other troops and give chase to the escapees. Ogrino didn't turn around. He ran until he was breathless, all the while trying not to make any noise. Razenbruck, behind him, kept turning his head to see if they were being followed. Every fifty meters or so the path would fork in two or three directions, and Razenbruck would unhesitatingly indicate one, which they would immediately rush into. Apparently they were safe now as they could neither see nor hear anything suspect. So little by little the tension dropped, and Ogrino stopped for breath.

'We'll rest later,' Razenbruck said in response, still anxious.

'But you distracted them by appearing in the opposite direction to set them on the wrong trail,' the little Ogre replied.

'You can't be too careful when the Militians are involved. They could retrace their path or cross straight through walls, thanks to their weapons or I don't know what kind of trickery.'

A screech from the sky made them lift their heads. A falcon was circling above them, observing them with its sharp eyes.

'That's not a good sign,' said Razenbruck. 'That cursed bird may well be in the Militians' service. It's spotted us and surely alerted them, and they won't waste any time in coming here. We must leave as quickly as possible, but first I've got something to do.'

With a soft tinkling of bells, Ogrino saw his friend disappear and a magnificent bald eagle that rose into the air at an astounding speed. The falcon was already fleeing, followed more and more closely by the eagle. Moved by a survival instinct, the bird dove toward its masters at top speed. Razenbruck accelerated even more and swooped down on his prey at the very moment that the first shots rang out. He crushed the falcon's neck with his powerful claws and let go of his victim just above the Militians. As they redoubled their efforts to shoot him, Razenbruck's vigorous wingbeats sent him out of range just in time. On high, he circled directly above his pursuers, taunting them with his calm, while they must have been boiling with rage at not being able to reach him. He doved and perched next to Ogrino, and transforming back, said to him, 'So we're safe for a little while now. Let's go!'

Legiferius's furor must have been inexhaustible, for they had barely taken up their path again when a torrent of explosions rained down around them, causing little fires to spring up and rapidly grow.

'Follow me and run as fast as you can. They must have calculated our position, and they're aiming at us blindly. Even if their shots may not be very accurate, they could hit us by chance.'

They began to flee once again, as behind them fountains of fire, earth, and smoke sprang up like gloomy fireworks.

After about fifteen minutes of frenzied running, Razenbruck judged that they were out of range and motioned to Ogrino to stop. The child could go no farther. So his friend opened a little pouch and took out one of Themistomene's cakes, which they shared. Although the quantity was minuscule in comparison with Ogrino's appetite, he could feel the pastry's benefits with each bite. He regained his strength and with it, his confidence.

'Let's start again now as we should leave the labyrinth before nightfall—it's safer.'

Gradually, evening fell and the light disappeared, making the place more sinister by the second. The thick, thorny bushes closed in on them as they went along. The labyrinth's walls formed a funnel, and with each step they had to be more careful not to cut themselves. During the long, arduous walk, Ogrino, who was having a lot of trouble avoiding the brambles, became more and more stressed. Finally Razenbruck signaled to him to stop. The alley they were in formed a cul-de-sac. They were stuck. *They had come all this way for nothing,* Ogrino thought, despairing. Razenbruck, on the other hand, closed his eyes and began to recite a spell in a language that Ogrino didn't understand, but found enchanting, so crystalline were its tones. And by magic, the bushes parted, giving way to a forest of outsized ferns. Razenbruck began to run again, getting a second wind, despite the surrounding night. Ogrino had trouble following him as he was tired from all their recent trials. Still, he tried not to let himself fall behind. He didn't know how long they would have to keep running like this, and he was beginning to despair, looking at all that was asked of him. Though he may have been an Ogre, he was nonetheless still a child. And then, all of a sudden, Razenbruck stopped short before a high wall, ivory in color that stuck out from behind the treelike ferns. The wall was smooth and, strangely, free from any moss or lichen growth. Nature seemed not to want to soil its surface as a mark of deference to what it represented. An arch was cut out of the wall, a cyclopsian eye allowing a glimpse of a path beyond the high wall. Razenbruck turned to his friend with a half-sad, half-joyful look.

'Here we are, at the place where my path ends and yours begins. I am not allowed to go any farther as this is the beginning of the Elf kingdom, and no Pixie, Gnome, or Sprite can enter here. You, on the other hand . . . you are invited and indeed eagerly awaited. So go, don't drag your feet! It's almost straight ahead, and anyway you'll have other guides. You can't go wrong. So go, follow your destiny. Goodbye! We'll meet again when this is all over.'

'Before we part ways,' said Ogrino, 'I wanted to tell you that our meeting has been one of the best gifts life has ever given me. I will never forget you, and you will always be my friend.'

A fat tear ran down his cheek and Razenbruck, his eyes brimming, smiled sadly.

He hugged Ogrino tightly, looked him straight in the eyes, and whispered, 'You must know that you have also given a lot to me. True friendship is always shared. I won't ever forget you, either. And now, Godspeed and farewell!' he called, and vanished in the darkness.

FELICIA REGINA

Ogrino stood there alone, a little indecisive, not knowing what to do. But his curiosity was so great that his desire to discover this strange and marvelous world won out. Night had fallen and enveloped the child in its inky blackness. It was at that moment that little fireflies began to circle about his face. His eyes widened as he saw that these seven minuscule luminous creatures were half-man, half-dragonfly. Their wings were translucent and yet emanated a soft, silvery light. The seven messengers fluttered around Ogrino for a few moments and then flew off in single file. Captivated, Ogrino could do nothing but follow them. As they progressed, it seemed to Ogrino that the night was fading as if the sun were timidly beginning to rise, but it was not even midnight. Gradually, a path appeared in the middle of a luminous meadow.

After a period of time that seemed both extremely long and quite short, Ogrino noticed that the whole forest was bathed in a silvery light. He looked more carefully marveled to see that this light was caused by the presences of millions and millions of elves who were waiting to welcome him. A soft, contagious joy emanated from this silent multitude.

With each step, Ogrino felt more and more joyful as if he were going to see someone dear to him that he had not seen in a long time. He had not felt so good since the time Tiboursio had caused his parents appear to him in the smoke from his magic fire.

At the end of a long curve in the path, he was astonished to see an immense tree appear, sparkling in a golden light. Its trunk was enormous as wide as eight castle-towers set side by side. And its height! It was as tall as twelve fortresses stacked one on top of another. It was conical like a gigantic fir tree, but its leaves were diamond-shaped, and its branches were so thick they made the tree look like a monumental pyramid.

Ogrino was enthralled by all this beauty. Such nobility. Such a feeling of strength and life emanated from this tree that the little Ogre almost expected it to speak. The most unbelievable part was that it was glittering, sparkling like a crystal, shining like a thousand suns. The closer Ogrino got, the more this botanical being's majesty impressed him. He felt that he was growing smaller and smaller, minuscule, like a tiny speck of dust compared to this oversized giant, with its enormous roots and its top that seemed to be planted in the sky.

'Gigantum' is the name that suddenly resounded in his head as if someone had spoken to him from within. It was very strange; the feeling of being insignificant was mixed with that of being welcomed like someone important. Small and large—that was how Ogrino felt as he approached this admirable tree.

Now he was very close, and he could make out the millions and millions of Elves that were practically encrusted in the tree's trunk, branches, and even leaves. Not a square centimeter of the immense being lacked an occupant. Ogrino would never have imagined that something so beautiful could exist, and yet he had the feeling that he had always been a part of this beauty since the dawn of time.

Still following his little guides, he found himself at the foot of the Gigantum, between two enormous roots as tall as city walls. They came together to an immense, majestic doorway, whose bark formed a very ancient script.

'Writing from before humans existed,' Ogrino thought.

The shapes looked indecipherable to him, and yet he automatically scanned them from left to right and a meaning popped into his head: 'Welcome all with pure intentions. Others will confront their personal demons.'

He would have liked to linger but already his guides were circling around his head and then lining up single-file again, inviting him to enter. As soon as he crossed the threshold, his wonderment grew. He felt as if he was going from surprise to surprise as if someone were giving him presents, each one better than the last.

Now he was in the heart of the tree if this being could still be called a tree. The inside was hollow at least as far as Ogrino could see. It looked like a gigantic cathedral with imposing columns, a ceiling so high it seemed invisible, and still this golden light emanating from everything. Before Ogrino's eyes, at the center of this sublime room, an immense, snow-white spiral staircase rose toward the sky like a majestic tree inside the Gigantum.

Ogrino could make out a translucent crystal egg with gold and silver highlights at the top of the stairs. From where he stood, the egg looked to be small, but it was so high above him. Ogrino felt calmly drawn to this egg as if he knew that something familiar awaited him there.

He crossed the room toward the staircase, preceded by his guides, and put his foot on the first step. Although nothing had moved, the staircase gave the impression of being alive or, rather, boiling with life. It seemed to be contagious, for suddenly Ogrino no longer felt tired from his long night-time run through the forest. He took the stairs four by four like it was nothing, and in no time, he was at the top of the staircase on a big white forecourt just in front of the egg, which now seemed monumental. It was made of crystal cut into diamond-shaped facets half as big as a hand, which were alternately silver and gold and others silver. In addition to the beauty of this geometry, pink, blue, and yellow reflections glinted through the egg periodically. From all this emanated an intense, invigorating feeling of life, even more powerful than what Ogrino had experienced stepping onto the staircase.

There was a large porch around the entrance to the egg as well. Engraved on the porch's summit were the same letters that had been on the arch. However, this time the phrase proved to be shorter, and only 'Welcome' was written as if having arrived here, he couldn't be otherwise. The fact of being able to climb all those stairs had to mean that one was expected and accepted.

When Ogrino entered the egg, a golden rain fell delicately on him and he felt a peaceful joy. All fear, anger, and desire for vengeance left him. He was now floating in total serenity. A gentle, yet profound feeling took hold in him. At the center of the egg, there was another staircase with very large, crescent-shaped steps that shimmered, as they appeared to be encrusted with diamonds. Half-blinded, Ogrino carefully climbed each of the nine steps that led to a vast platform. Seven large, concave seats were arranged in a semicircle there, the most majestic one in the centre towering over the others. It was decorated with the same ancient writing as the Gigantum. The letters gleamed brilliantly. 'Balance is in everything.' Ogrino had instinctively decoded the phrase, but, nevertheless, did not understand it. Then a pure, crystalline, melodious voice arose, a soft, feminine voice that inspired respect.

> *The ancient legacy has been entrusted to you.*
> *Link between the human world and our own,*
> *From the dawn of time, your destiny was known.*
> *You must be our ambassador to the world of men,*
> *That the Great Balance may be upheld again.*
>
> *Time is against us, that much is true,*
> *But rally each pure-hearted woman and man,*
> *And you may succeed in this grand, noble plan.*
> *In that, all creatures will come to your aid,*
> *All legendary peoples join in your crusade.*
>
> *They will answer at once, you need only ask,*
> *As you hold in your hands one particular prize.*
> *Your courage and will are your dearest allies,*
> *And thanks to what I give you now, you shall achieve your task.*

After a long silence, the one whose voice had enchanted Ogrino's heart came forward. He could finally see her clearly away from the throne's glare that had shielded her from view until now. She was a young, graceful woman. Everything about her radiated beauty. Her long hair was silver, and her face blindingly white, which brought out her emerald eyes, with their soft yet penetrating gaze that inspired trust. She was dressed in a long toga, also silver, that trailed on the ground as if she were one with the egg. Two large, translucent butterfly wings, gold and silver, sprung from her back and nearly met in front, giving her a large, queenly ruff. On her head, a silver crown with botanical designs completed her imperial look.

'Felicia Regina.' Ogrino immediately saw that the name fit her perfectly. He was standing before the Fairy Queen of the Elves, and he was charmed by her marvelous presence. His heart was beating very hard in his chest. He was so moved that he couldn't take another step, only look at her and bask in her aura.

He saw that people who had been sitting in the other chairs were now advancing toward him. Six tall men had made an arc around the queen, three on her left and three on the right. They, too, looked young and astonishingly like the queen, although they were larger and more muscular. Their delicate faces, their long silver hair, and their togas were completely identical to the queen's. They looked like septuplets.

The seven Elves approached and formed a circle around Ogrino, then they all rested a hand lightly on Ogrino's head and said in unison,

Ages upon ages before the first man's birth,
Already ancient was the great Gigantum.
It is the meeting point of heaven and earth,
Of all forms of Life, it is Father and sum.
The forces of the Great Balance live in this tree.
We are its seven branches and eternal guard,
So that its creative energy might ever flow free,
And earth's harmony never be marred.

Then they stopped. All was silent, and Ogrino felt a soft warmth radiate from their hands and travel through his head. Suddenly, ephemeral images passed before his eyes like a film on fast-forward. He saw the creation of the world, saw oceans form on the earth's surface, mountains rise into the sky, volcanoes erupt with torrents of lava, and the Gigantum appear, and then forests spread over the globe's surface, interspersed with verdant meadows. Then all sorts of living things paraded by. Elves by the millions, Sirens, Tritons, Pixies, Gnomes, Sprites, and a thousand and one other magical creatures. The Ogres were the last to appear, the last link on the long chain of the Legendary World. For each being, an unforgettable name rang out in Ogrino's head. Then he saw mornings, nights, dawns, and twilights, one after another on to infinity. Finally, innumerable animals of all sorts appeared, many unknown to him, and then the picture stopped with man, the final being of all creation.

> *The secrets of the Chain of Life unfurled*
> *Here, that you might realize what's at stake*
> *And in your quest protect all life you meet.*
> *You may call upon the vast Legendary World;*
> *All its beings will aid you for that name's sake*
> *And serve you as allies, until all is complete.*

Silence reigned once more, and Ogrino felt honored that these marvelous beings entrusted him with such precious knowledge. A feeling of great confidence came over him. He felt that from now on he could not fail in this mission. It seemed to him that he could not help but succeed and that it had been written this way always.

The six Elf guardians of the Gigantum retreated, leaving only the queen before Ogrino. She took off a necklace that dangled on her chest and placed it on Ogrino's neck. A shining diamond made of smaller gold and silver diamonds with pastel pink, blue, and yellow reflections hung from a silver thread—a leaf of the Gigantum. The little Ogre was sure of it, It was a leaf from the tree or perhaps a piece of the egg or even both at the same time as everything seemed to be one with everything else at the heart of Gigantum.

The queen looked Ogrino in the eyes for a long time, smiling, and he felt himself melt overcome by intense happiness. He was hypnotized; he could no longer look away from her. He would have happily stayed there for eternity, breathing in her fragrance, losing himself in the immense depth in her eyes. She spoke softly and Ogrino's heart leapt up.

This leaf is your link to our world; carry it wherever you go.
As you take it in your two hands, it will begin to glow,
And any creature you call upon will come be your escort,
For it will hear you leagues and leagues away.
You must return to the City, for time is short;
Our hopes and good wishes are with you every day.
Go confidently, fear nothing; you will never be alone again.

From their very first words, the queen and guards had spoken in verse, and this last line was only more powerful for its lack of rhyme. For years, ever since Legiferius had made him an orphan, Ogrino had felt frightfully alone, despite all the love and attention of his new friends. No one had been able to fill the empty place left by his real parents, not even Pantaleone or Slevania, and today, he felt deep within him that this long solitude had ended. An invisible, but very strong thread would connect him forevermore with these fantastic creatures who had paraded through his head and whose names he now knew. But above all, he felt personally linked to Felicia Regina. Felicia, the most marvelous of women, whom he had been privileged to meet. As he left, he had only one thought in his head—to see her again. When he arrived at the staircase, he saw with astonishment that it had become smooth; the steps had disappeared. It was now an immense slide. The seven little guides who had accompanied him thus far fluttered above its surface, inviting him to go down without fear. Ogrino joyfully threw himself forward and began to slide. He picked up more and more speed. The air against his face, the thousands of sparkles zooming past his eyes—it was magical and entirely intoxicating. He swirled around like this for long minutes and when he arrived at the bottom of the staircase, he naturally slowed down, without effort, and glided to a stop. As soon as he had set foot into the big room once more, it occurred to him that he needed a fast and reliable way to get back to Legiferius City. Of all the creatures that he had seen parading through his head, one had particularly struck him, and now was the time to call upon her. He took the leaf of the Gigantum, which was hanging on his necklace, in both hands and began to focus very hard on this creature, and then said her name. He opened his eyes but nothing seemed to have happened, no magical creature had appeared. Ogrino, disappointed, left the Gigantum and walked out into the forest. It was there that he saw her, a magical and peaceful being, feasting on the young grass not three hundred paces away. Had she always been there? Had she come to answer his call? Ogrino wasn't sure as she was so calm and looked so much a part of the area's beauty. A Unicorn!

Ogrino was utterly fascinated by this magnificent animal with her glittering white coat, long wavy mane, almond-shaped eyes, and spiraled horn. She stepped forward, powerful and proud, toward Ogrino.

'You called me. Here I am. My name is Viastella, and I will bring you where you need to go to complete your mission.'

This phrase sounded in Ogrino's head, and he was certain had come from the Unicorn, although she had not moved her lips. She lowered her head and turned toward Ogrino.

'Take my horn with both hands.'

The little Ogre didn't have to be asked twice. He gripped the horn and felt waves of gentleness emanating from it. The Unicorn lifted her head in one smooth motion, and suddenly, Ogrino found himself seated comfortably on the animal's back, and she began to walk. Ogrino, utterly filled with joy, said, 'We have to get to Legiferius City as fast as possible.'

He had barely finished his phrase when Viastella began to gallop. Ogrino could feel below him the powerful muscles of this animal at top speed. Despite this, he wasn't jolted around or shaken up at all. Rather, he felt like he was gliding along a frozen lake. It was altogether very agreeable. The trees flew past him at incredible speeds. Ogrino had never moved so fast. It was like leaping into open air, except that they were moving straight ahead. It was an incredibly exhilarating feeling. He was delightfully euphoric, though he had drunk no wine, no nectar. After the trees came two rows of faces, dozens and dozens of astonished yet smiling faces, lined up infinitely on either side of Viastella's rapid route. It took Ogrino a bit of time to realize what was going on. Drawn in both by the Unicorn and by the shining diamond worn by her rider, a multitude of forest creatures had gathered around their path. Ogrino now realized with amazement the incredible power of the leaf and through it, Felicia . . . unless it was the power of the Gigantum itself. Despite the intoxication of the journey, Ogrino suddenly felt the desire to stop and meet all these oncoming beings. He brushed Viastella's neck with his hand and, immediately, understanding, she slowed her pace and came to a gentle stop. At once, a circle of questioning eyes formed around them.

'My friends! We have been sent from Felicia Regina to fight Legiferius!' he announced at the top of his lungs, still seated on his mount.

The Gnomes, Pixies, and Leprechauns surrounding them looked perplexed.

'You will soon be attacked by humans, and you must prepare yourselves for this great battle. Until now, your families have been subject to soldiers' attacks, and perhaps you've lost some friends or even loved ones. But this is different, a battle of huge proportions. A real war is brewing, and no one will be safe from it. You must spread the news to everyone as fast as possible. Everyone must prepare themselves. Join together, find provisions, make weapons, and be ready, for in a few moons' time, there will be a big attack.'

As Ogrino spoke, the Gigantum leaf had begun to shimmer and then to shine with unequaled brightness. Seeing this, all the forest beings took off their bonnets, hats, and other head coverings and put a knee to the ground as a sign of allegiance. Ogrino didn't know what to do with himself; he was so intimidated by all of this. He, a child, a young Ogre, had hundreds bowing before him. Who was he to deserve such trust and respect? Henceforth, he felt a great responsibility toward all the peoples of the Legendary World. It was both a crushing and thrilling feeling. He found himself the defender of a strange, seductive, lively world, which had to rise up against a ruthless, cruel, and determined invader.

This was the path his life had taken since Legiferius had imprisoned him, or had it been before that, years before even, since that fateful hunt in which his parents from before had died? Unless it had always been written this way, and unless it was his destiny. A little voice inside him told him that he always had his free will. His life belonged to him. It was up to him to know where he wanted to go. So it was seeing the success of his improvised assembly that Ogrino had the idea to start over, farther back on the road leading to the city. Then he thought twice and realized that he would have to go warn and rally all the different communities, even daring to go see the Trolls.

'Change of plans', he thought.

Right away, Viastella began to move once more, slowly at first, then faster and faster, taking a right toward the Black Mountains, where the monstrous Trolls lived. Despite the fact that this foray into Troll territory was a long detour, they were there in no time at all, so nimble was Viastella's gallop. Night had just fallen so the time was ideal to meet the Trolls if one had to speak with them at all. While Ogrino was confident in the leaf's powers, he was, nevertheless, worried about the Trolls' reaction when they discovered an intruder venturing onto their land. Although he could not remember his fight with one of their kind, he had always carried within him an imprint of the fear these monsters inspired in him. Viastella, perceiving Ogrino's turmoil, told him, in a whisper inside his head, 'Do not fear. I am here, and Gigantum is present, too.'

Her words, once more ringing out in the child's head, were like a soothing balm to him, and he was filled with serenity.

Luckily, so, for at that moment, they heard a crackling on their left and turning their faces, they saw a couple of Trolls approaching, breaking branches on their way.

'Do nothing. Say nothing. Don't move. Only make sure the diamond is visible.'

The two Trolls, each one more than five meters tall, trained their glassy, myopic eyes on Ogrino, rumbling something that sounded like 'GROOMPF, GROOMPF.'

In Troll language, this meant, 'You are on our territory, and the punishment for this crime is death.'

Viastella lifted her head, and her declaration rang out thunderously in Ogrino's and the Trolls' heads.

'We have been sent by Felicia Regina, and the child bears the sacred leaf you see here.'

Ogrino stuck out his chest, pushing forward the Gigantum's leaf, which he took in his hand to display to the Trolls. The diamond began to sparkle and suddenly there was a light in the monsters' eyes. They tilted their heads and one of them said sharply, 'We could not have known. We respect Felicia even though we do not consider her our queen. What do you want?'

'War is on the horizon. The humans want to destroy us all,' said Viastella. 'Even the Trolls are threatened, and we must unite if we do not want to disappear.'

'We Trolls are not afraid to fight. Let the little humans come. We will make mash for our children out of them. We have already eaten dozens of them, but this will be a real feast.'

Ogrino could not understand what they were saying but saw that they did not want to cooperate.

He murmured to Viastella, 'Tell them that they have terrifying weapons, capable of destroying a horde of Trolls in just a few moments.'

Viastella relayed the information, and the Trolls began to laugh, throwing their heads back.

'Destroy a whole horde. Ha, ha, ha, that's impossible. It's never been done. Only old Trolls are sometimes captured by humans, but never young Trolls in their prime, and what's more, in groups. If that is all you have to say, then you can be on your way.'

'Do you think that Felicia would give one of Gigantum's leaves to a little Ogre if she had not given him an important mission?'

'That's true, it is strange. But we do not think the Trolls are in danger. No one comes through here. No man has ever ventured onto our territory. If it happens, we will gobble them up.'

'Except that they are armed, trained to fight you and they know your weak points,' said Ogrino. 'I've seen it with my own eyes. Trolls like you, prisoners in big glass tanks in Fort Legiferius. They looked pitiful in a state between life and death. The humans did horrible experiments on them to discover your weaknesses and to learn to destroy you more easily. What's more, they have giant weapons that can easily capture several Trolls at once. What they have done, they can do again, and this time on a larger scale. They are cruel and determined, so no one is safe. Join us so that we can crush Legiferius before they crush us.'

Viastella translated again. The Trolls looked at each other incredulously. They deliberated for a moment before announcing,

'What you say may be true, but until there has been a real threat to our people, we have no reason to take part in your war. We do not have a chief or a king. We live free. We gather from time to time to celebrate the full moon, but we are mostly solitary.

'The full moon is in four days,' Viastella said. 'I propose that you discuss this then, for maybe some of you have caught wind of some information. If you change your minds, form as large a group as possible, walk westward for seven nights, following the blue river, and wait for us by the big waterfall.'

'Bah! Why would we waste time doing that? We are not migrating birds, and we answer to no one.'

'Think about it. If there is great danger brewing and you are at Felicia's side, you can count on her magic. If not, you fight alone.'

'That is what we have always done. With that, goodbye!'

THE PRELATE'S HOMILY

For the final phase of his diabolical plan, Primus called in Tertius, who, immediately upon arriving heard this, 'I have a mission for you personally, Tertius, and when I say personally, I mean that I wish for only you to know about it. I want you to spy on the Prelate. I have need of him for our plans, but first, I want to be sure of his allegiance to our cause. So use any means in your power to find out what he thinks of our schemes. I also want a detailed report of our troops' morale levels and most of all of the opinions of the general population, who can be so unpredictable. For these two tasks, use your informers. I want as large a survey as possible so that we leave nothing to chance.'

'As always, you are very organized and forward-thinking, qualities of a truly great leader,' said Tertius obligingly. 'As far as the population, of course, I will survey them, but, you know, with all our propaganda about the dangers of creatures of the Legendary World and all the captures that have brought order to our villages, the citizens fully support us.'

'One can never be too sure,' Primus resolved.

'Of course, but I would be more careful of the Church, whose doctrine might, to some degree, differ from the Order's.'

'For the moment, we need the Church's support to ensure that our control of popular opinion remains complete. Later, we will see. Let us not forget that the Church existed before the Order and that we have been able to grow, thanks to my predecessors, by copying its structure, then improving our network and spreading it over the entire kingdom. From then on, we have been seen as the embodiment of power, but we cannot ignore the Church's influence on these ignorant, oblivious people who are still consoling themselves with religious fables.'

The Magnus Legifer paused briefly, then began to speak once more in a more imperative tone.

'I want you to make up a folder on the Prelate within the next week so that I can finalize my strategy toward the Church. I know your enthusiasm and I am convinced that you will carry off this difficult task brilliantly. Well, that's all there is to be said about that. Please excuse me, but I still have much work to attend to, so I won't accompany you. Goodbye, and thank you in advance for your valuable assistance.'

'It is always a challenge and a pleasure to work for the good of Legiferius,' said the Magnus Scrutator amusedly as he left.

'That Tertius is an intelligent man, and efficient, but he's one to watch out for, or someday he could overshadow me,' thought Primus, just before ringing for his secretary.

Ogrino had combed over a good bit of the forest, addressing families, packs, and sometimes crowds of magical creatures.

He was rather satisfied with these friendly meetings, the sudden support of Gnomes or Pixies, and most of all with the certainty that now there would be a whole host of peoples ready to mobilize against this absurd violence. His only regret was the Trolls' refusal to cooperate. He would have to spearhead the revolution, relying on Precelestine's, Themistomene's, and Delphoros' precious assistance. Before that, he wanted to warn Pantaleone and Slevania so that they could protect themselves. So he explained to Viastella that their tour was complete and asked her to head straight for the city. As always, the journey only seemed to last a few moments as they glided over the ground like ice skaters, simply and purely. They soon reached the edge of the forest, and Ogrino advised Viastella not to go out into the open. She risked attracting too much attention. He leapt to the ground just as a troop of Militians appeared in the distance, on the forest road. The Unicorn instantly disappeared, and Ogrino hid in the foliage. The patrol of soldiers passed right by him without even noticing. As soon as they were far enough, he began to run toward the fields. It would only take him a few hours to reach the outskirts of the city, and then he would walk by night so as not to attract attention.

Seven days had passed, and Tertius had just finished his presentation to Primus, advising him not to trust the Prelate. His report sat on the big oaken table.

'He is intellectually very honest, and his principles are deeply seated,' Tertius concluded. 'It will be difficult to make him take a position he doesn't entirely believe in. His attitude toward Legiferius is mixed. He recognizes the need for some kind of order to protect the kingdom and enforce laws, but our methods and dogmas irritate him. It would be desirable to take action to reduce his influence on the population. I recommend . . .'

'Thank you for your report and suggestions, ' Primus cuts in. 'I know what I have to do. I will make him a proposition he can't refuse. Leave me alone now. I must prepare for this meeting, for the Prelate will be arriving any minute now.'

Barely an hour later, the secretary knocked on his office door.

'Come in,' Primus said in a booming voice.

The man dressed all in purple entered the room.

'Ah, here you are at last, Prelate Johanes!' said the Magnus Legifer, irritated. 'I thought you'd never arrive. Legiferius should never be kept waiting.'

'I was kept by important business. I had to administer the Extreme Unction to a dying man and that cannot wait, you will agree?' the Prelate replied calmly.

'Perhaps! But I, too, have important business with you,' Primus declared, restraining himself. 'You are not unaware that we have been preparing, for months, to launch a large-scale battle against the evildoing creatures of the Legendary World, with the intent of destroying them forever.'

'Yes, I am up to date on your military preparations. In fact, who could fail to be with such tremendous measures being taken? War machines by the hundreds, men by the thousands, so many requisitions of objects and food, an infrastructure worthy of the greatest emperors of all the ages ! Really, even a blind man would notice your plans ! Aren't all these measures out of proportion while there are so many in need? Couldn't all this war money be used for more public aid?'

'Enough, be quiet! You do not realize how much is at stake. We must first eliminate the enemy before any peace will last, and only then can we dedicate ourselves to the well-being of the people. You deal with the spiritual realm and leave the material to us. That way everyone stays in his place, and everything works perfectly inside the Order.'

There was a pause and then Primus began again, 'In fact, it is to that end that I have something to ask of you. But let us first toast to the cooperation of the Order and the Church!'

He took out two silver metal cups filled with a dark brew and with a sardonic smile held one out to the Prelate, who took it, thanking him.

'Let us drink to the glory of Legiferius and the expansion of the Church, for through working together, we can build a vast and stable world where all subjects will submit, out of fear and respect, to the immovable, eternal Order.'

Although the Prelate did not seem to agree with what had just been announced, they drank in unison, their entire cups, as was the custom.

Then Primus declared, 'Don't you understand that a new era is dawning? We will wage war and destroy these evil breeds that cause trouble for the universal order, and the Church will greatly benefit as well. Just think, when the Legendary World is finally eliminated, the superstitions based on the creatures of nature will themselves disappear, leaving consciences clear, available for your wonderful teachings. Without their ancestral beliefs, men will be free to pursue another ideal—one nobler, purer, and more ordered—and all for the greater glory of the Church and of Legiferius.'

He had particularly emphasized this last word, which was not lost on the Prelate. The religious man added, 'That's all very well. In fact, until now the Church has always respected Legiferius's work, for in bringing order, they have also brought a kind of peace that is favorable to the growth of consciences. It's just that with time, the Order's power has become . . . how to say it, omnipresent, and somewhat stifling.'

'Stifling?' retorted Primus, 'whatever do you mean?'

'Only that your power reaches constantly farther throughout the land and even inside the Church, where the feeling of being observed, scrutinized, controlled, grows by the day. As if you had to know everything about everything,' the Prelate said, calmly but a little defiantly.

'Any organization has to keep itself informed. Information is the root of power. Do not think, however, that the Order wishes to control the Church. Each one has its duties and we would not be able to take your place.'

Primus pronounced this sagely, and yet his tone expressed some malice. The Prelate spoke once more. 'Actually, no human order can replace God's work as regards his creation. Any action contrary to the natural order is doomed to failure, sooner or later. I can assure you that the Church will always see to it that this is the case as that is our ultimate goal.'

He had said all this with unassailable aplomb and assurance.

'It is for that reason precisely that you are here, to take part in a great and noble mission for the restoration of the order of things. My army, as powerful as it is, needs motivation to become invincible and end this with a resounding victory, and the Church must play a crucial role in that,' Primus said in a frenzied, impassioned voice.

'Then what do you expect from me?' the Prelate inquired.

'Hardly anything—a simple intervention on your part at a key moment. I would like you to bless the Order's army during the annual Legiferius Day, with an eye toward the offensive that we will soon be mounting. I want a homily that will give them courage and comfort them in their mission that will strengthen their faith and that will make their will as hard and indestructible as bronze.'

Primus's voice quavered with excitement.

Johanes said calmly, 'And what would happen if the Church refused to participate in your crusade?'

'That is impossible. Our fates are closely linked. The Order's glory and the Church's greatness must increase together. We both have too much to gain from this business and too much to lose if we were to disagree. Isn't it obvious?' inquired the Magnus Legifer.

'Of course, you have too much to lose, that is obvious. On the other hand, however . . . collaborating with your war schemes could send the Church down a slippery slope, against its basic principles, which would tarnish its reputation with the clergy as well as among the populace, who are the soil in which the Church wishes to garden.'

'Nonsense, nothing but nonsense!' Primus declared. 'You mission is to help Legiferius, and nothing more. It is only thanks to me that your institution lives and grows . . . it would take nothing at all for me to crush you.'

The Magnus Legifer's face had become scarlet with rage. His fists clenched and his face threatening, he looked the Prelate up and down.

'Now, finally, you show your true colors. You care about the Church only for what you can take from it, and only because it ought to serve you docilely without a murmur, but let me assure you that that will never be the case. No political cause can suppress our existence. If there must be collaboration, it can only begin from a basis of respect and nurturing for all beings, not from their subjugation or even destruction.'

The Prelate had remained calm, but everything about him showed his deep, unshakeable resolve.

'I knew you were wily, but not this much,' Primus retorted. 'Regardless, you have no choice. You will help me, more than you could imagine.'

'That's out of the question,' Johanes asserted.

'Ohhh, but you will. You have no other choice. You belong to me now.'

'Meaning . . . ?'

'Your life is in my hands, Prelate!' Primus said, speaking contemptuously now. 'You will obey everything I say, or else . . .'

'Or else what? Even now, you wouldn't dare to lock me up?'

'I won't need to. You will cooperate on your own.'

'Never!'

'I have a proposition to make that will interest you extremely. Listen carefully. The beverage that you drank just now is in fact a powerful poison for which there is no antidote, except, of course, the one concocted by the Docts, which only Legiferius possesses.'

'You've poisoned me! You have dared to lay hands upon one of the Church's high representatives. You are a despicable criminal!'

'Hush! What does your passé criticism mean to me? I am the Magnus Legifer, and as such, I work for a cause much greater than myself. You ought to be able to understand that, with the position you hold in your institution. Legiferius's greatness must become dazzling to all, and sometimes that requires sacrifices. This war against the Legendary World is a holy crusade against a chaotic pest that prevents Legiferius from extending its power throughout the entire world. The Legendary World is an intolerable insult to the Order, and that is why our cause is just.'

Primus was now in a trance; his voice and even his body trembled. Flames danced in his eyes, seemingly consuming him to the very soul.

'That is the reason that I gave you that potion, so as to make a deal with you. I do not want you to die. Quite the opposite in fact. I merely knew because of your duplicity toward the Order that you would not cooperate easily. So I merely slightly, swayed the course of fate. So now you will either give a homily to the glory of God and the Order, or else you will be denied the antidote. Think carefully before you answer me as Legiferius's annual celebration is planned for three days from now, which means that you have no more than seventy-two hours to live if you do not accept my proposition.'

'A deal, is it? A deal with the devil, that's what you are offering me.'

'How could you compare me to that evil being who, by his own statement, rules over the Legendary World? I should have your head cut off for such slander!'

'Decidedly, with every passing moment you reveal your true nature a little more.'

'I say again, think twice before giving me your final answer. Your life depends on it.'

There was a long silence during which the Prelate put his hands together in prayer and closed his eyes. Only his lips moved slightly, though no sound escaped them. After minutes that seemed to last hours, Johanes opened his eyes and said simply, 'I will do this homily as you are forcing me to. I will do it as you wish in honor of God and the Order.'

'A wise decision! At last, you have become reasonable again. Let's forget that little quarrel, for now we are united by a great cause,' Primus said joyfully.

'You will excuse me if I do not entirely share your joy. Perhaps you forget that I have a deathly poison in my blood.'

'No, of course not! But in three short days, you will be freed from it as I will give you the antidote.'

'How do I know that you will do it? Why should I trust you?'

'I was waiting for that question. If you cooperate, I will have not the least reason in risking a scandal with the Church by killing one of its highest-ranking officials. That is why I will give you the antidote immediately after the homily. If, on the other hand, you betray me and criticize the order, I will have you arrested and thrown in prison, and if your weak heart can unfortunately not withstand such stress and quite unexpectedly stops beating, then I would regret that most deeply. Do you understand?'

Primus had said all this in a mocking, threatening tone that left the Prelate no doubt as to his intentions and determination.

'I believe this homily will go down in Legiferius's history,' the Prelate concluded in a tone he meant to sound conciliatory but which revealed a certain stiffness.

'I am delighted to hear it. As far as the ceremony's organization is concerned, my directors, along with your provosts, will see to the details of preparation. Everything must be perfect!' Primus said cheerfully. 'Let me accompany you, my dear friend,' he added, trying to sound amicable.

The Prelate walked toward the door Primus opened.

'Until we meet again—in three days!' Primus called gaily, as a farewell.

Johanes left without looking back, offering no goodbye. He was sickened by such Machiavellian treachery. The Prelate had barely disappeared when a messenger arrived, panting, at Primus's door. He knocked five times, respectfully, and waited. The door swung open to reveal the Magnus Legifer's shining face.

'A very urgent letter,' said the missive bringer, 'from the Magnus Scrutator,' he thought it wise to add, so as to impart a touch of solemnity to his mission.

'Very good, thank you,' Primus responded simply, without the slightest consideration for the man.

He quickly shut the door and opened the envelope nervously. What news could his favorite spy be sending him? 'News from the front lines, news of commandoes in good position', he thought excitedly. His face changed from jubilation to uncertainty. A young boy had been seen coming from the heart of the forest, riding a Unicorn and rallying, here and there, assemblies of all sorts of creatures such as Gnomes, Pixies, Ogres, and even Trolls, and then they had lost his trail. Whatever could this mean? Unless it was . . . ? No! Impossible! Could it be not a child but the young Ogre who had succeeded in escaping from Legiferius? If it were he, who perhaps knew the intricacies of Legiferius's building and underground, who was now allying himself with the members of the Legendary World. He was a very dangerous enemy and had to be destroyed as quickly as possible.

He took a parchment, scribbled a few words, and then folded it and stamped Legiferius's Seal of Extreme Priority into red wax. Then he pulled a lever. His personal secretary jumped up in surprise, hearing the bell ring above his head. He dove toward the padded door that separated him from his master and hurriedly entered the office.

He hadn't the time to say a word before Primus dryly ordered him, 'An extremely urgent letter for the Magnus Scrutator. Hurry!'

The secretary took the letter and nimbly departed, all the while regarding the letter he held in his hands. A letter of Extreme Priority—it had been a long time since he had seen one of those.

Three days had passed, and Primus's long-awaited moment had finally arrived. The celebration of the anniversary of the Order's founding had always been a major event for Legiferius. This intense moment strengthened the organization's cohesiveness. Today, this powerful time would prove even more crucial. Johanes arrived at the fortress at the agreed-upon hour and was led by Primus himself to the top of the ramparts. The Prelate discovered thousands of Militians assembled inside Legiferius's immense court. The men waited impassively, their eyes on him, and he felt the weighty responsibility for all that he was going to tell them. When silence reigned among the immense crowd of soldiers, the Prelate began his homily.

'Legiferius has asked me to grant you my blessing on the dawn of a great battle, which you must fight for the Order's and God's glory. I am very honored by this opportunity I have been given, to speak to you before such a decisive moment in your lives and the life of the Order.'

Hearing these words, Primus was overjoyed as the introduction was perfectly identical to the text of the speech that the Magnus Scrutator had brought him.

'Your orders are to bring home a resounding and complete victory over the Legendary World, exterminating all its creatures in one final battle. God is the keeper of the great universal order. He has created everything for his own reasons. We are too small and too limited to understand this. Nevertheless, man is blessed with intelligence and heart to guide him in his actions. Being a man of the Church, I am inspired with faith and compassion toward all living beings. You are soldiers, but above all you are men; you, too, are blessed with the same human qualities that live in me. So when you fight, you must ask yourselves why you act in such or such a manner. You must ask yourselves if your cause is just if your actions are consistent with what you feel inside, or better, with what is at the very heart of yourself.'

A grimace appeared on Primus's face, for these ideas were very different from those in the text he had before his eyes. The Prelate was improvising a homily. Could it be that he would dare to defy the Order, despite the threat hanging over his head? No! It must have been only a temporary digression, brought on by the stress of having to speak at such a solemn moment. He calmed himself and continued to listen.

'Who are we to decide what is good or bad, virtuous or evil? God created all kinds of creatures. Even venomous snakes serve a role in the Great Chain of Life. The Legendary World, too, is a divine creation, which thus has its place in the order of the universe, even if we humans do not understand it. As such, this world must be respected. Its complete disappearance would not only be an insult to the universal order, but also, I am certain, would lead to an unbelievable series of catastrophes.'

'He's really gone too far', thought Primus. The Prelate was transforming his homily into a defense of the Legendary

World, rather than Legiferius. It was an act of high treason that had to be halted immediately, without losing another second. He called his Inner Guard and frantically gave orders.

'The harmony of the Great Chain of Life cannot be broken, and regardless, should not be subject to the mere will of man. I call on your dormant consciences. May they awaken, that your eyes might be opened, and you might realize what you were made for, instead of following orders imposed upon you by others. From the bottom of my soul, I bless you all. May God light your life's path so that all that is true might triumph.'

Johanes dipped his right hand in the holy water and blessed the crowd, who all knelt and bowed their heads. Chaos ensued. Every Militian was talking to those beside him. Confusion sprang up among the soldiers, who were torn between their military education, based on obedience and loyalty, and this homily that invited them to think for themselves and doubt the Order's commands. Erasmus was the most confused of all, without, however, knowing why.

It was as if the Prelate were swallowed up from behind. Two powerful, determined hands had pulled him out of view of the crowd. A hand covered his mouth. 'Too late', he thought. Legiferius was arriving too late. He had been able to say all that he had wanted to say and a deep joy filled him even as the Magnus Legifer's Inner Guard jostled and manhandled him. He had fulfilled his mission and was at peace with himself. That was the important thing no matter what happened now. Never before, he thought, had he done something so honorable; he was serene. The Magnus Legifer appeared suddenly in his field of vision, filled with blinding rage.

'You betrayed me! You mocked me in front of my own Militians. It's an insult to the Order ! Do you know the consequences of defying Legiferius's authority? You will pay harshly for this!' Primus asserted in a wrathful voice.

'Do you then wish to enter into open war with the Church by making an attempt on the life of one of its highest representatives? I have made arrangements. If something were to happen to me, you would be held personally responsible.'

'And now you're threatening me. Do you even know how far my power reaches? I am the Magnus Legifer, the head of the Order, and no miserable Prelate will stand in the way of Legiferius's progress.'

'The Church, like the Order, also influences many people, and even if you eliminate me, I will become a martyr. Resistance to the Order's actions will grow, and you will be toppled sooner or later. If, on the contrary, you let me live, you will demonstrate to everyone your clemency and open-mindedness, which will not fail to attract the humble and powerful alike. You will come out of this only the greater, made more noble by your leniency.'

Primus paused, thinking of the pros and cons. If he let the Prelate live, the man would still be able to annoy him. Hadn't he braved death, risking and never receiving the antidote after his traitorous speech? This was certainly a daring, courageous man. Was he more of a bother dead than alive? That was the question. Primus, lost in thought, did not speak for a while.

Then suddenly he ordered, 'Let him go! Escort him to the infirmary with all the respect due to one of his rank.'

Then he turned away and disappeared into a large hallway. Johanes was elated; he had succeeded. Not only had he been able to give his subversive homily, but now his life was saved, for the doctors had no doubt been instructed to give him an antidote after the speech if everything went as planned. The guards escorted him to a heavy white door that stood out against the black marble of the long hallway that had led them there. Four medical Docts took over from the guards, who stood at attention at the office door.

'Please lie down,' one of the Docts said in a syrupy voice.

The Prelate obediently sat on the white bench that stood in the center of the room.

'We will give you an antidote which will counteract the poison's effects. It will sting your arm a little, at first, then you will feel quite warm. That's completely normal, nothing to worry about. Then you will feel heavy, heavier and heavier, before falling into a short sleep, from which you will emerge in full health.'

Johanes lay back, and everything happened as they had said it would. Still, as soon as he woke up, he asked, 'What am I doing here? Where am I?'

'You are in the infirmary. You fell ill during your homily praising the Order's mission. The heat and stress, no doubt.'

'Falling ill during my homily? I don't remember that at all. I can't even think of what I was saying. It's incredible.'

'That must be due to shock. A drop in blood pressure can lead to temporary amnesia, erasing the most recent memories. But they will return quickly, do not worry. If you would please sit up in order to reactivate blood flow throughout your entire body, this will bring oxygen to your brain, and you will be quite yourself again.'

He did as he was told, but no memories came back to him. A blank space as if the last two hours hadn't happened at all. Despite this, he felt good, euphoric. From this, he concluded that his homily must have gone well and that even if he didn't remember it, he must have spoken in accord with his conscience.

As soon as he was in the hallway, one of the Docts said, 'The Tormentine elixir has done its job admirably. He will not retain any trace of what happened, especially not his outrage at the Order.'

During this time, Primus, for his part, had energetically gotten the troops back under control. Immediately taking the stand, he had addressed the crowd in the guise of a conclusion to the Prelate's speech.

'Militians of the Order, on your shoulders rests the success of this great and good undertaking—that of securing peace and order, here and now. Our great Prelate has given you his blessing, for our cause is just. Certainly, God created everything, and we must not only respect his creation, but also protect it. If it were possible, as the Prelate recommends, I would be the first to reach out a hand to the beings of the Legendary World so that we could build an even better world together, where respect would be our top priority. Like the Prelate, I believe that the universal balance must be preserved. An abundant harvest fills the haylofts and brings prosperity to all. But what happens when innumerable hoards of mice arrive and devour the fruits of our labor, leaving nothing more than misery and desolation as a harsh winter approaches? What of the grand and beautiful, painstakingly built houses that end up destroyed by massive invasions of termites? I ask you, is the Great Balance being respected, if man, God's most beautiful creation, is threatened by stupid creatures merely because of their great and excessive numbers? What does the sensible farmer or carpenter do in the face of these pests? He exterminates and fumigates thoroughly, to eradicate the scourges threatening his goods. In the same way, so that the balance is respected and man can grow and develop in peace, we are forced to begin culling. Like a putrid swamp where plague and pestilence thrive, the threat of the Legendary World must be fought with as much determination as any other nuisance. Who does not know, among his family or friends, someone who has fallen victim to these vile creatures who steal children, set fire to barns, or decimate harvests? Who could stand by while Ogres and even Trolls walk with impunity through our villages, killing and destroying all in their paths? Luckily, Legiferius is here to watch over the kingdom's safety, and you, my brave Militians, you are the incarnation of the Order. You are the righteous arm brandishing the sword, the sword that will cut the rotten branch from the tree of Life and allow it to grow with renewed vigor ! Man will be able to flourish without hindrance after you, my faithful soldiers, have nipped in the bud this cancer corroding our society. May God light your way and give you the courage and strength to triumph, in your name and the Order's. Then the great harmony of the Chain of Life will be completely restored, and humanity will leave in peace forevermore. You are the hope of a new era, the pride of the Order, and your work will be greatly rewarded, for much is at stake. Bring victory to Legiferius and you will be covered in gold and honors!'

Primus had put particular emphasis and energy into this last sentence, certain that it would strike a chord with the men of his army. He was not disappointed as a great clamor arose below him. Thousands of voices rang out in unison for the Order's glory.

'WE ARE THE MILITIANS OF LEGIFERIUS, THE NATION'S ELITE. UPON US RESTS THE ORDER; WE ARE ITS CORNERSTONE, PAST, PRESENT, AND FUTURE.'

He had attained his goal. Once more, his eloquence had swept him away. He feared no orator. No one could best his rhetorical artistry; he possessed an unusual gift for persuasion. His charisma rounded it out, and thus won over the majority to his side. He was not the Primus Magnus Legifer for nothing. Even in his mother's womb, he had been destined to assume this supreme role. The Docts left nothing to chance; everything had been planned and controlled to the last detail, so that the Order would reign now and forever. Certainly, other Legifers would come after him to perpetuate Legiferius's rule, but today, he was the brilliant incarnation of the Order he loved so much, and which was his entire raison d'être. He snickered thinking of the images and arguments that he had used to win over these poor sheep who had been led astray by the Prelate's slanderous speech. Primus's eloquence had easily brushed aside all that the cleric had said. Certainly, the fact of having used the name of God several times to create links between the two speeches had been pure genius. Sometimes Primus astonished even himself with his immense capabilities. He had the talent of transforming obstacles into springboards to allow him to go further and accomplish more.

Completely satisfied with himself, he contemplated his army who, in hailing the Order, was giving him that most precious of gifts—blind devotion to a cause that he himself had created. What a wonderful idea he had had to create this antagonism between the Order and the Legendary World, to establish his power over the kingdom once and for all. He still could not believe how well his plan had succeeded in reinforcing the Order's presence in everyday society. Even the Church's influence was receding, faced with his institution's tenacity. Soon he would rule as a supreme leader and, who knew, perhaps thanks to the Docts' miraculous feats he could become immortal. Basking in these thoughts and the applause, he tasted the honey of those unique moments where power intoxicates you and lets you believe that nothing is impossible.

ERASMUS' REVELATION

'What can I do for you, Magnus Legifer?' asked the secretary.

'Call the Commander of the Aeronefs!'

'He has just returned from a mission at the edge of the kingdom and is no doubt very tired.'

'I do not need your commentary. I want to see him immediately. What does it matter to me if he's tired? He is above all a soldier and must obey orders, like all of you. Call him now!'

The secretary disappeared immediately and ran to knock on the Commander's door. He, like all of the Order's highest-ranking officials, lived at the very heart of Fort Legiferius, in the central L-shaped building.

'What is it?' the Commander asked in a deep voice.

'The Magnus Legifer wishes to see you for a detailed report of your mission.'

'But I've only just returned, and I haven't slept in two days. I'm exhausted—tell him that I will come in three hours, after having rested a little.'

'He has asked me to come find you and bring you to him as quickly as possible. I think he would be very irritated if you did not come with me now. He called upon your commitment as a soldier and your obligation to the Order.'

This speech electrified the Commander, who straightened his posture immediately. Forgetting his fatigue, he brushed off his uniform, polished his buttons, and swiftly opened the door. His tall figure was silhouetted in the doorway for a moment, then with a nimble step he followed the secretary, who was already striding hurriedly down the long hallway. Primus was pacing around his office when the knock on his door woke him from his reverie.

'My dear Quartus, I am so happy to see you again. You look very well. What news do you have?'

'Our mission was a success, despite difficult and changing winds. We flew over eighty percent of the area, that is, nearly two hundred thousand hectares of forest, and we located the target, the infamous Gigantum. It is approximately where the Docts calculated it would be, based on all the eyewitnesss' accounts previously gathered from prisoners from the Legendary World. This discovery is valuable, but military action can only be taken on the ground because the closer one gets to the target, the more violent and contrary the winds become, systematically pushing us away and threatening to damage the Aeronefs. It might be that the winds originate from the Gigantum itself as they form concentric circles around it, like the ripples from a stone thrown into water. It's strange, but it seemed as if it were conscious and was activating a kind of protection as it felt endangered because once we were far enough away from it, the winds died down immediately as if by enchantment.'

'Quartus!' Primus said in exultation, 'do you realize the importance of this discovery? We have here the confirmation of the Docts' suspicions—the Gigantum no doubt plays a fundamental role in the Legendary World to the point that it is powerfully protected. Do you see that if we are able to destroy it, we would very definitely set in motion a chain reaction that would destroy the entirety of these abominable fantastical creatures?'

'If it is well-protected aerially, it will also be terrestrially, perhaps even more so,' Quartus stressed. 'We will have to send a commando mission made up of our strongest units.'

'I have the elite team we need,' Primus proclaimed, 'and to that end, I beg you to work closely with Quintus, who as Commander of the Infantry will direct operations with your collaboration from the skies. And now, Quartus, this meeting is adjourned. Other tasks await me. Goodbye.'

The Commander took his leave, and Primus immediately called in the Magnus Scrutator for an overview on the map of the underground world. He could not wait to discover the networks of Precelestine's kingdom in detail. Immense riches lay there, and crucially, a most rare and precious object—an object worthy of Legiferius, though it came from the abominable magical world. Primus absolutely had to possess this gift so as to ensure the Order's supremacy until the end of time.

The next day as he entered the office Erasmus immediately noticed Quartus and Quintus flanking Magnus Legifer. To be summoned by Legiferius's supreme leader, along with two Commanders of that level, was a pleasure of the highest order, and Erasmus wondered to what he owed the honor.

'My dear Commander, may I call you Erasmus?' Primus said in a lightly honeyed voice.

'As you wish.'

'You are not unaware that we are preparing a crucial attack against our ancestral enemies. Our plans are nearly finished, and we are now reaching the final phase. We are aware of precisely what difficulties await us, notably one in particular. Of all the possible tactics we could use to reach our goal, we have discovered the most adept. Still, in order to complete our mission successfully, we will need the best of the Order.'

He paused theatrically before continuing, 'The mission will be extraordinarily secret and dangerous, so we thought of you—you, Erasmus—to lead it to success.'

The Militian was at once surprised and proud at this proclamation. He who had served Legiferius with enthusiasm and courage through long years was at last being recognized and promoted to great responsibility.

'You do me too much honor. Whatever this task may be, I will dedicate myself to it for the glory of the Order,' he said in a voice that was dignified, yet full of emotion.

'I expected nothing less of you. We made no mistake in choosing you. It is you and others of your ilk who make Legiferius great. This is what awaits you. You will leave with a handpicked crew of three hundred men. You will choose these men yourself, for the most part, on the basis of their loyalty, discretion, determination, and courage, not to mention their skill as warriors. Quintus, for his part, will select several Rectors who will work under your orders.'

'So here you are, de facto, appointed to the rank of division, Commander. This promotion is only just, considering all that you have accomplished in your career as a Militian. We are perfectly aware of all your achievements, your conquests, and your victories. Thanks to your unfailing contributions, the Docts, and thus the Order, have considerably advanced their knowledge of the enemy. More precisely, it is due to your great topographic abilities that you have been selected for this mission. You have completed numerous forays into the depths of the forest, giving you knowledge of many of its regions, and thanks to the Docts' maps, you will be well prepared to blaze a trail among its hills and dangers. You and your troops will need to go where no man has ever before set foot, crossing unexplored lands that will be full of obstacles we cannot even imagine. We have no doubts as to the outcome of your action. You will receive extensive training from the Docts as regards theory and, from Quartus and Quintus, on practical matters, for I want you and your men to be operating at maximum capacity. But first, I will need you to swear not to repeat what I am going to tell you. Only you will be in on the secret. It must not be revealed to anyone, neither man nor beast, even under torture. Is that quite clear?'

'It could not be clearer,' Erasmus replied, without any shadow of hesitation.

'Then listen well. The Docts, in their infinite wisdom, have been able to create an exceptional, absolute weapon. Its power is so great that it, and it alone will be able to forever rid us of this fount of evil that is gnawing away at our kingdom. To achieve that, it must reach its target, and you, Erasmus, will be responsible for concluding the act. You will bring your men to the boundaries of the known world, but it is you who must, in the greatest of secrecy, deal the final blow. No one must know. No one can be informed. Knowledge cannot be put in just any hands. Only those who are worthy deserve it, and you are in that group. Do not disappoint us, Erasmus.'

The Magnus Legifer had pronounced this last sentence in a friendly and yet military tone. Erasmus understood him perfectly. He had Legiferius's respect, however, failure was not an option.

'I will follow your orders with enthusiasm and determination until the end, even if I die doing so.'

'Here is a man worthy to be a division Commander. And now, I will ask you to please take your leave as we have much more to do.'

'Very well, I salute you, Sirs.'

'Farewell, Erasmus,' the high-ranking officials responded in chorus.

The door had barely closed after the Militian when Primus was already turning to Quintus, murmuring, 'We will have to take a second soldier into confidence. A soldier with very great discretion, for you never know, people are so volatile. I leave the choice of the soldier to you, but he, too, must be sworn to absolute secrecy.'

In the days that followed, Erasmus and the men of his division underwent thorough training. The days were endless. They were split between very physical military exercises and detailed instruction on the dangers of the various creatures of the Legendary World that lived in the forest. Quartus had initiated them into the world of the Aeronefs as they would be arriving by sky at first and then continuing on foot. At the end of this intensive training, the Militians were not only fully equipped for their mission; their motivation was also at its maximum. Their departure was planned for two days later so that they could rest a little. In the early morning, they left with their mounts on four Aeronefs, which were shaped like Legiferius's 'L.' They took flight and traveled for five days before arriving at the edge of the dark clouds.

'We can go no farther. It is too dangerous,' Quartus said to the mission. 'We risk damaging the wiring in turbulence or even attracting lightning. We will thus disembark here. Lower the platforms!'

The Militians uncoiled the ropes and attached them to enormous, shallow baskets. Then six horses and their riders climbed onto each of these wicker platforms. About forty men, their mounts, and their equipments began to descend in the storm, above the clearings. The wind was blowing forcefully and the platforms pitched about, making their riders motion sick. Still the first crews touched the ground safely if a bit shaken up. A second wave of Militians began their descent. The gusts were becoming stronger and the horses were growing very nervous. Some were rearing in fright, making them hardly controllable. The baskets were ever more shaken up and the men and their mounts fell heavily to the floor. The violent wind suddenly sent one of the platforms spinning on itself and its ropes twisted up. Then, like a top, it began to turn in the opposite direction, very quickly. Eight Militians were thrown overboard and four horses suffered broken legs. Seeing this, Quartus ordered the acceleration of the maneuver, and the baskets dropped to the ground as if weighted with lead. The landing was a bit painful but no damage was sustained. Erasmus was part of the third batch and knowing what awaited him, felt rather uneasy. The gusts and turbulence continued to grow stronger; the storm had become a gale. The rain now resembled a shower, soaking the men to their bones. They paid no more attention to the baskets-turned-spinning-tops; all the Militians' military capacities were needed to control the horses and equipments. Only a collision between two platforms darkened the scene. They lamented the loss of eleven soldiers and five horses. Having reached the ground, Erasmus did not bother to bury the dead as the mission could not be delayed. Thus, they continued under a driving rain, plunging ever deeper into the forest, and there, where no one had ever dared to venture.

They walked through the storm all night, savoring and delighting in the early-morning moment when the rain ceased. They stopped and ate their rations cold, unable to build a fire because it would attract attention. Then once more, they took up their forced march since it was absolutely necessary that they reach their stopping point before nightfall. To the surprise of all, no enemy had showed itself nor had any threat even been detected. Everything seemed unusually calm. Nevertheless, nearly a hundred men, doing their best to remain silent, could not reasonably pass unnoticed as they continuously approached the heart of the Legendary World. But nothing appeared, nothing at all, and Erasmus noticed his muscles beginning to tighten in anticipation of the worst. They continued in this way for much of the day after a pause of two hours, during which men and beasts were able to catch a bit of restorative sleep. That evening, the Militians reached a fortification of grey rock and the horses became slightly nervous. They walked along this sort of wall that seemed never to end. According to the Docts' instructions, however, there ought to have been an entryway somewhere further to the west. After an hour and a half of walking, a scout returned, confirming the presence of an archway that would allow passage on horseback. Erasmus brought his horse to a gallop so as to be the first to inspect the area. The long column of soldiers soon rejoined him, finding him on one knee to the ground, inspecting the soil on the other side of the opening. Seeing one of the Rectors advancing on horseback, Erasmus signaled to him to stop, but the man had already crossed through the archway. Immediately his horse reared and the Militian flew to the ground, falling heavily on his side. He let out a long moan as he stood up. His left shoulder looked very peculiar; it was visibly dislocated. Erasmus approached the Rector, examined him, then ordered him to kneel and lean forward slightly. Next he took the Rector's left arm and pulled it gently backward. Then Erasmus placed his left leg on the man's shoulder blade and pulled the arm toward him abruptly and violently. The man screamed before losing consciousness.

'His clavicle is back in place. Build a stretcher out of branches and blankets to carry him,' Erasmus ordered. 'This place stinks of trouble. The horses can smell it, and they become nervous, unpredictable, and difficult to control. From here on out, we will have the horses wear blinders and keep them on very short reins. Spread the word.'

From the moment they crossed into Elfin territory, a sense of danger arose, although no enemy was visible. They traveled in groups of four, spaced out, each soldier in the group, looking out in a different direction. Progress itself was not a difficult task as the ground proved rather flat. Nevertheless, discouragement and gloominess slowly descended upon the Militians. They would have certainly preferred a bloody campaign that would have awoken their assets as warriors. But here nothing was happening, no enemy made itself available. They sunk into boredom as they glided across this hostile clime. Little by little, as they went deeper into the forest, the feeling of a menacing atmosphere made itself evident. It seemed that all the plants, mosses, bushes, and even the trees were desperately trying to hinder the Militians' progress by scratching or wounding them or blocking their way. So the soldiers' progress only became slower and more painful. The animals struggled even more than the men, who were protected in their suits of armor. Not only were the beasts advancing against their will as they could feel an almost palpable danger, but they were also in agony because of ever deeper and more frequent wounds.

'Soon we will have to continue on foot if we do not wish to work our mounts to death. They are losing blood, and it is only getting worse,' said one of the team's Rectors.

Erasmus lifted his right arm as a signal for the column to stop as his own horse was bleeding copiously even as he bravely continued to blaze the trail. The Commander dismounted and immediately all of his men followed suit—luckily so, for the farther they traveled, the more overtly nature became an enemy. The plants became larger, thicker, hardier, and sharper. Saps spilled from their thorns and, even in the case of mere scratches, inflicted unbearable pain. Now they had to use machetes to clear themselves a path. It grew dark, ever darker, so the Militians lit their torches, which, despite their brilliance, only weakly illuminated their dark surroundings. The shadows themselves seemed to become denser.

'This is an evil place,' said the Rector. 'It stinks of a nearly palpable danger. Some kind of invisible power is ruling here, using the plants as weapons.'

'That means that we are very near to our goal,' retorted Erasmus. 'We are not here to complain but to fulfill a mission of the highest importance. According to the Docts' map, we have nearly reached our target. I do not want to hear another word, much less any sniveling. The first one to make the slightest peep will be severely punished. Absolute silence from here on out, understood?'

No one else dared voice any comment, and the Militians recommenced their slow progress in stony silence. Not only did the vegetation take even more aggressive forms now, but animals which until this point had remained invisible had also began to make brief appearances, such as tarantulas and venomous snakes that crawled along tree branches.

'Ready your crossbows,' whispered Erasmus.

The order was passed on down the line, and in an instant, all were armed, ready to shoot. A feeling of deep fear spread among the soldiers. Although these Militians were part of Legiferius's elite, this was the first time they had felt such hostility from nature itself. They had fulfilled dozens of dangerous missions, notably against the Trolls, but those had always been against an identifiable enemy, whose behavior could be studied and weaknesses found—all thanks, incidentally, to the Docts' research. This was completely different—the enemy was diffuse, intangible, and yet quite present and dangerous. Suddenly, a cry tore through the silence. A Militian was holding his throat and shaking violently. He fell, continuing to cry out and roll feverishly on the ground.

'Immobilize him,' said Erasmus.

He quickly set down his knapsack and took out a vial filled with a purplish liquid. Kneeling next to the wounded man, whose lips were trembling, Erasmus poured the contents into his mouth. The soldier, his eyes rolled back in his head, continued to twitch for another minute or two, then became still and immediately fell asleep.

'It was a snake, a damned snake that bit him in the neck. I've got it here, look!'

In fact, the soldier was holding, quite tightly in his right fist a reptile with white and black rings that was frantically contorting, though unable to escape from the grip encircling its neck. Erasmus approached hastily and carefully observed the thrashing animal. During this time, a great cry tore through the gathering. Another Militian was holding his throat, and the same scene played out again. Then a third and a fourth, then another, and another; the army was being attacked on all sides by reptiles who were dropping from trees and biting the Militians, most often on the face or neck. Suddenly, there was a dull buzzing sound, and the soldiers, dumbfounded, saw a thick grey cloud moving rapidly in their direction. Thousands and thousands of horseflies were descending upon them, followed by aggressive hornets. Their stings pierced the Militians' necks by the hundreds. The horses, stung until they bled, whinnied furiously and became entirely uncontrollable. Some reared up, others bucked, and others still ran in circles, trampling the men. Erasmus was disgusted. Never before had he seen such chaos among his troops, and certainly, he had never seen so many wounds, even in the harshest battles. The Rectors leapt from one victim to another, administering vials to neutralize the snakes' venom, all while battling the insects. Soon they had run out of elixirs. There were so many in need. Nearly half of the company had been affected.

'Turn back! We are turning back!' Erasmus decreed.

In the brouhaha and reigning panic, few heard him. The horses grew madder and madder and some began to flee, dragging many others in their wake. The Militians, who were busy aiding the victims, could not prevent the escapes of two thirds of the mounts. When some semblance of calm had returned, Erasmus reiterated his order, 'We are withdrawing. Place the ailing on the mounts that remain and let us clear out of here as quickly as possible.

The soldiers obeyed, and a long line set about the return path in a disorganized manner as the insects continued to pester the men and beasts.

'*No, it's too stupid! So close to our goal! I cannot abandon this now*,' thought Erasmus infuriated at the back of the line. 'Rector Nonetus!'

The Militian turned and responded, 'Yes, Commander?'

'Choose several trustworthy men and we will continue. The others will return and wait for us at the rock wall, so they will be safe. We should not need more than two hours and then we will rejoin them before dawn.'

The Rector listened with an impassive expression, but he could feel tension in all his limbs. His entire body was telling him to flee. Duty and discipline were stronger than fear. He had to obey, and he had to complete the mission, for the glory of Legiferius. He turned and shouted six names. The Militians rushed up immediately and stood frozen like statues. A seventh joined them.

'Rector Octavus! What are you doing here? I did not call your name.'

'I wish to participate in this mission. I want to be among those who receive the prize for courage, for having carried the Order's colors to the very depths of hell.'

Before such fervor, Nonentus could do nothing but nod, confirming to Octavus that he was accepted into the commando unit. Then he turned and called, 'Rector Septimus, the Commander wishes for the column to return to the wall and wait for us there as we continue to the target.'

The other Rector acquiesced, turned his back, and rejoined the end of the retreating troops. Erasmus unloaded a heavy, imposing sack from his horse. He carefully slipped it onto his back, then ordered everyone to put up their hoods to protect against the reptiles and insects. Then they began to walk again, ardently slashing at leaves and low branches with their machetes. Snakes and tarantulas were now literally raining down on them, but their uniforms, now impenetrable thanks to the goggles, protected them. The soldiers paid practically no more attention to this torrent of aggressors. As they advanced, they had the increasing impression of plunging into the heart of a canyon whose walls were closing in; however, it was difficult to tell because the vegetation was so lush. When they could finally touch the walls with their gloved hands, they realized that they were now in a narrow pass with sides made not of rock, but of wood.

'Here we are!' Erasmus rejoiced. 'We've nearly arrived.'

Comforted by this prospect, they began to make quicker progress. They continued to walk in this way for a hundred meters or so. Suddenly, the vegetation stopped completely, and they found themselves before a clearing surrounded by two walls of bark, which measured at least twelve meters high. A checkerboard had been drawn on the dirt, which was completely exposed here. Drawings and incomprehensible letters were carved into each square. Erasmus stood still at the edge of the board and studied, one by one, each of the squares, trying to decode from them a message. The Rector Nonentus came up level with Erasmus, knelt down, and reached out a hand to brush an image with his fingertips.

'Stop, for goodness' sake, you absolutely must not touch that.' Erasmus interrupted. 'I am unable to decode these abbreviations, but I believe it to be a kind of rebus that must be solved if we wish to cross this chessboard. The smallest false move could prove fatal, I'm convinced.'

He spent another several long minutes in silence, his eyes frenetically passing from one square to the next, sometimes horizontally and sometimes diagonally. Finally, he cried, 'I believe I've found it!'

He timidly stepped his right foot onto a square adorned with a symbol that vaguely recalled the letter alpha. He then placed his left foot on the same square and waited. A deathly silence fell. Nothing happened. Then he began again, setting his left foot on another square, two spaces away on the diagonal, atop a shape that resembled a sequoia. There he waited another moment, and given that again nothing happened, he jumped laterally to a stone three spaces away, with a jellyfish on it. Next he leapt onto a square holding a picture of an amphibian, four squares away in a straight line.

He carefully surveyed the grid and saw on his left, five spaces away, the image of a mammoth. With a swing of his arms, he jumped right in the middle of the animal. Then, looking all around him, he recognized a human form six squares to his right. He bent his legs all the way and launched himself forward. He landed on the intended stone, but his momentum caused him to set a hand on the one next to it. The entire board began to move, and the stones to sink slowly into the ground.

In a flash, he scanned the whole area in search of another sign, which he at last saw at the edge of the board, diagonal to him. Gathering his strength, he propelled himself like a spring, seven spaces away, to land on a drawing of the letter omega. Barely had his feet touched the stone when it tilted backward, and he was thrown off balance. With superhuman effort, he righted himself, allowing him to cling to the side of the earthen wall that emerged as everything behind him disappeared into a dark abyss. The dirt proved loose and his heavy backpack, loaded with the Tetrabomb, pulled him downward. Clenching his teeth and driven by despair, he was, nevertheless, able to pull himself up onto the ground, where he lay for several minutes trying to catch his breath. Finally, he sat up and turned to his men on the other side of the abyss.

'Throw the grappling hooks,' he shouted.

Immediately, eight hooked arrows planted themselves at his feet, each one linked to a rope that the soldiers were already securely attaching to tree trunks. Then the eight Militians began to travel over the void, suspended from the cords by their hands and feet.

'Does this remind you of your training at base?' Erasmus called out, amused.

They were halfway through their trajectory when a dull crack rang out. Suddenly, an enormous branch appeared above them. As it fell, it hit two of the soldiers, who let go, screaming. The imposing mass of wood cut through the ropes and pulled the men of the commando down with it. Only Octavus was able to cling to his cord, which swung and knocked him back against the wall. He held on and slowly climbed up the cliff face. Having arrived at the top, he signaled to Erasmus, shouting, 'I am safe and sound. I am going to try again to cross.'

'No, for goodness' sake. You will risk your life for nothing. Any other attempt will be fatal. Forces beyond our control are at work here. They are lying in wait for us and will kill us at the first opportunity. I will go on alone. Perhaps I'll have better luck. You go back and join the others. I will see you at base camp no more than six hours from now. Go along!'

Octavus saluted his Commander one last time and with a heavy heart, turned back. Erasmus was alone. He suddenly felt powerless, both appalled and revolted. He cried out in rage at having lost his best men, and his furor echoed in the forest for a long time. Finally, he shook off his stupor, filled with both disgust and a renewed will to definitively put an end to the nuisance of this cursed Legendary World. He was carrying the ultimate weapon. He had the advantage of unparalleled training. He had already lost much on this mission. He owed it to himself to succeed. So he leapt to standing, tore off his hood, and began to run toward his target which seemed so close, hidden behind the once-again lush vegetation. After more than an hour of swift running, the shrubs, treelike ferns, and underbrush grew scarcer, and Erasmus could finally see a clear horizon. He was met with a stunning vision.

An immense, ebony-black cone was rising before him. He could have believed it was a tree, but it was so dark that it more resembled a sort of monolith from another age. After sinuous detours due to the brambles and spines that covered the entire area protectively, Erasmus finally arrived before a kind of porch that led into the gigantic structure. Inscriptions adorned the door, certainly in Elfin language, which he was only roughly able to decode, but he understood the general meaning. It looked like a warning against imminent danger. He had barely finished scrutinizing these enigmatic symbols when a long shiver traveled up his spine. He took hold of himself and passed under the entryway. He had to complete this mission, whatever the cost, and he could not allow a simple threat to stop him.

Taking extreme caution, he advanced with slow, hushed steps onto the flagstone floor, his ears pricked up and all his other senses alert. He heard a rustling on the ground. Some kind of immense, dark carpet seemed to undulate as if lifted by an underground air current. Moving very slowly, he took a torch from his backpack and presently lit it. The horror was absolute! Millions of black rats swarmed on the gigantic indoor courtyard. Barely had they seen the light when they threw themselves at Erasmus, the first ones jumping onto his face. Even through his surprise, he waved his flaming torch through the air with ferocious energy, trying to fend off his innumerable assailants. The tide seemed unending, for even as the rats fell by the dozens, burned or clubbed, each one that succumbed was replaced by two or three more. There were so many that after a seemingly interminable battle, Erasmus, dragged down by the weight of his enemies, wobbled and fell backward. Immediately an immense and fetid wave covered him. He could smell their plague-like breath, feel their claws tearing at his neck and hands, sense their teeth avidly seeking his flesh. Fear and loathing intermixed, and he was suddenly nauseous. Never in his worst nightmares could he have imagined a more terrifying situation. He who felt such intense revulsion toward these vile beasts was now at their mercy. He could not perish like this as the prey of such repugnant predators—this sort of end was unworthy of him. Despite the mass smothering him, he was just able to direct his right hand to his belt, where various vials hung. With difficulty, he detached one. He succeeded in uncorking it with a trembling thumb and the liquid spread slowly along his uniform. He held his breath as a strong, nauseating odor was released. As if by a miracle, the sea of aggressors parted like a river flowing around a protruding rock. Freed from the crushing weight, Erasmus sat up with an irrepressible desire to vomit. Nausea overwhelmed him, and he regurgitated his last meal in a series of spasms. Relieved, he took a deep breath and looked around. The multitude of rats had disappeared.

He was now alone in this gigantic domicile. Each one of his steps resonated with the same echo one would hear in a cathedral.

At the shadowy center of the flagstone floor, Erasmus noticed a kind of well with no guard wall around it. When he arrived at the edge of the hole, he realized it was in fact a spiral staircase that led into the ground. Irresistibly attracted by a pale red light emanating from the depths of the earth, he began to descend the first ebony marble steps. The staircase seemed endless, for after he had rushed down hundreds and hundreds of steps, the fascinating light of the abyss was no closer. With every step, Erasmus felt the fatigue growing in his body, and his limbs grew ever weightier, slowing his progress.

Hours passed like this, and he became very weary. Erasmus was filled with a deep, melancholy whose cause he did not know. Nevertheless, he continued his descent and the light was now glowing quite brightly. He was very close to his goal, and at that idea, he felt only the smallest bit of bleak joy in his heart as he was so tired and subdued. A crystalline music arising from the bottom of the staircase reached Erasmus's ears, growing imperceptibly louder as he approached. Finally, he stepped onto a landing, whose floor was made of the same black marble as the staircase.

A majestic fire with undulating golden flames flickered at the center of the imposingly large room. The hearth literally sprung from the earth, expressing a subterranean force that was both peaceful and terrifying. He lifted his eyes and discovered that the room was pyramidal in shape and that its dark ochre-colored walls were adorned with innumerable inscriptions similar to those he had seen on the porch. Among these symbols, there were also pictograms, depicting all sorts of phantasmagorical creatures. Everything about this place emanated power, some strength from a time before time.

Erasmus felt small, crushed by an invisible hand that reminded him of his mediocrity, his insignificance compared to the forces that ruled the world. In addition, he vaguely recognized that he was in a sanctuary, a sacred place only accessible to those who were worthy. Despite the melancholy that had settled in during his descent, he found himself happy that he had been able to come this far. He was now certain that if someone had decided otherwise, he would never have reached at this apparently secret place safe and sound. He scanned the room, but at first glance, not a living soul seemed to be present. He decided to walk around the inferno that was blocking his view of much of the room. As he slowly approached the giant blaze, a powerful warmth entered his body and renewed his vigor. His sadness gradually dissipated, giving way to the desire to discover the mysteries of this place.

There, just behind the dancing flames, he caught a glimpse of human figures, and instinctively he took up his crossbow and loaded it. He circled the room very slowly, holding the bowstring taut. In spite of the fear constraining him, he was on the alert, ready to confront whatever awaited him. Arriving at the edge of the fire, he distinctively saw seven figures, who were observing him motionlessly. He took one more step to distance himself from the flames that were now roasting his skin. He placed one knee on the ground, aimed at the figures, and threatened,

'Not a move, or else you are dead. I am a Commander of the Order, a seasoned soldier, who never misses his target. What are you doing here?'

The others remained silent and still motionless.

'Are you fearful? Are you mute? Speak, for goodness' sake!'

Still no response, so Erasmus stood and went closer to the creatures. He saw them very clearly now—six old men surrounding one woman, and what a woman? She was of unrivaled beauty, dressed in a long, flowing red dress that gathered at her feet. Erasmus gazed deep into her eyes and was hypnotized. He dared not move, both fascinated and ashamed of having believed himself in danger while this woman projected nothing but bounty and respect. Felicia Regina, for her part, gave him a melancholic, compassionate smile.

'Why so much hate in your heart?
Violence only breeds sadness and pain.
Our lives and your own are not things apart;
We are links on the same chain.
You, Erasmus—for that is your name—are, yourself
The child of a human woman and an Elf
The gift of a great union, one of a kind.
Giving you life, your mother left hers behind.
But your father lives on still today, in you.
His presence and intellect make themselves known,
His strong will and intuition too.
Do you hear these words? You are one of our own.
Two separate worlds in you are twined.
If you wish, you can join us, enthroned.'

At these words, Erasmus dissolved into tears. All his life, he had fought against the Legendary World for the greater glory of Legiferius. All these efforts, these sacrifices, these ignominies, only to finally learn that the world he had fought, with such rage, was his own. Somewhere within him he had felt many times, in flashes, that his battles were groundless as the world the Order described as dangerous was not, after all, so terrible, and the creatures within it were most often wily, but harmless. However, save for these brief moments of lucidity the Order's indoctrination had won out, and Erasmus had only become more and more murderous. He fell to his knees, his body wracked with deep sobs. He trembled with sorrow and rage. Scenes of hunts, pursuits, violent captures, and massacres played in his memory like a horror film. His hands, so delicate and yet so strong, now inspired disgust. They had clubbed, clawed, tortured, strangled, and sliced. So many victims' faces, uneasy, frightened, incredulous, tormented, horrified, imploring, and so sorrowfully resigned before the Order's power and Erasmus's own power. What had he done? What had he done with his life? A life spent sowing terror and fear everywhere he went. Had that been his life's purpose? Could he be proud of all this? He was seized by a blind rage against himself, and he pulled his dagger from the sheath that hung from his belt. He raised his arm quickly, ready to plunge the knife into his heart.

NO! Stay your hand—there is a better way
To heal these wounds, than one more death today.

This gentle, yet imperious voice had appeared in Erasmus's mind like a peaceful, refreshing spring. His anger dissipated, his heart rate slowed, and little by little, his arm fell. He let go of the dagger, which clanged on the ground. The echo seemed to Erasmus to be deafening as if it were weighted with his entire past which was falling from him.

May the spirit of war become that of peace;
May the will to destroy learn to create;
May the hand that defiled now preserve without cease;
You are the author of your own fate.

Erasmus picked up the dagger, stood, and approached the Fairy-Queen. He held it out horizontally before her, one hand on the hilt and one on the blade. He put a knee to the ground. Then Felicia Regina came quite close to him and placed her hand delicately atop his head. That was when he felt a river of goodwill flow into his mind and his body. A myriad of silver sparks passed before his eyes, exuding a calm and profound joy. Delicate scents reached his nostrils, unknown yet familiar perfumes that delighted his soul. He began to cry again, no longer from rage, but from happiness. He was one with this marvelous world that held such riches, such beauty, such . . . bounty. He realized how much he now wished to remain one with this sweet and marvelous universe. It seemed that here no hate and no abomination could persist. All dark feelings vanished from him, in contact with so much natural harmony. Felicia Regina took a step back, and all became clear to Erasmus. He suddenly realized what he had to do. Standing, he looked straight into Felicia's eyes and said to her,

'I feel that I am part of this world and that this world is part of me. A powerful energy lies within me, and I wish to surrender to it. I have denied my nature for so long.'

Felicia continued in a murmur,

Your gifts are finally revealed.
You will require them every day.
Your task is now to find a way.

To stand up and begin to heal
The wounds left by humans gone astray.

She smiled at him, and Erasmus understood that the time had come for him to depart. He looked around once more, taking in the vision of Felicia and the old men, and then turned toward the staircase. Just as he was about to place his foot on the first step, a rock toppled on its side, and a door opened in the room's central column. He entered into the alcove and, lifting his head, saw that he was in a very long tube. The door had barely reclosed when a bluish light descended upon him. He was immediately vacuumed upwards. Seeing the joins of the wall fly by him, he understood that in only a few seconds, he would arrive at the top. When he was no more than ten meters away, his ascent slowed, and he found himself gently deposited into the large entry-room. This time he found no rats, no fear; he felt at home. He exited. The starry night unfolded before him, cloudless. He took up the same path he had followed there, this time with changed intentions. He had to act quickly as the threat was great and every moment counted. He attempted to run and realized the weight he was carrying on his back. So he set his heavy pack on the ground and dug inside of it.

'Here you are at last! Have you succeeded then?'

He turned around, already knowing who was calling to him, for he had immediately recognized Octavus's voice.

'What are you doing here? I ordered you to join the others. And, anyway, the last time I saw you, you were on the other side of the chasm.'

'After much effort, I was able to cross the abyss, despite all the branches that fell, by inching along the side of the cliff step by step. The Order's crampons and my training worked wonders. I followed you in case.'

'In case of what?'

'In case you were not able to complete the mission. In fact, you did not answer me. Have you succeeded?'

'No! Unfortunately, it is impossible to continue. This path is a dead end.'

'I have here some explosives which will surely create a breach and allow us to pass through.'

'The wall is far too thick and our weapons are not powerful enough.'

'Even if we cannot pass, we can at least leave the Tetrabomb.'

'The Tetra . . . how did you know?'

'I was specially appointed to this mission by the Magnus Legifer himself, and nothing can stop me. We must return there and set off the bomb. Even if we do not reach the target itself, the explosion should be powerful enough to finish the job. Let us go!'

'I have told you, it is impossible.'

'That attitude is not worthy of the Order. Nothing can stand up to Legiferius. How could a Commander use such language?'

'Silence! That is an order! We will return to our troops and that is final.'

'We cannot go back. It would be an act of high treason. For me it is unthinkable. I serve the Order and I will finish this out. Give me the Tetrabomb.'

'I take no orders from you. You do not even know what is at stake.'

'I will ask you once more,' Octavus declared. 'Give me the bomb.'

'You have no right to speak to me in that tone.'

'If you refuse, you are a traitor!' shouted Octavus.

He leapt at Erasmus who, rolling backward, threw him to the ground. The two Militians were standing again within a quarter of a second. Erasmus turned to his left to avoid a shot from Octavus's crossbow; the arrow grazed his side. At the same time, the Commander had also aimed and destroyed his opponent's weapon. So Octavus took out his dagger and rushed forward. Erasmus unsheathed his own and a violent struggle began. The Militians crossed swords with a clash, but neither was able to take the upper hand as both were so strong and experienced.

The duel lasted a long time and little by little fatigue set in. As he was attempting to avoid a hit, Erasmus caught his foot on a root and found himself unbalanced, his back against a tree. Octavus threw himself upon the Commander furiously. With superhuman effort, Erasmus pushed off with his legs and to his surprise, found himself two meters in the air, above his adversary. Octavus, carried by his momentum, ran into the trunk. Erasmus landed behind him at the ready for when his rival turned around. Strangely, Octavus remained still, pressed up against the tree. Erasmus advanced slowly, fearing a trap. Still no reaction. He seized the man and turned him slowly, discovering a red mark at the level of his heart. A branch had pierced his ribcage. He touched Octavus's neck and felt no pulse. He was dead.

Erasmus felt both sorrow and relief, for he had not really wanted to kill this man. Fate had decided it thus, but was it really fate? He remained intrigued by his leap. Never before, even during training, had he been able to jump so high. He decided to try again and pushed himself forward. He was astonished to discover that he could literally fly. In fact, he landed over ten meters from where he began. He repeated the act several times to convince himself that he was not dreaming. With each leap, he improved, now reaching fifteen meters. His training could not be the reason. Something else was now expressing itself within him, he was sure. His father's gifts had at last revealed themselves. Perhaps other abilities still lay dormant within him. He would have to discover them, one at a time. It was both fantastic and exciting. Perhaps he would not even uncover all his talents in this lifetime, who knew? Filled with these stimulating thoughts, he took the Tetrabomb out of his pack, removed the detonator, and threw the weapon into the void. The abyss was so expansive that Erasmus did not even hear the thud when the bomb reached the bottom.

Then he turned to Octavus's limp body. He could not bring himself to leave it there to spoil or to be torn to shreds by animals, so he sought out a hollow in the ground, pulled the deceased there, and buried him with stones. This work completed, he judged the burial decent, befitting a courageous soldier. He reclosed his pack and donned it, ready to continue on his way with a lighter load and heart. He found himself at the edge of the cliff where most of his men had succumbed. His men! What a peculiar idea, now. All his certainty, the meaning of his life even had been turned on its head by a simple meeting with that woman, that Fairy who had revealed him to himself. He was lost in reflection when he noticed a movement to his left. A long vine hung before him. He studied it carefully and realized that it would become his vehicle for crossing the chasm. He clung to it securely, ran back, and threw himself into the void. He easily and delicately debarked on the other side. He began to run and discovered that his speed was continually increasing, without his feeling the least bit tired. His journey proved leisurely, and he arrived astonishingly quickly at the edge of the forest, the border of the human world. Now he needed a plan.

THE WIND PEOPLE

After many long days in captivity, Pantaleone, Slevania, and the other captured members of the circus had at last been released. Weak and ragged, they rejoined their friends, who were both glad to see them again, and grieved to find them in such a pitiful state. The endless interrogations along with a lack of food and sleep had exhausted them. Seeing the troupe reunited to welcome them, Slevania's bright smile returned, and she declared, 'Not only did we reveal nothing to Legiferius, but we have returned determined to resist this idiotic, barren Order, which understands nothing!'

This was met with cheerful hurrahs, and weaving through the crowd, Slevania saw a little brown head pop up and immediately recognized it. Her heart skipped a beat the moment Ogrino leapt into her arms.

'Mama, I'm so happy to see you,' he said, covering her with kisses. 'I missed you. I have so much to tell you, and Pantaleone too.'

He lunged toward his adoptive father and clung to his neck, kissing him loudly.

'I have seen and done such marvelous, beautiful things, but the situation is grave and dangerous, and I have a great responsibility I would like to share with you.'

Saying this, he took his parents by the hand and led them to their wagon. Over the next several hours, he told them in detail of his adventures since their tragic separation. Pantaleone and Slevania could not believe their ears. All the splendors, all the strange and fascinating creatures that their little boy had been so fortunate to meet, and most of all this sublime woman, this Felicia Regina, who seemed straight out of the most fabulous of fairy tales. Ogrino's account filled them with enthusiasm and hope. So there really was a Legendary World, complete with structure, representatives, and ethics. This meant that Legiferius was attempting to destroy a whole world and not merely some isolated, bizarre creatures. The Order's plan seemed even more horrible now than they had initially thought. Eliminating so much beauty, such rich souls, could not be tolerated. They had to form a plan to counter this atrocity. Slevania fell into a long silence; her sorrow was visible. Pantaleone caught her eye, and they gazed deeply at one another for a long time. Ogrino, too, was silent before his parents' grief. Then Pantaleone turned to him, his eyes moist, and spoke in a sorrowful tone that the little Ogre had never heard from the mouth of his always-jovial adoptive father.

'The Wind People, the nomads, will be the Order's next victims. When it has lain waste to the creatures of the Legendary World, it will turn to those who refuse to be shut up in a straitjacket where everything is forever in the Order's control. For we are the sons of liberty; our symbol is the wheel, the one painted on my wagon. The wheel means movement, and it cannot be enclosed in Legiferius's box, or it will die. I am a son of this People, the Wind People, and that is why I started this circus. It allows me to travel constantly, to be free to go wherever I wish and meet all kinds of people and creatures and sometimes come into contact with the Legendary World, even as I did with you, Ogrino. When I took you in, I knew that you were not a human child, but I took pity on a little abandoned creature, all alone. Legiferius does not like those who are different, those who do not feel they belong to any particular group; that scares the Order because it likes control. If you travel, are always on the move, then you have a more progressive view. You question yourself; you have a more developed critical eye and do not accept the Order's ideas as if they were absolute truth, and so Legiferius knows everything about us; it tolerates us as it watches us constantly. One day it will forbid us to travel, the better to control us, and those who refuse will be imprisoned or even put to death.

'If what you say is true,' Ogrino interrupted, 'you cannot just sit here twiddling your thumbs, waiting. At Felicia's request, I was able to convince the different parties of the Legendary World to ally themselves to march against the Order, except for, unfortunately, the Trolls. If you could help us too, that would take Legiferius by surprise and give us a greater chance of success.'

The conversation was interrupted by cries and the sounds of falling objects. Ogrino peeked out the window and saw the Messeyer brothers on either side of a man who was flailing in all directions, trying to hit them. Othello, the juggler, hit the man on the head with a bowling pin, which quickly subdued him. He was tied up and brought into the main tent. There, he was doused with a bucketful of water to wake him.

'Who are you? And what were you doing hiding and spying?'

'I was not spying on anyone. I love the circus and only wanted to know how the artists live when they are not performing.'

'You lie!' said Othello. 'What is your name?'

'Jaspar!'

They searched him and found a symbol of the Order on him.

'You are a Militian, a spy. What are you looking for?'

'I am a simple shopkeeper, fascinated by the circus.'

At that moment, Cordicello slapped him hard across the face.

'You will talk or else!'

The man fell sullenly mute and did not make another peep.

'He won't say anything more. The Order's soldiers are trained to resist all kinds of suffering. His silence says more than any speech would. He was spying on us, and I would not be surprised if he were here in search of Ogrino.'

Pantaleone reacted at once.

'We will leave him in the middle of the countryside in a hayloft. By the time, the Order finds him, we will have had time to decide on a plan of action.'

At that, Cordicello climbed atop Colossus, the soldier was laid on his stomach across the Clydesdale's neck, and straightaway they were off.

'This regrettable incident is just one more proof that the Order mistrusts us and is constantly watching us. Sooner or later, we will have to fight the Order, so it is better to take the initiative rather than wait for further oppression. It's settled. We will help Ogrino in his task, not only so that justice may triumph, but also for our own freedom.'

'Tomorrow morning,' said Slevania, 'we will leave at dawn to meet our brothers, those Wind People who live in the Emerald Valley.'

And so they all went off to bed without any further delay, for the night would be short. In fact, as soon as the first light of day arrived, Pantaleone came to rouse Ogrino. They washed their faces together, above a bowl of water that the child found very cold. As soon as they arrived in the main room of the wagon, they saw that Slevania had prepared a nice breakfast with steaming milk and honey, whose aroma filled Ogrino's nostrils pleasantly. Mountains of croissants and pastries awaited them, recalling memories of times gone by. Ogrino felt very lucky to have found his adoptive parents and to be setting off with them. He had the vague idea that they could be a very great help in the task Felicia had given him, and these Wind People intrigued him. He was eager to meet them. If it were true that they held nature's secrets, as Themistomene had said, then certainly their involvement would be very valuable if they agreed to assist the Legendary World. Once more, Ogrino would have to find the right words.

As the sun peeked over the horizon, glowing red, the circus's long caravan was already on the move. Still on their eastward route, they crossed much of the kingdom, passing over hills, prairies, and forests, finally, arriving four days later in the center of a wide valley. The grass looked like the lawn of a garden extending as far as the eye could see. The more they walked along this spongy carpet, the further it seemed to stretch out before them. A feeling of vastness slowly settled in, accentuated by the bright, almost shining, distinctive green of these blades of grass.

In the distance, Ogrino could make out broad, dark masses creeping along. He questioned Pantaleone, who told him that they were bison. The bison accounted for the riches of the Wind People. They lived in symbiosis with these animals, which provided all that they needed—meat, milk, and fat for nourishment; skin for clothing and boots; and horns and bones for tools or weapons. But beyond these benefits, the spirit of the Wind People was closely connected with the spirit of the bison. In fact, the tribe's shaman was able to communicate with it through the spirit pathway. So the two peoples shared a mutual respect, and never did the humans, in their hunt, endanger the survival of the herd. They took only what they needed to survive, never more.

Geometric forms appeared before them, rising out of the landscape. As the circus people advanced, Ogrino was able to distinguish wagons and funny sorts of triangles from which clouds emerged. When they had arrived, they were welcomed by wolfdogs who rushed forward noisily to meet them, leaping, followed by smiling children. They completed their journey amidst laughs and hurrahs and entered into the mobile village. The wagons were set out in a circle around teepees from whose tops smoke was escaping. A delicious smell wafted through the air, and Ogrino heard his stomach rumble. The chief of the village, Rostropov, came out of his tent to welcome them with a warm embrace, first for Pantaleone and Slevania, then for all the circus troupe as if they were his own brothers and sisters. Soon he was rejoined by the whole tribe, its members more numerous than Ogrino could count. It looked like they were emerging from all over, still more children by the dozens, vigorous elders, women carrying baskets, and robust men transporting all sorts of various objects. Ogrino felt a deep joy emanating from these people who were at once so diverse, in their colored costumes, and yet gave an impression of great unity. They were one as a tribe and one with the natural world surrounding them. Ogrino now understood what he had felt among the circus troupe, that feeling of a great big family whose members were all joined by a powerful, invisible link. Here that sentiment was ten times as strong, thanks to the number of people. The boy felt at home, although he knew no one in the tribe.

'My friends, I must speak with our brothers,' Rostropov said. 'We will meet again tonight for a celebration in honor of their visit.'

As the crowd dispersed, Rostropov had Pantaleone and Slevania come into his teepee while Ogrino found himself being led into the village by the children. They ran along, laughing, between the wagons, and Ogrino discovered a whirlwind of activity. Everyone was occupied with a specific task; the women were weaving blankets or wicker baskets, and the men were carving wooden boxes and making bags from skins. Ogrino learned from his companions that the Wind People traded with cities and villages, selling artisanal objects. They also did minor domestic work, such as repairing fences or roofs, painting houses, or even sharpening knives, and many other useful things. In this way the Wind People, different though they were, had always been warmly welcomed everywhere they traveled, for through their work and their good spirits, they brought a sense of festivity to each of their stopping points.

The day thus passed in a delicious manner for Ogrino, who, after a gargantuan snack had taken part in all sorts of games such as archery, tetherball, and a frenzied horse race. At the end of the afternoon, he felt tired but pleased with all he had seen and done with his new friends. At nightfall, a great fire lit in the center of the village was quickly surrounded by a number of barbeques. A very long table which formed a circle around the blaze was set, and the guests sat down. Toasts were given in their honor, and then the meal began in a joyous commotion. Once more, Ogrino's appetite was a subject of attention, and it quickly became legendary among the community.

At the end of the banquet, when everyone was sated, Rostropov stood to officially mark the beginning of the ball. For this, he climbed onto the table and, as the staccato music of violins and tambourines started up, he began to dance energetically, tapping the heels of his boots with his hands. Men were whistling along with the beat and others cried out, 'Ho, ho!' Then the women climbed onto the table and, taking their long dresses in one hand, began to spin around, faster and faster. More instruments joined in, enriching the melody. Flutes, oboes, guitars, cellos, and above all accordions had begun to play. A real orchestra was now at work, giving the dance quite a festive and harmonic air. Irresistibly drawn on by the music and the dancers' graceful movements, Ogrino couldn't help but climb onto the table as well. He was joined by his parents, who never missed an opportunity to enjoy themselves, especially after what they had experienced in Legiferius's jails. In the space of a single day, Ogrino had forgotten the tragic events in the making and had once more tasted of life's simple joys, thanks to this humble yet tremendous society, which emanated a pure feeling of freedom.

Having reached Fort Legiferius, Erasmus presented himself before Primus's secretary and asked for an immediate audience.

'That will be difficult,' the secretary announced, 'as his schedule is very full in this time of preparation. Make a report to your superiors. They will transmit it.'

'What I have to say to him must not wait,' he replied authoritatively. 'It could prove crucial for the Order.'

Disconcerted by Erasmus's self-assurance, the secretary finally pressed a round button. After five seconds, an irritated voice rang out from a metal horn.

'What is it? I explicitly forbade you to disturb me.'

'Commander Erasmus wishes to speak with you on an important subject.'

'Erasmus! Have him come in at once.'

As if suddenly electrified, the secretary passed in front of Erasmus and led him to Primus's office. He disappeared at the last moment to allow the Commander to enter alone.

'I heard of your tribulations at least six hours ago, yet you are only now arriving. Did you dawdle on the way back, or what? It is useless to tell you that your failure deeply damages the Order. So I will listen. Explain to me in detail why you failed. Do not omit anything. Be concise, for my time is precious.'

Astonishingly calm in the face of the Magnus Legifer's threats and aggressive tone, Erasmus gave his account tranquilly.

'The target is defended by evil forces which transform every living being—animals, insects, and even plants—into an enemy. We lost half of our soldiers and more than a third of our mounts. I personally lost my best men to the depths of an abyss that opened up beneath our feet. I, too, nearly died in that chasm, only scarcely escaping. However, unfortunately, it claimed the Tetrabomb. After that, I had to return with what was left of my unharmed troops as well as the numerous injured. The overland route is essentially impassable; the obstacles are legion and our forces are too limited.'

'I must say that you possess a certain gift for camouflaging your mediocrity. A Commander of the Order, worthy of that name, would not allow himself to deviate from his goal even if met with the devil in person. I had placed such hope in you, and you have utterly disappointed me. Do you realize what the loss of the Tetrabomb means to the Order? Are you even aware of the massive sums of intelligence and effort necessary to create such a weapon? Do you know how long it will take to build another? What's more, it is your fault that the target is still intact and our plan thus is greatly affected. For this you will be punished.'

'Magnus Legifer!' Erasmus interrupted, in a deferent, yet firm voice. 'I recognize that I did not live up to the confidence you placed in me. I failed, and I admit that. Still, I went farther than any man has ever gone before. I was within striking distance of the target. What's more, I have memorized the area and its dangers. In short, I am the best-suited to lead another expedition, and this time, succeed.'

Primus was pensive and did not respond for a time.

'Time is running out. Your suggestion is not so bad,' he finally said. 'The issue of the Tetrabomb remains. We absolutely need another one as that is the only weapon that could eliminate the target. I will speak to the Docts, but I am not hopeful of obtaining one in the time given. If that is the case, the mission will be cancelled.'

'As I told you, I was near enough to the target that our next mission will permit us to break through its last lines of defense and reach its heart. There, a relatively large mass of classical explosives will suffice to eliminate the target. Thus, we do not necessarily need the Tetrabomb in order to succeed. We must keep at this mission, whatever the cost.'

'I am glad to see your enthusiasm and desire to make up for your failure. Consequently, I assign you to this new mission whether the Tetrabomb is ready or not.'

'It shall be carried out according to your orders. I have only one request. I wish to choose each one of my men myself. I will need an entire garrison as the dangers are many and the potential losses very high. I will also need a dozen Terranefs to make our progression easier.'

'As far as the men, you shall have them. Concerning the Terranefs, that is different. You have neither the rank nor the training to operate such machines. I need them for other missions. However, I agree to set one aside for you to clear your path. A large convoy would attract too much attention from the enemy, in any case, and we would lose the element of surprise.'

'But . . .'

'That is all. I want you to be ready to leave at any moment as soon as the new bomb is finished if that proves to be possible in the time which remains to us. If not, I will provide you with ten tons of dynamite. Erasmus, this time do not fail. I am giving you a second chance and the means to succeed. If you are victorious, a brilliant career with the Order awaits you. If you fail . . . ' He trailed off.

'I thank you for your leniency and your support, Magnus Legifer, and I can assure you that I will do everything in my power to complete the mission I have dedicated myself to.'

'Good, I will give the necessary authorizations for you to obtain the materials and Militians you need for this mission. With that, I bid you farewell.'

As he left, Erasmus could not help but smile to himself, thinking of what he had been able to obtain from the Order. His plan was taking shape; now he needed to put it into action. That part would be the longest and most dangerous of all.

THE ORDER'S LAST BATTLE

For the first time, the Council of the Elders met along with a child, for the hour was grave and the guest very special. Romcunda, the shaman of the Wind People, had in fact detected the great depth of the little man's soul and knew also that he was carrying out an important mission. And so, before the Council, Ogrino divulged the extent of his knowledge about the different kingdoms of the Legendary World's plans of defense as well as of Legiferius's intended attacks. After the long explanation, during which all had been silent and attentive, Rostropov, the chief, and also the eldest began to speak.

'Taking into account the Order's power, we must battle them on two fronts. The first is that of classical warfare, in which our ingenuity and knowledge of the battleground will give us the advantage. We should be capable of giving our adversaries some trouble. However, without the aid of our second front, victory is far from certain. We hardly have a choice. We must invoke the spirits.

He turned to Romcunda, seeking his approval.

'Rostropov speaks the truth,' said the shaman. 'Without help from the Legendary World's deceased, we cannot defeat such a vast, battle-hardened army.'

'How can they help us combat the Order's armies?' Pantaleone asked.

'It is simple!' Romcunda spoke up again. 'They will sow terror and fear among our enemies by their mere presence, and especially by their touch, which will cause the most alarming of frights in their adversaries.'

Romcunda was blind, but far from being a handicap, his disability had always allowed him access to a world unknown to humans. He had the power to communicate with the spirits of the dead. Today, he would call upon those killed by the Order. These ghostly beings, though immaterial, were not necessarily harmless. On the contrary, they could prove to be formidable adversaries as they had an unquenchable thirst for vengeance against their enemies.

'Usually, I take this path alone,' Romcunda announced in a loud voice. 'But on this very special day, we will have to go as a pair on this journey to the shores of the spirit world. The little man, or rather, I should say the Ogre-child, will come along with me, as he is the link between humans and the Legendary World.

A pipe was filled with aromatic plants with ecstatic properties, whose secrets were known only to the shamans. Romcunda took a few puffs and the pipe glowed red. He passed the piece to Ogrino, who copied him. The harsh smoke irritated his lungs. He coughed violently and his head spun. He felt intoxicated as if by a wine that was both sweet and rough, then his eyes rolled backward in his head, and he began to tremble ever so slightly and then his body stiffened. His head jerked from side to side and incomprehensible sounds escaped from his throat.

Carried by their trance, Romcunda's and Ogrino's spirits rose up like two eagles and quickly passed through several planes of the world of the deceased as if crossing through clouds. Then they stopped hand in hand. A weak, pale light emanated from them in the surrounding darkness. Nothing happened for a long while, and then slowly, very slowly, shapes—beings—timidly approached the light. Little by little a group accumulated, then a second and a third, until a numerous crowd had gathered around Romcunda and Ogrino. The shaman chose the right moment to begin a low, hypnotic chant and the light emanating from him grew stronger, until it shone like the sun reflecting on the sea. Ogrino's light too, brightened by Romcunda's, began to shine like the full moon in the dark night.

Ogrino, irresistibly drawn on by the moving shapes slowly gliding around him, let go of the shaman's hand and moved toward them, arms outstretched. At first, the closest spirits recoiled, then seeing that the child had stopped moving, they came close again, nearly brushing up against him. One of the spirits, perhaps bolder than the others, even touched him, and then two, three, four, did the same, and others followed suit. Ogrino took one by the hand gently and signaled to him to do the same with his neighbor. In a short time, everyone was joined in a long chain. Ogrino felt compassion for these immaterial creatures who seemed so melancholy, and yet must have once been joyful in life. These feelings caused his light to subtly change color, veering toward the orange of the setting sun.

Little by little, each spirit of the deceased, each shaped in the chain began to emit a dull light as well. The crowd then became a pale-glowing ring around the shaman and the little Ogre. Then Romcunda began to speak in a slow monotone.

'The time has come for your spirits to quench your thirst and finally achieve peace. We are at a crossroads. The order of the world below is on the point of toppling, thanks to the men of Legiferius. You were once victims. Today, you can be conquerors. I can show you the way back to the world of the living. If you have not forgotten who you were and who you loved, then you can follow me. In exchange for your assistance, I promise an end to your suffering. May those who feel ready to confront their past follow in my footsteps. But I warn you, if your will is too weak you will remain forever caught in the intermediary planes of the world of the dead. On the other hand, after your intervention in the material world, you will be liberated.'

Barely had he spoken these words when something that was closer to a long wail than a murmur spread throughout the assembly. Some lights became stronger while others flickered. Romcunda, remaining silent, began his slow descent toward the lower planes, pulling Ogrino along by a firm grip on his wrist. More than three quarters of the spirits followed them, others separated from the group like fireflies were growing paler each moment. The return was more tedious than the ascent had been as Romcunda had to make sure that the spirits that had been called were able to follow along. Dark, grasping entities attempted to join this downward procession like leeches greedy for energy. Several spirits fell victim to these attacks, their lights extinguishing before Romcunda could do anything. Ogrino felt steely sharp teeth plant themselves in his spirit body. He wanted to escape, but the three or four ghosts assaulting him literally stuck to his skin. He tried to detach them by pulling and pushing on them, waving his free arm through the air or trying to shake them off, but nothing worked. He felt his strength drain slowly as the ghosts sucked away his life force.

Romcunda concentrated on passing from one plane to another as they descended and had noticed nothing. Automatically, looking backward, he suddenly saw the attacks and shouted a particularly acute spell, and the sticky beings let out sharp cries, retreating like leaves blown in a strong wind. Ogrino, relieved, nevertheless, felt worn out and frozen as well. Their arrival into the world of the living proceeded without further mishaps. Romcunda awoke from his trance and his rolled-back eyes returned to their normal position.

He declared vibrantly, 'They are here. They came attracted by the child's light. He was able to 'speak' to them better than I could have. His heart is pure and loving, and the spirits felt it. He was able to create a link with them very naturally. Now thousands of them are ready to assist us in our struggle, thanks to this child.'

Ogrino, for his part, had not yet regained consciousness. His face was still pallid and his body cold.

'Bring hot water and blankets, quickly!' Romcunda ordered after having rapidly examined the child.

A woman brought a steaming bowl into which the shaman sprinkled dried herbs. He then lifted the child's head, parted his lips with a finger and poured the liquid slowly into his mouth. The crowd stood, petrified, waiting for something to happen.

'He was attacked fiercely, and his spirit body was gravely damaged. The most important thing now is that he does not fall into a deep coma, for then his spirit would remain forever stuck in one of the intermediate planes of the world of the dead. Wake up!' he said, now addressing the child.

Ogrino could not hear the shaman. He was floating about in a grey world where up and down meant nothing. He felt profoundly sad without knowing why. He had a vague desire to find someone but did not remember who. He felt he would remain here for eternity in a sort of infinite melancholy. Suddenly, a light appeared, dancing along furtively, now silver, now golden. A soft, yet imperious voice spoke, 'Your time has not come, Ogrino. Your task is not yet finished. You have achieved great things, and there are more to come. You will return to the world of the living, for I will guide you.'

'*That voice! I recognize it,*' thought Ogrino. 'It's the lovely, marvelous voice of Felicia.'

'Felicia. Will I see my parents again?' he asked, addressing the light, which was now taking shape. Little by little a face came into view, and what a face? Felicia Regina smiled tenderly. Her gaze, full of goodwill, inspired confidence.

'When your mission is complete and when the hour has come, then yes, you will be able to see them. Now follow me.'

She took Ogrino by the hand and pulled him gently downward, toward the human world.

Romcunda observed the child very carefully on the lookout for any movement that would indicate that his spirit was coming back to his body. He heard a gurgle escape from the little Ogre's mouth and jumped for joy.

'He's returning, this is it, he's on his way back. My potion has worked.'

Still, Ogrino took a long time to return to consciousness as he had been so exhausted. His stay in the land of the dead, nevertheless, left him with a glad feeling, not only because he had succeeded in attracting the spirits to the human world, but most of all also because he had seen Felicia again, and what's more, she had given him the hope of one day being able to see his parents again.

Gathered under the teepee, everyone felt more light-hearted now that they knew Ogrino was not in danger. Still, they were incredulous of the shaman's claim that the spirits had come because no one could see anything at all. If one were really attentive, he might have noticed the feeling of a presence, but nothing more. The shaman put out some of the candles, allowing darkness to settle in, and then they saw. Under the tent alone there must have been at least thirty of them—little ones, enormous ones, giants, glowing and floating shapes, kinds of transparent veils in the moonlight. Now that he had returned to the world of the living, only Ogrino was not squinting like the other members of the crowd. In fact, they had never seen ghosts in their life and judging by their tensed faces, it made them uncomfortable. After this initial sentiment of repulsion, they began to look at who these indistinct forms were and discovered a whole people whom they recognized. Pixies and Sprites gamboled about between the legs of a Troll who would have crushed Korrigans and Naiads without a second thought. The shaman was very satisfied, for although some of the spirits had disappeared during the journey, a great many had succeeded in reaching the human world. This army would be very valuable in their fight against the oppressor as Romcunda was convinced that Legiferius would not be expecting adversaries of that kind. Instinctively, the spirits gathered around Ogrino, who was still lying down, for though he was living, he was still one of their kind. They tried to touch him, but their hands passed through his body. With each point of contact, Ogrino felt heat that both warmed and reinvigorated him. It was a delicious sensation after the cold and his weariness from the journey, where he had been bitten by the clinging ghosts. In a short time, he felt entirely back to normal and leapt nimbly to both feet.

'I'm hungry!' he proclaimed. 'All that drama gave me an appetite. I could eat a whole pig.'

'The child is right,' said Rostropov. 'It is time to sit down and draw up our plans over a good meal.'

Primus was closely studying the map of the battle plan drawn up by his Docts and Commanders. Everything seemed calculated, thought-out, and designed to perfection. The different divisions' trajectories, the method of surrounding the enemy, the destructive attacks down to the last detail, everything was carefully dictated. Victory was all but inevitable as the plan was clearly the product of so much concentrated intellect. Primus was, of course, quite proud as he had instigated the idea. Still, he had to admit that the Docts, as well, had done excellent work. The various companies of Militians were perfectly suited to their respective missions. The Docts' knowledge of the terrain and the number and location of enemy hordes would make his army's task much easier. Everything was for the best, then. All he had to do now was gather his Commanders to go over the practical details of combat.

He seized his bullhorn and frantically shouted, 'Call all the Commanders as well as the Magnus Doct! Meeting in my office in five minutes.'

'Very well, Magnus Legifer,' said the secretary meekly, 'I will contact them at once.'

Less than four minutes later, they were all there in front of the Magnus Legifer's personal office. Quartus knocked and upon hearing Primus's 'Enter,' he opened the heavy door with no further ado, followed by his fellow officers and Segundus.

'My dear friends, I am overjoyed to see you as I am very eager to study the details of these battle plans together. I have carefully analyzed their overall strategy, and it seems wonderfully appropriate to me. There are several points in particular that I would like to go over with each of you, specifically concerning logistics. Our army will be large, consisting of exactly six hundred thirty-nine thousand seven hundred men, of whom sixty percent are in Infantry, thirty percent in Aviation, and ten percent in the Navy. This military mass will be unable to abide any delay due to purely logistical causes. I want the provision of equipment, weaponry, first aid, and food to be considered with as much care as the combat strategies themselves. I will not tolerate any wrench in the gears of your organization. So my good men, I am ready to hear from you regarding this.'

Quintus spoke up first, for thanks to the number of his Infantry troops, logistics were a vital part of his regiments' decisive entrance onto the battlefield.

'We will create a support base for each attacking company to provide for all their needs for the entire mission. Apart from all the equipment, these bases will hold fresh troops. They will move along at the same rate as our companies, no more than a half-day's travel from the front lines.'

'That seems satisfactory to me,' said Primus. 'It will be necessary, however, to make sure that the bases' supply chain is protected from interruption. Sentries will have to be posted at regular intervals, with visual contact between them.'

'It shall be done,' concluded Quintus.

'And you, Quartus, as Commander of the Aeronefs, you will play a decisive role both in destroying enemy strongholds and in providing coverage for Quintus's men on the ground.'

Now Quartus, in turn, described his entire plan, as well as the offensive and defensive preparations he had undertaken so that nothing would be left to chance. Then it was Sextus' turn to speak. His role as Commander of the Navy consisted of taking control of all of the coastal and inland waterways, keeping in mind that the main part of the attack would have to take place in the very center of enemy territory, far below the ocean's surface.

After three hours of intense, lively discussion, Primus was satisfied with all the improvements, adjustments, and alterations he had brought to his Commanders' initial, overall strategy.

'We have here quite an impressive plan, as soon as you integrate my suggestions,' he said to conclude the meeting. 'You may go back to your commanding bases. There will have to be a military parade before the attack, so that I can assess our troops' quality and readiness. My good men, you are well aware: we are taking part in a historic moment as Commanders. Your names will be carved into the public memory forever. Victory, in fact, bestows eternal glory upon the triumphant. Defeat is impossible: your honor is at stake. Your lives are at stake. Is that clear?'

'WE ARE THE ORDER, WE ARE LEGIFERIUS. VICTORY OR DEATH, SUCH IS OUR LAW!' the three Commanders chanted in unison.

There was a long silence during which each man reflected inwardly, wanting to give an almost sacred feeling to this declaration of faith.

'If I may allow myself,' the Magnus Doct said, voluntarily ending the solemn moment, 'I would like to offer my modest contribution to this magnificent body of work. A clock, no matter how accurate, is not immune to a speck of dust that could jam its gears and stop the whole operation. So that our organization might reach maximum efficiency, I have come up with one last element which will secure us victory. I call it 'the Eradication Elixir.''

'Oh? Do elaborate,' said Primus, seeming very interested.

Segundus, overjoyed at the chance to shine in front of Primus, thanked him with a nod of the head as he continued in a syrupy voice:

'My dear Primus, you are not unaware that my medical Docts have been working for months on a substance that would stimulate belligerence at a cellular level in the brain. Thanks to this elixir, we are now capable of inducing more aggressive behavior in our Militians.'

'Our soldiers are already very hardened,' Quintus interrupted. 'What more can your 'substance' contribute?' Irritation had crept into his voice.

Segundus addressed the Commanders in a pedantic tone, looking Quintus in particular straight in the eyes.

'In no way am I calling into question the capabilities of our army, which has been trained very well, incidentally, according to the Docts' regulations. What I wish to emphasize is that due to fatigue, or even to the destructive psychological influence of the Dissidents, our Militians could find their will to fight weakened. Our elixir acts in two parts. First of all, it will give them an immediate impulse to fight. Then, more importantly, as the battle continues they will begin to feel the desire to demolish, to exterminate the enemy. That is why it is called 'the Eradication Elixir.' With this increased motivation, our troops will abolish these despicable creatures, whose mere presence casts disgrace on the Order, from the face of the earth.'

Primus rejoiced. He had known that the Docts were ingenious but this finding, which would stimulate his troops, was a pure miracle.

'I am delighted with this news, and must once more congratulate my dear medical Docts. However, due to the size of our army, we will need a very great quantity of this product and, importantly, it will have to be included in the daily food rations just like meat or bread.'

'Let me then reassure you, dear Primus. Production began several months ago and our stocks are more than sufficient to provide for the short period that our soldiers will be in combat.'

'How secretive you have been, Segundus. You had neglected to inform me of that good news,' said Primus with amusement.

'I wished to be certain that all the preparations were in place before making an official announcement.'

'You are forgiven. And now let us drink to Legiferius's good health and to the Order's success.'

Ogrino had not wanted to leave the Wind People, but he had to continue his mission. After the evening meal, he had once more called upon Viastella and ridden to the waterfall on the blue river, hoping to find an entire colony of Trolls there. Arriving at the site, he saw no one, not even a rock out of place nor a broken tree, no trace of their passage. The Trolls had completely ignored the warning they had been given. They must have selfishly pushed into the depths of the forest with no thought to the fate of the Legendary World. Ogrino was disappointed, for he was losing a valuable ally in the Trolls.

Viastella, feeling his pain, whispered, 'Do not be sad. Everyone is free to go his own way. The Trolls have chosen theirs. Perhaps it is a wise decision for their people . . . we must not judge them, for everyone is acting according to his conscience.'

'It's ridiculous. They could have been a major source of support in our fight. They are so strong and robust they could sweep aside the Militians with no effort at all. They're too stupid.'

'Do not be so harsh. If they are not participating in our fight, there must be a reason.'

'I don't care about reason. So many people are risking their lives and little creatures much more frail than the Trolls are taking part in this war, so why not them?'

'I have told you, the meaning may escape us, but we have to trust in fate, and in Felicia. Now let us go! We should not stay here. We have much work still ahead of us.'

At that, the Unicorn leapt forward with a majestic bound, and they resumed their frenzied course toward the city.

The Golden Stag Tavern was famous for its well-brewed barley beer and fragrant wine as well as for its assortment of spiced sausages, hams, and so forth. It was a place where all sorts of people gathered—merchants from faraway countries, migrants in search of work, vagabonds, and soldiers. A small group of these soldiers was assembled in the tavern's darkest corner, and their voices were inaudible over the animated roar of the other clients. It's true that there was but one subject on everyone's lips—Legiferius's grand maneuvers in preparation for the coming war against the magical creatures. So no one heard Regalus, one of the Militians of the Order, speaking to the other soldiers at his table.

'Some of our own have been imprisoned because they were caught holding a conversation that the Order deemed blasphemous. They have been baptized the 'Dissidents' and have been tortured for their anti-establishment positions. I myself have participated in discussions, at night in my room, in which I learned that many of my companions felt tormented inside. I do not see the harm in speaking what one believes, even if it is against Legiferius's ideas. We are soldiers, it's true, but also men with the ability to think and to judge for ourselves. The Prelate's homily moved me. It shook me to the core. I have lost my convictions. Is the Order's crusade against the Legendary World as just as they would have us believe?'

'You're right,' added the soldier named Pertius. 'I, too, have been asking myself the same questions since the Prelate's speech. What if all this was nothing but a put-on? If magical creatures weren't so dangerous after all?'

'Maybe they are even useful,' chimed in another named Gladius.

'Yes, I no longer feel ready to participate in a mission. I don't believe in it any more. My convictions have dried up,' concluded Regalus.

'What should we do?' asked one of the Militians named Philbus. 'If we announce that, we don't want to go off to war, they will convict us for treason, and we'll end up in prison, or else be shot.'

'I myself cannot do something I no longer believe in,' added Quercius.

'But still, we couldn't rebel against the Order? We are stuck.'

'Maybe there is a solution,' said a voice from the shadows.

Everyone was startled. Someone had discovered their conversation. Regalus stood, his hand on the hilt of his dagger.

'Calm yourselves. You have nothing to fear from me. I am here to help you. I have a proposition to make.'

The man walked out of the darkness and most of the Militians, recognizing him, could not relax but remained tense.

'I have had the same thoughts as you and have arrived at the conclusion that we must stop the Order from carrying out their nefarious plans, whatever the cost,' Erasmus stated calmly. 'I came to this place precisely because I knew I could meet soldiers like you here. To openly stand up against Legiferius is tantamount to suicide. That is why I propose another path, which will allow you not only to stay alive, but also to act in accordance with your deepest convictions . . . unless you are cowards.'

'Cowards! Who do you take us for? You yourself are a soldier of the Order and you know very well that there are no cowards among us.'

Erasmus rejoiced. All was going as he had intended; he had cut his companions to the quick and was sure now that they would follow him in this undertaking. He explained to them in detail what he expected of them, and after a lively discussion, all enthusiastically signed on to his cause. They exchanged a warm embrace before parting. Erasmus watched them leave with a growing feeling of hope for his plan. He now had to continue his clandestine recruitment to put together an entire garrison of Dissidents. He wrapped himself in his cape and left. The night would be a long one, for he still had many inns left to visit.

Primus and his highest-ranking Commanders had drawn up a hub-and-spokes plan of attack, starting from the City. The geography and topology of the area particularly lent themselves to this idea. The gist of it was that they would comb over and secure the whole region around Fort Legiferius to then attack the areas most infested with magical creatures. The troops would be deployed in the four cardinal directions, meaning that their battlefields would be to the South, the Austral Sea; to the West, the Occidental mountains and caves; to the East, the Oriental hills and plains; and to the North, the dense Boreal forest. A large map of the kingdom displayed the sequence of operations, with symbols and arrows representing the different corps of the army and their respective pathways on the terrain. At the end of a very long, final meeting, Primus declared himself satisfied with the preparations and invited his Commanders to dine with him. Wine and good food allowed them to somewhat drop the tension of the last few days, each of which had seemed too short to deal with all the organizational problems and unexpected factors that arose without cease. Their energy drained, they retired to their rooms in order to be fresh and ready for the next day's dawning as the big day was nearing. Only sixty hours remained until it would all begin.

In the middle of the night, a furtive shape swept through the city's alleyways. Leaping from porch to porch, hiding in the shadows, the figure escaped the eyes of the few people still out at such a late hour. When a troop of sentries passed by, it stayed still until the street was clear once more. Then, as quickly as a jackrabbit, it ran along the road and crossed the intersection with care. Its journey led to the foot of Fort Legiferius. Crouched in the shadow of a carriage entrance, it waited until a military convoy passed through and then surreptitiously slipped between the wheels and clung to the underside of a cart. The line of soldiers entered into Fort Legiferius's courtyard, put the carriages away in the shed, and went to their barracks. When all was calm once more, Gumbo slipped out of his hiding place. Seeing that the sentries on the lookout towers were surveying the city, and none were looking in his direction, Gumbo scaled the wall of the central building as a spider might. Having reached the top, he leapt onto a pretty balcony bordering a spacious office whose many windows made it resemble a sunroom. One of the panels on the top row of windows had been left open. He climbed up its frame and jumped through the opening into the room. Chandeliers lit up a vast library and furniture stacked high with books and scrolls. On a long table, a colorful and complicated map was unrolled. Gumbo recalled Ogrino's instructions and, as best he could, folded the large scroll that held Legiferius's plans of attack. He pushed the paper into his sack and retraced his path with no problem. However, on the way out, he had to pass over the surrounding wall as the carriage door seemed irrevocably closed. His task would be more difficult than entering had been, for there were many guards, and they passed very near him. He had to use a thousand and one strategies to stay out of sight. Suddenly, as he was running along the path atop the wall, he heard a bellow from the top of the fortress itself.

'An intruder on the outside wall!'

An arrow came crashing against the ramparts just two inches from Gumbo's head. Despairing, he climbed onto the crenellations just as four guards ran toward him. He peered over the edge. The wall was too flat for him to be able to climb down rapidly enough, given the situation. As he turned his head, there they were, their hands outstretched and ready to seize him. With a bound, he leapt over the guards' heads and bolted. The men took aim and fired. Gumbo's innate sense of danger saved him at the last moment. He launched himself forward and slid on his belly for two meters as the arrows grazed the hair on his back. Before the sentries could reload their bows, he took three torches from the wall and threw them toward the men, forcing them to protect themselves. One of the torches fell onto a chariot that had remained in the fortress's court. Taking advantage of the distraction, the chimpanzee quickly pulled a sort of lasso out from his sack and looped it around one of the crenellations. A new volley of projectiles rained down on him, and this time, he could not avoid them. One of the arrows struck his left shoulder, passing all the way through it. He clenched his teeth in pain, making a face that resembled a mocking smile. Other voices piped up on his left. Six sentries were upon him . . .

All of a sudden, the sound of thunder rang out, creating panic among the Militians. The fallen torch had caused a barrel of powder to explode, and the blast had forced the pursuing soldiers up against the wall. Gumbo did not waste a second in taking advantage of this brief respite. He leapt over the crenellations, holding the rope in one hand. After rebounding once against the fortress wall, hitting his head, the chimpanzee found himself dangling fifteen meters above the ground. He felt somewhat dizzy, and his shoulder hurt. The sentries were firing once more, but Gumbo's slight swaying protected him; only one arrow pierced his left leg. He slid along the rope and reached the ground in no time at all. He limped across the plaza surrounding Fort Legiferius under yet another shower of arrows. Luckily, by zigzagging he was able to reach one of the adjacent streets safe and sound, and he disappeared into the darkness. The Militians immediately sent out patrols to find him, but Gumbo had retreated into the sewers and was slowly making his way to the edge of the city through that labyrinth of tunnels.

Primus was furious that the secret plans had been stolen right under the nose of the most powerful army in the world, and what's more, from his own office. This offense was unforgivable, and an example had to be made of the incompetents who had allowed this to happen. He immediately woke the Fortress's entire garrison, and, though it was the middle of the night, a scaffold was erected. The poor sentries who had let the intruder—a lowly monkey—escape had their head and hands enclosed in a pillory. The executioner unleashed a torrent of lashes onto their bare backs. All the Militians were gathered before the morbid spectacle. Primus began to speak from atop the outside walls.

'You are all Legiferius! Without your dedication and excellence, we have nothing. But thanks to the Docts' knowledge and the Commanders' vision, along with your commitment, nothing can stand in our way. We shall conquer new horizons, and you will be the first to benefit. In this marvelous plan, there is no place for those who doubt, hesitate, or fail. The Order embodies strength, efficiency, and intelligence. That is why punishment is necessary. It should fortify one's motivation by imprinting into the body those errors that must not be repeated.'

During this speech, the executioner had not stopped his whipping, and the condemned now lay motionless and bleeding.

'My tolerance is great, and my forgiveness infinite. These Militians are as dear to me as sons, and they will return to their places in our ranks with dignity once they have recovered. They will have learned their lesson for good, I am sure, and will thank me for that later. I want you all to conduct this war with unwavering enthusiasm and determination, for that is the secret to our victory and to the advent of the Order's brilliant glory.'

At these words, the crowd began to roar, filling Primus with unspeakable pleasure. He saluted his men and retired to his chamber, followed by his Ccommanders-in-chief.

'We have to change our plans at once,' said Quintus. 'If the enemy knows in advance where our troops will move, we lose the element of surprise, and they will be able to organize a counter-attack.'

'No,' Primus cut in. 'It is too late to adjust our strategy. We do not have the time. What do they know, thanks to that map? They know our general angles of attack but neither the volume of manpower we will have nor the speed of our progress. What's more, the owners of that thieving monkey are surely not linked to the Legendary World, which limits the spread of the confidential information. In brief, this theft will have a very limited impact.'

'Could it be the Dissidents?' asked Quintus.

'It is possible,' Primus responded.

'Then they would be able to take advantage of the data to work against us.'

'Even so. They are few as we have imprisoned most of them, and thus I am not so very concerned,' Primus concluded. 'Here is what we will do. We will attack twenty-four hours sooner than scheduled to catch our foes unaware, and you will watch your men closely for any signs of rebellion. At the end of the day, this theft is for the best because it forces us to do our utmost to have the odds on our side.'

With this, he ended the meeting and everyone returned to his tasks, for now each minute counted. The plan would take shape quickly, for all the high-ranking officers were frantic, and orders were being issued in all directions, making the army look like a teeming anthill. The war machines were lined up in the central courtyard. Some soldiers were oiling the Terranefs's tracks as others polished the machines' crossbow-cannons. The Aeronefs, anchored to the ground for the moment, had their Zeppelins filled with gas. The convoys of food and ammunition formed slowly in single-file lines, awaiting orders to depart. Soldiers ran back and forth and orders were shouted without cease. Everyone was double-checking his pack's contents and shining his weapons.

Gumbo arrived, exhausted, at the edge of the city where Ogrino and his friends were supposed to be waiting for him. At first, none of them saw him, for the morning fog obscured their view, and they were busy making coffee to warm themselves. There was a little group there consisting of the Messeyer brothers, Othello, Cordicello, Camillo, and, of course, Pantaleone and Slevania. Ogrino, who was impatiently waiting seated atop Colossus, saw Gumbo first and ran to meet him. Discovering that he was wounded, he called Slevania, and they brought him over to the fire. Pantaleone opened the backpack while Slevania took care of Gumbo. Ogrino couldn't tear his gaze from the suffering animal, who was staring straight into his eyes. The chimpanzee slowly relaxed as the ointments Slevania had applied to his wounds took effect.

Ogrino said admiringly, 'You were extraordinarily brave and clever.'

'This was a remarkable task,' said Pantaleone. 'He has brought us Legiferius's plans of attack. We know exactly what they are going to do. We must return to the Wind People as quickly as possible.'

They wrapped Gumbo in a blanket. Pantaleone mounted Colossus, and Slevania placed the monkey into his arms.

'Let's go. Everyone saddle up! We are leaving at once. The alert must have been given, and the Militians are surely looking for him.'

'I am not coming with you,' said Ogrino, 'for as you know, I have a mission of my own to complete. Give me the map as it will be useful when I meet with the beings of the Legendary World.'

So Pantaleone took out the scroll and scrutinized it so as to memorize every detail, then handed it to Ogrino.

'I wish you could stay with us. It would be safer for you, but you must go your own way.'

'Take care of yourself,' said Slevania sadly. 'Do not take any needless risks.'

'Do not worry. Someone is watching over me.'

Saying that, he clasped the leaf of the Gigantum in his hands and thought hard of Viastella, who came out of the mist as if by magic. He smiled at her as his companions looked on dumbfounded, filled with wonder at the creature's grace. In a bound, he was astride her back. They approached Gumbo, and Ogrino kissed him on the forehead. Next it was Pantaleone and Slevania's turn. Then he waved to his friends and disappeared into the mist.

Finally, the Militians received the order to depart a little before dawn, and long convoys issued from the fortress toward their positions of attack in accordance with the plan. The hub-and-spokes strategy conceived by the Docts was taking shape, little by little, and operations would soon be ready to commence on all four fronts.

On the western front, the task was apparently complex. Not only did the Order have to hunt their enemies on the surface, but also below ground through tunnels, passageways, and caves. Their orders were clear. No being could be allowed to escape. The Pixies of the world below were, in fact, classified by Legiferius among the most malignant of creatures as they could easily infiltrate any space thanks to their tunnels. In addition, one commando had been assigned the special mission of bringing back an item of immeasurable strategic value for Legiferius's triumph. Most of the Militians underground had easily penetrated into one of the main passageways through a little temple whose door was obstructed by the corpse of one of their own, deceased on a previous mission. The others took alternate tunnels whose entrances had been meticulously catalogued by the Docts. Some even started from the underground pathways beneath Fort Legiferius itself.

The Scavanef, one of the Order's most tremendous inventions, was to leave from the Fort's crypt. It was an imposing tracked vehicle with the general shape of a conch shell and a massive, spiraled drill in front. With a deafening clanking, the machine began to move toward the western edge of the crypt. Having reached the wall, the drill began to turn at full speed, digging the beginnings of a tunnel. After only a few dozen meters, the Scavanef reached a narrow underground passageway and its progress quickened. As it advanced, Legiferius's troops rushed forth easily in its wake.

Elsewhere, other soldiers were exploring the subterranean maze at a run, armed with torches and diligently eliminating the poor wretched creatures that had the misfortune to cross their path. Those in the main passageway, equipped with light cannons, were massacring the Komodo dragons, whom they annihilated as soon as the reptiles tried to attack them. In this way, they were able to proceed without hindrance up to an old bridge over an underground river. After that, their trail became less evident, due to the multiple mazes of tunnels before them. Here again, the Docts' research was doing its part. The maps that the Militians held seemed to be relatively faithful in their description of the labyrinth of tunnels they were weaving through. So as to cover major portion of the ground, they separated into several battalions which plunged bravely into the entrails of the earth.

At the surface, the troops' progress had begun according to schedule and encountered hardly any resistance. It is true that in general Sprites, Kobolds, Groundlings, and Will'-o'-the-Wisps made up only small and, for the most part, harmless groups. The Terranefs blazed the trail, driving out with their shots the poor creatures hidden under boulders, behind tree stumps, or in burrows. Terrified, the Dracs, Mutins, and other Imps fled in a chaotic jumble. The soldiers only had to load their crossbows with grenades that, as they exploded, mowed down the creatures as they ran. The flying nets also caused a veritable massacre, capturing whole families of distraught Imps, Alfas, and Genies. Then the soldiers would exterminate them without mercy, shooting at point-blank range. It looked like nothing could stop this slaughter until, strangely, all of the Terranefs simultaneously stopped in their tracks. The drivers did their best to restart the engines, but without success. Even the crossbow-cannons would not shoot.

So the Militians found themselves transformed from assailants into prey, before the surging mass of combatants that was now upon them. Themistomene, seated on a young Processionaire, was at the front, boldly leading his troops into battle. A cavalry composed of Gnomes and Korrigans mounted on countless giant crickets crashed through enemy lines, easily jumping over the volleys of arrows, bullets, and other projectiles. Equipped with ebony breastplates and shields of bramble, the cavaliers threw blinding pollen at their adversaries, whipped them with thorny vines, or poured stinging sap on them. Many of the Militians were wailing in pain, rolling on the ground, or sobbing like children. Still, after their initial surprise, little by little the soldiers were able to counter the attack. Nets flew out, stopping numerous crickets in mid-air, and jets of tar glued others to the ground just as they were about to take off. Then the Order's soldiers threw themselves upon their enemies, brutally wounding their faces or shooting armor-piercing arrows through their breastplates. The losses on both sides were now heavy, and the battle's outcome became more uncertain.

During this time, Erasmus and his men had reached the aqueduct over the wide Saint Michael fault, a hundred meters deep. Apart from the transport of potable water, the bridge's large scale offered a shortcut to the forest for convoys, troops, and most of all the Terranefs. Although this place was not the only point of access to the heart of the Legendary World for Legiferius, it was crucially strategic. That was why two Dissidents had already leapt into the void, suspended on ropes in order to position themselves on either side of the bridge's western end. They meant to mine the abutments supporting the aqueduct. Concentrated on their delicate and perilous mission in which they were manipulating several kilograms of dynamite, they did not notice the clicking sound of tracks on the bridge above. Erasmus, seeing three Terranefs beginning to cross at the other end of the viaduct, immediately gave the order to shoot. The sole Terranef of the Dissidents fired, annihilating one of the enemy war-machine on the other side of the bridge. Legiferius's Militians, surprised to be attacked by soldiers wearing the uniform of the Order, hesitated, allowing time for another shot that destroyed the Terranef on the right. The response was definitive. Before it could fire a third shot, the Dissidents' Terranef vaporized in a terrible commotion. Hundreds of pieces of metal rained down on Erasmus's nearby soldiers, causing many injuries and deaths. The Militians advanced onto the bridge rapidly, following behind the Terranef which was shooting one cannonball after another. Having finished their work, the two Dissident pyrotechnists climbed slowly back up the bridge's abutments. The Order's artillerymen were now very close. The Dissidents were continually shooting to repulse their assailants; some had drawn their daggers, ready for hand-to-hand combat. As soon as the two miners had reached the bridge, they began to unwind the wires connected to the explosives. One of them was struck with an arrow in the center of his back, and he crumpled down dead. The second ran to take the bobbin of cord from his unfortunate companion and continued the operation until he reached the edge of the fault. There he attached the wires to the detonator and signaled to Erasmus.

'Retreat, retreat!' called the latter.

The Dissidents fled the bridge at full speed, still spraying their enemies with heavy fire. The Militians, taking advantage of the retreat, were hot on their heels. And then apocalypse. An explosion loud enough to burst eardrums tore cries of pain from the Militians. These transformed into fearful screams as they saw that the aqueduct was buckling, inching them inexorably toward the abyss. The bridge was fractured in several places and entire sections were now falling into the void along with the horses, men, and equipment they had held. In less than thirty seconds, the magnificent construction had sunk into the chasm with a sinister crackling, taking with it a whole division of Legiferius. Despite the deaths of many friends, Erasmus was very satisfied as not only was one of Legiferius's main attack routes now severed, but the Order had also just suffered a heavy loss. Exhilarated by victory, Erasmus felt as if he could do anything. He wanted to move on to other bold acts that would bring down the enemy. He felt sure that all the Dissidents scattered throughout Legiferius's ranks would follow his orders. However, the pressure on the Order would have to be increased in order to significantly weaken the forces of destruction and give the Legendary World a chance at victory, no matter how small. He opened his back and freed a pigeon carrying a message for Primus.

On the southern front, the Militians' troops were few, in accordance to the Order's plans, but, nonetheless, devastating. Small skiffs floated down rivers and streams, dragging behind them metallic nets that captured all kinds of aquatic life.

Each time the nets were drawn up, a teeming mass of pike, carp, salmon, and trout was revealed. Sporadically, Nymphs, and Dryads would turn up and be immediately put to death with a lance or harpoon. At the same time, large crafts such as galleons, caravels, and other warships were forming a veritable armada, which would comb the coasts or cross the seas at the southern border of the kingdom. Through a system of acoustic emission, the vessels attracted undersea creatures who became hypnotized and gathered around the boats. Then the soldiers would throw barrels filled with dynamite overboard. These would explode as they sank, devastating everything within a hundred-meter radius. And so the poor Tritons, Sirens, and other mer-people perished by the dozens in these detonations.

On the eastern front, the flying ghosts made up a translucent grey cloud, visible only when the sun's rays passed through it. Lacking that, nothing warned of their presence. Still, Vintunus, one of the Rectors of the first battalion, noticed a blur undulating in the sky and immediately gave the order to fire. Thanks to their goggles, the Militians could divine, rather than see, exactly, the mass of ghosts descending upon them. They shot electric arrows which sizzled as they tore through the air. Several of the ghosts contorted in pain, but most were passing through their enemies' bodies, filling them with dread. The Militians fell to their knees, crying like babies, trembling in fear, and calling for their mothers. Vintunus couldn't believe his eyes. Soldiers that he himself had trained, men who had fought a thousand battles, some of whom had endured serious injuries without so much as a groan, were now reduced to the state of a whimpering child. A disgrace!

'Stand up and fight! You are Militians of the Order, for heaven's sake!'

Before he could say another word, a Goblin spirit attached itself to him, and he immediately felt a suffocating horror that flung him to the ground, terrified. As the mass of spirits spread, the army turned into a panicked mob. It was at that moment that a great cloud of dust appeared in the distance, producing a deafening roar that grew continually louder. A tide of countless bison covering the whole width of the plain was advancing rapidly toward the soldiers. Several Commanders and Rectors gave the order to the Terranefs and to the men to shoot. Under the impact, clumps of earth and animals' bodies flew up, but the pack skirted around these obstacles without slowing in the least. The ghosts continued to wreak havoc, and most of the Militians were completely overcome with fear. So when Romcunda arrived at the enemy front lines astride a bison, no shots were fired. He was followed by the immense herd. The men of the Wind People, armed with rifles, sat atop the first row of animals. Romcunda, followed by his clan, passed through the Order's battalions as if they were mere wisps of straw. A few more shots rang out from the Terranefs just before the cloud of ghosts reached them, and then nothing could be heard but cries of horror and the dull roar of hooves on dry earth. The tide of bison continued to roll by, leaving only death in its wake. As it left the plain, the herd turned now inexorably toward the hills, still led by the blind shaman.

It was on the northern front that the confrontation would be most brutal, for much was at stake. Legiferius's aim was to destroy the Gigantum, whatever the cost, and most of its means were concentrated on that aim. In fact, Primus had only limited faith in the commando led by Erasmus. Hadn't they already failed once? Better to be safe than sorry. Another commando, this one airborne, was meant to reach the target through the skies. An all-star team led by Quartus himself would to drop the last available Tetrabomb onto the Gigantum. The Aeronef that held it was smaller than the others, and thus more easily controllable and most importantly, more protected. Covered in metal, its balloon would be impenetrable under almost any circumstances, and its compartment, completely airtight, should easily resist the attacks of flying magical creatures. The number of propellers had been increased to eight, as opposed to the usual two, in order to increase its forward power and effectively counter the violent winds that arose to repulse intruders as they neared the Gigantum. Even so, in order for the aerial attack to succeed, a diversion would have to be created to keep a maximum of the enemy forces on the ground. That was the task of the infantry, where many of the Order's troops had been positioned throughout the area.

Faced with this system of destruction, the peoples of the Legendary World and especially Felicia Regina had to prevent this tragedy from playing out, for the equilibrium of the whole world was at risk. Ogrino's role in the drama would be important. He would now discover whether his mission of associating the various clans of magical creatures had been successful and whether their alliance would allow them to counter the Order effectively. At this critical moment, he was wracked with anxiety, all the more so because the Trolls had not responded to the call. Ha! How far away now was the sweet serenity he had felt in Felicia's presence. Then, to calm himself, he watched the Gigantum's leaf shimmer in the sunlight, and his confidence returned.

Far above him, the fleet of airborne troops was rapidly approaching its target. The sky was clear and a tailwind pushed the zeppelins along quickly toward the top of the Gigantum, which one could make out against the backdrop of the forest canopy. On the ground, the Terranefs were advancing in 'V' formations, which blazed wide trails, crushing all vegetation in their way. Then, with no trouble at all, the foot soldiers flushed out the Drakes, Drows, Efritts, and still more genies of the woods who fled through the shrubbery, terrorized by the cannon shots. The Militians skewered them easily with arrows, and their haul was impressive.

On the eastern front, Themistomene's troops had received reinforcements in the form of an enormous fleet of Hobgoblins, sitting astride innumerable squadrons of wild geese, which bombarded the enemy with exploding pumpkins. The blasts made holes in Legiferius's well-aligned ranks, sowing panic and disorder among the Militians. Taking advantage of the chaos, Jinns, Sprites, and Will-o'-the-Wisps cut through the Order's battalions, which then found themselves unable to reorganize. The soldiers were, nevertheless, fighting forcefully, spurred on not only by the pride instilled in them by their military education, but also by the mad desire to destroy this pitiful people who, for the first time, were daring to oppose them. 'Defeat' was not a part of Legiferius's vocabulary, and they had to defend the flag of the Order. The desire to crush the enemy was in their very bones. Little by little, the units regrouped around the Rectors, who took control, and the battle raged once more. Flurries of explosive arrows discharged in mid-air, releasing cobwebs against the sky. Many geese and their riders were caught in these nets, and still more fell to the ground, their mounts' heads or wings burned. Seeing this, Themistomene signaled to the heads of each squadron, who rather than stopping the battle, rose higher in the sky to avoid the enemy fire. Once out of range, they let loose a shower of dust which became a thick cloud upon reaching the ground. There, the Militians began to sneeze, couch, and spit while the Korrigans, Jinns, and Gnomes, who were quite comfortable, stabbed at their sides. The soldiers of the Order were dropping like flies, their ranks thinning before Themistomene's very eyes. The monarch smiled; victory was not far off and soon they would be marching rapidly toward their goal.

Underground, on the western front, Precelestine had ordered his people to stop the persistent excavator aimed straight at his throne, whatever the cost. Djill had had the brilliant idea of suggesting to his king that the snails might be used to obstruct the passageway. And so more than a thousand of these mollusks were piled up in the Scavanef's path, making up a thick, solid wall. The Pixies stood behind the barricade of snails, ready to intervene if necessary. A dull noise, growing louder, along with the trembling of the earth, alerted them that the terrible machine must be very near. When Commander Trezius, who was piloting the Scavanef, saw the wall of snails from his porthole, he slowed the rotation of the drill bit as well as the speed of the craft itself. The machine thus sank with apparent gentleness into the mass of shell and flesh. It was a bloodbath; the snails' mutilated bodies released a torrent of entrails and slime, causing the Scavanef to zigzag. The Militians following behind it found themselves stuck in this viscous fluid that covered the ground. Although its trajectory was difficult to control, the Scavanef was able to penetrate the wall of mollusks, and it arrived in a high tunnel with a sloping floor. Its tracks covered in slime, the craft began to slide dangerously toward the precipice below. The driver turned one hundred and eighty degrees, and the Scavanef, still slipping, now faced away from the abyss. So he pressed the gas to the floor, and as stones clattered into the chasm, the machine stopped sliding and ground to a halt, the back of its tracks over the cliff's edge. The Pixies took advantage of the situation to attack the Militians who were still caught in the deceased snails' mucus. The soldiers' arrows could not pierce the Pixies' coats of armor, and so the creatures approached with impunity. Using their swords and daggers, they soon eliminated the invaders.

The Scavanef was being attacked on all sides and was fighting to distance itself from the abyss as well as to avoid the jets of lava launched by the Pixies and the stalactites dropping onto it from above. In a final effort, the machine sputtered forward violently just as an enormous column of rock crashed into its cockpit. Despite the damage, it continued moving at an impressive speed while the Little Folk struggled to keep up. Thus Trezius encountered no more interference before reaching a point where several tunnels branched off. From what he could see, the members of his team were the only survivors of Legiferius's main underground battalion. Nevertheless, he had to continue the mission at any cost. According to the Docts' plans, he ought to take the second tunnel from the left, which proved to be the narrowest. The drill bit worked wonders again, despite the hardness of the rock, which crumbled with an incessant eruption of sparks. Suddenly, a frightful shockwave tore through the air. Everything exploded into a cloud of light and dust. The grotto's ceiling collapsed, crushing the Scavanef and leaving nothing but tatters of metal and flesh among the rocky debris.

On the southern front, the rivers roiled with a multitude of fish below the Order's watchful barges. As they tried to pull up the too-heavy nets, the sailors were shocked by electric eels. Many of them fell overboard, where they were devoured by piranhas before they could climb back onto their boats. During this time, the imprisoned Tritons and Naiads were freed by schools of pikes, who cut the nets holding them.

At sea, the galleons continued their gruesome harvest of the bodies that floated to the surface after detonations. Suddenly, the admiral's ship tilted bizarrely starboard, though there was hardly any wind. The sailors on other ships could see the crew struggling against an invisible enemy, which seemed to be pulling the ship downward. Faced with the slaughter of his people, Delphoros had attacked with his largest and most powerful squid—the Kraken. These primitive creatures were, nonetheless, formidable opponents, and the element of surprise was on their side. The flagship was pitching dangerously, irrevocably turned on its right side while torrents of water poured in through its cannon holes. The sailors tried to sever the thick tentacles of the two Kraken attached to the masts and rails. The monsters, though bleeding from the cuts, did not release their grip, and the ship sank ever more below the water's surface.

All of a sudden, it toppled completely and turned upside-down so that only the curve of its hull emerged. The seamen rose slowly to the surface, swimming toward the light. They were very quickly joined by a great many white sharks, which swallowed the poor men in a single mouthful. In very little time, nothing remained but a floating blood-red cloud around the ship. Not a single survivor had escaped these marine carnivores. Delphoros's cruel response to Legiferius's attack was valuable as a warning. Indeed, Rector Tilvarius of the captain's ship took very seriously what he had been able to witness through his telescope.

'Form a circle!' he shouted at once.

Immediately light signals were exchanged between the ships, which rearranged themselves to form an immense ring, and a good thing too, for already tentacles were flying through the air, catching a guardrail here, a bow there. Four caravels were attacked in this way. As soon as he realized the danger, Tilvarius ordered the entire fleet to shoot. All of the warships simultaneously fired their cannons toward the threatened caravels, taking aim at the enormous grey masses that could be made out below the surface. Geysers of blood spurted up from the depths of the sea, and the tentacles immediately uncoiled, letting go of their prey. They slid limply across the boats' bridges and then disappeared, engulfed by the sea. A 'hurrah!' resounded among the crews of the caravels. They were rejoicing when a thud was heard below the ship. A violent tremor passed from the hull all the way to the crow's nest, unbalancing the lookout sailor, who fell from the top of the mast to the Rector's feet, his neck broken.

'Incoming water!' one of the soldiers cried out from below deck.

Tilvarius leaned over and was stupefied to see a long fissure appearing in the center of the hull. Before he could react another tremor arrived, and nearly everyone fell to the ground. This time a large hole formed and roiling water was filling the depths of the ship.

'We are sinking! Everyone to the lifeboats!' Tilvarius shouted. 'Bring your weapons!'

A third tremor and tragedy struck. This time the ship broke into two and the sailors slid down the deck, which had become a diabolical slope, toward the sea which swallowed them instantly. None of the seamen reappeared. Only those who had been able to hang on to a cord or guardrail were not sucked into the waves, but their fate too was sealed, for in a short time, the flotsam they clung to was struck by the mouths of sperm whales. The other crews began to feel a great apprehension, wondering who would be next. They sent out a flood of underwater bombs, more as a general precaution than against any identified threat. The waters shuddered heavily at the detonations, and then the sea became astonishingly calm. The Militians breathed a sigh of relief. Then a heavy silence took hold in which everyone kept their eyes peeled on the surface and remained perfectly vigilant at their posts.

Now flying over the great north, Quartus marveled at having been able to come so far, for all the previous missions had failed well before this point. He contemplated the vast forest that extended as far as the eye could see, like an immense continent of greenery. Finally, he saw the outsized silhouette of the Gigantum jutting from the horizon. It was unbelievably enormous so much so that it seemed not a gigantic tree, but rather the peak of a botanical mountain. It was surrounded by immense sequoias which, despite their impressive dimensions, were like dwarves next to the Gigantum. As clouds passed over it, it seemed to Quartus that the giant tree was sparkling like the surface of a lake beneath the sun. He was surprised to be moved by its beauty.

'Commander! Threat at three o'clock!'

The lookout's cry pulled him suddenly from his reverie. A dark mass was headed straight for them.

'Ready your weapons!'

Millions and millions of birds had formed a teeming cloud which was growing before their eyes. Never in their lives had they seen so many birds. They were able to make out eagles, ospreys, vultures, and sparrowhawks. Most of these birds of prey were ridden by a multitude of Imps—Bogans, Gullters, Ozegans, and Brownies, all minuscule and coiffed with multicolored pointed hats. Their numbers blocked out the sky as they approached the Aeronefs.

'FIRE!'

Barely had the shells been fired when the cloud of birds dispersed to form a ring around the vessels. It seemed that the Pixies could anticipate the soldiers' next moves. Salvos of machine-gun fire sounded, again without success; the birds rapidly and easily moved downwind. The Militians fired again and again, spitefully and obstinately, but in vain. Quartus gave the order to speed up, all the while keeping up a crossfire in which each Aeronef protected the others. He hoped that they could continue to keep their assailants at bay this way while still gaining ground toward their target since the winds remained favorable.

All of a sudden, it seemed that one of the Imps, wearing a harlequin-patterned hat, gave an order, and immediately one line of the raptors dove toward the first Aeronef's balloon at an incredible speed. The impact of their steel-sharp beaks and talons on the fabric tore deeply into the material, leaving a hole gaping like a wound. Before losing even one of their own, the birds had dispersed once more, and others, using the same technique, had attacked the craft at the end of the line. The Commanders of the affected Aeronefs were having trouble maintaining their altitude as the damages were severe. Teams of repairmen had already climbed up to the balloons and were doing their best to stop up the leaks. The more areas they patched, the more new damage the raptors caused, and the men wore themselves out with the task. Despite his artillery fire, Quartus was unable to prevent his four accompanying zeppelins from grave mutilation. Slowly they were pulled downward, brushing dangerously against the treetops.

At that moment, a strong west wind began to blow, unexpectedly, hitting them on the left. The Aeronefs pitched dramatically; the one Quartus was in did a two hundred and seventy degrees turn and rocked onto its side. When he regained his balance and was able to look through the porthole, Quartus saw that the other machines had crashed onto the canopy. The balloons, entirely destroyed, lay atop the trees. Of the splintered cabins, only fragments were visible. Not a living soul was in sight. The soldiers had essentially been swallowed up by this wide, deep green sea. Quartus was left alone with his men, the Tetrabomb, and a mission to accomplish. The cloud of birds had returned, denser than ever. However, their flagship was admirably resistant to the attacks, thanks to the Docts' technology. This time the machine guns did their job, decimating hundreds of birds and their riders. Despite the losses, the attackers were crowding ever closer to the Aeronef, now able to touch it. It was dark as if night had suddenly fallen. Even when the cloud of raptors backed off, it remained just as dark inside the vessel. All of the portholes had become opaque, covered in glue and feathers. The craft, although blind, stayed on course thanks to its compass and other orienting tools.

'Clean those windows for me. I want visibility,' Quartus ordered.

So soldiers began to unscrew the frames of the portholes. As soon as they were opened, a raging torrent of sparrowhawks dove into the cabin, filling the space with hostile claws and beaks. The Militians continually waved their hands, armed with daggers, through the air, trying to disembowel as many raptors as possible but the influx was too great, and they were completely overwhelmed. The soldiers were left screaming and clutching their faces, their eyes punctured. Quartus just had the time to descend into the hold and close the door above him. Five sparrowhawks which had managed to follow him were circling about his head menacingly. Simultaneously, he put a mask over his face and pulled out a vial from his belt, which he then threw to the ground. A thick green smoke rose up, and, immediately, the birds dropped to the ground, dead. The hold having no windows other than the minuscule airlock in the floor, Quartus could rely only on his pocket compass, which indicated that they were still on course. However, he could tell that the vessel was slowing down. Outside, the Bogans were steadily winding vines around the propellers, which, one after another, stopped turning. The Aeronef hovered for a moment, and then Quartus felt it moving backward.

Little by little, he came to feel the craft rotating; the Aeronef had turned into a sort of spinning-top. Quartus was thrust against the wall by the centrifugal force. With a heroic effort, he managed to take out a scrap of parchment and scribble a few words on it. Then, with some contortion, he took a small box from his backpack. He slipped the message into the collar of the pigeon that was curled up there. Then he turned over and, like a snake, crawled along on his belly as best he could down the wall and then on the floor toward the center of the craft. Having reached the airlock, he opened it and clung firmly to the tiny opening with his left hand, feeling a strong urge to vomit. Overcoming his nausea, he inhaled deeply and, with mechanical motions, detached four spheres from his belt, then threw them out of the opening. Barely had they fallen out of the craft when they exploded, expelling a thick, green, toxic-smelling smoke. Quartus gathered his strength and hoisted himself up to peer through the opening. He was pleased to see that the cloud of birds had dispersed. He threw the box into the air. After falling several dozen meters, it opened with a click, and the carrier pigeon was released. When the bird got its balance, it began to wing its way toward Legiferius. Unable to track his messenger by sight, Quartus could only hope that his strategy had prevented the raptors from spotting it. The Aeronef was spinning faster and faster now, and Quartus could no longer curb his need to vomit. His stomach did a somersault, and he let go, distracted, and was thrown against the side of the craft. His head collided violently with the wall, and he lost consciousness. He did not see the great north winds rise up and carry his frail skiff, now directionless, well beyond land and sea.

On the northern front, one section of the Terranefs had arrived at the bottom of a basin and was preparing to climb out of it. Suddenly, the machines began to slow, then to turn to the right, moving in large circles. They stopped, and their pilots got out to see what was happening. There were no obvious problems or anomalies, and yet the tracks on the right side of each machine were stuck.

A mechanic shouted, 'Sabotage, sabotage! The axle of this Terranef is damaged.'

'Here too, someone bent one of our axles!' another soldier agreed.

'This is the work of the Dissidents, curse them a thousand times,' added a Rector.

'How much time will you need to repair this?'

Before an answer could be given, a clamor was heard from above, and the Militians saw an alarming number of giant pumpkins rolling toward them. The oversized vegetables knocked over and crushed the first lines of soldiers. Those who had taken shelter behind Terranefs or boulders now saw a motley army advancing upon them. There were Efritts, Groundlings, Fradets, Korils, Gullins, Follets, and Drows led by a plump child mounted on a Unicorn. With the Terranefs now useless, nothing could stop the tidal wave of little creatures. The Fradets were the first to cross enemy lines, avoiding fire thanks to their legendary speed. With Herculean strength, they snapped soldiers in two or else tossed them into the air. The Efritts were sending swarms of thousands of wasps to sting the artillerymen while the carnivorous Korils were eating soldiers alive. The Gullins, for their part, were successfully bewitching their adversaries with their lively music. Despite the protective helmets they wore, the Militians became babbling marionettes with idiotic smiles plastered on their faces. Other soldiers became completely insane in the presence of the Follets and began to laugh madly. Confronted with this, the remaining Militians, spurred on by the Elixir of Eradication, threw themselves savagely and hatefully on their victims, slaughtering them with a demonic grin. Ogrino, revolted by these horrors, dove into the melee, carried by Viastella. His burning desire to strike down this vile and contemptible enemy made him ten times stronger.

He sprang onto three Militians, shouting, 'You don't know, you don't know, you don't know WHO I AM!'

Before they had time to understand what was happening, the soldiers found themselves unconscious on the ground, their bones broken. Ogrino was already throwing himself upon other combatants as Viastella followed closely, watching over him. The child was fighting a good hundred men all by himself. He was doing so much and so well that he gave the forest genies hope and energy, despite their heavy losses. Moved by the belief that they were defending a just cause, they were victorious in the battle, taking a maximum of prisoners. They left these hanging from the branches of trees, bound in groups of ten in large nets woven by the Floreannes. Again mounted on Viastella, Ogrino took the lead once more, ready to face new and inevitable clashes.

On the eastern front, the bison had now reached the green hills and were delighting in the lush grasses after their long and exhausting journey. As planned, the men had rejoined their spouses, and Pantaleone clasped Slevania tenderly in his arms. The circus troupe was once more complete, for even Gumbo, Colossus, Herculium, and Royal were there. Night had now fallen, and the lights of the military encampments appeared below.

'We could ambush them during the night,' said Pantaleone to Romcunda.

'No, the bison are tired. They must rest for tomorrow.'

'Still, we must seize this opportunity. We cannot let the survivors reorganize. They will only be more dangerous. I propose that we attack as soon as they are asleep.'

And so they waited patiently until the middle of the night to attack by the light of the moon. Having reached their posts, everyone carried out the agreed-upon plan simultaneously. Pantaleone entered the encampment atop Herculium, who was trumpeting loudly while the Messeyer brothers and Othello, riding Colossus, took care of the guards with slingshots, and Royal spooked the horses. At the same moment, Pianissimo and Camillo used torches to set fire to the tents. The Militians promptly came out in their underwear to escape the flames. With his tusks, Herculium easily dispatched with the still half-sleeping soldiers. During this time, the other members of the circus were throwing daggers, methodically eliminating their enemies one by one. Hardly a single shot or arrow was fired by the Militians, so quick was the attack. Atop the hill, Romcunda smiled, for despite his blindness, he could perceive the favorable outcome of the battle playing out before his eyes.

Underground, Precelestine was now leading a veritable army of giant ants into combat. The Militians' arrows ricocheted off their exoskeletons while with their mandibles the insects tirelessly bisected everything in their paths. The many shots fired from portable cannons could not overcome this outsized ant colony, and the soldiers' losses were so heavy that their ranks thinned quickly. The Pixies continued to throw torrents of knives, javelins, and darts, hitting their marks every time. The genies of the Little Folk were known not only as master metalworkers, but also as fierce warriors. The fight became more and more unbalanced, and the Militians began little by little to retreat. However, some still affected by the Elixir of Eradication, preferred to sacrifice their lives, blowing themselves up in the midst of their enemies so as to kill the greatest number.

Weary of watching his children suffer and be destroyed, Precelestine ordered the withdrawal of his troops even though the battle was turning out in his favor. The Pixies began to retreat and a clamor of victory spread through the Militians' ranks. Their voices were, however, quickly drowned out by a low rumbling. The soldiers barely had the time to lift their heads to see a cascade of stalactites raining down on them. When all was silent once more, not a single soldier had survived. Only corpses were visible—crushed, impaled, or skewered by the limestone arrows that now served as tombstones in an immense cemetery. Precelestine, atop his royal snail, took the lead again, and the long column of his army began to march eastward.

On the northern front, despite the losses suffered by their central faction, the Order's army continued its arc-shaped advance, plunging ever deeper into the forest. The first Terranef was blazing the trail for the formation, climbing up the side of a hill. In a flash, the machine was struck full force with a fast-moving tree trunk, which terminated in a metal ram's head. The impact smashed the front of the tank, and its occupants were crushed against the cockpit. Then other trunks, each held by a cord, began to fall from the trees like the pendulums of clocks, mowing down men and machines with each sweep. The turrets of many Terranefs were knocked off as well as their crossbow-cannons. Before the intact Terranefs could return fire, most of them fell into wide holes that had been admirably well concealed beneath blankets of grasses and moss. Then a forest of spears, harpoons, axes, and maces appeared in the hands of a proud horde of Ogres. Tiboursio lowered his right arm and his fighters ran forward with terrifying cries. Three-meter-long harpoons flew through the air by the dozens, skewering the Militians four at a time. Then came a flood of spiked maces and torrents of stones the size of ostrich eggs, launched by slings. The Ogres' skill was impressive, for the soldiers suffered great losses despite their training. Nevertheless, their response was matched to the attack. The Militians shot arrows dipped in acid that would eat away at muscle tissue. Fragmentation grenades tore at the Ogres' legs and torsos, and jets of a viscous green paste burned their eyes. A wave of Ogres swung from the trees on vines, decapitating soldiers by the dozens with their axes. Tiboursio and, behind him, a whole mob of his kind, threw themselves on the survivors. The surrounded Militians fought courageously, spurred on by the Elixir of Eradication, but that wasn't enough to counter the raging Ogres who were cutting them in two with scythes as easily as they might slice through reeds. In very little time, not a single soldier was left standing. The battlefield was a bloody massacre where Ogres jumped for joy among the dismembered corpses.

'We have achieved a great victory over a powerful and an insidious enemy,' proclaimed Tiboursio, standing above the crowd on a boulder. 'These men have now paid for having stolen our women and children through treachery. They have no sense of honor. They slip into our villages furtively while we are out hunting and decimate our families. Today, we have cleansed with blood the loss of our nearest and dearest. But the enemy will not stop at this. They will always and forever pursue their schemes of destruction. So we have no choice, we must continue fighting them until our victory is complete. The map Ogrino gave us will allow us to set more traps for them as efficient as the ones here. And now let us go, toward the gorges to arrange another, even bloodier ambush for our enemies.'

'WE WILL CRUSH EVERY LAST ONE OF THEM,' shouted the chiefs of each clan.

Intoxicated by the smell of the blood covering their garments, the groups of Ogres set off with joy in their hearts, ready to embrace danger and death once more.

On the eastern front, the soldiers were blinded by a cloud of gnats produced by the Kobolds. Although harmless, the insects prevented them from fighting, and the Korrigans took advantage of this, slashing the Militians' calves and thus pinning them to the ground. The Floreannes conjured up fields of roses whose spiny stems instantly wove together, forming great cages which imprisoned the fighters. The flowers' sweet smell filled the air, sending the men into a deep sleep. At the Alfs' command, ivy sprang from the ground and laced around the soldiers' legs, making them easy prey. The Jinns turned the Militians into inflating balloons, and they suffocated in their now-too-small uniforms. They rolled about on the ground like eggs, unable to find balance, and so the area was cleared, and Themistomene's troops could continue freely toward the City.

THE MAELSTROM INCANTATION

The few reports that reached Primus all depicted an alarming situation. Under enemy pressure, the Militians were retreating on all four fronts. Thousands of men had been lost. Those that had held out were becoming weaker and weaker. Rations were lacking, for grains were rotting in the stockrooms and nothing was growing in the fields any more. Water was becoming scarce too as wells dried up one after another. The Dissidents were multiplying, and their sabotages were now beyond counting. It had begun with the poisoning of the water, which had caused dysentery among the soldiers, and then there had been the destruction of the bridges, the horse thefts, and the sabotage of wheels and wagons. All of this had interfered with the transport of convoys of food and ammunition. It had reached its height with the incineration of the pigeon-house in which most of the birds had perished. Communication within the army had suffered greatly. Not content to leave it at that, these traitors had gone so far as to transmit false messages and turn whole battalions away from their targets, sending them on invented missions. Not to mention the mass resignations which had crippled the army's ranks. Faced with this situation, where everything seemed to be conspiring against him, Primus felt both disappointment and a furious will to continue fighting, knowing that he was so close to his goal. Whatever the cost, the men had to keep their positions long enough to act as a distraction and allow his commandos to reach their goal.

Ogrino, riding Viastella, was leading a motley, yet vast and courageous army toward the city. Among the crowd were representatives of the various peoples of the Legendary World. Those from the moors stood alongside those from the World Below, who mingled with those from the forests, and so on. With Herculean force, the Sprites were gathering all sorts of objects in the alleys to throw them at the soldiers, who were knocked senseless by the dozens. The Will-o'-the-Wisps were launching their invisible spears at the Militians, thinning out the enemy ranks, which made the Little Folk's advance all the easier. Korrigans, blowing into goats' horns at the top of their lungs, produced a strident sound that tore through their adversaries' eardrums. Despite their soundproofing equipment, the soldiers were obliged to hold their ears as the great number of 'musicians' elevated the noise to levels the Docts had not anticipated. Hobgoblins threw themselves on the survivors, who lost all energy and fell to the ground, exhausted, at the creatures' mere touch. Perched atop the nearby roofs, the Order's archers inundated the streets with arrows, decimating by the dozens the attackers within their range. Before this flood of projectiles, Ogrino instinctively raised his arms in protection, but incredibly, not a single one touched him. He realized with amazement that as they approached him, the arrows were transforming into rose petals. Viastella smiled serenely, amused.

'What is this miracle?' cried the child.

'If your heart remains calm, nothing can hurt you. If you let fear take hold in you, then anything can happen.'

Ogrino could not believe his ears. Viastella, with her composure, had become untouchable. He would have loved to do the same, but he was no Unicorn. Still, this allowed him to move ever closer to Legiferius without any danger, bringing along a whole host of combatants behind him. From above, clouds of bats descended upon the archers' faces, putting their eyes out. So the shots severely dwindled, and, gradually, the attackers arranged themselves to escape the few remaining volleys of arrows.

To face this formidable column of invaders, the Militians activated the last Terranefs kept in reserve. They were positioned on the eight main roads leading to Legiferius's central plaza. Before Ogrino could understand what was happening, the first one fired at Viastella. The explosion was violent, and although she was unhurt, Viastella reared suddenly in surprise. Ogrino was thrown and fell to the ground. A second shot hit a section of the wall and the little Ogre just had the time to roll sideways so as not to be crushed. He stood up but blinded by the dust, he was unable to make out anything, but the crowd swimming before him, and hear cries of pain. Other explosions filled the air with fury and death, and Ogrino threw himself to the ground once more to escape the metal and stone debris flying in all directions. When the clouds of ash disappeared, he saw that he was now alone, for the others had retreated.

The moon had risen, round and full, lighting the earth and sky with its soft pearly glow. As night fell, the ground began to tremble irregularly, and the city's inhabitants, already frightened by the violent combat, expected the worst. Some herd of wild animals must have been approaching the capital.

The sound of their galloping was now deafening. The people were dumbfounded and most of all terrorized when they discovered that it was not a pack of animals rushing through the streets, but rather an astounding number of Trolls who were destroying everything in their path. The few people who had remained outdoors despite the clashes were now running in all directions, desperately, and stealthily shutting themselves away in their houses. Everything that lay in the streets was swallowed up by this tide of monsters. Chariots, those storefronts that were still standing, signs: everything fell to pieces below the mass of bodies advancing with dogged determination toward Legiferius. In each street, the first line of Trolls pushed an enormous round rock ahead of them, which both protected them and cleared their way.

The only one to rejoice at the sight of this horde of monsters was Ogrino. He was unabashedly triumphant. His appeal had not been in vain. Actually, he could not have imagined how much he had directly contributed to their coming. One of the Troll spirits that he had brought back from his journey to the world of the dead had appeared one night to an assembly of his own kind. He had convinced them to join the little Ogre with a big heart. That was why they were here today. The involvement of these warriors, with their tremendous strength, surely guaranteed victory.

The last archers remaining on the roofs continued to shoot tirelessly to no effect. The arrows seemed to bother the Trolls less than mosquitoes' bites, and their progress was not slowed in the slightest. They were moving so quickly that the Terranefs only had the time to fire one round, which destroyed the enormous boulders, causing them to explode into thousands of tiny pieces. Before another shot could be fired, the Trolls expertly launched a barrage of stones, which crushed the Terranefs and buried them entirely. So in just a few minutes, they were at the foot of the fortress. There cannon shots decimated the first line of assailants with some Trolls utterly flattened.

Faced with the deaths of their friends, the pack dispersed, surrounding the outside walls. A group of about twenty Trolls hid themselves in an alleyway near Fort Legiferius's main door. A long, hoarse cry rang out and then dozens of massive rocks flew toward the top of the ramparts, crashing through the top edge of the walls in some areas. The Order's cannons were instantly reduced to rubble. Several sentries perished after a long fall, knocked down by enormous pieces of rock. At the same time, the twenty Trolls left their hiding place and rushed toward the colossal entryway to throw huge stones at that as well. The impact, though dreadfully strong, was not enough to break through the thick door. Each side of the arched doorway, reinforced with metal, was hardly damaged—just slightly twisted, opening a crack in the center so thin that not even the smallest Gnome could slip through. A new volley of shots and more sentries were killed while the door once more received its allotment of stones. This time the doors parted a little more.

Shooting from narrow gaps in the walls, archers rained arrows down onto the Trolls near the door as they were preparing their third attack. Hardly bothered by these minuscule stings, the twenty armed themselves for a synchronized assault. The onslaught, however, never took place, for they all fell simultaneously to the ground. Their glassy eyes became yellow, and their skin rapidly grayed. Other Trolls were rushing up, but seeing the tragic spectacle took a step back, frightened. The sight of their wounded comrades was horrifying to behold. Their skin was falling in sheets, revealing first muscles, then bones. A nauseating odor emanated from their decaying corpses. A great wail of distress and disgust escaped from the throats of many Trolls before this abomination. After revulsion came hate, for those who could commit such a despicable act.

The Trolls dispersed once more, looking for cover, then they systematically broke through the doors of the houses nearest to the fortress and climbed to the highest floors. From there, they began to throw rocks once more, aiming both at the gaps in the walls, where the archers stood, and at the pathway atop the rampart. While some fired, others gathered ammunition, and so an unimaginable quantity of rocks, slabs, and stones crashed down upon the whole of the wall encircling Fort Legiferius, causing grave damage. In places, the top part of the wall had been destroyed, leaving only a great jagged notch as if a giant had bitten into the stone. In addition, the neat gaps had disappeared, replaced by wide fissures. It seemed that the influx of stones would never end as the Trolls, who were proving to be indefatigable, had gathered up an abundance.

Under this rocky rain, the Militians' shots had practically ceased. Thrown off by the force of the attack, they were having severe trouble regaining their famous efficiency. Nevertheless, after a certain time had passed, the order was finally given to change strategy. Forming small, mobile units, the soldiers began to fire while constantly moving about. Their ammunition was different as well, and, as the Trolls noticed quickly, more effective. Explosions of a bitter green vapor erupted everywhere, blinding and choking everything in a thirty-meter radius. The grenades that had come through the windows flooded the houses with smoke, and many of the Trolls died of asphyxiation, caught off guard by weapons they did not understand. Others leapt out of the windows, frightened, and still others hid in the cellars to protect themselves. The assailants' attack had swiftly come to an end. Ogrino, who was keenly following the various stages of the battle, privately hoped that the Trolls would not give up.

New explosions rang out, but this time, there was no effect on the houses. So Ogrino dared to take a peek and discovered that Pixies, mounted on wild geese and ducks, were throwing explosive pumpkins onto the path atop the fortress walls. The soldiers still at their posts had to retreat at the volume of this enemy fire. Seeing that the path was clear, the Floreannes began to throw the seeds of giant ivy into the cracks between the stones of the plaza. Thanks to their ultra-quick growth, vines instantly climbed to the top of the ramparts. These botanical staircases allowed a multitude of besiegers to quickly launch the attack on the walls. At the same time, out of nowhere, a long line of Pixies infiltrated the fortress through the crack in the main entryway.

Primus held in his shaking hand the report from Quartus, informing him of the failure of that mission. If the Gigantum could not be destroyed, the keystone of his plan was crumbling. He felt both wounded and infuriated but most of all exhausted for so much energy had been expended for such meager results. He had been able to greatly weaken the enemy, but not to destroy it. He would have a more accurate impression of the situation in the hours to come as not all of his commandos had yet made their report. He would have to change his tactics then, in response.

The fortress's court was now completely covered with all sorts of creatures from the Legendary World. Apart from Ogrino, who had succeeded in slipping through the doorway despite his roundness, one could see Gnomes, Pixies and Korrigans aplenty. Even some of the Little Folk were there, for their giant ants had succeeded in digging tunnels reaching underneath the center of the fortress. Only the Trolls were absent, for, with daybreak nearing, they had had to return to their caverns to protect themselves from the sunlight, so as not to transform into statues.

The Militians had all taken refuge in the main building, where the Docts lived and worked. An enormous, heavy portcullis blocked the entrance, which was further barred by a thick iron door. Behind it, the soldiers had placed huge blocks of granite, eliminating access with this makeshift wall.

Some Fijns, forest beings who resembled moss, rushed up the walls of this stronghold, covering them with a thick vegetal cloak that closed off all gaps, fissures, and windows as it climbed. Soon all the openings to Legiferius's central building were blocked. Primus, informed of the state of siege in which they found themselves, ordered the use of their last line of defense. Dozens of men descended into the cellars and opened great gates. Several minutes later, a thick liquid was spreading throughout the court, through the first-floor gaps, oozing through the cover of moss. Apart from the substance's nauseating odor, the Gnomes, Korrigans, and all the others found that it bogged them down and prevented them from moving about. Suddenly, a torch fell from a window high on the central building. The moment it touched the ground, everything went up in flames.

'Petrol!' cried Ogrino. 'Save yourselves, QUICK!'

He ran as fast as he could toward the main door. The crowd rushing through it had formed a bottleneck, and he had to climb onto some boxes of weaponry to escape the flames. Just as he was about to jump through, outside the walls, the shockwave of an explosion sent him flying face-first into a cart of hay, which softened the blow. He turned to contemplate the apocalyptic scene. Hundreds of little beings scrambling, screaming, their clothes on fire while others fell to the ground, charred. Even where Ogrino was sitting, the heat was unbearable. The flames reached four meters, creating an impassible wall, even for Trolls. Access to the heart of Fort Legiferius seemed impossible. The Magnus Legifer had certainly lost the battle, but he was not ready to admit defeat. Who knew what other evil potions he might be able to concoct, locked in that tower? All of a sudden, a marvelous idea popped into Ogrino's mind. He ran to a place sheltered from the flames, then took the leaf of Gigantum in his hands and intently called to Viastella.

During this time, somewhere below the surface of the seas, Edwimus was rejoicing. His idea of using drills had been, quite simply, ingenious. In the end, the drills had succeeded in creating long, thin tunnels in the sarcophagus of ice surrounding the Aquanef. Soon all the sticks of dynamite would be inserted and lit. Twenty or thirty minutes later, there was a deafening noise and the thick, frozen sheath exploded, flinging enormous blocks of ice far and wide. The Aquanef's hull shook, but there was no damage, not a single leak. It was a total success. The machine could once more move freely. An immense 'HOURRAH!' of relief was heard throughout the whole crew.

Stimulated by the episode, everyone was working hard, and the submarine went hurtling off in a cloud of fat bubbles, which were furiously pouring out of its wide frontal chimney. The machine and all its occupants were resolutely set on their goal, and henceforth, nothing and no one could stand in their way. Exalting, Edwimus had only a single idea in his mind—to immediately inform the Magnus Legifer that his mission had resumed and of its inevitably favorable outcome. He was delighted to discover that these imbecilic fish-men, so sure of their victory, had not even thought to cut the telegraph wire. A coded message was sent off to Legiferius straightaway.

After days and days of watching the icy sarcophagus—from afar, so as not to become deafened—Delphoros's sentries were practically half-asleep. So at the moment of the thunderous, destructive explosion, they were all the more surprised and panicked. What they had thought was only routine surveillance had now turned into the beginning of the end of Delphoros' kingdom. If even the Metanor had failed to eliminate the enemy, who could possibly succeed? A messenger immediately departed for the palace to communicate the frightful news.

The Aquanef was moving at its full capacity, even faster than the maximum speed predicted by the Docts. This was not the moment for such details, for they had to make up for lost time at any cost and reach their target on schedule in accordance with the plan the Magnus Legifer had drawn up. The submersible sped over the seafloor like a tortoise transformed into a hare, leaving behind it a foamy wake. Not the glistening hills of algae or the sandy plains or even the steep mountains could slow the machine's incredible momentum. It seemed to have taken on a life of its own. Every second brought it a little bit closer to its goal. According to Edwimus's plans, once they reached the top of the mountain road, they were now climbing, and they would have an unobstructed view of the rest of their path to the target. Only a few dozen more meters, only a few more meters . . .

As they reached the edge of the cliff, Edwimus was stunned to see just before him, floating in the open sea, hundreds and hundreds of Sirens looking at him, or rather, at the craft and smiling. They seemed to be completely unafraid, and yet, that was impossible. Wasn't the Aquanef of the Legiferius a most devastating weapon? But what was really most incomprehensible was that they were so close while the sonar was still running, and their eardrums should have exploded from the ultrasound. But no! There they were, floating peacefully, taunting him. Though he couldn't understand by what magic this would be possible, such insolence warranted a good lesson.

Before he had time to give the slightest order, a harmonious melody filled the cabin, and all of the soldiers immediately stopped what they had been doing, utterly enthralled by the song. Each man's lips curved into a beatific smile. Even Edwimus smiled so broadly that his gold teeth were visible on the sides. Then the soldiers went back to work, seeming content but still very busy. The Aquanef began to move again. Curiously, it was no longer following the road cut into the side of the mountain, but rather heading straight for the Sirens, toward the sheer drop. The men redoubled their efforts as if to hasten this fatal outcome. The machine had regained its cruising speed and, having reached the edge of the precipice, glided off into the open sea for a moment and then took a nosedive. Picking up speed, it plunged through the cloud of Sirens, who delicately parted to let the craft fall. As they passed quite nearby, Edwimus saw that the Sirens' heads were all covered with glass helmets like upturned fishbowls. At that moment, he regained his lucidity, for the song had stopped, and too late, he understood the deception. The Sirens, with their enchanting voices, had charmed them all and led them into a trap.

The Aquanef sank inexorably into a dark abyss that only grew darker. The body of the machine began to creak under the increasing pressure of the mass of water above it. Since the submarine was falling straight down, Edwimus found himself pressed up against the porthole of the commanding cabin. In order to reach the bottom of the room, he had to pull himself along with great effort, using drawers, levers, and shelves as so many steps on an improvised staircase. Finally, he reached the transmitter and, contorting to arrange himself perpendicular to the instrument, immediately typed out a final message to the Magnus Legifer. Before he was entirely finished, the Aquanef, now shooting toward the depths as fast as a rocket, was stopped in its tracks for a fraction of a second. The bobbin of telegraph cable having unwound completely, the cord snapped with a metallic 'pop' and the Aquanef continued on its course. The hull emitted low groans reminiscent of a large, wounded animal.

The soldiers, both frightened and resigned, did not speak. Some were gripping onto anything that would serve as a handle or foothold and some were curled up in cabins, closets, or pieces of furniture for protection. Everyone was waiting for the final impact. Leaks began to appear, like automatic showers flicked on by a capricious switch. The cabin lights suddenly went off and everything was plunged into absolute blackness. Not a single ray of light penetrated deep enough to illuminate this sad, unknown world. The long and dreadful minutes seemed to last for hours. Edwimus and the other men began to hope that the end would come soon, for all this waiting was becoming intolerable. Then came the impact, sudden and violent. The Aquanef, Legiferius's pride and joy, disappeared in an explosion of rare intensity. Upon impact, the Tetrabomb had released its phenomenal destructive power. A gigantic orange sphere arose and grew like a sun, illuminating and burning everything in its path. The water began to boil, cooking the marine insects, crustaceans, fish, and giant squid at the bottom of the sea. The shockwave rose toward the surface and the Sirens had to flee at top speed to avoid being thrown against the cliff wall by the lethal force of the blast. The devastating effect disappeared as quickly as it had arisen, the large sun shrinking down into a minuscule red star that was soon absorbed by the surrounding darkness.

The sound of the explosion reached Delphoros's palace so clearly that by the time the Sirens arrived at the grotto to make their report, the whole of the Grand Council had already guessed the outcome. The Sirens were congratulated for their courage and the success of their performance, but the very highest praises went to Razenbruck for his idea of the spherical helmets, which had permitted the Sirens to approach the enemy closely enough to act.

At that exact moment, he was receiving these honors, Razenbruck was careful not to mention that Ogrino had come up with the idea when they were on the way to Felicia's domain. Delphoros began to speak solemnly.

'You who were banished have been redeemed. You in whom I had no trust have proven your loyalty. You whom I hated, I have learned to like, and you now have my friendship. If you have any wish, please tell me, as I would like to officially thank you for your contribution to saving the Kingdom.

'Sire, I appreciate your gratitude, and nothing would give me more pleasure than to become a part of your family by taking your daughter's hand in marriage—if, of course, she herself consents.'

'My daughter? But, poor fool, you know only too well that I no longer have a daughter. She belongs to the Metanor.'

'No, my King! It was specified in the agreement that the Metanor's mission had to be a success, and he has failed, for the enemy freed themselves and continued their attack, which, as we now know, could have proven incredibly bloody.'

'You speak the truth. So I am delivered from my promise. Triaos and two Tritons from my guard must go at once to fetch my beloved daughter.'

'If I may permit myself to ask, I would like to be in that delegation. A bit of magic could prove useful, and in any case, I want to be able to announce the news to Delphania myself if you do not mind.'

'How could it be otherwise? My greatest wish is my daughter's happiness, and only she can decide who will be her heart's chosen one. Her choice is my choice, and now, enough talk. Go, and bring back what is dearest to me in the world.'

At that, the four emissaries leapt into a chariot and were off like a shot.

The secretary, trembling, tapped on the heavy office door. Primus started, suddenly torn from his contemplation.

'ENTER!' he shouted.

'Two top-priority messages from the Aquanef and from Commander Erasmus,' the secretary said in as neutral a voice as possible. 'The first was cut off,' he added apologetically.

'Cut off? Have you responded to the Aquanef to try to discover why?'

'Yes, of course, Magnus Legifer! But without success, the lines of communication seem to be down. It is possible the submarine has reached the depths where communication is no longer possible.'

'Do not invent stories. There must be another reason. Enough talk, give me this message!'

The servant handed over the two papers with a slightly wavering hand, which Primus did not fail to remark as he seized the telegrams in one swift movement. First, he read through the text quickly, then not believing his eyes, read it again, very attentively. With a snap of his fingers, he dismissed the secretary, who disappeared. Then nervously, he unsealed the message from Erasmus. He learned that the Dissidents had devastated his division and taken control of the Terranef and explosives. Erasmus said that he would try to join a nearby infantry corps along with the troops he had left. In any case, he could no longer pursue his goal, his commando mission of destroying the Gigantum.

The Magnus Legifer felt severe irritation, which quickly became powerful exasperation and, finally, blazing, growing rage. This rage transformed into unspeakable loathing. He was overcome by a feeling of pure hate. Incredible violence arose in him, his eyes grew bloodshot, and his lips began to tremble. A lust for murder, mass murder, extermination, and filled his mind. This feeling took over his body and soul.

He nearly shouted, in a trembling, hysterical voice, THIS TIME IT IS TOO MUCH. WE MUST FIGHT FIRE WITH FIRE, EVIL WITH EVIL! The Maelstrom incantation, the ultimate weapon, that's what I need. I will break all my oaths. I will do the unthinkable, and no one will ever have any idea. Only the glory of Legiferius means anything, only victory. Utter and absolute victory. The Order will be forever freed of this revolting Legendary World, which dares to defy us, which has disseminated its venom of disorder among the populace in the center of the City, even within the Order itself, at the heart of its army. All that I detest. All that I loathe has come to pass. Such an abomination cannot stand much longer. I must put an end to it at once.'

His hands were quivering; shivers of hate were passing through his body. He had only one obsession now—the complete destruction of the Order's ancient enemy.

'GUARDS, GUARDS!'

He was now shouting frantically. Two guards entered promptly, thinking that their master was in grave danger. They were worried to discover an unrecognizable Magnus Legifer, his hair disheveled, his eyes red, his forehead creased, his features hardened, his face scarlet, and his body excessively tense. He embodied fanaticism in its purest form, and they were frightened.

'Go and get me the Encyclopedia Legendaris Mundi. Come back straightaway. Your life depends on it. Go!'

He gave them a written order bearing a 'high-priority' seal. One of the soldiers seized the missive and, terrified, they began to run through the endless halls until they reached the Docts' enormous library. They opened the door noisily in their great haste. A surprised Doct was suddenly torn from the meticulous work he had been engaged in.

'How dare you disturb a Doct at work without warning and so crudely!' he exclaimed in an imperious tone.

'The Encyclopedia, quickly! We don't have time to lose with chatter. Here is the urgent order from the Magnus Legifer, which demands the Encyclopedia at once. Our lives depend on it!' the two guards said in unison.

The Doct took the letter, unsealed it roughly and avidly read the short sentence. His eyes quivered as if he had received an electrical shock.

'Librarian Docts, fetch the Encyclopedia Legendaris Mundi at once and help these guards bring it to the Magnus Legifer as quickly as possible!' he shouted in a high, strident voice.

'Guards! Go and help the Docts,' he added authoritatively.

The guards ran into the large room, which contained thousands of projects. If they had had the time, they might have perused all these books filled with precious knowledge in all fields. They covered everything from metaphysics to social sciences, passing by history, botany, medicine, astrology, physics, and still more along the way. But for the moment, at the height of stress, they fluttered frantically around the Docts, who were taking from a chest an immense, half-charred tome of which some sections had been burned away. They carefully slid it onto a wheeled cart, covering it with a white sheet and rolling the table toward the exit. The guards rushed ahead, opening the double doors just in time for the cart to pass through, then joining the Docts in pushing the precious cargo through Legiferius's long halls at top speed.

'What have they gotten into? It has been more than three minutes since they left, they should be here already. They will be punished for their slowness.'

Primus had barely finished this phrase when the door to his office opened with a crash, sending splinters of wood flying.

'Here we are, Master!' the first guard said proudly and yet with a tinge of fear.

'Poor fools, with your recklessness you might have spoiled an extremely valuable volume. For that, you will suffer my wrath, but later. For now, place the Encyclopedia on the pulpit and leave me alone, and most of all I do not want to be disturbed for any reason. FOR ANY REASON, do you understand? No matter what might happen. Is that quite clear?'

The inflections of his voice, his tone, the volume—everything about what had just been said commanded complete obedience and indicated that there would be no further discussion.

'Also, I want an entire garrison of my bodyguards to be posted outside the door to my office. They must fight to the death, if necessary, to prevent anyone from entering this room. NOW!'

Everyone left immediately as frightened as if they had seen a terrifying specter straight from hell. Finally alone, Primus closed the heavy door and then took out a strange apparatus that emitted very, very high ultrasounds so that no magical creature, be they invisible or able to walk through walls could remain in the room. Then with a look of great anticipation and lips parted, he bent eagerly over the Encyclopedia, as one might over a loved one. Carefully, but with feverishly trembling fingertips, he began to leaf through the magnificent volume's charred pages. A great rictus, rather than a smile, suddenly spread across his face. Recklessly and violently, he flipped over hundreds of pages at a time until he saw those much-desired words.

There it was, the Maelstrom incantation, before his very eyes. He was teary with excitement. The fire had only very slightly damaged the precious phrases, and Primus's prodigious memory and great knowledge of the Encyclopedia would easily allow him to fill in the few missing words. He was rejoicing, for soon absolute power would be bestowed upon him. He decoded the incomplete phrases with the speed of a crossword champion, and in less than fifteen minutes, he had filled in the blanks, drunk with exhilaration. Then, with a sweeping gesture, he closed the curtains over the enormous window in his office. He lit up the four stately candelabras, and in this hushed, mysterious setting, he stood solemnly before his desk, where the Encyclopedia lay. Reading a text that looked like an archaic form of Latin, he chanted:

> *Zephirium, supreme spirit of the winds,*
> *I call upon your eternal power*
> *Escumpta belgansis*
> *Méréumna altivarum*
> *Boreala ostransis*
> *Urlitum atlantarum*
> *May your power be in my hands amassed.*

Outside a thick fog—rare in this season—began to form around Fort Legiferius and slowly spread throughout the entire city. The birds suddenly ceased to sing and a heavy, deathly silence took hold.

Epsilonium, omegansis
Sputatum versatum
Australus perlantis
Repandistum voltarum
May gales, tornadoes, and cyclones all become ONE.

Violent winds were now blowing throughout the entire kingdom, gathering up leaves, twigs, insects, linens, dishes, tools, chairs, shingles, branches, flowerpots, tavern signs, shutters, and chimneys in a whirlwind.

Expectora mega
Mutantis circulum
Propensis maretum
Alpha zircontis
May this force spread over the land so vast.

All the winds came together, little by little, forming a single and colossal storm, which slowly began to twirl around Fort Legiferius. A multitude of gray clouds had merged to form an enormous fluffy ring, which expanded ever farther so that not only was the entire kingdom covered, but also that dark mist now encroached on the sea.

Summum crescendis
Spenderum murus
Distrugerus omnia
Spiralus elevaris
May Zephirium's destructive eye open at last.

The sun had disappeared from the surface of all known land and seas, giving way to crushing darkness. It seemed that nothing could escape the fury of these unrestrained elements. Monsoons beat down on the forests and plains, battering or drowning small animals from field mice to foxes. Violent rivers of mud coursed over boars, badgers, skunks, and fawns.

Nor were the beings of the Legendary World spared. The Forest People suffered greatly in the storm. Falling trees crushed climbing Thilomills and gliding, bushy-tailed Guerliguets. Rockslides buried rodent—Gnomes, Gardinelles, and Minutets alive, and lightning struck down winged Fairies and Fijns by the dozens. The tempest also took a heavy toll on the creatures of the moors and hills, such as Satyrs, Fauns, Korrigans, Imps, and other Sprites. Some were sucked into tornadoes while others were thrown against tree trunks or quickly swallowed up by rivers that had flooded out of their beds. It was a massacre.

The people of the Empire Below—Pixies, Knackers, Telchines, and Cabeiri—saw their underground tunnels filled with gushing water that ravaged their homes, carried away their elderly and children, and left behind only grief and desolation.

Although it might seem they would be sheltered from the effects of the massive storm, even the creatures of the seas were troubled. Devastating underwater typhoons left death in their wake, pulling Tritons, Hooks, Octopus-men, Ellylldans, Ondines, Sirens, and Nymphs into a violent *danse macabre*. Frighteningly powerful tidal waves rocked the ocean floor, smashing Mermen, Naiads, Shark-Tritons, Bosches, and many other creatures against the rocks.

Delphoros was at once devastated to see his people destroyed and terrified by the idea that he, too, might disappear, leaving the survivors on their own like orphans or, who knew, to be conquered by the Metanor. His gloomiest thought was for his beloved daughter, whom he would perhaps never see again. At least, the Metanor would protect her, and she would not succumb in this calamity, which could not be of human origin, Delphoros was sure. The ocean's currents became ever more violent and soon he would have to close his shell, and so cut himself off from the world. He hated the thought of it and intended to delay that moment as long as possible.

On the surface, there was lightning everywhere, striking mountains and hills, exploding rocks, charring trees, and killing creatures by the dozen. In this murderous storm, not even specters were spared. A bolt of lightning suddenly pierced their cloud, and the shock was so strong that it spread throughout all the ethereal bodies. The spirits instantly evaporated into thin air. At the very same instant, Romcunda, rain running down his face as he sat astride his totem-bison, lifted his eyes to the sky and loudly called out this entreaty:

'MAY THE SPIRITS WHICH TOOK ON LIFE-FORCE NOW BE FREED AND REJOIN THE OCEAN OF ETERNAL PEACE!'

At these words, a vertical rainbow appeared, stretching from Romcunda to the very highest point of the skies. Despite the hurricane swirling about it, an inexpressible calmness reigned in that column of colored light, which, an instant later, disappeared. Then the white bison carrying Romcunda began the slow journey back to its native plains, braving the raging elements, and followed by its immense and loyal herd.

The cyclone grew stronger each moment, and the atmospheric winds had now reached dizzying speeds, even making the Gigantum's canopy sway dangerously as bolts of lightning reached ever closer. The omnipresent danger was now palpable; everyone could feel it. Even the humans were holing up in their cottages, houses, cellars or other shelters, without feeling safe at all. The now-phenomenal windpower was uprooting everything in its path. Carts were airborne, trees falling, huts collapsing, and whole roofs flying off.

Potentum spendum
Ira devastensis
Omnia potentis
Mortes venire
May ultimate destruction . . .

An explosion of glass and wood interrupted Primus's mid-incantation. Countless shards of glass flew into the room, and the draperies which had been covering the window fell loudly to the floor. A violent gust of wind immediately entered the office, sending sheets of paper and parchment flying. The candles went out and in the half-darkness, Primus thought he saw the curtain come to life, like an inflating animal. Eyes wide, he saw a shape come out from under the thick fabric, a sort of large dog, or no, a human form reduced to the size of a pygmy. No, that wasn't it. His eyes, growing accustomed to the darkness, were ever better able to make out the figure rising before him with difficulty. Could it be possible that it was . . . him? Him, that insignificant creature, how could he have spoiled the work of a lifetime. How could he have prevented the rise of the Order? A murderous rage entered Primus's eyes; he was filled with an irrepressible urge to kill.

'I WILL DESTROY YOU BEFORE YOU DESTROY MY WORK!'

He looked furtively to his right and left, but among all the papers flying, he could not see any object that could serve as a weapon. So he threw himself on the little man staggering before him and knocked him over, flat on the ground. Primus's hands, filled with hate, encircled the child's throat, and he squeezed them like a vice, crushing his victim's Adam's apple. The little Ogre could hardly breathe.

Still dazed from his fall from the Icarius to the terrace of Legiferius, he had just begun to recover, only to find himself attacked by this man, whom he recognized as the Magnus Legifer. He could not inhale, his face was becoming red, but hate for the one who had killed his parents gave him a bit of energy. He clutched at Primus's hands and tried to make him let go, but in vain. So he scratched; he scratched as hard as he could, with all his loathing and despair. Despite the sharp pain, Primus did not release his hold—his desire to kill was too strong. Ogrino tried to kick his aggressor in the groin, but, pinned under Primus's body, he was unable. His head began to spin and his thoughts became more and more muddled. He saw his mother smile, his father carry him valiantly atop his broad shoulders, the sun shining through foliage, Professor Lovestone, the Baron of Swordscar, Razenbruck, Slevania, and Pantaleone, and Felicia too. He hardly noticed the wind growing stronger inside the room, becoming a real vortex that pulled everything into its swirl. The great wooden door had just opened and in his half-conscious state, he could hazily make out a dark shape that rapidly approached.

'Guard! Come and help me!' cried Primus. 'The wind is pulling me away. Take out your sword and kill this evil creature.'

The soldier unsheathed a dagger and plunged it into the arm of the reclining man, who let out a cry of pain, the weapon having plunged deep into the bone. The vise around Ogrino's neck was released and oxygen began to flow once more, bringing him back to consciousness. Primus was now standing, despite his wound, in furious combat with a soldier of the Order. It was a surprising scene, to say the least; Ogrino thought he must be hallucinating.

Small objects were flying through the air at high speed. The chairs, tables, stools, and books had also begun to make a circuit of the room. At the center of this whirlwind, the two adversaries were trading kicks and punches.

The wind became more intense every moment, and now heavy objects were flying about, brushing past the walls. So as to avoid a blow to the face, Erasmus—for it was indeed he who was fighting the Magnus Legifer—stepped backward, and a chair that was circling at the height of a man crashed into his head. Slightly stunned, he fell to his knees. Primus, taking advantage of the reprieve, picked up a candelabra in his unhurt hand and raised it high above his head to use it as a bludgeon.

Suddenly, with an immense cracking, a bolt of lightning tore through the air and struck the metal candleholder. Primus, caught in the explosion, instantly froze like a statue, his hair on end, his skin crimson, and his clothes smoking and torn to shreds. The tornado grew still more intense and everything began to fly. Ogrino and Erasmus came to their senses at the same time as Primus, who seemed to still be alive. Ogrino noticed that gradually, fewer and fewer objects were twirling about. He saw that a long line of various items had formed and was disappearing into the chimney, swallowed up by a sort of gigantic Ogre's mouth. As if by telepathy, Erasmus had the same idea at the same moment. He tried to swim through the storm toward Ogrino, but the wind pushed him off balance and sent him crashing against the shelves of the library. Ogrino, too, batted his arms like a bird toward Erasmus, but he had a hard time keeping a straight course, as he continually had to dodge a flurry of tools, now transformed into projectiles, coming at him from all angles. Using his legs to push off from a corner, Erasmus threw himself upon the child and grabbed his arm tightly, and then they anchored themselves, face-to-face as they were blown around the room. Primus, with his last bit of energy, had succeeded in catching onto the Encyclopedia and, despite his wounded arm, was hugging it to his chest like a loved one. He was propelled to the top of the tornado ravaging the room, then pulled into the descending column of air, and with a whooshing sound, sucked into the chimney. He was shot like a cannonball high into the sky and then the terrifying winds carried him away at a dizzying speed. He disappeared forever, beyond the confines of the kingdom.

At the same moment, Ogrino said in a loud and determined voice, 'ANZOUSTRADIM POTENTAS SUMMER GICTERE, protect us with the unbreakable sphere!'

Immediately, a bubble formed around them, just as they too were pulled toward the chimney. The sphere lodged in the frame of the fireplace and, despite the strong suction, ceased to move. They had to wait long hours for the winds to die down enough for them to leave their protective bubble. Erasmus explained to the young Ogre how he had overcome the guards who were blocking off Primus's office.

'It is not possible for a single man to conquer an entire garrison of elite soldiers. I know something about that. You are not telling me the whole truth. Who are you really?'

Erasmus hesitated and then murmured, 'I am rather like you, a meeting between two worlds, although in a different way. Elfin blood runs in my veins.'

'You are an Elf? A son of Felicia?'

'No! My mother was a human and my father an Elf whom I know nothing about. Felicia revealed my identity to me and little by little, I am rediscovering my dormant gifts. The mastery of my new powers allowed me to easily avoid the shots and blows of the guards and reach Primus's door with the firm intention of killing the man behind this whole disaster. Promise me you will never tell my secret to anyone.'

'I promise on my life.'

After the long silence that had followed the Maelstrom, it was now time for an explosion of life. Noisy birds filled the air with their joyful melodies. Ogrino and Erasmus, barely recovered from their trauma, took this as a sign of hope and renewal to come.

EPILOGUE

Scarcely a year had gone by since the end of the war. Both humans and the creatures of the Legendary World were recovering. There had been an impressive number of births among both peoples. It was as if the forces of the Great Balance were trying to erase the horrors committed against the harmony of the universe. Life was springing forth from death. The great spiral of evolution inexorably unwound, toward a better world.

Everything was back on track, then, but differently. Legiferius had been dissolved after the Dissidents took the fortress. Most of the Docts and Militians had perished or fled. Those who had stayed had agreed to use their knowledge to serve the community. A new administration based on radically different ideas had arisen. Its representatives were chosen by the people from among the people. A Council of twelve sages now governed the kingdom. A farmer, a blacksmith, a carpenter, a mason, and a baker represented the wisdom of the populace and the essential knowledge for village life. A musician, a painter, and Theophilas brought to the table an eye for beauty, refinement, and the spiritual world, all indispensable for the elevation of the mind. The Baron of Swordscar, Professor

Lovestone, Ogrino, and last but not least Erasmus, constituted the forces of order and innovation necessary for the kingdom's future. Each person had an equal vote, and it was rare that their agreement was not unanimous.

The Council was responsible for the justice system and the police, for the army no longer existed. Erasmus had naturally been designated the permanent representative of these groups to the Council while their other members did not join the general assembly except as needed. Nothing was left to chance in the great celestial plan. Without anyone's knowledge, fate had placed Erasmus in a key position, he, the link between the ancient legacy of man and of the Legendary World. The Dissidents, too, had played a large role in this nomination, publicly extolling the merits of the Commander who had not blindly followed along with the Order's schemes but had dared to rise up against injustice and cruelty. He was well-respected, and his innate authority had made him a natural favorite for election to the Council. Ogrino, for his part, had been chosen for his courage, determination, and decisive action against Legiferius. Though he was still a child, the adults had detected in him the will to bring everyone together despite their differences. Thus, perhaps precisely because of his youth which embodied the future, he was allowed to sit on the Council, where his contributions were always valuable.

Ogrino recalled how he had reached his current state. One year previously, with Viastella, he had returned to the hill where the Icarius was left and had been able to achieve liftoff on his own. Buffeted by capricious winds, he had thought he would never reach Fort Legiferius. That was when he had heard Felicia's sweet voice in his head, saying, 'I am here alongside you, and I believe in you.' That had encouraged him and, pushed on by a mysterious tailwind, he had resolutely set off for the city. Then while he was struggling against Primus, the Dissidents in the fortress had led an insurrection and taken control of the bottom floor. They had opened the entrance, allowing those magical creatures that had survived the Maelstrom to enter the building. This had created a diversion, allowing Erasmus and his troops to enter the fortress as well. Once inside, they had fought all the way up to Primus's office, not without heavy losses. On the top floor, the remaining Dissidents had all succumbed to Legiferius's elite garrison. The sole survivor, Erasmus had battled once more, now against Primus's bodyguards. Thanks to his awakened Elfin powers, he was able to avoid their shots, leaping from wall to wall, all the while dealing out fatal wounds with his dagger. In a final parry, he had bounded over them and eliminated the last soldiers with a flurry of crossbow fire. That was how he had found himself alone against his worst enemy and had been able to overpower him and save Ogrino.

Just after the fall of Legiferius, all of the Order's prisoners were freed from the underground jails—Aristophanes, who was still recovering, among them. At Erasmus's request, the repentant Docts had freed the hundreds of magical creatures who were imprisoned in jars in a state of hibernation. Ogrino had regained his memory thanks to a tonic Themistomene had made of Herb Paris. This little plant was in fact the antidote to the sap of the Tormentine, the bush Ogrino had fallen into three years earlier. What a joy to suddenly be overcome with a mountain of happy memories and to be able to look for his parents with their faces clear in his mind, and no longer only hazy images.

His surprise had been complete when during the release of the prisoners, the largest aquariums had been opened and a pair of Ogres had appeared. He had recognized them instantly. They were still wearing the same clothes as they had been on the day of their capture; they were as beautiful and majestic as in his memories, if a little pale. So Ogrino had leapt at them with squeals of joy. Loganda, her eyes tearful, had hugged him against her heart. She felt as if she were awakening from a long, drab, and joyless dream, and finally, coming back to life. Hogar had stood up to his full height and taken the child in his arms. Ogrino had been both moved and impressed by his father's size and strength. With infinite tenderness, the Ogre had kissed his son's forehead, then looked him deeply in the eyes.

'You've changed!' he had said. 'You are no longer the little boy I knew before. You really have the eyes of an Ogre now. You must have faced many trials to have such a gaze.'

'I fought those who wanted to do us harm and, along with all sorts of friends, helped bring about their downfall.'

'Your son is exceptionally courageous,' Erasmus had added in Ogre language. 'You are here in the fortress of the old Order, which persecuted and fought against Ogres and all the creatures of the Legendary World. It is thanks to your son, who led the revolt, that you are free today, and safe from danger tomorrow. Your family is reunited. You can live in peace now. However, nothing will ever be like before, for now your son has certain responsibilities. He is no more the innocent child that you last knew. He is now the symbol of a renaissance, and the link between your world and that of humans.'

'It's true, Papa! Among everything else that happened to me, I gained a second family, an adoptive, human mother and father who loved me and raised me. Through them I discovered the human world, and I want to preserve the precious bond that has been created.'

Hogar was dumbfounded by what he was hearing. Too much that he did not understand had happened during his long sleep. He had just been reunited with his son, only to learn that he was drifting away. Hogar had only one desire, and that was to leave these stifling walls and return to the wide-open spaces of the forest, alone with his family. Loganda spoke up.

'All these things you are saying are too much for us right now. We need time to understand them. Let us go back into the forest so that we can talk at length with our child. Then we will make the best decisions for all involved.'

'Indeed, let it be so!' Erasmus agreed.

It was only after meeting Pantaleone and Slevania that Loganda understood the importance of her son's relationships with humans. She was thus able to convince Hogar not only to allow their son to see the members of the circus regularly, but also to sit on the Council, even if she personally could not see the point of it. Hogar and Loganda were also fortunate enough to be invited to Razenbruck's marriage, and so plunged into the magic of the undersea kingdom. Despite Ogrino's tales, Hogar had not really been able to believe that his son had traveled to so many fantastic worlds until the moment Welchar carried them into Delphoros's great palace. The ceremony would be spectacular in keeping with Razenbruck's and Delphania's great joy. The wedding was full of songs, melodies, and feasts and lasted for three days and three nights. The occasion was also a contemplative one, for it symbolized the people of the seas' freedom not only from Legiferius, but also from the Metanor, which to Delphoros seemed more important.

Under the rule of the twelve sages, the kingdom now experienced a period of peace and prosperity, marked by mutual respect between humans and the peoples of the Legendary World. The harvests were more abundant, the fruits more plentiful, the rivers more full of fish, and the cows fatter. Industry and commerce thrived on a basis of mutual aid between the two communities.

All would have been for the best in this best of all possible worlds if it weren't for the disturbing rumors emerging from the south. Sailors, peddlers, and travelers were all reporting a growing threat from the depths of those remote lands beyond the Austral Sea, south of nowhere. For the moment, there was no evidence that the kingdom was in danger, but no one could deny that trouble was brewing. A serpent of evil lay coiled—ready, perhaps, at any moment, to strike.